THE

SAGAS

OF

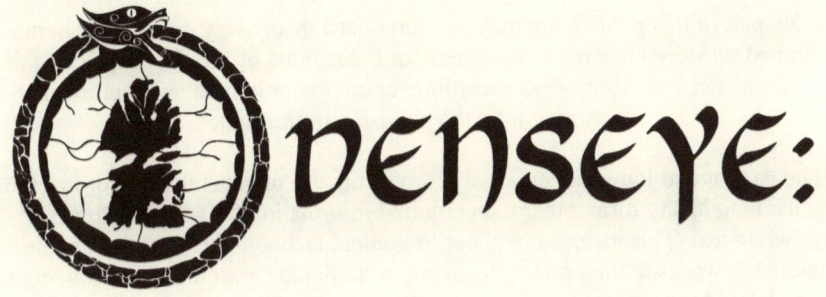

OVENSEYE:

CONQUERING AUTUMN

By

JD McLucas

&

Ryan McGuire

Pathfinder Media Group

Harrisburg, Pennsylvania, USA
publishing@pathfinderops.org
media.pathfinderops.org

Conquering Autumn – Book One of The Sagas of Odenseye

Disclaimer:

All characters and events portrayed in this book are fictitious. Any similarity to real persons, living or dead, is purely coincidental, and not intended by the author.

The content of this book or series may cover controversial or sensitive topics to include violence, loss, trauma, warfare, hatred, or other potential triggers. Readers' discretion is advised.

This work was created in its entirety without the use of Artificial Intelligence or Language Models of any type.

ISBN (Paperback): (978-1-970018-22-6)
ISBN (eBook): (978-1-970018-23-3)

From the Authors: This book is the culmination of a decade of work building a world and pouring our hearts and souls into it. For those who believed, those who supported, and those who shared our hope, you have our eternal thanks. This work exists because of you, and it is dedicated to all of you.

maps and calendar

map of ovenseye's northwest – se'vikoral, elysia, islands

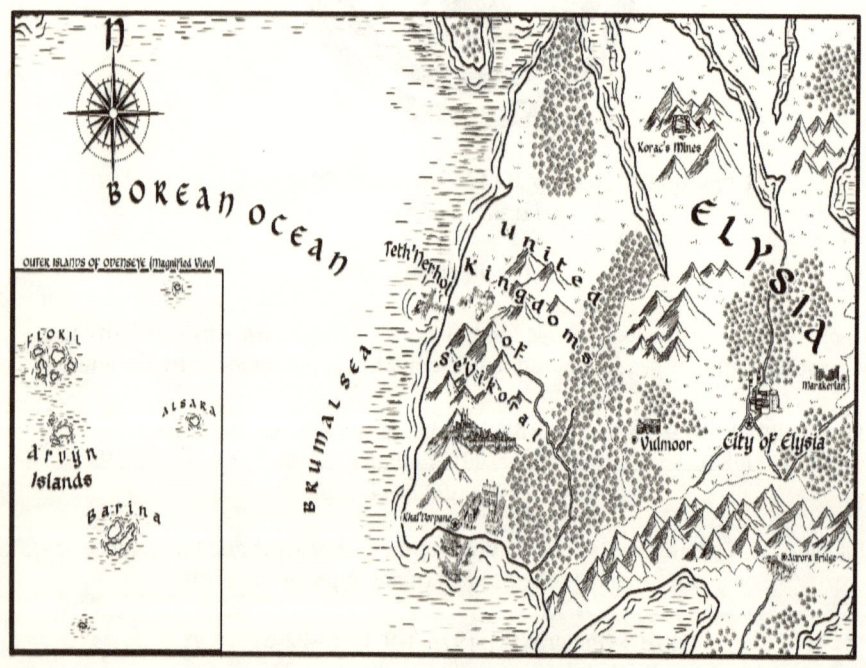

FULL ODENSEYE MAP

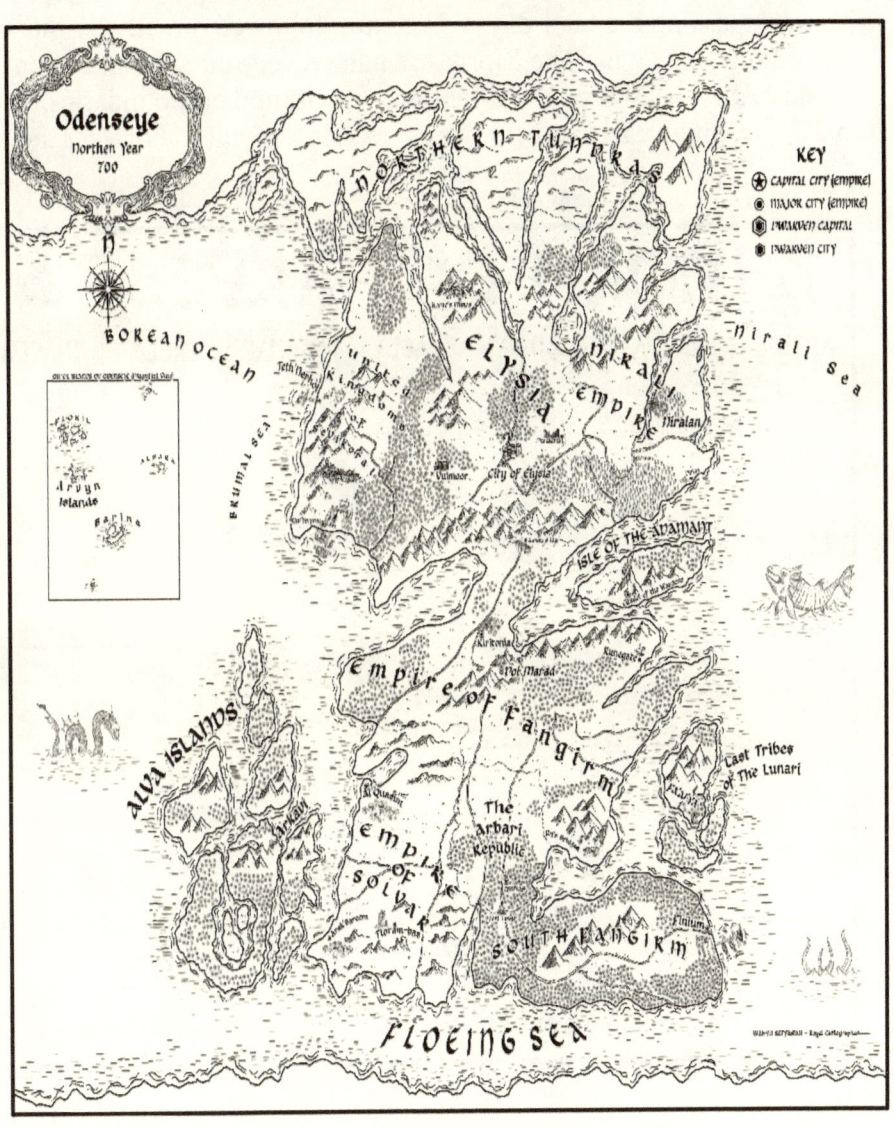

See more at Odenseye.wiki

NORTHERN CALENDAR EXAMPLE

The Northern year is comprised of thirteen months (referred hereto by their native term of Morn), with each having forty-two days. The Morn of Harvest, pictured here, is the ninth Morn of the year, encompassing the later days of autumn, followed directly by the Morn of Bare Trees. The Morns are named very directly and often describe a season or event that occurs within their boundaries, making it much easier for foreigners to glean what time of year they represent.

MORN OF HARVEST

AMEDA	VAEDA	CAEDAR	BRAELA	THAEDAR	SAELA	MAEDA
1	2	3	4	5	6	7
8	9	10	11	12	13	14
15	16	17	18 Harvests' Dawn Begins (Empires)	19	20	21
22	23 Festival of the Fallen Leaves (Elysia)	24	25	26	27	28
29	30	31	32 Festival of Kedja's Ascension (Arvyn)	33	34	35
36	37	38	39	40	41	42 Harvests' Dawn Ends (Empires)

Odenseye is a place of many cultures, very different from ours, and their names often prove difficult for foreigners to master. For ease of reading, a pronunciation guide for a few recurring names has been provided.

Niralan: Near-ah-lawn

Elysia: Ee-lee-see-uh

Se'Vikoral: Seh-vih-kor-ahl

Alauren: Ah-lore-en

Edlevin: Eddle-vin

Valin: Vah-lin

Arvyn: Arr-vin

Skylörek: Skull-deer-EK

Jqrtura - Yor-toh-RA

Redja: Red-yah

Thjodhild: Th-yo-d-hill-d

Eira, Thyra: Eer-ah, Theer-rah

Karlmaðr: Karl-muh-deer

Table of Contents

PROLOGUE:

FALL OF AN EMPIRE

The dawn shivers, and the greatest Empire on the continent topples before its mighty quakes.

Elysia, my country and my city in the north, greatest of the Nations, bastions against the brutal tyranny of Niralan, have come under siege for the first time in centuries, left to our fate by all but a seldom few of our allies. The wolves gnaw at the gates, rabid and slavering, eager to feed on the flesh within. I have heard in hushed tones, in mutters spoken by men of the sword, that the thresholds are failing as fast as morale. They believe the animals will have their feast.

Should these truly be the last days of Elysia, my duty is as solemn as it is critical. I write these words as a testament to the will of the free peoples of Odenseye, The Elysian and the Fangirmish, the valiant hearts willing to defend justice and the freedom of man to the biting of the ground. Their story will be told, dark and impossible as it may be.

I am not one for foolish legend or outlandish claims. History is our most valuable possession, a reminder of the nameless workers and soldiers that built our great Gem in the North, generations of work toward a common good that deserves proper appreciation. I would die before I sullied such a sacred idea.

Trust that I do not exaggerate, then, when I tell you that our enemy is an abomination, a stain on the purity of nature. He wakes from death, hungering for the blood of our great Empire. Twenty years ago, we sent the Grand Marshal of Niralan to the east, heartless, to rest among his brethren in his shattered homeland.

It was not enough.

Karsus is alive, beyond all explanation, one of the many drool-soaked animals who now pound against our doors. Niralan follows the command of a dead man, and so we fight to the last, each soldier's sacrifice recorded in the eternal histories.

This is the end. May any gods that care for what is good and just help us in this zealous struggle.

Gauis Truvani, Royal Historian

(Gauis Truvani, Royal Historian)

SIXTH OF THE MORN OF LONG DAYS
NORTHERN YEAR 715

For a moment, there was only a muffled din, like the pounding of rain on a roof on an otherwise silent night. These moments were to be savored, these precious few seconds that seemed to linger the length of winter, all the might of its frosted embrace closing in at once, the icy touch of death a mere handbreadth away. All the experience of life had led to this, one fractured moment in time whose shards each held their own futures, their own consequences. A single second could yield glorious victory or eternal darkness, yet there was no quiver in the soul of the armored General of the Nirali. He stood within the grand city of Elysia, the heart of his enemy, and from that thumping font of life he would draw blood.

His mind became clear once more, and the thunder of his own sabatons upon the cobblestone streets of Elysia's grand entry courtyard became the dominant sound. Ahead of him laid a shield wall, and behind those gilded blockers stood the Elysian Royal Guard, their ornate armor shining in the summer sun, reflecting from opal and gold fringe that seemed to line every crevice of the protective shells. All the while, their steel blades stood ready, eagerly awaiting the first of the enemy to crash upon their defensive line. To the side, a golden statue of Talis, the Elysian uniter and first emperor, stood watch over the coming violence. General Morvin shrugged within his armor, a set of silver-colored plate with etchings of ancient wars covering most every piece, readjusting to ensure his gaps were covered before meeting his foes.

Morvin grinned wickedly under his helmet. With a few final strides, he sprung himself forward as best as his heavy armor would allow, jumping into the defensive line and impacting two of the enemy shields, one with each knee. The Elysians crumpled under the weight of their heavily armored opponent, tumbling onto their backs as the General landed between them. His blade was ready, and he wasted no time in sliding it across the momentarily exposed necks of his foes. Within a breath, he drew his body tightly inward, closing his armor's gaps and locking each piece together as if they were pieces of a puzzle.

Blades thundered against the plate, yet a runic empowerment had been placed upon it by the Dwarves, creating what they called *Nasgadh*, the Skin of the Mountain. No sword found a gap, and neither did the armor crack or dent under the relentless assault, absorbing each blow as if they were little more than strikes from rodent.

Moments after the initial clash, a crush of silver armor, similar to Morvin's yet lacking the detailed etchings, slammed into the broken shield wall with the force of a typhoon. The Nirali, each as ready to die for their country as the last, swept over the Elysian battle line with a burning zeal, fighting savagely in close quarters. Their plate protected them well, but gaps could still be found; even with their numbers, many attackers fell at the feet of the Elysian guard, though their deaths only made the ground more treacherous for those defending it.

"Come on, then, up you go!" an energetic voice cried out from behind, knocking on the back of Morvin's chestplate. It was Skarde, his Lieutenant General and executive officer. The man was, even in the din of battle, chippy and energetic, and his words dripped with excitement. "You're not going to be happy with just two, are you? Look!" He pointed to a massive marble archway on the other side of the courtyard, flanked by solid walls. Two large gates still stood agape under the awning, waiting for the beleaguered defenders to retreat. "They left the door open!"

Morvin stood and chuckled, a sound that thundered in his helm and vibrated the metal. "Nirali! Push! Push to the keep! One more step!"

"ONE MORE STEP!" Dozens of voices chorused.

Seeing more Nirali pouring through the city's main gates a good distance behind their vanguard, the Elysians disengaged where they could and fell where they could not, choosing either living to fight another day or forging a final glory in the fires of war. Morvin kept a dogged pursuit, ensuring that he reached the gates mere steps behind the enemy.

Grabbing the gate on the left, he threw it open wide, catching a few arrows on the ridges of his armor for his trouble. Skarde mirrored the action on the right, clearing the way for a cadre of Nirali to secure the portcullis within. Resistance inside was light, despite the close quarters of the checkpoint, and so Morvin found himself stepping into the opulent glory of the main thoroughfare of Elysia in good time.

The ground here was a smooth, white marble, a carefully chosen variety of the stone that showed no wear under decades of constant use by the economic and political forces of the entire north. The midday sun reflected from the rock, sending a soothing, otherworldly glow and a soft warmth cascading to the silver armor of the advancing invaders. Houses and businesses lined either side of the road, each made of a similar marble, soft and beautifully crafted with rounded edges, each having small alleys on either side leading to back streets. Every step seemed to make these places more impressive, more awe-inspiring, growing in their glory as they neared the heart of the Empire of the Elysian Fields, and thus the power and riches held within the gilded walls.

Morvin paid them little mind, for the enemy stood ahead, occupying a chokepoint where two buildings jutted out into the main street. The Nirali troops, without need for instructions, closed ranks around their General, awaiting their next move. Morvin strode forward with squared shoulders and heavy steps, smirking under his helm. His troops followed suit, each betraying no emotion in their stance, only presenting a stoic calm. The Elysians formed a shield wall, readying for the encroaching tide.

The Nirali, following their officer, thundered forward with a bestial vigor as the sun glimmered from their armor, painting the street with flashes of light that darted this way and that as the invaders moved about. Morvin gripped his sword tightly, readying to drink once more from the blood of Elysia's sons.

In a single moment, the Elysians dropped their wall and charged forward with a booming battle cry. Though the maneuver was surprising, it only turned the fire in the General's heart to an inferno, and the savage grin under his helmet grew more with every thundering step. Two rivers of metal slammed against one another, bringing the respective charges to a grinding halt as they met in the middle.

Morvin shouldered his first target to the ground brutally, moving with near unnatural speed to plunge his blade into the man's neck before the gap could be closed. The General kept up his momentum, bringing his sword back to bear and leveling it straight forward, placing it harmlessly under another Elysian's arm as the distance between the two was closed. The enemy took the opportunity to drop his arm and lock it against his chest, meaning to clamp and disable Morvin's weapon, as Elysian plate protected the area well.

The General kept his charge going, though, throwing all his weight forward. The clamped blade acted as a point of leverage, allowing the Nirali commander to roughly spin the Elysian, putting him off balance. Skarde took advantage, running his sword up through a gap in the plate near the man's waist and ending him with a huff of breath and a soft gurgle. The enemy's arm went limp, and the Nirali weapon that he had clamped to his side was freed.

Morvin had already turned back to the fight, taking a breath to survey the scene. Chaos had erupted; a torrent of ear-splintering screams and the clashing of metal filled streets that were quickly becoming stained with blood. Gory splatter sprayed onto the fine marble of the buildings, seeping deeply into the porous stone, the meticulously crafted beauty becoming stricken with the scars of war as the sins of this gilded empire were paid back to it in full.

The road behind was empty, mysteriously missing the expected second wave of Nirali troops. Morvin's eyes widened as a hauntingly familiar memory peeked through the bloodlust that dominated his mind. "Retreat!" called the General. "Back! Back!"

The remaining Nirali disengaged where they could, with some choosing to stay to keep their enemy occupied, heroes that Morvin would ensure were remembered forevermore. The eastern troops gathered in a defensive line, while the Elysians had no choice but to do the same, with many of their soldiers lost within the chaos.

"Skarde," Morvin growled, "they'll be coming from the sides. Take ten of the company, help our second wave with whatever is holding them up, then pour down these alleys. The rest of us will hold here."

"Aye!" Skarde yelled, running back and tapping ten troops as he went, all of them dutifully following without question.

Morvin heaved with breath, looking on to the remaining twenty-four Nirali soldiers. "We hold, and this day will be won!" he yelled with a fiery vigor. "Form up and keep them busy! To the last drop of blood, we take no step back!"

The soldiers roared their approval, hunkering down, allowing Morvin to form the centerpiece of a silver wall that spanned the street, the shining plate of the Nirali leaving no gap to be found in their lines.

The Elysians charged again, taking a wedge formation with their shields, with the center aimed directly at the Nirali General. Leading the charge was an Elysian Royal Commander, a massive man in armor gilded with glittering rubies and sparkling diamonds, gems that twinkled brilliantly in the soft light of the street. Morvin braced, steadying his helm.

The Commander slammed shield-first into the General, pushing with all his might, a strained growl and drops of spittle escaping from his helm all the while. Morvin's feet skidded on the marble, yielding to the raw strength of the titanic human. Ground was steadily lost, forming a dangerous salient in the center of the line while the rest of the Nirali soldiers held fast. The Elysian, all the while, stabbed with his weapon, a short sword, unsuccessfully attempting to find an opening in his opponent's armor.

Morvin, waiting for a particularly heavy strike from the Commander, suddenly leapt back, quite agile despite his heavy plate. The Elysian overcommitted and stumbled forward, clanking and crashing as he fell onto his belly, his impressive strength unable to save him from his own momentum.

Instantly, Morvin stepped over the man, filling the gap in the lines. He locked his armor together, standing firm as if he were a statue, listening with joy as the Elysian Commander was brutally dispatched by another Nirali behind the fray. Impacts of swords and shields thundered off the General's armor, each failing to crack the metal, and each failing to push him back. One blade, however, found a small hairline gap near the belly, lacerating the General's lower ribs on the surface. He grit his teeth, pushing away the pain, for it would be among the most glorious of his many scars.

The marble shook under his feet as the second Nirali wave approached from behind; some poured down the alleys, while others moved to reinforce the front line. Morvin cackled madly, unlocking his armor and shoving away the nearest Elysian guard like he was a mere child. Much like the Eastmen minutes beforehand, the Elysian's assault had been costly, with several Royal Guards lying dead at the feet of the invaders. They attempted to pull back, scattering like fluff in the wind, sprinting down the main street to the chokepoint they had so foolishly abandoned. Elysian conscripts, dressed in gambesons and armed with pikes, poured out of the alleys ahead, unable to flank their opponents as they had been commanded, their only choice now being to link up with the remnants of the more trained troops.

"Forward!" Morvin cried. "Run them down!"

The minutes of combat that followed became a blur to the General, each son of Elysia that he sent to the dust being a just vengeance for the pain and sorrow of the past, for the horrors of the wars before, and a respite from the weight of the dead which had rested on his shoulders for two decades. Each successful strike of the blade was a promise fulfilled, a fallen comrade who could find their rest at last, comfortable in the knowledge that their sacrifice had not been in vain. On this day, Morvin's blade drank so deeply from the blood of Elysia that even he himself lost count, cackling like a madman as his rampant slaughter continued on.

Eventually, with his blade plunging through a prone man's gambeson, there were no more left to kill, and the few remaining of Elysia's forces retreated frantically toward the keep. Morvin, drenched in blood, stood tall, the viscous, crimson liquid streaming through the etchings on his armor like a forest brook, painting the graven visages of ancient battles with the glory of a new war.

"Sir!" Skarde yelped from behind. "A small contingent of Royal Guard was holding the gates, but we've cleared it out. Our counterattack surprised them. They are routed!" He was clearly beaming under his helm, his typical grin likely wider than ever. "We're encountering civilians, though. Bakers, drunks, the like. What should we do?"

"If they stand, run them down," Morvin growled. "If they let us pass, preserve them."

"Aye, sir," replied the Lieutenant. "One final push, General. The keep awaits."

Morvin peered at the grand palace of Elysia, sitting atop a hill, sunbeams shining through the clouds to brush upon the seat of Elysian power.

Morvin breathed deep, savoring the moment. "One more step."

"Damned of a thing, isn't it, Sir?" Skarde asked, removing his helmet to reveal a pearly white, wide smile. Black hair trickled over emerald eyes and a face that, though painted in blood, seemed to radiate only warmth and confidence. "The gates fall at dawn, and before sunset we stand..." He splayed his arms out, twirling, taking in the glory. "Here!"

The Nirali, now wearing their traditional black cloaks atop the silvery armor, stood in the throne room of Elysia, where every wall was gilded with masterful frescos and every bare spot on the marble floor had been covered over with intricate rugs from the lands of the Solvari, the Sun Elves. The T-shaped room was now swarming with Eastmen, while the Elysian Emperor sat on his throne at the center crossroads of the letter, rubbing his temple as he overlooked his ultimate failure. Where once the seat was meant to be an example of opulence to visitors and dignitaries, a way to show that business with Elysia meant riches beyond imagination, it now stood as a monument to the fall of an empire.

"Indeed," Morvin replied, leaning against one of the marble pillars that lined each side of the room, his helm still steady upon his head. "I'm just sorry that they surrendered before my blade could find their Emperor."

Skarde chuckled. "Even an Elysian has a point where their ego dies, and they must admit the battle is lost. Besides, a peaceful surrender means that Karsus himself can oversee the transfer of power." He leaned against the pillar opposite Morvin, tossing a thought. "I've been wondering, General... How did you know their plan, anyway? The attempt to flank us? It seems like that was quite the turning point."

Morvin glanced to the Elysian Emperor, Talisia, a man of gray hair and wrinkled skin, still flanked by beleaguered royal guards, though they now lacked arms and armor. They had surrendered soon after the baileys of the keep were breached, seeking a final end to the violence, though the corpses of a few of their more zealous soldiers still laid here and there in the hall, cut down where they stood, unwilling to sully their honor by giving up the fight.

Morvin turned his attention back to his Lieutenant General. "They reused tactics, Skarde, from Marakerlan. There, their elite forces held us back while their rank-and-file flanked through thick forest outside the city. It is impossible to forget the chaos, how everything suddenly turned inward despite the wide road we attacked from, leaving us barely any room to breathe." He inhaled deeply. "There, the Elysian tactics broke us. Here, they did little but allow me a chance to respond with a full understanding of their battle plan." He chuckled. "Just like the Elysians to believe that we wouldn't remember. Creatures of hubris, all of them."

Skarde nodded deeply. "And now, one more step has been taken. Our fallen souls can find their rest." The words brought another grin onto his face, almost in disbelief at their achievement. "With respect sir, take off your damn helmet and enjoy this moment."

Morvin, after a breath of consideration, obliged, removing his helm to reveal short, salt-and-pepper hair that was still drenched in sweat. An old scar, thin yet clearly visible, ran diagonally across the ridges of his pale face, terminating just above his brow. Hazel eyes looked over the throne room, the lights of chandeliers above reflecting within the depths of the world-weary soldier's gaze. "Twenty-two years, Skarde," murmured the General. "Twenty-two years of wailing ghosts following my every move." His words became choked for a moment as he looked down upon his trembling hands. "We fulfilled our promise."

"Damn right we did!" Skarde exclaimed exuberantly. He abruptly stood straight as a board, eyeing the throne room's main door. "Looks like another one is about to be fulfilled, as well."

Morvin turned and stood at attention just as quickly as his subordinate, for Karsus, Grand Marshal of Niralan, strode through the threshold with an icy confidence. The General had seen the man many times before, in both life and death, but he had never grown accustomed to the unsettling cold with which his leader carried himself.

Karsus wore a full suit of old Nirali plate, complemented by a ridged and angular helmet; the metal of these relics were covered in dents and bits of rust, the old scars of an old war, blemishes that reflected the torment of their bearer. In his hands he carried a massive, two-handed battleaxe, serrated near the top with a clean, curved edge on the bottom, while a single massive spike jutted out from the rear. Ivy vines wrapped around the hilt, seemingly growing from a dark crystal pommel.

Karsus strode past his commanders without acknowledgment. The determined gaze that lay behind the shadows of his helm was locked on to the Elysian Emperor, who could do little but quiver in place. Even Talisia's well-groomed beard seemed to tremble before the gravity of the figure that now stood over him, peering down with a crushing darkness.

"Kneel," Karsus said, calmly and coldly, hardly an emotion betrayed.

The Elysian ruler recoiled at the word, but quickly gathered himself. "I would bargain for my people."

"Your people are now mine," growled the Marshal. "Kneel."

Talisia stood from his throne, allowing a gilded white cape to fall away from his back. "I have no living heirs. I would ask for exile, never to return."

"Many of my country have no living heirs because of you and your bloodline," Karsus rumbled. "Kneel, or your people will know the pain that has thrusted upon the Nirali for centuries."

Talisia took a deep breath, steadying himself, though a quiver erupted in his lips, followed by tears which broke through the wall of strength that he attempted to project. Without a further word, he nodded and kneeled. Karsus raised his axe and paused for a moment. "Your line has ended."

Morvin watched with starry eyes as the axe fell, its blade wailing like a sorrowful phantom as it sliced through air and flesh, finalizing the victory of the Nirali. Karsus turned and strode out of the keep without a further word, leaving the remaining invaders alone with their thoughts and the pooling blood of the Imperial line.

"The greatest empire on the continent falls," Skarde said, his voice painted with amazement, like someone who had just seen the night sky for the first time. "Our victory is final. We won."

Morvin rumbled an indistinct agreement as two figures in obsidian black robes entered the throne room, wearing tightly wrapped hoods under which only their lower jaws could be seen, each painted a deep purple. Their mouths emanated mist, dissipating like fog under the morning sun soon after the breath left their lungs. They kneeled and pawed at the dead Elysian guards, inspecting them closely.

"We should go," Skarde mumbled. "We've got work to do, and there's no sense in being around for this."

Morvin, nodding in wholehearted agreement, led the way out of the keep and into the red glow of the sunset, the last light that would ever paint the Empire of the Elysian Fields.

PART ONE:

THE CHANGING SEASONS

CHAPTER ONE:

SMALL TOWN LIFE

4th OF THE MORN OF HARVEST
NORTHERN YEAR 715

On a planet called Jǫrtúra there was a continent known as Odenseye, towering and vast, a sprawling scar on the wild, dangerous oceans that encompassed the vibrant green, brown and white of the land. This was a place of empires, of sprawling domains and fluttering flags, of violent war and undying strife. Even so, peace could be found nestled within its nooks and crannies, like the nest of a songbird that has made its home in the enclosed trunk of a tree.

One such pocket of peace was called Teth'Nerhol (Teth, in shorthand), a small village in the remote Northwest of Odenseye. The United Kingdoms of Se'Vikoral laid claim to the area, yet the creeping fingers of power seldom found a reason to bother with what was, in all reality, little more than a speck of a fishing town on the coast.

A vassal of sorts to Elysia, Se'Vikoral was generally a quiet, peaceful nation, albeit lacking in much of the splendor and opulence of the neighboring empire. Commerce and advantageous terrain had saved them from total conquest in ages past; even so, they still found themselves owing tacit allegiance to the Empire of the Elysian Fields. They were independent kingdoms, yet it was well known that they remained so at the behest of their masters, their rural and meager country treated like a prize hound for the true power in the north.

Within Teth, near the water's edge, there was a smithy, a simple structure, enclosed by three stone walls with a wooden countertop in the front for interacting with customers. The roof was made of a royal purple canvas (a rare color in such places as Teth) that protected thick wooden support beams from the rage of the sea and weather alike. With a single pull of a rope, the open-air stall would collapse into a private, dome-shaped tent, heated by the warmth of the ever-glowing furnace.

Inside the structure, a blacksmith worked dutifully, going about her daily routine with as much enthusiasm as she could muster. She wore a leather apron on top of a pocketed vest and toolbelt, under which lay a well-fitting button-up shirt of an off-white color; loose cloth trousers of a dulled gray hue, meanwhile, had been hastily tucked into tightly tied leather boots. Deep brown hair drooped haphazardly over her chestnut eyes, pointed ears, and milky, almost golden skin. She was a well-toned woman, her muscles perfectly fitting for her smaller frame, being neither too large nor too small, and she wielded her lithe form with a deceptive strength, swinging her heavy hammer as if it were a wooden toy. Many travelers from the lands beyond her quaint village would guess that she was an Elf; in truth, she was a mix of species, yet the specifics of her bloodline were a long-forgotten mystery. It didn't matter, in the end, for the simple folk of Teth cared only for her masterful creations and good company.

She supplied ships and shops alike across the Northwest of the continent, taking orders as fast as she could fulfill them, using her decades of practice to produce some of the finest metal in the north. Regardless of her success, she had kept her place small and tidy, choosing to spend much of her gold elysium coins on exotic food and drink that often passed by in the wagons of foreign merchants. Splendor was little more than a waste to her, a trait that had been appreciated by those residents who had become her neighbors, all of them living a simple and proud life.

Today, though, her typical shuffling haste was not present, and it would be clear to anyone who knew her that something was, simply put, wrong. She paced back and forth in her shop, eyeing the forge warily, her mind and body uncharacteristically in unrest.

It isn't hot enough, thought the smith. *Why?*

She began to inspect the outside of the large, scorching structure, being careful not to touch its searing stone walls. It appeared as little more than a large, rounded boulder with a conical cap, yet there was a deceptive complexity to it; each curve and opening had been carefully placed to keep a steady, high temperature upon the metals that liquified within. Even so, the smith's well-trained eyes came upon the problem almost instantly: a crack near the rear of the forge, and not the first in that spot.

Instantly flying into a rage, the blacksmith grabbed her hammer from her belt and whipped it across the structure, where it clattered on a pile of swords before coming to a quiet rest upon the dirt floor. "Damn it all!"

"Oh, this should be good," a familiar, soothing voice trilled from the shop's only entrance, a wooden door next to the counter. "Sounds like Angry Alauren is visiting."

The voice belonged to Edlevin, an older human who had been Alauren's closest friend since they had first met over fifteen years ago. A large man, Ed stood a head taller than most humans, while his perfect posture was clearly indicative of a military history. His face was hardened by wars and wrinkled by years, yet the old soldier still managed to display the same soft look of concern and amusement that had first greeted the blacksmith when he retired to her quiet village. Even back then, he had a perpetually disheveled look, bearing wrinkled black clothes and messy salt-and-pepper hair, complemented by a permanent growth of stubble that he shaved infrequently. Still, he was a dignified man, proud, and a single look easily revealed the quiet strength hiding underneath the façade.

Alauren smiled at the man and gave him a quick hug, which he returned in kind. "Seems like everything that could be going wrong, is," she said, letting go. "First my favorite crucible cracks and falls apart, then my nails come out warped, and now I find the culprit has likely damaged a lot of the goods I shipped without me even knowing it."

Edlevin smirked warmly, raising an eyebrow. "Maybe I can help. What's the cause?"

"My forge has a crack in the back. Same place as before. Here – look." She led him to the damage and pointed, following up the gesture with an exasperated shrug.

"Ah, it's nothing! Watch," Edlevin said, procuring a small pouch from one of his black tunic pockets and donning a pair of thick leather gloves. He used a small bowl to gather some water from Alauren's 'reservoir' (in reality, just a hole in the ground that helped her avoid running to the well or ocean again and again). "I bought this stuff, Vragad, from a particularly loud but exceptionally clear Dwarf." He pinched a small amount of the putty-like material from the pouch and carefully placed it over the crack, taking care to cover every piece of the fracture. He moved quickly to pour water on the patch, causing it to harden instantly, even before the sweltering furnace could turn the liquid to steam. "Easy," he warbled, smug and self-satisfied.

Alauren crossed her arms. "Don't get too proud of yourself, now. I could have fixed it."

"You would have just paid Varuk to do it, and he always overcharges you," Edlevin dismissed with a laugh and a wave. "In any case, I accept your silent thanks!"

Alauren nodded, but the smile disappeared from her face as her mind shifted back to her work, uncharacteristically unwilling to argue the point.

"Hey," Edlevin said in a fatherly voice, removing the gloves. "I know you. A crack in your forge wouldn't upset you enough to mistreat your equipment or miss an opportunity to give me a hard time when I'm being prideful. What's bothering you?"

Alauren shrugged. "I don't know, Ed. It's everything combined, I suppose. Elysia's fall, the Norts to the north, the fact that there seem to be dark days ahead, in general. I'll bet you my hammer that the winter will be tough, too. The air already has a bite to it, doesn't it?" As if on cue, a crisp wind blew through the forge, drawing out an extended sigh from the smith as she exhaled with the breeze. "Worst of all, Martin told me yesterday that the Inn is running low on ale. There's a lot to be worried about."

"True," Edlevin conceded, smirking. "But you must not let the weight of the world rest upon your shoulders. It is something I did for too long." He leaned backwards on the tent's front desk, lounging with a continuing smile upon his face. "Are you happy, here at your forge?"

"You know I am," the woman replied.

"Then let yourself focus on that," Edlevin said. "Do not think to lift the world alone! No Man, Dwarf or Elf can do so single-handedly. We will persevere together. For now, focus on your forge. Focus on helping to arm the guards and keep us safe. Find strength in those around you. That's the only way I survived the war, and the sorrow that followed."

"I don't know, Ed," Alauren replied unsurely, crossing her arms in response to another chill gust. "I can narrow my focus all that I want, but those problems still exist. They still press on my mind. What will we do if Niralan shows up here? What will we do if the Norts try to raid us? There are certain realities we should be prepared for, right?"

The old soldier maintained his smirk. "Again, we persevere together. We will face those challenges, should they come. All you can do is be prepared to stand up and do your part."

Alauren opened her mouth to thank her friend for his comforting words, but was interrupted by a whooshing sound as a bright light erupted between them, briefly interrupting the autumn wind.

After the light had gone, it became apparent that a Dwarf had appeared, materializing from seemingly thin air. He was, like all Dwarves, short and stout. He stood half of Edlevin's height and sported a black, tangled beard and long hair that drooped over intricate (but exceedingly ragged) red and black robes. He held in his hand a war scythe; black smoke poured from its ivory-white (and only slightly curved) blade, a smog which quickly dissipated into nothing as the wind began to shuffle through the shop once more. The black metal shaft of the scythe was adorned by wicked red thorns, having two smooth areas with which to hold the weapon, each matching the blade in color.

"Aw, damn it, ye arse, I was havin' fun!" the Dwarf exclaimed, talking to seemingly nobody. "Now where have ye taken me?"

He suddenly perked up, noticing the two disturbed residents peering at him with slack jaws and wide eyes. He turned to Alauren and grinned, displaying a set of slightly yellowed teeth.

"Ay, lass!" bellowed the Dwarf. "Where's the pub?"

CHAPTER TWO:

AND THEN THERE WAS A DWARF

The race of the Dwarves were largely native to the underground of Odenseye, and those typical to the surface were "Shortbeards" (so named for their trimmed facial hair, which is less of a burden in combat). Usually, these stout warriors were simple mercenaries taking on contracts in order to take wealth back to their homes in the deep. This one, though, had a long and flowing beard indicative of aristocracy, a true oddity in the lands which were touched by sunlight.

"Excuse me? Who are you?" queried the smith, her eyes wide with a clear shock.

"Nevermind that, lass!" the Dwarf grumbled gruffly. "THE. PUB. Where is it?"

Alauren felt a sudden fury build up within her, a growing indignancy that needed an outlet. A slap impacted the Dwarf hard across the face, eliciting a yelp from the stout stranger. "Any who enter MY forge say a proper greeting first, short one," growled the smith.

The Dwarf furrowed his brow for a moment, processing the sting on his cheek. After a moment, he nodded, and the grin appeared on his face once more. "HA! Me apologies, lass. I'm not so good at the social parts o' life, bein' a wanderer. My name is Valin. Valin Runesorrow."

Alauren glanced at Edlevin, who was still staring with a twisted, nearly comical face of disbelief. His gaze seemed to focus intently on the scythe, and his eyes intensely watched the smog pour from the blade.

"See, politeness isn't so hard," grumbled the smith, returning her attention to the sudden visitor. "Now, how did you get in my forge, and what are you doing in my forge?"

"Eh?" Valin grunted. "I dunno, lass. Ye'd have t' ask Drell. He controls the teleporty contraption."

Alauren sighed deeply and rubbed her temple, doing her best to tamp down her annoyance. "Okay. Who is Drell?"

"Oh!" the Dwarf laughed. "Ye can't hear him. I sometimes forget, given that he's such a loud wank. He's an old sorcerer. Lives in me Scythe and talks in me head. Varsa Drell."

"Varsa Drell," Edlevin repeated skeptically, narrowing his eyes. "That's a name from the story books, Dwarf. A children's tale. You're seriously telling me that he lives in that weapon?"

Valin smiled, his yellow teeth just barely showing from under the scraggly beard. "Aye, his soul's in there, or some such thing! He gets on me nerves sometimes, the loudmouth."

"Ed?" Alauren asked incredulously, finally giving in to the creeping confusion. "What the *fuck*?"

Edlevin simply shrugged with bewilderment, content to explain what little he could. "Varsa Drell, by the word of the stories, dabbled in magic that was beyond any other. He could move objects across great distances with a thought, transporting them with little more than a flash of light and a light puff." He cocked an eyebrow and leaned in closer to the Dwarf, inspecting every smudge of dirt and grime upon the stout fellow's skin. "That is, until he teleported himself to a place beyond the stars." He shook his head, dismissing further consideration. "It's all bunk, in any case. Magic is too fickle for such things, too hard to master. It is impossible."

Valin looked to his scythe for a moment before speaking. "Drell says that's all a load o' shite. He knew what he was doin', and judgin' by me presence here, it's not so impossible, is it?"

Edlevin shrugged. "It's tall tales. I'm just quoting what I've read." His gaze turned stern. "Besides, if someone like Drell was in that weapon, a vagabond like you would hardly be able to hold it without falling victim to him. The stories told of him turning others to ash with hardly a broken sweat." He smirked and crossed his arms. "You look like you can barely control your own beard hairs, Dwarf."

"Naaaaaw!" Valin droned in protest. "I'm more powerful than this old dustrag! HAHAHA!" A momentary glance at his weapon followed the guffaw, his face suddenly becoming painted with annoyance. "I am too, ye knob!" the Dwarf shouted at the blade, as if he were yelling in someone's face. "Not arguin' it with ye again, and if ye wanna prove otherwise ye best come outta there and prove it rightly!"

"I am so confused," Alauren groaned, breaking the convoluted conversation.

"As am I," Edlevin agreed. "Whatever the truth is, the Marchioness needs to be made aware of this new visitor. Dwarf, with me." He beckoned heavily towards the stout stranger, while the steely cold of his face left no room for argument.

"Alright," Valin replied calmly, unfazed by the events, as if it were a particularly boring day at work. "Can we stop by the pub first?"

"No," Edlevin calmly replied. "They're nearly out of ale anyway."

For the first time since he had arrived, genuine concern painted Valin's face.

The inside of the grand longhouse reeked of incense and wood fire, smells which caused the new arrival to wrinkle his bulbous nose in a barely hidden disgust. The building was a simple, narrow hall leading to a few steps and a carved wooden throne, behind which several candles flickered dimly. A number of doors on either side led to the ruler's various living and dining areas, away from the general din of the main court. Though it appeared small, the building was a maze of its own, and each of the myriad of thresholds opened to larger chambers beyond.

A gathered Counsel, the official title of a moot in Se'Vikoral, looked upon the strange visitor with equal parts fear and curiosity. They were influential fishers, merchants, and the captain of the town guard, all men and women of prominence who had been the de-facto government of the town for decades, each owing their loyalty to the local ruler, who took the traditional moniker of Marchioness. Once, the epithet was given only to women, who were viewed as subservient in the ancient, fractured Se'Vikoran lands. Long ago, however, the title had been forcibly bestowed upon the vassals who found themselves conquered by a woman named Se'lah, the unifier of the United Kingdoms, and the first female ruler of the Se'Vikoran people.

At the center of the mass stood Marchioness Sortul himself, his perfect posture and still-dark hair obfuscating his true age. He was an older man, in truth, who had once stood as the greatest among the guards in the capital city of Khal'Dorpane. Now, though, he had grown far more round with his docile years of service to the people, forgoing the jewels and splendor of other rulers for white fur robes and a crown of simple, twisting wood. Still, the air he carried along with him was as dignified and respected as that of an Elysian Emperor.

After much arguing (and a brief entanglement of blows), Valin had been allowed inside with his weapon, with Edlevin stressing, however unsurely, that the scythe was safest with the Dwarf. Alauren waited next to the stout stranger patiently while Edlevin told the group's short, strange story.

Sortul stood silent for a few moments after Edlevin had finished, his left eyebrow raised nearly to his hairline as his mind tried to make sense of the nonsensical. "He just… appeared?"

"Out of thin air, Marchioness," Edlevin repeated, shrugging in response to the ruler's confused glare. "It is due to his artifact, I think. It is a relic of power. A relic of Varsa Drell, according to Valin."

Sortul looked on in even greater confusion. "Ed, you've never told me any tall tales before. Why start now?"

Edlevin looked to the smith, silently asking for support with a half-shrug and a questioning tilt of the head.

"He's telling the truth, Marchioness," Alauren testified firmly. She was quite unused to speaking publicly, as evidenced by the rapidity with which the words were delivered. "I saw it all myself."

"This is a portent, Lord," the Captain of the Guard spouted, glaring angrily at the Dwarf. "A sign from the gods!"

"Yes, Dalvon." Edlevin replied with a dripping sarcasm, practically spitting each word. It was known to the smith that her old friend respected the Captain, more so than he did many others in Teth, but the old soldier also rarely hesitated to prod the proud man when he was being short-sighted. "I too recall all the times the gods used half-drunk Dwarves to deliver their warnings."

"Two thirds drunk!" Valin corrected, which drew glares all around.

Dalvon, ever the firebrand, flushed red with fury at the comment. "Do you have any other explanation?" he snapped, glowering at Edlevin. "We have Norts camped to the north. Eight hundred of them!" He shifted uneasily in place, his anger giving way to worry for a split second. "We lose Elysia, our protectors from the Eastern hordes, and now this. The world is turning sour."

Valin spoke up, breaking his amused silence. "Yer borin' me with yer panicked notions o' war." He slammed the pommel of his weapon hard on the wooden floor, drawing an echoing boom which, after a few gasps, brought utter silence to the room and full attention to himself. "I'm here because Drell is an absolute arsehole o' a prisoner who likes t' drop me halfway across the continent at random," the Dwarf elaborated calmly, his tone noticeably more tactful and diplomatic than it had been just moments before. "Just last week, he had me briefly pop in on the Fangirmish royalty. They didn't appreciate the company." The dry comment drew chuckles from some of the gathered Nobles, which seemed to please the stout stranger. "I don't mean ye any harm, truly, nor am I some sorta portent of darker days. I'm just a wanderer, lookin' fer me next pint."

"Bah!" Dalvon yelled. "Why would he tell us the truth?"

"'Cause I'm not drunk enough t' lie, wanker!" Valin shot back with a growl, regaining his more flippant attitude.

"You are an agent of forces that would see us die!" Dalvon shrieked, having fully lost his temper. He wheeled on the Marchioness, his patchwork armor clacking against itself at the sudden motion. "My Lord, we must make ready for an immediate attack. The Norts mean to confuse us before they destroy us!"

Sortul gave no reply, staring forward with empty, bewildered eyes.

"I don't think they do, Dalvon," Edlevin soothed, stepping forward and obscuring the Dwarf behind him. "Such a small number is rare for the Northmen. When they raid, it is usually in the thousands. Strength in numbers and a wide front are their advantages."

"You always stress readiness," Dalvon quickly countered, his voice gruff and uncompromising. "Always be ready for the tide, you often say. The Norts are the tide, and they are here for a reason! By your own words, we are fools to do nothing!"

"We are fools to antagonize them without reason!" Edlevin contested, his brow furrowing incredulously. "We can't send a bunch of armored townsfolk to fight them should we manage to piss them off, can we?"

"We would fight valiantly!" Dalvon proclaimed proudly, thumping his fist on his chestplate.

"You would die quickly, at least," Edlevin replied, following the comment with an involuntary (and quite regrettable) yelp of a laugh.

The room abruptly delved into absolute chaos, with all parties voicing their sides of the argument in a calm and orderly manner, if your definition of calm and orderly is exemplified by a tavern at midnight. Various fiery opinions on the Nort predicament echoed off the walls and vibrated the floorboards, a veritable flood of ideas and suggestions that could be held back no longer.

"We'll just kill 'em all, yeah!" one man yelled.

"We'll give 'em a bunch of bycatch tah eat, tell 'em tah bugger off in return," a woman shouted.

"If the Norts sent him, let's use the ol' catapult and launch the Dwarf back at 'em!" a light voice yelled, hardly holding back his following cackle.

Sortul let his head fall into his hands, rubbing his eyes in frustration as the 'solutions' became ever more absurd.

Alauren, ever reticent to engage in what Edlevin called 'lively debate', stayed silent, watching the red faces of the Counsel as they bellowed their thoughts. She glanced at Valin, who simply returned a smirk and a roll of the eyes. The smith sighed, exasperated, and gathered the will to speak. "Why don't you just talk to them?" she proposed quietly.

Subdued as the words were, they were heard by the only person whose opinion would, at the end of the day, matter. "Quiet!" thundered the Marchioness, snapping his head up and drawing an instant end to the clamor of voices.

Silence fell over the room as all eyes were drawn first to Sortul, whose gaze led to Alauren.

"Isn't it always simplest to just talk to them, even if they're Norts?" the smith presented. She chuckled to herself, tossing an absurd thought. "If it will get me back to my forge before sundown today, I'll do it myself, tomorrow."

Sortul looked to the woman for a while, sifting an idea, seeping a deep dread into the pit of her stomach as his intense gaze focused in on her own. He shifted his eyes to Edlevin, who nodded with a knowing smile. "What a splendid idea," said the Marchioness, smirking devilishly. "If the Norts hold any ill will, we must approach this situation with the utmost caution. I would ask you to personally bring them a sword of the finest quality, as a gift and token of our desire for peaceful relations. I will, of course, provide materials."

Alauren took a shocked a step back, as if she had been struck by a heavy gale, her eyes as wide as the moons. "My lord, I was only jesting. I'm not fit for such a task." She looked to Edlevin for support, yet found only a barely contained amusement returning the glance, leaving her standing alone. "I haven't left this town in decades, and I don't mean to now."

"Yes," Sortul continued, ignoring the blacksmith's feeble pleas for mercy entirely. "A personal delivery from a smith of your quality is the finest gift I could imagine. Such situations outweigh your personal desires." He chuckled. "I commend you for bringing up the idea in this meeting, Alauren. You will depart as soon as the blade is ready. Until then, focus on this task."

"The Dwarf, sir?" Dalvon asked, unhappy yet willing to accept the judgement of his superior.

"Sequester him in a room at Martin's," Sortul instructed. "We'll see how this goes before we make our decision on him."

Alauren could only stand frozen in horror as the gathered crowds were dismissed back to their homes, satisfied with the night's unexpected entertainment.

CHAPTER THREE:

A GIFT BEFITTING

5th OF THE MORN OF HARVEST
NORTHERN YEAR 715

"I wasn't serious!" Alauren exclaimed, her voice sharp and anxious. She carefully strained to set a large, red gem into the bottom of a bronze-hued hilt, held vertically by a vice. She stood towards the front of her forge, where the light was strongest, struggling to hold her hands steady in the shadows of the tent. The afternoon was fresh, standing at odds with the smith, who could find barely a wink of sleep in the night, choosing instead to start her work well before the sun peeked over the western reaches of the ocean. For her tireless efforts, a completed blade had taken shape, and not even the tremors of her nerves could have hoped to reduce the quality of her work.

"I know you're anxious, but I'll be there with you," Edlevin soothed. Indeed, he had volunteered to escort the smith safely to her destination. "There is no need to worry, truly. The legends of the Northmen are often overblown. They are people, just like us. I promise you that."

"You know this…" Alauren inquired, looking up; though her eyes were hidden behind a pair of protective goggles, the tilt in her eyebrow was still easily visible. "How? You've rarely mentioned them."

"You know I've been to the north before," the old soldier answered proudly. "Even in the safest lands of Northern Se'Vikoral, one rubs shoulders with a diverse lot."

Alauren's brow fully furrowed in equal parts skepticism and amusement. "Ed, I've had to listen to a billion and a half of your stories, and you've mentioned Northmen a total of twice. Once when you were drunkenly listing off the 'right bastards of Odenseye' and once when you said they made good shields." She returned her eyes to her work. "They seem like the kind of folk you'd remember a bit more of than that."

Edlevin laughed heartily and shrugged. "I'm getting old, Ally. Memories don't come without prompting anymore."

Alauren shook her head, snickering with derision. "Sure, blame the age and not all those nights at the Inn. I can't imagine Martin's 'Mind Eraser' concoction has helped any."

Edlevin returned the mirth with a conceding smile and nod as the smith turned back to her task. He resolved to be quieter, choosing to let his friend work while admiring her new creation. It was a fusion between a short sword and a saber, a brilliantly creative blend of southern elegance and northern hardiness. Steel shimmered on a blade that curved ever so slightly near the tip, while the base terminated in a heavy, protective crossguard, whose arms turned downward, forming a cage for the fingers. Its edges were awe-inducing even at first glance, sharp enough to cut bones with ease, and a single bronze strip of metal ran over the weapon's upper curve, terminating in the hilt and reinforcing the structure. There were no blemishes from the working or grinding of the metal, the marks of what Alauren often called a 'lesser smith'.

"Done!" the blacksmith yelped gleefully as she bent the last metal shim of the pommel down, sealing the gem within. "How does it look?"

"With the Norts, it's not about looks," Edlevin replied calmly, snatching the sword from its vice. He cut a series of mock blows through the air, finding the balance and weight to be perfect as he sliced the flesh of his invisible enemy to tatters. Even the slight curvature of the blade was carefully designed, giving every slash the potential to cut deep. "It performs beautifully, my friend," he beamed, smiling as he carefully ran his fingers across the edges. "The design is familiar to me, yet you've changed it for the better. It will be accepted gratefully, I think."

"It had better be, for both our sakes," Alauren replied anxiously, brushing back her hair. "I don't know if I can do this, Edlevin."

The old soldier smiled and took a deep breath. "The doing is not the hard part, it's the thinking about it. Come on, the Inn should still have some ale left to ease our minds a bit."

Alauren nodded, cleaning her hands in a bucket of water before attaching the sword to her waist with a fine leather scabbard and belt, a piece acquired from traveling merchants decades ago, simply awaiting a blade that would fit. She allowed her goggles to slip down onto her neck and followed her friend out of the forge with a nervous spring in her step, trying to push away thoughts of the future.

The FishInn was a simple but effective design, being a single-story building of unblemished oaken boards and beams. A large dining area, lit by hanging torches, laid to the left of the main door, while the right led to the bar, where a slab of solid redwood served as the dining surface. Every seat in the establishment was carved of fine wood by the Innkeeper himself, a red-haired, stout, and plump man with a large nose and a state of near-perpetual drunkenness. The lone occupied stool at the bar held a fisherman, looking down at his drink worriedly.

Edlevin had wasted no time in his rush to the bar, taking a seat one down from the fisherman. Alauren settled in next to her old friend, who was already ordering drinks. "Ed," she grumbled, "my nerves are on fire."

"I know, Ally. We'll be okay," replied the old soldier. "Focus on the ale for now."

Alauren looked on in horror as Martin plunked a mug onto the dark wooden bar. He prided himself on his work just as much as Alauren did her own, typically leading to the finest selection of ales and stouts on the coast; most were his own make, though he always kept the finest of Elysian brews stocked in brighter times.

The beverage in front of them today, though, was siltier than a riverbed and smelled of something mysteriously sour, while flakes of an unknown origin swirled within the dark brown depths. It looked, truthfully, like someone had managed to liquify and ferment the slag from the smith's furnace.

"Shit, Edlevin," Alauren recoiled, picking up the drink and swishing it about. "I feel like taking a swig out of the ocean would be cleaner."

Edlevin's cup was already tipped high as he gulped down the murky concoction loudly and without hesitation. He suddenly slammed the mug down hard onto the bar, sending a *thwock* sound echoing across the room. "If I had such nervousness as you do," he said amidst a gasp for breath, "I would rather be trying to calm those nerves than talking. Drink!"

Alauren peered down at the cup, again watching the dark flakes drift within. "Martin!" she yelped suddenly. "Your beer looks like shit!"

Instead of being offended, Martin simply let out a guffaw that echoed around the building. "That it doesh!" he slurred. "Almosht out. 'Bout 8 cupsh left in the barrel, I think. Shit getsh sssilty when it'sh old. All I got 'til the next batch ish ready, though."

Alauren smiled, daring to take a sip. The ale was predictably bitter and more than a little sour, lighting up the tip of her tongue as if it had been stung by a wasp. "Ed," gasped the smith, holding a hand close to her mouth as she recoiled, "how did you chug this?"

Edlevin's only reply was a hearty chortle. "Martin! Another!"

Martin grabbed Edlevin's cup and attempted to use a small tap on a barrel built into the rear wall to fill the vessel, yet he found only drips spattering forth.

"What?" the keep queried to himself, incredulous. "I checked earlier. I had more than thish!" He flew through the kitchen door with an unmatchable zeal to investigate the issue.

"Well," Edlevin said, watching the stout man retreat to his back rooms. "I'm sufficiently inebriated to talk about tomorrow. How about you?"

Alauren could not respond with anything but a light gurgle as she forced the brew down. She eventually laid the cup gingerly onto the bar, her face scrunched like she had just eaten a plump insect raw. "Alright," she struggled, her voice low and guttural, forcing back a gag reflex. "Now I am."

"We leave tomorrow at sunrise," Edlevin instructed. "I think it would take about a day's travel by horse. I'll requisition a few from the Marchioness."

Alauren squirmed in her seat, pushing her empty cup around aimlessly. "You know how long it's been since I left town, Ed?"

Edlevin smiled and shook his head, leaning his elbows on the bar. "You've been here ever since I arrived. So, quite a while."

"I don't talk about it much, but there's something about being out there. I just…" Alauren explained, trying to choose her words as best she could. "I never feel safe."

Edlevin smiled warmly. "Such feelings are often nothing more than homesickness, Ally. Once you are again in the open fields and forests, I know you will be able to find your center, to find strength that can only come from being out there, away from it all. Give your spirit rest, and know that it will be well for the fresh air and sounds of-"

Alauren rolled her eyes, bracing for another long-winded explanation of just how much beauty the old soldier had found in his travels. Instead, her friend was interrupted by a loud scuffle in the kitchen, shortly followed by Valin being thrown through the kitchen door. Splinters rocketed from the stout man's impact point as the slab of wood cracked in two and clattered to the floor. The Dwarf's upper back slammed off the inner rim of the bar with a great rumbling sound, but he jumped to his feet quickly and hopped over the redwood surface, rushing towards the nearest exit before the enraged innkeep could close the distance.

"Thief!" Martin shrieked, grabbing a large kitchen knife.

"Now's a good time t' teleport me, ye daft arse!" Valin yelled intently at his weapon, plowing through the front doors shoulder-first.

Martin, amazingly fast for his size and intoxication, hopped the bar in a single bound and followed the Dwarf out the door, screaming swears all the while.

Edlevin stood, grabbed the fisherman's drink (who was clearly grateful to be rid of the swill), and downed it with a surprising speed. "Come on," he grumbled. "I should step in."

Alauren jumped from her seat and followed the sounds of curses into the main square, where the keep was already in a standoff with the snarling Dwarf. The human wielded his blade threateningly with bear-like hands, while Valin waved his scythe about feebly, like he was swatting at a swarm of disturbed hornets. He was pressed up against the town's center sign, caught between two planks that pointed to other communities throughout the kingdoms, and on either side sat small market stalls with annoyed shopkeepers looking on from within.

"Alright, gentlemen. Time to break it-" Edlevin began, interrupted by a stumble as his foot caught a rock. He blinked rapidly and looked down, wobbling, recentering himself and causing the smith to roll her eyes.

"Let's figure this out, yes?" The old soldier proposed, once he was solidly on his feet.

"There'sh nothing to figure out!" yelled the Innkeep, who was wavering from side to side with each utterance of a word. The commotion grew a large crowd around them, eager to see what drama the stranger had stirred up. "He shtole from meh!"

"If ye'd have served me, I wouldn't o' had t' tap it meself, would I?" Valin retorted, similarly wavering.

Martin only grew angrier at the comment. "I told ya, I'd only serve localsh because I was almosht out!" The crowd's opinion seemed to shift heavily behind their giver of alcohol and his convincing argument.

"Let's just calm down, my people, and breathe for a moment," Edlevin petitioned, his voice booming around the square with ease. "Martin, talk to me inside. I'll make sure you're compensated."

"Compenshation my ash!" Martin yelled. "He shtole from meh! He needsh to stand trial." The crowd loudly enforced their agreement.

"His is a rare kind among us, Martin," the old soldier pointed out, his voice taking on an air of experienced diplomacy. "We must keep in mind his own customs. They differ from ours, you know, quite drastically. I, for one, have traveled the southern lands, often bumping shoulders with the Shortbeard warriors of the Garradh. I'm familiar with them."

"Yeah? Howsh about doesh their customsh work?" Martin snapped skeptically.

"The weakest, most pathetic, and most destitute among the Dwarves are often granted access to take ale and small amounts of food for free, as long as they stay out of trouble with the city guard," Edlevin bellowed with extreme surety, planting one hand on his hip while the other confidently pointed to the sky, accentuating his words. "Clearly such a pitiful one was not aware of our selfish customs. He has been here but hours, and what seems to us to be malice is simply an act of utter foolishness; idiocy, even, lacking the good sense to ask us first."

"That's not-" Valin yelled angrily, before abruptly cooling down after a glance to the scythe. "That's not entirely inaccurate. I'm new here, and I've spent many days on the road."

Martin rocked back and forth repeatedly for a few moments, locking eyes with the Dwarf. A hatred burned within them, an anger that could be held only by a man separated from his vice, but they soon softened as he considered the words of his more experienced neighbor. "Fine, you short shlummy. But shomebody is payin' me!" He whirled and stumbled past Edlevin, towards the Inn.

"I'll take care of it," the old soldier assured calmly, patting the Innkeep on the shoulder before rejoining the blacksmith.

"I do believe you made all that up," she said, a sly smile on her face.

Edlevin returned the expression in kind, shrugging his shoulders. "A good story solves a multitude, especially when all parties are drunk." He beckoned Valin over with a wave of his hand.

Valin joined them quickly, looking at both with relief. "Ye have me thanks," he muttered gratefully. "I owe ye."

"Yes, you do," Edlevin replied with a furrowed brow. "You'll be leaving town. Today." He took a deep breath. "Ally, I need to make amends here. Take him a few hours outside of town and make camp."

Alauren's eyes went wide. "What? Alone?" she yelped. "I can't do that!"

Edlevin replied with a hard glare and crossed arms. "You can, Ally. Responsibility is responsibility, and we've managed to saddle ourselves with this one, however unfortunate that may be. I have to settle things here and I would rather not leave him unsupervised any further. Besides, with him, you'll have a…" He gestured vaguely to Valin. "A Dwarf whatever-he-is with you."

The stout stranger replied only with an amused, toothy smile.

"How are you sure he wants to come, anyway?" Alauren questioned anxiously. "You didn't ask him."

Edlevin looked to the Dwarf and ground his teeth for a moment. "He has no choice, in any case. He needs to leave before Martin stuffs him in a crab trap. We'll be on the road regardless, so we might as well bring him along."

"No ale makes fer a borin' town anyway, lass," Valin agreed. "This sounds like fun."

Alauren looked pleadingly towards Edlevin, who only replied with a serious frown.

"Go to your forge and make a travel pack," instructed the old soldier. "You have the sword for any defensive needs. Camp next to Bleeding Creek off the main road, and I'll meet you first thing in the morning." He smiled warmly, attempting to comfort his old friend. "It's just a few hours, Ally. You'll be alright."

Alauren sighed nervously and looked down at the Dwarf, only to see that he was already bounding towards her forge. "Come on lass!" he bellowed. "We're burnin' daylight!"

"Ed," asked the smith, "are you sure we can trust him?"

Edlevin shrugged. "Sometimes we're left with no choice but to find out. He's a mystery, certainly, but to unravel it we'll need to get him out of here and keep him close." He chuckled lightly. "Besides, any being as loud as him tends to have a hard time hiding any ill intent."

Alauren peered towards her shop with uncertainty, but willed herself to follow the instructions, even if her mind screamed at her with every step.

CHAPTER FOUR:

THE WORLD OUTSIDE

Dwarves are a peculiar race on Odenseye, due to both their stature and their way of life. They are distrustful of surface dwellers (wise, in my mind), and their interests in this world seem to lie only in the sprawling caverns that they have colonized far to the south, under the feet of the Fangirmish people. While the roots of many races upon Odenseye can be traced to small details, with change over periods of millennia directly observable through inspection of ancient crypts and barrows, Dwarves have shown no growth, in looks or in mindset, since the day that our fledgling kingdoms first discovered these elusive tunnelers in the dark. Ancient remains have shown the same stubbornness in evolution, raising questions about their origin as well as their genetic hardiness. In any case, they are a people that warrant study, for the secrets they keep could very well prove to be of value.

– Gauis Truvani, in the prelude to "A Complete History of the People of the Rock"

Autumn marched ever forward, dutiful in its steady pace, quite like a well-drilled soldier on parade. Rarely did it miss a step, and never could the world stand resolute against its coming. The forests surrounding the town of Teth were daubed with a swatch of brilliant colors, stretching along the road ahead. Red, green, yellow; even some black in the occasional shadowbeech tree could be found here and there. The grass, however, was a muted green color, and the vibrant life that had once claimed this place as its own had begun to succumb to the slow, steadily deepening cold of the unstoppable seasons. Flowers still managed to poke up here and there, though, coloring the drab ground in patchy fragments of white and pink, like drips of fresh paint on a faded canvas. The Tail of Se'Vikoral, a magnificent range of spiky, craggy mountains that separated the western coast from the interior, served as a snow-capped backdrop to the brilliant colors of the lowlands. Even in the dimming light of the evening, the view was striking.

The atmosphere did little to ease the smith's fluttering heart as she walked purposefully down the main road, attempting to remain focused on the ground beneath her feet. It was no more than a flat (by a loose definition of the word) stretch of dirt and rocks, flanked by small drainage channels on either side, though frequent use by traders and merchants meant that it was kept up relatively well, as compared to many other routes in the north. Groves of trees came and went, rustling in the wind while the nervous traveler below their branches managed to put one foot in front of another.

"…And that's why ye never leave yer pack alone in woods like this," Valin wrapped up, continuing a stream of advice that fell on deaf ears.

Alauren simply stared forward, her mind focused on driving her next step. It seemed that every movement of the muscle took all the effort of a day at the forge, bringing on an exhaustion that she knew to be more than physical.

"Eh?" the Dwarf grunted, realizing his words had gone unnoticed. "Ye'd do well t' listen up, lass!"

Alauren grimaced at the Dwarf, finding her nerves easily alight, but quickly softened her gaze. "I'm sorry, Valin," she said midst a sigh. "My focus is on staying calm. Hearing stories of thieves and sprites within the woods hardly helps."

"Heh!" Valin cackled. "If ye don't know of 'em, how are ye gonna deal with 'em if they show up?"

"I just planned to throw you at them," jabbed the smith, shooting her newfound companion a wry smile.

"If ye could lift me!" Valin replied jubilantly. He grabbed his husky belly and jiggled it up and down, an action accompanied by a deep, vibrating chuckle from the stout man.

A small laugh managed to erupt from the nervous smith. "Are all Dwarves quite as boisterous as you?"

"Most," Valin replied. "Well, except fer a few. I used t' be a Priest, before they kicked me out. Them types have got some prickly sticks so far up their arse they get splinters in their gullet."

"You were a priest?" Alauren chortled skeptically. "I hesitate to believe that."

The Dwarf's wrinkly face flushed bright red, reacting strongly to the innocuous comment. After a deep breath, he pushed the anger away and, slowly, found his calm. "Sorry, lass," he murmured, knowing that his emotions were clearly betrayed. "It's a bit o' a sore spot fer me."

"My apologies," the smith said softly. "I didn't mean any offense. Did something happen to you?"

Valin nodded solemnly. "I was a member o' the clergy, the wielders o' the Forge God's sacred magic. Damn good one, too. Dedicated me life t' it." He kicked a rock, winding up the blow before sending it sailing into a hedge on the side of the road. "They took that from me."

"Edlevin mentioned the Forge God a couple of years ago in one of his stories. Was it Tarlak?" asked the blacksmith, struggling with the pronunciation.

"Tearlach," Valin spurted expertly.

"Teerlock?" Alauren recited, attempting to match the throaty sounds of her traveling companion.

"Ha!" Valin huffed, visibly amused. "Close enough. Some sounds are only meant fer the Dwarves, I suppose."

"I digress," the smith dismissed, waving her hand. "What happened?"

Valin continued on with vigor. "Well, the Dwarves have a sacred burial ritual called stonebindin', where our dead are turned t' rock t' stand as monuments t' our memory. The magic was stolen from us." He shook his head and wobbled his scythe about. "Give ye one guess as t' which goat's scrote was behind it."

"Drell?" queried the smith. "He could steal a god's magic?"

"No," Valin replied. "He could simply cut us off. Used whatever dark nonsense he learned in life t' mess with our heads, t' isolate us. Was as good as stealin' it, though. I put a stop t' it."

"For what purpose?" Alauren asked. "Did he get anything out of it?"

"I'll ask him," the Dwarf sputtered through a snicker. He stared intensely at the scythe for a moment before erupting in a toothy smile. "He's givin' me the silent treatment, I'm afraid. Didn't like the question, I reckon."

"Is that a first?" queried the blacksmith, smirking.

"Yeah, ye seem t' shut him up," Valin replied, his tone one of mild surprise and admiration bundled neatly into one. "First time fer everything, I guess."

"Indeed," Alauren concurred. "How did this get you kicked out? If you helped restore magic to your people, shouldn't you be hailed as a hero?"

"If I did it meself, sure," the Dwarf grumbled, attempting to kick another rock but missing it cleanly. "Outside magic is strictly forbidden by me people. I had help from Elysian scholars." He tried his punt again, this time succeeding in sending the stone airborne. "They saved me people and died doin' it. Now, not even the empire they served remains. It's a sorrowful history, lass."

"I'm sorry," Alauren murmured. "Still, you were successful. Why kick you out?"

"Old, bloated bastards unwilling t' listen t' any's views but their own," Valin spat venomously. "Ignorant arseholes, stuck in their ways, unwilling t' change. Just like old Varsy here, ain't that right?" He waved the scythe about wildly, with a few self-amused chortles. After a moment, though, his face scrunched up, glaring incredulously at the weapon.

"What is it?" Alauren asked.

"I made him angry," answered the Dwarf, rumbling with a chuckle. "He keeps tryin' t' shatter the scythe,"

Alauren took a swift step to the side, keeping a respectful distance. "I'll be over here."

"BaHA!" Valin barked with a toothy grin. "Don't let it worry ye. I can't stop his teleportin' me, being that I don't understand that magic very well." He rubbed his beard, making a fine scratching sound. "Any worse spells, I can control. I think, anyway."

Alauren chuckled (though some unsurety remained), and she shifted her attention back to the path ahead, making good use of the momentary warmth that the short distraction had brought along with it. She took the opportunity to take in her surroundings, inhaling a deep breath that smelled of freshly fallen leaves whose rustic colors had abandoned their comfortable homes in the branches to seek the cold embrace of the ground. The sounds of birds chirping and wind whispering through the rows of tall trees broke an otherwise silent world, producing an ethereal atmosphere of calm. Gone were the days of summer, when the air would have been brightened with an orchestra of insects and amphibians alike, and their warm melody now gave way to a crisp gust that rolled down from the mountains to sweep across the land.

Alauren's anxiety came flooding back, though, when she returned her gaze to Valin, who had stopped a few steps behind her. "Valin, what-"

"Shush, girl!" chirped the Dwarf. "Someone's comin'!"

Alauren quickly moved to the edge of the road, near the tree line. Valin joined her, kneeling and trying to keep a low profile despite the noticeability inherent in his appearance.

"Ye hear it, girly?" he asked.

The smith listened carefully, hearing the birds and wind as she had before. It had been a dozen morns since she had used such skills, and her ears were now more used to the shuffling and banging typical of the fishing town. However, she was able to make out a single, distinctive sound among the others: a repeated *clip-clop* in the distance that she quickly recognized as a horse galloping. She rested her hand on the ruby-pommeled sword, forcing a calm while readying herself for whatever might be coming, though she could not help but succumb to light quakes as the crisp air brushed across her skin.

They knelt for a while, listening to the sound growing near while the wind whistled by. *Clip-clop, clip-clop,* ever louder, ever closer. The birds grew quiet, content to silently observe the events below as the horse came into view.

The two travelers remained still for what seemed to the smith to be hours before the cause of the sound ventured close enough to make out details: a large, blonde-haired rider was mounted atop a midnight black steed, both of them seeming to have an incredible urgency in their demeanor.

Valin stood cautiously and moved to the center of the road, despite Alauren's silent protests and bewildered glare.

The sound of the galloping animal grew thunderous as it approached. It was a breed from the far north, standing head and shoulders above both the Dwarf and the smith, were they stacked on top of one another. A few like it would come through Teth occasionally, accompanied by adventurers and unsavory types; the creatures always carried a majestic (yet deeply intimidating) air about them. The steed reared up high as it reached the stout man, stopping in place.

Alauren stood, moving cautiously to Valin's side. The man atop the dark steed was clearly a Nort, his large stature and lanky muscles indicating his bloodlines clearly. His blue eyes were widened and bloodshot, and they held what was instantly recognized by the smith as intense fear. He was covered from head to toe in dried blood and heavy lacerations, many of which still leaked small trickles of plasma from under the coagulation. The fluid stained his ragged clothes and his sundered Nortish armor, leaving every bit caked in aged, brown viscera.

"Out of the way, fools?" he bellowed with a clear unsurety. "I must Go south." His voice wavered wildly with every word, changing inflection, as if each one was part of a different sentence. "South!"

"What're ye on about?" Valin growled. "We were just goin' t' see yer kin! Think ye can guide us?"

The Nort seemed to grow even more uneasy at the delay, deaf to Valin's words. "The future Marches forward, and I must go… g… g…" he stumbled over his words. "south?"

"Slow down and tell us what in bollocks you're talkin' about!" the Dwarf snapped, softer this time. "Ye sound like ye need our help as much as we need yours."

"No time, no; none At all," the Northman rambled, urging his horse forward. It obeyed with blinding speed, missing Valin by a hair as he bounded clear of the thundering hooves. In an instant, the Nort was gone, racing off into the deepening darkness.

Alauren hurried to the Dwarf and heaved him up, feeling surprisingly calm in the moment of stress. "Did you get any of that?"

Valin brushed dusty streaks from his intricate robes with a huff. "Just that he's a madman. In any case, he's gone now."

"Madman. Some would say the same about you," jabbed the smith, grinning uneasily, eager to lighten the situation.

Valin simply returned the joke with a low grunt. He sighed with exaggerated exasperation and gestured heavily forward. "Come on, then. Let's get t' the campsite before I get sick o' ye."

After another hour of walking and the disappearance of the sun, the travelers at last came upon their sanctuary. Bleeding Creek was a narrow, shallow rut, only measuring about two strides wide, but the waters that poured forth from its underground sources were said to be especially refreshing (after a good boil, of course), due to a myriad of minerals that were purportedly carried from the mountains above. These minerals also gave the waterway a rusty red hue and, therefore, served as the decidedly innocent reason behind such a grim sounding name.

The travelers, at the forceful and uncompromising insistence of the smith, had found a remote place deep in a clustered grove and down small a hill, hidden from most that were not actively looking for them; even the glow of their coming fire would be nearly unnoticeable from the road above, providing some semblance of security to salve the woman's ever-present worries.

Alauren, parched, moved swiftly to gather water with a pail procured from her travel pack before setting up their bedrolls. Valin cleared a small area among the dark trees to lay when they needed to sleep, and proceeded with his further duties by gathering firewood and tinder.

Their work was overseen by Etia, the greater moon, hovering above and displaying the shining glory of its full face. Meanwhile, the lesser moon, Misele, had just begun to show from behind its much larger master; the celestial titans were caught in an eternal, spiraling dance, forever drawn towards one another, yet never able to fully embrace nor escape. Together, they painted the land in a pale glow, where every tree cast long shadows that danced back and forth when the chill wind breezed through their leaves. Those old, wooden giants stepped in a wondrous ballet of motion, each movement seeming precisely chosen as they bounced in a unified rhythm.

The air was intoxicating, especially compared to the forge that Alauren had spent so many days within. Free from the acridity of melted slag and boiling metal, the creek's freshwater aroma rode with the breeze, mixing in with the fallen leaves and the late flowers of the season to produce a smooth, invigorating fragrance. Meanwhile, the mountains to the east stood as magnificent white-capped giants, glowing indigo in the gloam, yearningly reaching toward the bright stars of the night sky.

Alauren, though she had insisted on finding a good hiding place and had, in the end, chosen this grove, still felt open and exposed. Her nerves, while temporarily relieved by busywork, still played havoc in her thoughts. Despite her lack of sleep the evening prior, it was already clear that rest would be difficult, even in a place of such seeming peace. She was anxious, fearful of the present and the future, and there was an unnerving feeling in her chest that she found difficult to fight off, like an insect that flitted around her head, unable to be swatted away.

Even so, the blacksmith was grateful to have this leg of the journey done, and she felt a noticeable sense of satisfaction grow within her. The path ahead was still long and the road unbroken to a potential foe, yet there was a warmth, driven by a familiar but faded memory that swam in her mind. She sat cross-legged on her bedroll, closed her eyes, and breathed deeply, finding her center in the moment. She had been out here in the world before, among the trees and the birds, and though those days were many human lifetimes ago, she was able to find something resembling peace within the small comfort of her winnowed recollection.

She focused her thoughts inward, seizing the opportunity to find calm. The fluttering, insulating anxiety fought a pitched battle with her feeling of peace as each combatant locked in a bloody, muddy struggle to dominate the moment. The latter prevailed, eventually, leaving her with calm thoughts, though she knew them to be temporary; still, she supposed, a momentary victory was still a triumph. She opened her eyes, finding solace in the well-built nook of a campsite that had been prepared.

She breathed deeply and tried to match her breath with the wind, heaving in and out as the gusts came and went, and she even began to sway lightly as the fresh air brushed over her skin. Her mind leveled and calmed, becoming even keeled and strong, as if she was one of the trees, looking on at the march of the world with hardly any care paid towards the thunderous steps it took.

This feeling was something impossible to find within civilization, where the incessant noise of chattering merchants and the assault of smells never ceased. As much of a homebody as she was, the smith had to admit that there was wisdom in Edlevin's often verbose descriptions of what was out here, beyond Teth's walls. It refreshed the soul in an unexplainable way, planting a seed of excitement within. Her daily life was filled with distractions, a rush that kept her mind occupied, yet it only served to push her anxiety away, rather than overcoming it. She closed her eyes once more, breathing deeply and steadily.

"Eh?" Valin grunted, throwing down a bedroll near Alauren's, opposite the makeshift fire pit. He had built a flat, beautiful campsite, indicative of many days on the road. "Ye asleep already?"

"No," the smith replied calmly, opening her eyes slowly. "Just enjoying the moment while you fetched your roll. Let's see if I still remember how to do this."

She placed a small bit of dried moss down in the flat dirt bed, which was surrounded by small, rounded rocks arranged in a perfect circle. Ensuring that the lichen was packed tightly, she positioned small sticks in a crisscross pattern over it, followed by hand-broken, larger branches in a tent-like cone. By the end, the fire was a conical piece of art, needing only a flame to complete the ensemble.

"Fer someone who hasn't been out here in a while, ye seem quite adept. Perhaps ye embellished yer inexperience?" the Dwarf chirped.

"I run a forge," Alauren stated flatly, prodding at the wooden structure to ensure its strength. "If I can't build a simple campfire, I'd be all sorts of knackered, wouldn't I?"

"Eh," Valin grunted. "Forges are easy. Ye don't have a nice, contained environment here."

Alauren responded with a rude gesture and a smile, which was returned doubly by her stout traveling companion. She reached into the main pack of her pouch, seeking her starter kit.

"Oh, bollocks," groaned the smith, the words accompanied by the flushing of her cheeks. She began to dig madly through her pack, searching in vain, before falling back in exasperation and slapping a hand onto her forehead. "I was in such a rush that I forgot the flint."

Valin let out a huge, exaggerated sigh, blowing a few of the longer hairs of his beard around in the action. "How the mighty master o' the campfire has fallen," he mocked, quite dramatically. "I suppose I, lowly servant o' the world, must step in t' do me part."

Alauren's response was a flat, unamused glare. "You do have something, though?"

Valin silently reached into one of his robe's pockets and pulled forth a small piece of charcoal, wrapped in a wax cover. "Ye got a piece o' parchment?"

Alauren shook her head, confused. "No. What exactly is a piece of charcoal going to do for us without something to light it?"

"Shush, lass, and let me work!" Valin chided. He picked up a nearby leaf, crackling it between his large fingers. "This'll have t' do."

He drew something on the leaf, biting his lower lip as he focused his thick fingers on the delicate task. After finishing, he flipped it over and showed the smith, letting a sly smile cross his face.

On the rusty red color lie a "🝰" symbol in black, though it was only just visible to the blacksmith in the twilight.

"What does it mean?" Alauren asked.

"This here's a Dwarven rune," Valin explained exuberantly. "The meanin' is in the action. Watch this, lassie!"

Valin placed the leaf carefully among the branches, laying it into the bed of dry moss and gazing toward it with starry eyes, as if it was a crystal ball that swirled with images of the future. "Teine!" he squawked, quietly, but with determination. "Teine!"

Alauren watched in amazement as the scrawling began to glow a dull burgundy hue. "Valin, what-"

"Teine!" the Dwarf yelped a final time, deaf to the blacksmith's words as he completed his incantation. The final utterance brought with it a sudden burst of light; the campfire sprung to life in a brilliant crimson flame, roaring as the rune combusted and engulfed the tinder. It was unlike any fire Alauren had seen before, carrying a strong heat along with the soft glow, but one that wafted over the campsite and provided a remarkably even warmth, exactly as comfortable on the smith's side as it was on the Dwarf's.

"Dwarven runefire," Valin proclaimed, slumping back with pride.

"H-how?" Alauren stammered.

"It's the job o' the Priests t' control this magic and use it fer the good o' our people," the Dwarf replied. "Our stonebindin' was rune magic, too. I was well trained before I had to go." His eyes looked deeply into the fire. "The torches outside me favorite bakery back home used t' be lit like this, every day." He sighed. "Seems like an eternity since I was in Dol Marad."

"What was it like?" Alauren asked, her curiosity piqued. She picked up the pail of water, sitting it carefully on the now-raging fire. "I've never even read about a Dwarven city, to be honest."

"Most humans and elves would call it a clustered nightmare," Valin murmured, allowing a slight smile to creep onto his face as the memory went by. "Massive roads that ran in a circle, surrounded by nearly sheer walls that had homes and shops built into 'em. In Dol Marad, we found it easier t' build up, rather than out."

"Sounds practical," observed the smith.

"Ye just described me people in a word," Valin agreed with a nod. "We all have our jobs t' do, and we do 'em. Well, until we get unjustly kicked out, anyways." He ground his teeth. "It's been six years, I think. Six years o' wanderin'."

"I'm sorry," Alauren replied. Red light and shadow swept over her face, dancing in turns as the twirling storm of the runefire ebbed and flowed. "What have you been doing, if you can't go home?"

"Walkin'. Gettin' drunk. Waitin'," muttered the Dwarf. "Tearlach has a purpose fer me, that I know. I can do nothin' but stay vigilant." He winced at a memory, freshly kicked up in his head. "I don't wanna talk about it anymore, lass. Now, I think I deserve some answers outta you."

Alauren nodded. "Fair enough."

"This whole time, I've been wonderin' how a young, pretty Half-Elf lass can avoid all yer town's young men hangin' 'round ye," Valin continued. "Ye must do somethin' t' scare 'em off, eh?"

Alauren laughed boisterously. "It has more to do with the fact that I've known most of them since they were kids."

"Eh?" grunted the Dwarf, visibly confused at the words.

Alauren's brow rose at the looseness of her own lips. The detail had escaped her mouth without a chance to truly consider it, a rare slip of the tongue when talking about such things. She sighed, conceding to the fact that she had to elaborate. "I'm probably older than you, short one. I'm *definitely* older than Edlevin."

"If yer older than that fossil, me beard's a wizard!" Valin bellowed.

Alauren shook her head, deadly serious. "By my count, which is very rough, I'm four hundred and twenty-seven, by the Northern calendar."

Valin sprung to his feet in wide-eyed shock, knocking his scythe and bedroll to the side as he ascended. "Right!" he roared with an exaggerated waggle of the head. "And I'm restraint personified!"

Alauren simply shook her head, smiling in amusement.

Valin calmed quickly and flopped back to the ground. "Yer serious? That's absurdly long, even fer a Half-Elf."

"The forge keeps me fit!" Alauren explained. "I've been in that village for an age, Valin. When I said it had been a long time since I left, I meant that it was a *long* time."

Valin retrieved his scythe, leaning it on his shoulder. "No wonder ye had such trouble comin' out here."

"I'm still having trouble just *being* out here," barked the smith. "It's hard being so unfamiliar with my surroundings. Where's the warmth of the forge, or the bite of the ale? It is peaceful, but at a cost. I like familiarity and consistency. I like my home."

Valin nodded and stared deeply into the crimson flames, while the light from the fire flickered over his face in irregular intervals. "There is an allure t' the world we've worked out fer ourselves, I agree," he murmured. "I had planned t' spend me life goin' t' the same damn bakery in the same damn district o' Dol Marad every day, 'till I keeled over and was bound in stone. Then, it all came crashin' down 'cause o' a duty I could not refuse." He shook his head. "I learned that day that 'familiar' is a luxury. The ability t' have a comfortable world, t' be surrounded by things and people that you recognize, is somethin' that can be lost at any time."

"That's rather dark," Alauren countered. "You think places like Teth are that fragile? The town hasn't changed in two centuries, and even then, it was just a few buildings going up. I can't see that come crashing down anytime soon."

"Lass, I lived in a city where everyone did the same thing every single day, without fail," the Dwarf stated. "Me people are a precise lot who keep t' their schedules with painful efficiency, unbothered by any o' the annoyances o' the surface world. If that isolationist world can be robbed, any other can be, too."

Alauren gave him a distraught glare, clearly skeptical of his pessimism.

"I don't mean t' be all doom and gloom," Valin quickly eased, waving his hands disarmingly. "My point is, lass, that there was somethin' that had t' be done, and I could do it or walk away. That choice took everythin' from me, but I'd do it again in a heartbeat. If there's slack, *somebody* has t' pick it up."

Alauren turned her gaze from Valin to the fire, its hypnotic dance seeming to accentuate the Dwarf's words as they rumbled forth.

"In all those centuries," Valin continued, "it's just odds that ye would eventually have t' be the one t' step up." He pointed at the sword. "Fer yer risk deliverin' that, people like that arsefaced innkeep can continue wastin' space unbothered!"

Alauren's grave expression broke into a chortle as her eyes averted from the flame. "And here Edlevin told me 'Dwarvish Wisdom' was just ale recipes!"

"Shall I give him a speech, too?" Valin asked, followed by a yawn.

"He'll give you one right back," the smith warned. "I remember when the Marchioness tried to lecture him on proper home upkeep. Sortul said that 'his house always looks like it's been commandeered by the military'. Ed spent the next three hours reminding the Marchioness of his 'gallant service'."

Valin chortled mightily. "He was a warrior, eh? Seems more like an ambassador now."

Alauren nodded and pulled her knees close to her chest, hugging them to keep warm in the deepening cold. "He was in the Fangirmish military during the Eastern War. Caught a lot of the worst of it, or so he says. You can ask him tomorrow."

Valin chuckled. "Not without ale to numb me head, first. He seems like a talker."

Alauren nodded with a smile. "He is, but there's a lot behind his bluster. If you can filter out the more, shall we say, *inflated* parts, he's got quite the sharp mind."

"My filterin' ain't so good, lass," Valin countered. "Probably best I remain generally skeptical, eh?"

"Probably," the smith replied in a matter-of-fact deadpan. A few moments of silence followed as both travelers looked deeply into the flames once more, letting their minds wander to other thoughts.

"Ay, lass," muttered the Dwarf. "Somethin' I've been wonderin' if ye don't mind me askin' about yer past a wee bit more."

Alauren smirked. "Depends on the question. Go on."

"Ye've got quite the name there, eh?" Valin asked. "Doesn't sound like many other names up here on the surface. I've been from one end o' this continent t' another, and I don't see any trace o' a culture I know in it."

Alauren nodded and gathered her words for a moment. "The memory is a bit fuzzy for me, but it's from when I first arrived in Teth. Apparently, for the first few morns, I only said a single word. Or, what the townsfolk figured was a word, I guess." She grabbed a stick and poked at the fire, exposing a few glowing embers. "Aki, the Captain of the Guard at the time, wrote it down as 'Ahloorawn'. People seemed quite happy calling me that, and I didn't mind. Once I learned the trade tongue, I prettied it up a bit and got Alauren."

"Hm," Valin grunted. "As good o' a root as any, I suppose."

"Indeed." Alauren replied. "How about you?"

"Eh?" grunted the Dwarf.

"Your name," the smith clarified. "I don't know much of the Dwarves. Is there meaning behind it?"

"Ah, not so much," Valin rumbled. "For first names, we tend t' take on somethin' that sounds good, and then pay honor t' our ancestors by completin' it with a part o' their name. Me pappy was named Linfi, for instance. Va-lin."

"Interesting," Alauren said, again poking at the fire. "What about Runesorrow?"

Valin's demeanor darkened noticeably at the question. "That's…" He bit his lip for a moment, thinking. "It's a mark. Dwarven Priests all take on a singular name, Runeforger. If one is t' break our code…"

"They break your name," the smith finished with a nod. "Runesorrow."

"Aye, lass," Valin replied quietly. "Now, if ye'll excuse me rudeness, I swiped some salted meats from that innkeep o' yours before I left, and I'd like t' use me jaws fer somethin' other than jawin'!"

Alauren chuckled. "You are excused, as long as you share!"

The final hour of the deepening night was spent with a meal and the cleansed water of Bleeding Creek, among friendly stories and idle conversation, until the runefire turned to long-burning embers, and the travelers lay down in their bedrolls to ward off the cold.

CHAPTER FIVE:

DENTED HISTORY

Fear most the ones with gray in their hair and rust
upon their armor, for they are greater than you.

– Nort Adage

6th OF THE MORN OF HARVEST
NORTHERN YEAR 715

The morning was ushered in by the glow of the sun painting the land in a deep maroon, the warm beams broken only by the whispering of the trees still flitting back and forth, though in a greatly lessened frenzy than the previous night. The air was largely still and comfortable, having only a slight trace of the chill that had blown through the evening before, and even the occasional gust of wind seemed to yield to the dawn's demand for warmth.

Alauren was the first to rise, stirred by nerves that had also awoken in full form; meanwhile, the Dwarf was slumbering away with his head tucked into his bedroll to avoid the light of morning, and the warm mist of his breath poured from within a gap in the crumpled leather blanket, looking quite like the exhaust pipe of the blacksmith's furnace. He was comfortable, clearly, and so she saw no reason to bother him until it became necessary.

Alauren sat up on her own bedroll, yawning. The birds sung with a renewed vigor while their melody bounced off the trees from every direction, echoing throughout the forest and meadow. The air still held the pure and fresh smell of the creek, bubbling a short distance from camp.

She stood, stretching in the warmth of the rising sun. The night had been frigid, but the intense, focused heat from the runefire embers kept the area consistently warm, spreading heat evenly and comfortably around. Now, it was nothing but a rapidly cooling pile of ash, with hardly a glowing speck to be found in the gray mound.

Her old friend would arrive with horses, eventually, but the smith was all too familiar with Edlevin's unique concept of time. He had promised to leave at dawn, so the smith knew it would be hours before he arrived, and still more if he found someone to talk to.

Initially, she passed the time by cleaning the campsite and double-checking her pack, but as the morning wore on, she found her list of tasks dwindling to nothing. She could only sit on her bedroll and think, ruminating over this and that. Her mind wasn't used to being so unoccupied; usually, she would have a dozen boatswains clamoring for a weld or new parts for their riggings at the first light of dawn, rather than an unsettlingly placid silence. Thoughts of the future sent great waves through her spine, drawing her breath short and ragged.

What would the Norts be like? Hostile? she thought to herself. *Will they kill us before or after stealing everything we have on us? Will our heads be rammed onto pikes?*

The ideas and images in her mind's eye raced like speeding horses, coming and going so fast that the smith hardly had time to consider whether they merited further thought. In her state of near-panic, one idea seemed just as reasonable as the next, and each served to strengthen the rising feeling of pressure in her chest.

Edlevin had taught her over the years how to focus in on her surroundings; how to push out the fear and anxiety by appreciating the world around her. With great effort, she managed to narrow her mind, seeking the advice of a day long past while struggling to control her breath.

'I've walked among the curdling screams and the stinking rot of a lucid nightmare, leaving my mind scarred with visions of the past that are ever looking for their chance to surface,' Edlevin had once said, in one of his more sober moments. *'The only escape I find from those memories is realizing that nightmare didn't follow me. I survived, I escaped, and I'm in a much more beautiful and peaceful place now. If you ever feel under assault, just look around, with all your senses.'*

Following the advice, Alauren's eyes locked on a small red squirrel, patterned with stripes of gray across his belly, the sure sign of a male. He sprinted up the side of a gargantuan shadowbeech tree, smuggling something in his bulging cheeks. He made his home within a knot of the deep obsidian wood, braving the viscous, flammable sap within to keep warm in the winter.

'Shadowbeeches saved my skin more than once,' Edlevin's voice again whispered from an old memory. *'The absolute-black color of the leaves and bark absorb light all year round, providing easy warmth during cold winters. They are of great comfort to me, for they are givers of life.'*

Her eyes shifted to the mysterious Dwarf, whose face was still buried in his scrunched-up bedroll. He was an affable fellow by Alauren's estimation, even if he was a bit flagrant in his manner of speaking. She liked him well enough, but his true intentions were yet to be seen.

'Trust should be hard to come by. Giving it or accepting it easily can end poorly. Measure a person by what they do for you, in both the light and the shadows.'

Alauren centered herself and closed her eyes, finally letting Edlevin's voice bleed out of her mind. She counted the different bird songs, hearing a variety of unique performances, from the steady *chirp chirp chirp* of a cardinal to the thunderous shriek of a passing gloamhawk, stalking the fields for prey.

Bleeding Creek, nearly drowned out by the animals, bubbled softly in the background. The smith could hear the occasional native fish jump *splish-splash* out of (and back into) the water, feeding on insects that spawned on the surface.

Edlevin was right. Through the small reminders of her reality, held ever within the passing of the moment, she felt herself steady. Her mind focused not on the Nort camp ahead, but rather on the world's striking of her senses, and each impact of its hammer brought her closer to the present, closer to calm.

There was something else there, though, a sound unlike the others, growing in intensity, jagged and grinding, like a rock sliding down a hill; every moment brought it more clarity, more strength.

Hear me.

Alauren's eyes shot open with panic, but her sight was greeted only by the slumbering Dwarf and the pristine forest around her. She rose quickly, unsheathing the sword and letting its blade shine in the soft rays of the morning sun. Nothing stirred save for the rise and fall of Valin's chest and the birds flying above. She closed her eyes and listened for anything out of the ordinary, focusing in.

You heard, the voice returned. It was rough and raspy, addled by age. *Fascinating.*

Alauren again opened her eyes, slowly this time, yet was again greeted by the confusing sight of nothing at all. She snapped them back closed, determined to find the source of the words.

Who are you? she thought, seemingly talking to herself. Much to her surprise, an answer came.

I am the one you know as Drell. He chuckled through a throat that was dry and shaky, and he sounded as if he was on the other side of a wooden wall, muffled and subdued. *You are someone who interests me greatly. I wish to speak in more detail.*

We can speak now, thought the smith.

Only at great effort, all of which is my own, Drell replied. *You have vision, yet you stumble through the world. Take the scythe. Let us talk.*

Alauren's eyes rocketed back open. Her mind brimmed with equal parts confusion and excitement; her gaze fell immediately on the scythe, lying flat next to Valin. The world was peaceful, and it would be hours still before Edlevin arrived.

The smith looked at the Dwarf, still sleeping, and furrowed her brow.

He won't mind, Drell assured. *I promise.*

Alauren inched closer to the scythe, taken in by the unique experience. Even under the spell of curiosity, she hesitated, remembering Edlevin's stories of an ancient evil.

I was a sorcerer, long ago, Drell elaborated, somehow feeling the smith's apprehension. *Now I'm little aside from an imprisoned old failure, being carried by the most annoying man on the continent. Indulge me, I beg of you, if for no other reason than to sate the boredom of us both.*

Alauren sighed, but gingerly stepped to Valin's weapon. She was careful to avoid the wicked looking thorns, whose surfaces seemed to shift like billowing clouds, choosing instead to let her fingers carefully float towards the smooth, ivory grip midway down the shaft of the weapon. Her nerves were conspicuously absent, a realization that disappeared as fast as it had materialized in her mind.

Alauren, taking a deep breath, wrapped her hand around the

handle. Her vision instantly went white, as if the world had ceased to exist, leaving only a cold emptiness behind. Gone were the sights and sounds of the forest, the rise and fall of Valin's breathing. It was as if she stood in an endless, bright void, her mind unable to comprehend even a concept as simple as which way was up.

Someone appeared in front of the smith, popping into her view in less than a blink. He was an old man, his hair thin and strung out, with a gray beard that was draped upon his dark blue robes. He had no legs, and his garments turned to ragged strips as he floated in place, like a phantom of legend. His blue eyes met hers, and he spoke.

"Thank you," rasped the sorcerer. His voice carried with it the wear and tear of age, magnified by a thousand lifetimes. "It has been centuries since I've had a visitor that wasn't an overly short drunkard."

"Well met, I suppose," Alauren greeted shakily, still getting her bearings. "You said I interest you?"

"You interest many people, me included," Drell confirmed. "When close enough, they can hear you as I can, for you stumble along your path in the world like you were plowing through dozens of chairs and tables along the way."

Alauren's face scrunched up in confusion. "I think I'm pretty light-footed, actually."

Drell smiled and shook his head. "The other world. My world."

The smith crossed her arms and narrowed her eyes. "Magic?"

Drell nodded.

"I've read some of the histories, Drell," Alauren replied. "I know where magic gets you. It is something that we cannot be trusted with."

"Skepticism is a reasonable measure when discussing such a power," the sorcerer agreed. "Magic is a fine asset, though, should you have the skill and dedication to harness it."

"Right," the smith snapped sarcastically. "Tell me, where did magic get you?"

"In this prison, I admit," Drell acknowledged, splaying out his arms to the empty depths beyond. "However, it was voluntary."

Alauren cocked an eyebrow, surprised. "You submitted yourself to this willingly?"

"I saw people who needed my help, and I helped them," Drell confirmed. "Now, I want to do the same for you." He extended his hand. "Take it. Let me share my knowledge with you."

Alauren hesitated, backing away. "I'm not sure that's a good idea."

"Even for answers about how you ended up in your town?" the Sorcerer posited with a toothy, broken smile. "I can't tell you directly, but I can give you the tools to find out. Dreams that will reveal all, should you know the way to dredge them up."

"I took a risk even picking up the scythe," Alauren stated. "No. Not today."

Drell sighed. He seemed to twitch slightly, but the microscopic movement carried him forward to the smith in an instant. He grabbed her hand, and her world became an inferno.

It was like a forge had been ignited in her throat before being fed by the gust of the largest bellows ever built. Intense heat pushed forcefully out of her head through her nose, mouth, and eyes, incinerating any organs or flesh that stood in its way. At the same moment, it felt as if her skeleton had crumbled to dust, leaving every nerve exposed to the blistering heat from the embers within.

"It wasn't a choice!" the sorcerer snarled menacingly, his voice echoing a thousand times in the walls of the smith's mind. "I need a vessel that can hold me, and you need a guide. We will make a fine-"

The pain stopped. Alauren found herself lying on her back, her vision suddenly filled with tree branches and the morning sky. Her body ached from head to toe, and her muscles twitched involuntarily, not yet realizing that the pain had gone.

"Are ye daft, girl?" Valin scolded frantically. "Come on, stay with me, ye wee idiot."

Alauren, blinking, was suddenly aware that her traveling companion was shaking her violently. She began to wriggle, eager to stop the panicked Dwarf's agitations.

"I'm... I'm fine. I just need a... a moment," she stammered weakly, pushing the Dwarf away as she sat up on the grass. "What just happened?"

Valin grunted vaguely. "I'm wonderin' the same thing! I woke up t' find ye screamin' bloody murder and clutching me scythe."

Alauren shook her head, clearing her vision. "I was meditating," she explained amidst a still-wavering voice. "I was trying to keep my nerves under control. I heard Drell speak to me, as if he were reaching out into my thoughts."

Valin's face softened. "I'm sorry, lass. I've never seen him try t' be sociable before. T' be truthful, I can't even hear his voice unless I'm real close t' the scythe, thank the forge god for that." He rubbed his beard between two fingers. "Interestin' that you could hear him."

"Drell?" Alauren asked, her voice still wavering. "That *was* Drell, right?"

"Old wanker, bad hair, no legs, impatient?" the Dwarf prompted. Alauren nodded.

"Aye, then that's him," Valin said with a sigh. "Always comin' up with new tricks. Come here." He reached for the smith's hands.

Alauren pulled them back instinctively, taking Valin by surprise.

"He touched ye?" asked the Dwarf.

Alauren, again, nodded silently.

Valin ground his teeth for a moment, chewing a few stray beard hairs. "He wanted t' take yer body. I've seen him turn people t' ash tryin' t' make that leap." He again beckoned for the blacksmith's hands.

Alauren nodded this time, extending them. They were spotless, as if nothing had happened at all.

"Interestin'," the Dwarf observed with clear interest. "No burns. Yer lucky."

Alauren breathed deeply and stood. "Let's take advantage of good fortune, then. We should get moving."

"Lass," Valin cut off, clearly not willing to let the matter go. "Did he say anything t' ye?"

"Not much," replied the smith with a shake of her head. "He was just trying to confuse me."

"Good," Valin rumbled. He finally allowed himself to breathe, taking a moment to regain his senses after a rude awakening. "Let's get packed up and get on the main road where the old man can see us. Oh, and... don't worry him with this, eh? I don't feel like havin' me head bashed in."

"Of course," Alauren agreed. "I'd like to put it behind me, as well. Come on."

A few hours passed as the travelers sat idly by the road. The red hue of dawn that had once glimmered upon the dew had now faded for the coming of the day, ushering in a bright blue sky, free of clouds.

Alauren wrung her hands nervously. She could still catch a whisper of Drell now and then, reaching into her mind like a frigid claw. A silent insult would push him away, yet he was persistent, only backing down for good when the smith neared the end of her expansive vocabulary.

She took a deep breath. The sorcerer couldn't hurt her, Valin had assured, unless she laid hands upon the scythe again. Even so, the fragments of his raspy voice on the wind sent shivers down her spine, unnerving her.

She took comfort in a growing silhouette, someone on horseback, coming from Teth's direction. It could have been Edlevin, but the man was dressed in old, dented plate mail, showing decades of clear disuse. A shining silver coloration upon the metal itself had given way to tones of black and rusty red, speckled across every piece of the full suit of armor. Only the sword looked like it had seen the sun in the last decade, having often been worked on and refined by the resident smith. Its hilt was wrapped in leather and its blade was tucked into a simple leather sheath, which was strapped to his back. Underneath, a patch of Alauren's purple forge tent, typically stored away under her counter for any needed repairs, served as a cloak. He towed another horse and a smaller pony along at his side.

"Hail, travelers!" bellowed the new arrival, removing his helmet and hanging it on the side of the horse via a leather strap. It was Edlevin, indeed, grinning widely. "What is your intention, friend or foe?"

"With you approaching in that getup, I'm not sure," Alauren jabbed. "You've never shown me that before."

Edlevin chuckled and hopped off his horse, his ragged armor clanking all the way. He banged on the helmet, drawing out a dull, hollow thud. "No reason to, now that it's in such poor condition."

Alauren inspected the helm, finding that it had aged most poorly. Its sloped edges were covered with water spots and a large dent lay on the left side. The separate metal faceplate, which could swing up to reveal the eyes and brow, had been hastily reattached with ill-fitting pins, likely 'borrowed' from the blacksmith's shop. Looking over the rest of the armor, she noted that some of the leather straps securing it to the man's body were rotted and sinewy, while others looked as if they had been repaired or replaced by the work of an unskilled hand.

"I could fix it up, you know," offered the smith. "With some sanding and reinforcement, it would be good as new."

Edlevin waved the suggestion away. "It's not meant to be perfect, Ally. It's only here as a memory, a memento of the past." He smiled with pride. "Every dent means something to me. I wouldn't have it any other way."

"Well, it's an open offer," Alauren said as she shifted her attention off of the old relics.

Edlevin nodded in thanks but moved the conversation along. "How was the night? It felt a bit snippy back at Teth."

"Valin's runefire kept us warm," the smith replied. "Remarkable, how he can turn a drawing into fire."

"Not just fire!" Valin interjected. "Wind, rock, concussive force… Ye name it!"

"Hopefully, we won't need that last one," laughed the old soldier. "Anything else?"

"Yeah, we encountered a Nort," Alauren said. "Strange fellow."

"Strange me arse, he was madder than hell!" Valin corrected boisterously. "Rambled about needin' t' go south. Sounded like he was delirious."

"Curious. I didn't encounter anyone, nor did anyone of the sort come through Teth, at least that I'm aware of," Edlevin mumbled, his brow furrowing like a sail while he rubbed at his stubble. "I suppose the Nort way of life can easily lead to such madness. All the violence, death, rampaging…"

"You're really not helping me find the confidence to get this done," growled the smith, punching her old friend in the shoulder plate. "Any more… *descriptive* words and I'll make you deliver it alone."

"My apologies, Queen of the Forge!" Edlevin bellowed, mock-bowing and twirling his hand elegantly under his chest. "I will be sure to avoid any talk of reality and how the world works in the future."

Alauren punched her old friend once more, eliciting a yelp from the man and a huff of laughter from the Dwarf.

"Come on," grumbled the smith, climbing her horse. "Let's get this over with."

CHAPTER SIX:

REFLECTIONS

The road sprang on ahead of the trio, stretching towards hills that were, for the moment, distant. The scenery remained remarkably consistent as they made steady progress on their journey; this part of Se'Vikoral was defined by the mildness of the flora and fauna, making for easy roads and a comfortable journey in the afternoon light.

Alauren's thoughts were finally at ease, knowing that Edlevin was near. As ridiculous as he looked, the clanking of the old armor was a reassurance in and of itself, a reminder that adventures such as these were nothing new to the old soldier. For the first time, the smith felt as if she could genuinely enjoy her surroundings, for she no longer stood alone.

She breathed deeply of the cool air and stroked her horse's mane, letting the coarse strands of hair glide between her fingers. The songs of nature around her were broken only by the resounding snores of the Dwarf as he dozed in his saddle between the two, half-hunched. The birds, meanwhile, seemed content to simply talk over the slumbrous Priest, chattering away with little more than mild annoyance at the nasally rumbling below.

The smith's happiness was not lost on her old friend, who smiled warmly at the woman. "Ally, I haven't seen you this happy since you got that shipment of Ghaldevhal ore into your forge."

"It's a nice day," Alauren replied matter-of-factly, careful not to betray any emotion.

"Come now, we both know that it's more than that," Edlevin quickly shot back, his voice taking on an inquisitive air. "A life cannot be spent in a cramped forge or inn. We are defined by what we see and what we do!"

Alauren cocked her head in slight confusion, shooting a skeptical glare towards her old friend. "I've seen much and done much, Edlevin."

"Have you?" the man countered with a smarmy smirk. "You've been in that town for as long as anyone can remember." He pointed to the sky and twirled his hand, letting the exaggerated emphasis in his gesture strengthen his words. "Tell me of your great adventures within your forge! Tell me of the horrors of a cracked furnace! Tell me of the wisdom you have gained beyond your hammer!"

"I've gained the wisdom to know when you're about to go off on a tangent," the smith riposted with a roll of the eyes.

Edlevin confirmed his friend's intuition, ignoring her words completely. "I thought not! A life without incident is no life at all. Hardships and challenges are a necessary part of life."

"You're saying I have it easy?" Alauren yelped, quite indignant.

"I'm saying that up until now, you've been content with the mundane," the old soldier retorted. "Happy to see the familiar faces pass by, all on a tight and regular schedule." He met her eyes and erupted into the smarmiest grin the smith had ever seen from the man, a true miracle of a feat, given the competition. "Perhaps that has changed?"

Alauren shrugged. "I like it out here, that's all. Doesn't mean I don't want to get back home."

"Home will be there, Ally, yet experiences like this are once in a lifetime!" Edlevin exclaimed. "Come to the Southlands with me this winter and let me prove it to you in full. Fangirm is beautiful year-round." He was caught up on the thought, and took a moment to consider it further. "Well, the part of Fangirm we'd visit, at least."

Alauren shook her head. "It's one thing to be a messenger going a day's journey from home. It's another thing entirely to sail halfway across the continent. It wouldn't be good for me."

Edlevin shrugged and splayed his arms out towards the sprawling road. "How can you know if you have not experienced it?" He took a deep breath and looked to the horizon with intensity. "Wisdom, my girl!"

Alauren simply shook her head. "It's too far for me, Ed. You know how I get."

"But now you know how you feel once you experience the world!" Edlevin countered, determined to get the smith out of her shell. "Does that do nothing to grow your appetite? There is a continent to explore. Can you really say you have no interest in-"

The old soldier went silent suddenly and pulled his horse to a stop, his mirth dying in an instant as he focused ahead with an expression of stone. There was a rustling in the bushes beyond the trio as two colossal men melded from the forest, as if they had been a natural part of the flora just moments earlier. Their exposed arms were covered in tattoos of serpents and swords, all expertly applied in a deep, black ink. They took a place in the middle of the road, while another appeared behind the travelers, cutting them off from any retreat.

One of the men stepped forward. An intimidating figure, he easily met Alauren's height, even from her place on her saddle. Crimson red hair was complemented by a matching, braided beard, while sky blue eyes inspected the travelers warily. His armor was protective but light, consisting of a simple chestplate which was backed up by a layer of light chain mail and some fur for the coming months of cold. Though he bore two axes, they remained upon his back, in their sheaths.

Valin awoke from his slumber with a start, reacting to the sudden halt of his steed. "Eh?" he grunted questioningly, looking to his flanks.

"No quick movements," Edlevin whispered. "Norts."

"Northmen to you, rusted one," the red-haired Northerner growled. His was a light accent, rolling often when speaking in the trade tongue. Some words were protracted, while others were cut short, yet there was a notable elegance in his manner of speaking.

"Of course, Northman," Edlevin replied diplomatically, finding no hesitation in his words. "We are messengers from the town of Teth'Nerhol. We bring gifts."

The man ignored the old soldier, instead looking intensely at Alauren with eyes that contained a wild, crushing confidence in their infinite depths of opal. "Odd to see a Half-Elf this far north," he observed calmly.

Alauren found no response. All the anxieties and the fears that had melted away over the last day came rushing back as if a dam had burst, sending a white wall of water thundering forward. Her hands shook with tremors as her mouth hung agape, trying to stammer an answer. "I... I..."

The other two Norts looked mildly amused at the spectacle, but the leader retained a stern gaze. "You say you come from Teth, a human settlement, but only one of you is human." He backed away and splayed his arms out questioningly. "How can I trust such an oddity?"

Edlevin maintained his confident, reasonable demeanor. "We could exchange names, for one. I am Edlevin, joined by my closest friend, Alauren." He gestured to the smith. "She is one of the finest craftsman north of the Spine Mountains, and has lived in our town for many years." He glanced at the woman, silently begging her to calm, before moving on with a point to the stout drop-in. "We're joined by our newest guest, Valin. He's… well, he's a long story."

The Nort looked to the Dwarf, who returned the wary gaze with a toothy, entertained smile. "Hope ye've got some ale, laddie. Can't tell a story sober, that's the rule!"

The Northman stood in silence for a long while, looking the trio over carefully. To the smith, it felt as if her very mind was being ransacked, like every thought held was at risk simply because of the Nort's burning gaze.

"Ronnok," the Nort stated, breaking his silence and his stare. "Chieftain of Nordiska and protector of my people." He gestured to the young, black-haired man flanking him. "This is Bjorn."

The Nort nodded silently in greeting.

"We are also joined by his father, Harald," Ronnok furthered, pointing to the gray-haired Nort sauntering up from behind the trio. "He collects teeth."

The older Northman jingled a small leather sack that hung from his neck, erupting in a gruff chuckle as he passed by the travelers.

Ronnok, after a moment, continued. "You will tell me the story of the Dwarf, as well as any more you may have." He pointed to Edlevin's helmet. "Has that armor always belonged to you?"

Edlevin smiled proudly. "It has."

"Such worn metal must be met with respect. You will return with me to my people." He shot a stern look at the smith, who was already subconsciously shaking her head. "All of you."

The Norts, now seated on their own horses, escorted the trio swiftly through the forest, finding themselves atop the formerly distant hills. The Northmen's mounts were of the same species witnessed the previous day, towering over the slenderer southern steeds. The animals had bright white hair and tufts of similarly covered fur that drooped over their large hooves, while their muscular legs pranced in precise rhythm. These details were all the smith could glean, for she couldn't bring herself to raise her eyes any higher.

Despite Edlevin's repeated attempts to start friendly conversation, the Northmen remained largely silent throughout the journey. They occasionally stared at Alauren, studying her with curiosity. In response, she simply kept her gaze down as much as possible, feeling a profound sense of vulnerability when her eyes met with even the slightest glimpse of theirs.

It was for this reason that she did not see the forest growing thin around her, nor did she take notice of the ever-shrinking mountains behind. She focused in on controlling her nerves, closing her eyes for prolonged periods of time as the men guided her further north.

She had pushed every thought of her current predicament out of her mind, allowing herself to trust completely in Edlevin. For the last leg of their journey, she focused on finding some sort of serenity amongst the pressures of the world, something to lean on besides the comforting presence of her old friend.

The fear of the unknown wracked the blacksmith, yet there was a strange rush of energy with it, an excitement that fluttered about in her chest, seeming to be at once unpleasant and invigorating. More memories were stirred, reminders of days long past.

The fog of time was heavy in these distant recollections, blurring the finer points. Still, they had remained as whispers in the back of her mind for nearly half a millennium, weathering the sands of time and the new experiences that piled atop them.

She knew the smell of mountain air and the rough hair of a horse's mane. She knew the taste of fresh spring water, and the warmth of a campfire. She could recall looking down upon lush oceans of forest from atop soaring mountains, where clouds seemed to hang just a mere jump from her head. She had never given these memories much thought, believing them to be unimportant glimpses of a past life that she barely knew she had.

They gave her a strange comfort now, even if that comfort was only the realization that this world outside wasn't completely unfamiliar to her. Though she remembered little of it now, her path to Teth was one that had taken her over mountain and river alike, an arduous youth of wandering and seeking a home. If she could conquer these challenges as a child, she could conquer them now.

In that thought, a realization occurred: Edlevin was, despite his penchant for bluster, right yet again. Millions of memories of Teth had blended in her centuries of life. Could she name the taste of a beer on a certain visit to the Inn? The smells of the bakery on a certain day?

Of course not! She remembered things such as exciting bar fights and odd visitors, yet the small pleasures of those days were not carried along with those more varied memories. The intricacies of the normal and mundane life she cherished were, in the end, as fleeting as ale on a weekend.

Those other memories, though, hundreds of years old, managed to retain specific, finer details, even if they did lose most everything else. Only in the smith's separation from her familiar life did she realize how little the prosaic things of the world moved her. In one day beyond her home, she felt as if she had lived through a hundred sunrises, and the memories of the world around her became vivid etchings within her mind.

She would return home, as was so desired, but she resolved that it would not be before the making of another memory to carry along with her, another experience that would survive the erosion of time. For the first time, the smith's soul felt ready to endure whatever was to come.

Her thoughts were interrupted by a rough nudge from the left. She jumped with a small fright, opening her eyes to see Valin chuckling at her.

"Welcome back t' reality, lass!" bellowed the smirk-wearing Dwarf. "Yer eyes were so distant I'd thought we'd have t' chase after 'em!" He pointed forward vigorously. "Take a look!"

They stood upon the last of the Tail's foothills, gaining clear sight of the open land ahead. The trees halted in their place at the crest of the summit, leaving tall brown grass to grow unhindered over the sprawling plains below. A great distance to the west, they could see the gray beaches and white cliffs of the Borean Coast as the furious Brumal Sea crashed and foamed against them. The vast fields and meadows stretched to the horizon before them, unbroken save for a few rolling hills.

A small distance into the plains lay an enormous encampment, a bustling metropolis of life among the dying grass. Though there was still much ground to cover, one could easily make out a myriad of tents, as well as the hustle and bustle of hundreds of the Northmen people as they went about their day. Pillars of smoke rose steadily over the roofs of the canvas structures, easily carried away by the whipping of the ocean wind. The layout of the camp was neat and organized, and the Northmen had even possessed the forethought to arrange their homes in blocks, with small streets in between them.

"It's beautiful," the smith gasped, finding the words escaping before she had a chance to notice them. "I've never seen anything like it."

Edlevin returned the comment with a sly smirk. "I see you've recognized that beauty can come from places other than a mug."

Ronnok smiled slightly at the comment, but was quick to return to his steely demeanor. "Enough," growled the Nort. "Keep moving."

CHAPTER SEVEN:

MORE THAN MEETS THE EYE

The smell of the Nort village was quite strong, ever more noticeable as the group grew closer to the tents. It was hardly an offensive odor, but rather, a homelike one; the sweetness of baking bread and juicy meats filled the air, wafting around along with puffs of smoke from wood fires, each mixing perfectly with the others. Only sight could betray that this place was a dwelling of the Northmen, for the fragrance and sounds of life were remarkably akin to the coziest of rural villages.

The tents that comprised the encampment were enormous, triply as long as they were tall; massive cloth walls and towering canvas roofs engulfed ornately decorated wooden supports placed evenly down the sides like ribcages, seen occasionally as the wind whipped the soft materials about. Each dwelling had a small hole at the top, directly in the center, allowing columns of smoke to escape into the wind.

Ronnok leaped from his horse, landing upon the soft grass with a muffled thud. He quickly moved to Alauren, pulled her from her saddle, and guided her to the ground, a task that he seemed to accomplish with relative ease. Edlevin and Valin silently followed the implied instruction, dismounting from their own steeds.

A small crowd gathered to ogle the strange newcomers, muttering in a language unfamiliar to the smith. The Norts all shared Ronnok's large, lanky features, and each stood well over even Edlevin's head. Their hair colors varied widely between shades of red, golden, brown, and silver, as did the hues of their irises; more than one even had eyes of two different colors, though all gazed at the visitors with equal curiosity.

"Talk to nobody unless I grant permission," the Chieftain instructed. "Accept our customs without question, and make your stories entertaining."

Edlevin nodded with a smile. "They always are."

Alauren opened her mouth to object, but her words were cut off by a flurry of motion within the crowd. A white figure, moving incredibly fast, bolted towards Edlevin in a blur.

It was a dog, clearly, but enormous in size, double that of the typical northern hounds. It tackled Edlevin roughly and leaped atop him, burying its face in the old man's and thrashing wildly about.

"Edlevin!" yelped the smith, peering on in confused horror.

Her growing fears were interrupted by the sound of shrill laughter from behind her, quickly followed by Edlevin's own chuckles.

"I must still smell of the Inn!" he giggled, distracting the animal with strokes as he returned to his feet. He tried feebly to clean the slobber from his face and armor, but soon realized the futility of the task; he chose instead to reassure his old friend with a pat on the shoulder, smiling as he joyfully shared some of the grime.

"Thanks, Ed," the smith rumbled, wiping the substance off of her shirt with the canvas of her pack.

"My apologies," Ronnok stated flatly. He procured a cloth from one of his saddlebags and tossed it to the old soldier. "The wolf belongs to Froli, and he is once again failing to tend to his charge. A not uncommon occurrence"

Alauren took a breath and turned her attention back to the village. Two small girls approached Ronnok from behind, though their gaze seemed to be fixated intently on the smith. Their hair (blonde and red, respectively) had been braided into ornate shapes and tied tightly behind their head. One wore a fine blue dress, decorated with visages of white flowers, while the second girl's garment was identical save for a reversal of the colors. A master craftsman had clearly sewn each, someone who took great care in ensuring that each stitch was perfect, and that no color had bled.

They spoke a few phrases in their native language, accompanied by points and giggles towards the new arrivals. The words were thick and flowing, rolling off the tongue like honey dribbling from a spoon. It was a language that, though gentle from the sound of a little girl, became far more menacing when spoken by one of the large warriors.

Ronnok shot the girls a sly smile. "Karlmaðr," he said with a laugh, repeating one of their words.

"Karlmadeer?" Edlevin echoed phonetically. Though he failed to find the more intricate rolling of the tongue that seemed natural to the Northmen, his pronunciation was remarkably close. "Did she call me old?"

"She did," confirmed the Chieftain, who maintained his bright smile. "Do not take it as an insult. Rather, as respect. An old warrior is something not often seen."

Edlevin held his chin high. "As you say."

"They are quite beautiful," Alauren complimented. "May I know their names?"

Ronnok stood in silence for a while, taking a moment to stare into the smith's eyes once more, as if the answer to her question lay within his silent, sky-blue gaze. Abruptly, he turned around and grabbed the girls, one in each arm, and twirled them around in the air. The massive Chieftain let out a decidedly nonthreatening scream, smiling and laughing with just as much genuine mirth as the children. He collapsed to his knees abruptly, pretending to grow tired and weak.

"These are my daughters!" the Chieftain said with feigned exhaustion and an undying grin. "Alvilda in blue, with blonde hair, and Solveig in white, with red hair."

"They're beautiful," Alauren murmured, enamored (and a little unsettled) by the large man's sudden change in demeanor.

"Yes, they are!" Ronnok affirmed, enveloping the girls in a tight embrace. Solveig pulled lightly on his beard, which he met with wide eyes and an exaggerated bellow.

Alauren laughed reservedly and tried to let the genuine warmth she felt towards the girls break through her fluttering nerves, attempting to tell them without words that she could be a friend.

Alvilda broke away from her father's embrace briefly, running to the smith. The Nort girl studied the older woman intently for a moment before producing a small, red flower from a pocket on her dress, which she offered sheepishly.

"For me?" Alauren asked, pointing to her own chest.

The girl giggled shyly and extended the flower even further.

The smith accepted the gift and placed it in the top buttonhole of her tunic, at the collar. Alvilda, meanwhile, smiled timidly and ran back to her father, burying her face in his arms.

"She likes you," Ronnok observed, running his fingers through the girl's hair. "Come, you may get to know each other better over a feast, once proper introductions are had."

"Now yer speakin' me language, sonny!" Valin said, breaking his bored silence. He bolted past Ronnok, motioning intently for the group to get a move on.

Nort feasts were traditionally boisterous affairs, having massive amounts of roasted meat and finely baked confectioneries to gorge upon, and the present moment did not stand at odds with that longstanding custom. The group had been led to a noticeably ornate tent, having a canopy decorated on the inside and out with fine gold trim. Despite its cramped appearance when viewed from without, the interior within was cavernous and roomy, and it was lit effectively by several lanterns that hung from the wooden skeleton of the structure.

A long table, packed with food, had been arranged for the revelers, who were each seated in a large wooden chair. The Chieftain sat at the head, nearest to the door; flanking him on either side, two seats down, were Edlevin and Alauren, with Valin taking a standing place on his seat at the far end of the table.

Once everyone was armored down and seated comfortably, Ronnok poured a large amount of mead into his cup and downed it with a single swig. "Skol!" he bellowed, slamming the empty vessel down.

"I'll drink to that!" Valin replied, pouring his own cup of mead while greedily grabbing large chunks of meat from a serving tray.

"Will your family not be joining us?" Edlevin asked, an air of suspicion about his words. "I do not mean to demand that they be here, but I would like to get to know them better, if that is agreeable to you."

"Only once I am sure you are who you say you are," Ronnok replied. "I am still wary of such a diverse group coming from a human village."

Edlevin chuckled and nodded. "Of course. We are a unique combination; I'll give you that. Though we are from Teth, none of us can call it our original home."

Alauren nodded in agreement. "I cannot remember where I hail from, only that Teth has become my home."

"She was there when I arrived, around fifteen years ago," Edlevin added. "Nobody had any knowledge of her origins, just that she was a fine blacksmith."

"Oh?" Ronnok asked after taking a swig of mead. "Such a small figure, working metal?"

Alauren smiled and rolled up her sleeve, showing a well-toned muscle on her arm. "It takes equal parts strength and a delicate touch. I have both in spades."

The Nort chortled and nodded. "So you do!" His attention turned to the old human. "What about you, soldier? From where do you hail?"

"First, a question, if I may?" Edlevin ventured.

Ronnok nodded and gestured for the man to go ahead.

"You knew I was a soldier," Edlevin continued. "How?"

"Combat etches itself into your eyes, Karlmaðr," the Chieftain rumbled in a dark murmur. "Like a great wood carving, it tells a story, intricate and unmistakable to those who know what to look for. It is permanent, only cleansed by fire." He smirked. "Now, truly, where among the nations do you come from?"

The old soldier looked at the table briefly, a brief sadness washing over him. "Fangirm. I left my home a long time ago, running from the war that seems to constantly engulf the nations of the world." He smiled warmly at Alauren. "I wandered for a long time, but I found a home in Teth, a family."

"You two are close," Ronnok observed.

"We are," confirmed the smith. "He's a mentor and a good friend, the closest thing I've ever had to a father, mind-numbing lectures and all."

"Wisdom often comes through boring means!" Ronnok laughed, drawing a side-eyed glance from his human guest. "What of the Dwarf?"

"Well…" Alauren said, struggling to find words. "He just… appeared. Literally out of thin air."

The Nort Chieftain cocked his head in confusion.

"Itsh me shtaff," Valin said through a mouth full of sweetroll. "Itsh Magic. Don't worry, it won't harm ye, jusht don't touch it."

Edlevin nodded at the Dwarf. "He's an interesting specimen, but one that has been friendly enough since his arrival."

Ronnok sat back for a moment, thinking over the situation

carefully. "Fair enough," he said after a moment. "Each of you have seemed troubled from the moment I laid eyes upon you. That is why I have been so cautious. Friendliness and a reasonable demeanor seem to be increasingly rare in the world, and these are often used as deception."

Edlevin sat back in his chair, sipping mead. "Indeed. However, there is much to be troubled about, isn't there?"

Ronnok nodded. "Too much. Nordiska has moved many times. Never in its history, though, have we been driven so far from our homeland against our will. Something stirs in the east."

Edlevin nodded. "The Empire of Niralan has risen again. By our most recent knowledge, even mighty Elysia has fallen."

Ronnok thought for a moment, biting his lip. "I know these names, and their might. We have faced something different." He shook his head as a clear sorrow overtook his voice. "Something much worse."

Edlevin leaned forward, curious. "I know of no other threats. What have you seen?"

"Strength," Ronnok stated. A darkness fully washed over his face in the shadows of the tent, the empty gaze of his eyes staring into the past. "Their armor is like rock and their swords can cleave great oaks with ease. These beings are larger than us, and stronger. In the earliest days of their attack, even our fleet of longships had no choice but to flee the fjords of our home, unable to risk being caught by the destructive grasp of these warriors." His eyes returned to the present as he rumbled in subdued frustration. "The rest of us have stood little chance, only being able to retreat overland and do our best to stay alive."

"Your fleet left you?" Edlevin asked, cocking an eyebrow.

"Our ships are our life," Ronnok replied with a nod. "Without those vessels, the Northmen are nothing. We cannot trade and fish, nor can we explore the lands beyond. The majority of us could not make it to them before we were set upon." He swallowed hard and ground his teeth for a moment. "These beings were a grave enough threat that any lives lost running on the land were worth the cost. The decision was the right one, yet it still cost us hundreds of kin."

"You don't know who these attackers are?" Alauren asked, feeling her own concern growing.

Ronnok shook his head. "We only know that they wanted us out of the north, by any means necessary. Many of my people died to get us away from them."

Edlevin stood abruptly, sporting a furrowed brow of urgency. "We must return to Teth with this knowledge. We had not heard of this force, and our town should be ready if they encroach."

"They follow us no longer," soothed the Chieftain. "For the last half-morn, they have stayed on their side of the mountains, in the interior. Our scouts have reported no movement from the enemy, at least not yet." He erupted into a lopsided smile. "Besides, would you dishonor my feast by leaving early? Your road has been long, and you need rest."

"I'm with him!" Valin blurted through a meat-stuffed mouth, the words accompanied by a floppy point towards the Chieftain.

Edlevin regained his composure and calmly sat back down with a sigh. "My apologies. Alauren will tell you that I can get worked up."

The smith chuckled derisively. "I think 'worked up' may be too light of a term."

The jest drew a chuckle from the Nort Chieftain, fully washing away the somber mood. He banged on the table loudly, which was followed by the rustling of the tent's entrance flap as it parted before his family, who rushed to join. Alvilda and Solveig were followed by two Nort women; each looked nearly identical to each other, as well as to the girls standing in front of them.

"My newfound friends, allow me to introduce you to Eira and Thyra, my wives," the Chieftain stated proudly.

Each woman wore a fine green dress with white trim, complementing their blonde hair well. They carried themselves with clear pride, gliding themselves into their seats at the table, flanking Ronnok.

"Seveli," each said in unison.

"That means 'hello' in our tongue," Ronnok explained.

"Seveli," Alauren replied politely, which drew smiles from the gathered Norts.

"They look quite alike," Edlevin observed. "Are they related?"

Ronnok nodded. "Sisters."

Edlevin scratched his stubble in thought. "I am familiar with many of your customs, including polygamy, but I have not heard of a man choosing to be joined to both sisters."

Ronnok wore a wide grin. "Your mistake is thinking that it was my choice! They would not have it any other way." He smiled at the women, who returned the expression fully. "We do not place restrictions on our love, as the nations do. So long as those involved are adults and are agreeable to the union, the Norts accept their wishes warmly."

"Soundsh like fun!" Valin blurted between swigs.

Ronnok brushed off the comment with a friendly chuckle and a light point towards the stout visitor. "I like you, Dwarf."

Valin returned the mirth. "Keep the food comin' and ye just might make it onto me good side as well!"

Alauren, all the while, had wanted to speak, but found herself enamored by the unfamiliar world: the good food, the odd customs, the beautiful architecture, and the unexpectedly warm company. After some time (and a bit of mead), she began to find words. "Ronnok, I must admit, I did not expect your society to be so…"

"Civilized?" the Chieftain finished instantly, bearing a thin, knowing smile.

Alauren nodded shyly. "For tribes, you seem to have a mind for the finer things."

"As we always have," Ronnok affirmed proudly. "If it were not for the harsh conditions of our ancestor's home, they may have settled into the mundane, as your people did, finding more joy in excessive ale and food than the great struggles of a hard life."

Alauren laughed, finally letting go of her apprehension. "I can't argue with you. Our biggest problem was our Inn running out of alcohol!"

"Even so, a nightmare!" Ronnok yelled with a laugh. "Here, though, the mead never stops flowing, and we ensure so ourselves."

"That's what I like to hear!" Alauren chortled. Indeed, her cup never seemed to empty, and all the while realistic stories and unexaggerated experiences were shared under the careful guidance of increasingly intoxicated minds.

The feast was capped off by a performance of the harp by Eira and Thyra, the instruments bearing fine carvings, masterfully crafted down to the smooth curves. Each of the women plucked at their strings in perfect harmony with one another, reciting an ancient Nortish tune effortlessly, as if their minds were linked in an unshakable rhythm. The music echoed through the tent, wafting a sense of calm and relaxation over the weary inhabitants.

The group had moved from the table onto soft, fur bedrolls, listening to the light melody as sleep began to snake its creeping tendrils around their minds. Alauren felt the numbing effects of the mead, allowing her to enjoy the experience with little of her previous anxiety. Valin and Edlevin had both fallen fast asleep almost instantly, for their part, leaving only Alauren, Ronnok, and his family awake.

"It has been a long while since I've heard this instrument," Alauren whispered to her host, careful not to interrupt the music. "It is beyond beautiful."

Ronnok smiled and pointed to the instruments. "Do you see the etchings in the wood?"

"They are elegant. I see dragons, warriors, boats…" the smith listed. "Fine work."

"It took me many hours," beamed the Chieftain, a clear pride in his gruff voice.

Alauren was briefly taken aback. "Oh?"

"I do not possess the skill to play them, but I can construct them well, yes," Ronnok confirmed. "Norts are as much craftsman as they are warriors, though some are more inclined to either pursuit."

"Still, it's not a feat I would expect of you at first glance," replied the smith.

Ronnok chuckled. "Many feel the same way, only because they do not look hard enough. Norts learned quickly that our lives cannot be only fighting and violence. That is the fastest way to madness."

"Why *do* you fight, anyway?" Alauren asked bluntly. "Your people have a reputation for being ruthless invaders, pillagers of towns, yet you have such gentle skill in your other crafts. Your food, your clothes, your instruments… Why be violent?"

Ronnok thought for a moment before speaking, something the smith was noticing to be a common occurrence. "Could you so easily give up your forge?" he asked, to which Alauren shook her head. He continued. "Combat is in my blood. In all of our blood." He swept his hand around the tent. "Our prowess in battle is a gift from the gods, but so too is our skill at the craftsman's table."

"Who are your gods, then?" Alauren asked. "I know very little of them. They seem like interesting beings. Varied."

"If I told you now, would you have a reason to return?" Ronnok asked with a chuckle.

Alauren smiled warmly. "You would invite us back?"

"So long as our enemy does not pursue us once more, we will remain here, eagerly awaiting your visits," the Chieftain replied, matching the smile. "You have treated us with respect and good spirits, the first on our long and arduous road from our homes. You look at us with curiosity rather than fear. Your company has been most welcome."

"Truthfully, I was afraid, before we arrived here," the smith said, shifting in her bedroll. "I expected you to rob us or kill us."

"Yet, when we stopped you, you did not attack," Ronnok pointed out. "When we stared at you, you did not meet us with anger. Your fear did not guide you to unnecessary violence. That sets you apart."

Alauren remained silent, digesting the words. She removed her scabbard from her belt. "I was told to present you with this," she said. "As a token of Teth's commitment to peace. It's my own creation."

Ronnok smiled, accepted the gift, and removed the blade from its sheath. The sharp edge shined in the dim glow, and the ruby of the hilt sent points of light cascading around the tent whenever it caught the flickering of the lanterns.

Ronnok's large hands barely fit around the handle. The blade looked more like a machete in his sizeable paws, though the Chieftain hardly seemed to notice as he swiped it here and there with a noticeable appreciation.

"How does it feel?" asked the smith, eager for an assessment of her talents.

"Like a skinning blade made with an unrivaled skill," the Chieftain replied, placing the weapon back in its scabbard. "Your gesture is appreciated, but this sword would perform its best in your hands."

Alauren chuckled. "I'm not a fighter."

"Not yet, you're not," Ronnok countered. "Return, and we will change that."

Alauren took the blade back with a nod, setting it beside her. "An intriguing thought for the morning. The mead is starting to pull covers over my eyes."

"Of course!" Ronnok said. "Enjoy your slumber, knowing that all of Nordiska watches over you."

The smith nodded and, slowly, allowed the comforting darkness of sleep to envelop her.

CHAPTER EIGHT:

EMBERS

7th OF THE MORN OF HARVEST
NORTHERN YEAR 715

The world seemed to be richer in the senses of the smith as she rode alongside her compatriots, though the forests around her were the very same that had been traveled through the previous day, changed only by the blowing of the wind. Much to her old friend's surprise, Alauren had been favorable to staying with the Norts for a few more hours, but Edlevin insisted that they embark on that cold autumn morning.

The old soldier seemed troubled, though he would never allow his outward expression to show such a thing. He masked the feeling, as he was wont to do, by making small talk, going from this topic to that in a clear bid to keep his mind busy. Even after a warm farewell from Ronnok and hours traveled by horse, the erudite human still managed to draw stories to tell, as increasingly dubious as they had to be.

"…And that's why you shouldn't mix Dwarven Flamewater with Ale. I'm pretty sure I was fully dead for at least an hour!" he said with a half-hearted huff of laughter, a sound which was echoed only by a whinny from his horse.

"I bet ye were still talkin' as ye expired," Valin quipped, a clear annoyance seeping into his voice. The comment drew a hearty laugh from Alauren and a scowl from her old friend.

"He was," the smith confirmed. "This one happens to be true, and I was there."

"You were?" Edlevin asked. "I don't remember that."

"You don't remember because it was your first night in town and you ended up passed out face-down on the docks," Alauren quickly shot back.

"Ah, yes!" Edlevin bellowed with a chuckle. "In the south, they call that a Dwarven Housewarming."

"Only counts as a housewarmin' if ye drink in the mornin', too,"

Valin deadpanned.

"And what makes you think I didn't?" the old soldier countered instantly. "Hair of the dog!"

Alauren chortled and shook her head. "It seems like that was a century ago, now."

"Fifteen years come the first of the Morn of Cold," Edlevin corrected.

"Seems like a lot longer," the smith mused. "You know, in all that time, I don't think I've seen you as uneasy as you are now. You talk when you're nervous, you know."

"I'm just eager to get news of whatever is attacking the Norts to the Marchioness," Edlevin hastily explained, sniffling and rubbing his moist nose as the brisk air passed over it. "I have some theories, none of them are good."

"Theories such as...?" Alauren trailed off, allowing for elaboration.

"Well, the North Elysians were never exactly the most loyal to the throne," the old soldier proposed with a rub of the chin. "They can be manipulated by strength, and that's one thing Niralan has an abundance of."

"Going up against Norts, though?" the smith pointed out. "You saw how big they are. I don't believe it."

"That's true," Edlevin conceded. "A force of North Elysians alone might not be able to take them on, but supported by Niralan? They can't be underestimated." He sighed and shrugged. "The only other answer that makes sense to me is mercenaries from this island or that, beyond the Nirali Sea. Big ships and a wealth of weapons."

"I suppose," Alauren said. "Still, the Norts don't seem like they could be so easily driven away by humans."

Edlevin chuckled. "Anyone can be defeated, Ally. Back when I was running cargo for the Sun Elves, we ran into all sorts of nasties. Burrowers, pirates, slavers, all in strengths tripling our own."

"Eh?" Valin grunted, attempting to break up the speech. "Ye see that?" He nodded his thick brow towards a thin stream of black smoke, rising to the sky in the distance ahead.

The words were hardly heard by the old soldier, who continued unabated. "We defeated them all, with some difficulty. Certainly, my own skill would come into play, but we had solid strategies."

"Edlevin!" Alauren snapped, drawing the man's annoyed attention. "Valin is right. Look!"

The human's eyes snapped ahead and caught sight of the plume. "That's not smoke from a hearth fire," he murmured as his face darkened with concern. "Have your weapons ready."

Teth was dead.

Buildings, including Edlevin's house and Alauren's smith, smoldered with red embers. Only the longhouse remained standing tall, scorched with black streaks, but intact. Parts of the town's stone wall had fallen, and the main gates on the north and south ends laid flat on the ground, far from their hinges, pressed into the dirt as if a thousand horses had thundered over the old wood. The docks looked to be the only thing undamaged, and even then, all but a single small skiff moored a small distance from the pier had been sunk. The trio gawked at the destruction as they rode into town and dismounted in the square, swords (and scythe) ready.

"Edlevin…" Alauren quaked, her breath ragged. "The Norts?"

"I don't know, Ally," the old soldier replied, an unfamiliar fear dripping from his voice. The tip of his sword shook lightly, mirroring his own tremors as he looked over the scene. The town was blanketed in total silence save for the ocean's dull roar and the crackling of embers, leaving the returning company in an eerie, otherworldly calm.

Alauren cautiously moved to the longhouse doors and placed her hand briefly on the handle to check for heat. "Looks mostly intact," she reported nervously. She glanced inquisitively at Edlevin, who gave her a nod.

She pulled the door towards her, but found it to be unyielding. "I think it's locked from the inside."

Edlevin disappeared behind the longhouse for a moment before returning. "The back is locked, as well. We need to find the keys."

Valin silently stepped to the front door next to Alauren and shooed her away with a push. He procured a piece of charcoal from his pack and scrawled a "ᛈ" symbol on the door. He backed up several steps.

"Briste! Briste!" squawked the Dwarf.

The door cracked and shattered as splintering wood was sent soaring across the square. The trio ducked down, attempting to avoid the airborne projectiles that whistled through the air. Soon enough, the wood cracked into two jagged pieces, falling away from the threshold.

Alauren, after being sure that no more splinters would rain down, returned to her feet. She was a few steps away from the longhouse, yet she could still easily see what lay within with an unbearable clarity. Her milky skin went a pale white, and her jaw fell open.

Fishers, laborers, watchers, servants, and even the Marchioness himself lay scattered about the narrow hall. Their eyes were a solid, bloody red, wide open in terror, while their pupils had dilated to their fullest extent. The color of their skin had been turned a sickly green, and many clutched at their throats, frozen in the last throes of death. The walls were lined with scratch marks and dents from men and women trying desperately to escape whatever had happened within. These were the final etchings of the people of Teth, a graven epitaph that recounted the agony of their last moments.

Alauren broke her horrified gaze and promptly vomited off the side of the stairway. A deep fear mixed with a primal disgust, forming a potent poison within her stomach, an acidic ichor that burned through flesh and bone. It hobbled her legs and threatened to send her tumbling to the ground in a heap. Only Edlevin grabbing her by the shoulders allowed the smith to avoid collapsing into the dirt.

"Edlevin?" she asked between sickly heaves. "What…?"

"I still don't know, Ally," the old soldier hissed. He perked up abruptly, lifting the smith fully onto her feet. "Though, I have a feeling we're about to find out. Stand, and stand tall."

The blacksmith obeyed, finding three figures approaching from the south in glimmering, bronze-colored armor. A shiny, blackened metal coursed through grooves on the surface in a spiraling, knot-like pattern, causing Alauren to gawk wide-eyed at the masterful touch of the maker, the skill necessary for such a thing unrivaled even in her extensive experience. The heavy plate was smooth, yet angled where necessary, expertly crafted down to the folds, resembling classical, feudal designs despite the alien nature of the aesthetic itself. The edges, trimmed and rounded, were meticulously crafted to guide a blade far from its intended target, making even a strike at a gap a risky maneuver. The bearers were massive beings, even compared to the Norts, and each wore a large, concealing helmet.

The centermost figure was armed with a longsword of a brilliant, shining steel that matched his armor in craftsmanship perfectly. He planted his blade into the ground, burrowing it a hand's length into the soil, and leaned upon it, like a knight of old posing for a painting.

The beings stood for a long while, silent and still, like stone guardians of a royal tomb. No breath could be heard behind their helms, nor did their armor let out a single creak. Even so, there was a weight thrusted upon the trio of locals, a crushing gravity that poured from the darkness behind the helms of the imposing knights.

Edlevin, after a fleeting moment of clear fear, broke the silence. "We are travelers from the Southlands. Mercenaries attending an urgent matter to the north. We are returning home. Friend or foe?"

The only response was the crackling of the embers and the wind, which whistled shrilly through the armor of the phantom-like knights that stood before them.

"We stumbled upon this place moments ago," the old soldier continued. "We wish to pass with no trouble, as our road home is long."

Again, no response came. The center man lifted his sword, finally breaking his perfect stillness.

"We will defend ourselves, if necessary," Edlevin warned. "Let us pass."

"Rarely do we slumber long enough to see the end of a Dream," the centermost knight said, his low, slithering voice crawling on the wind and scurrying down the smith's spine, eliciting a heavy shiver. He tilted his helm toward Alauren. "With her death, we will wake."

Edlevin grit his teeth and brought his sword up in front of him, recognizing the cold truth. He shoved Alauren behind him and stared sternly at the men from under his helm, though his trembling hands betrayed his fear.

The center knight brought his blade to bear. The metallic sheen glinted gold in the sun, like flakes of the precious metal had been inlaid throughout the length of the weapon. The two men flanking him mirrored his action, drawing simple steel swords, held with both hands. The man in the center locked the gaze of his helmet on to the smith, holding it steady.

"I don't know what's going on, but it's about to go south quickly," Edlevin muttered to his compatriots. "If we fight, fight them like Norts. Keep your distance and make them overcommit."

"Who are they?" Alauren asked with a quiver, drawing her weapon.

"If we're lucky?" Edlevin replied coldly. "Dead men. Get ready."

Each of the three smaller combatants took their pick of opponent. Edlevin squared himself at the center, drawing the attention of the leftmost knight while the others paced wide. The center enemy kept his focus on Alauren, cautiously picking his steps.

The smith breathed heavily and focused in on the colossal man standing before her. A single glance at his log-sized arms told her that any strike, no matter how glancing, would likely mean instant death, leaving no room for error. She still heaved occasionally in disgust, but the images of the longhouse were largely pushed out of her mind by the stress. She focused and breathed deeply.

Alauren's opponent was the first to move, followed quickly by the other two. The smith, feeling her fear leave her for the moment, held her ground before ducking into a forward roll just as the man fully closed the distance. His sword sailed a mere hair above her head, close enough that she felt the wind from the near miss brushing against her scalp. She was back on her feet in a second, allowing her to dodge yet another blow, and another, and another, all in quick and frantic succession, a desperate struggle to avoid the swinging steel.

Edlevin met his target full on, using the broad side of his blade to intercept three quick blows thrown at him from his lower left. Each drove him backwards, impacting on his sword like he had been hit by a boulder. Still, he held his ground, though he couldn't help but skid on the dirt and gravel as the thunderous blows slammed against him.

The knight, in a feat of unnatural speed, suddenly swung his blade up and reversed it back down. The entire U-shaped motion of his sword took less than a second, and he guided the hefty slab of steel like it was a wooden toy.

Edlevin could only look on with wide eyes as the blow plunged towards his head. He raised his wrist and closed his eyes, dropping hard onto one knee and bracing for the impact.

Clunk!

Time seemed to freeze for the two combatants as the knight

looked on confusedly. His sword had met its target with pinpoint precision, but it had stopped dead against Edlevin's bracer, like it had hit the side of a solid cliff.

The old soldier wasted no more time. He sprung up and rammed his sword hard into an exposed opening of the enemy's armor at the armpit, producing a moist crunching sound and a pained gasp as it drove through the man's ribcage and lungs. Edlevin jammed the tip of the blade up and through the man's neck, a wound from which a greasy, sickly gray liquid poured forth. Eager to be away, the human ripped the sword out and let the knight fall to the ground, where a puddle of the muted blood began to form amid the gurgling struggles for life.

Valin, meanwhile, had attempted to charge in and surprise his opponent. Instead, he found himself teleporting randomly about the enemy. The thin, ashy smoke that wafted in the air distorted with each low *thump* from the stout Priest's sudden, repeated appearance and disappearance.

"STOP - IT - YE - ARSE - FACED – WIZARD!" Valin wailed as he phased in and out of reality. His opponent tried to keep track, but failed to land any blows in the confused fracas.

Alauren's target, who had been momentarily distracted by the death of his fellow, suddenly wheeled around to face her. He strode forward with his weapon held to his right, perfectly still.

The knight abruptly ran forward and struck out low with his blade, carrying the momentum into an upward swing. The smith lunged backwards and dropped to the ground upon her back, desperately avoiding the blow as it sailed a finger's length from her chest.

Her enemy suddenly twirled, bringing his sword up to block an attack by Edlevin. The smith jumped swiftly to her feet and, with hardly a thought, charged at the distracted man, sprinting silently towards his unguarded backside with her small blade. Even in the heat of combat, she was able to pick out several gaps in the armor, a skill learned over years of her career at the forge. She chose an opening, a seam at the waist, and brought her sword into position, driving it forward with zeal. At the last second, the knight's hand appeared in her vision, hurtling backwards.

For a moment, the world was nothing but white. The next, the blacksmith was lying face down on the ground in a pool of gray, viscous liquid. The left side of her face bled and swelled, pulsing with pain, while her arms shook with uncontrollable tremors. She attempted to stand, but only found herself vomiting at the effort. The world was blurry and confused, yet she could still barely make out Edlevin fighting and Valin still teleporting about.

Edlevin's panicked, screaming voice got her attention. "GO, ALLY! RUN!" he grunted as he intercepted and deflected a blow from the enemy. "TO THE NORTS! GO!"

Alauren rose shakily and stumbled towards the north side of the village, giving the combatants a wide berth. The gray fluid stuck to her skin and caused her to dry heave at the smell; it was a stinging, metallic odor, quite reminiscent of her forge's emissions, had they been saved up for a week before being released directly into her mouth. She shambled away as fast as her feet would carry her, though she found a great deal of difficulty as her legs wobbled unsurely beneath her.

Valin's target noticed the smith's attempted escape and moved to intercept. Instead of reaching his quarry, though, he found himself literally tripping over a swearing Dwarf who appeared under his legs. The knight fell hard onto the ground with a growl, losing his sword in the process.

Valin crumpled just behind him, dropping his weapon while groaning and cursing incomprehensibly.

The enemy fumbled around for his weapon, but instead found it grasping the hilt of the scythe. Seeming to find the pointed edge agreeable enough for his purpose, he rose and strode quickly to the smith, who could only stumble away madly, half-conscious, yet fully aware of the specter that was ever stalking towards her.

The knight stopped abruptly, his body seizing up. He stood motionless in mid-stride, as if he had been turned to stone, locked into place by some infernal curse. He grunted several times, like the air was being forced out of his lungs repeatedly by swift blows to the gut.

"Well, ye'll regret that one, laddie," Valin grumbled with a wicked grin.

Black soot and ash, thick as the eruption of a volcano, began to pour from the knight's helmet. His bronze armor began to glow white, sparking violently with each of his convulsions. After a few prolonged moments, he let out a blood-curdling scream, a deafening howl that echoed off the mountains and across the ocean, shrill and awful. One final blast of black smoke poured from his armor before the plate plunged to the ground, empty save for bits of ash.

"GO, LASSIE!" Valin directed, snatching his scythe before bounding off to assist Edlevin.

Alauren, finally finding some semblance of balance, carried herself away. She made it to the gate quickly and ran to where the horses were tied, a large log just outside of town.

The two larger mounts had, at some point, had become frightened and broken their ties on the old piece of wood. The smith barely noticed, as her focus had to be on carefully untying Valin's pony. She hopped on to the saddle and rode forward, as fast as she could away from a waking nightmare.

Edlevin, though cautious, stole the occasional glance to make sure that his old friend had made it beyond the walls; while the Norts had not fully earned his trust, he knew that she would be safest with those warriors, and they were more likely to be able to protect her from the thunderous strikes of this enemy than his own waning strength. His breath had become ever heavier, the toil of moving his blade and armor dragging on his lungs, yet he fought on.

Though his foe was bigger, stronger, more agile than he, there was a distinct caution around the knight's movements, careful to avoid the old soldier's blade as the attack was driven, the sole saving grace that kept the fight resembling an even match. The enemy would try to step around him, to chase after what seemed to be his primary prey, but a flurry from the human would set him back upon his heels, as if the sword bore with it an aura of strength beyond that of the wielder.

"VALIN!" Edlevin yelled, finding a moment to catch his breath as the knight reset his stance. "Go! Get out!"

"Aye laddie!" cried the Dwarf, his voice already distant.

The knight moved again, thrusting forward with his sword like its weight was little more than that of a hollow piece of deadfall. The attack was narrowly dodged as the old soldier ducked to the left, throwing out a stab of his own toward the gap in the enemy's knee armor while he carried out the maneuver. His movements were controlled, precise, executed without a hint of decay despite the decades since he had seen combat.

The blow connected, driving with enough force to impale even a gambeson-wearing combatant cleanly through. Edlevin shifted his weight forward and erupted into a run, repositioning himself behind the knight while attempting to drag the blade through the enemy's tendons, hoping to immobilize him.

Only after the maneuver was complete did the soldier realize that his sword had stopped dead upon the flesh of this mysterious enemy, while the sharp edge had been heavily blunted by the dragging motion. It was as if he had struck a solid anvil, carving the metal of his sword away as it slid across the unyielding surface. He backed up slowly, staring in disbelief as the enemy stood tall and wheeled around.

"Your blade sings," hissed the knight, bringing his own weapon back to bear. "Yet, there is little power in its voice."

Edlevin ignored the nonsensical ranting entirely, planting himself in a defensive stance. He caught sight of Valin, running back through the gates. "No horses!" yelped the Dwarf. "Hold tight!" He sprinted off towards the dock, making for the last available way out.

"Come on, then," Edlevin growled, shifting his attention back to the knight. "Come and get me."

The titan shifted his weight to his left leg and planted his sword in the ground, uttering a single word, his voice calm and collected: "No."

Edlevin wasted no time, charging forward at the utterance of the rebuttal, hoping to catch the enemy off guard. He struck out at gap after gap in the enemy's armor, seeking to find an opening to the soft flesh that surely laid beneath, but each blow was met only with a muffled thud, each hope that a strike could be true dashed by an adamant resistance. All the while, the armored giant stood tall and still.

The knight, after taking several harmless blows without so much as a flinch, shot out his arm with an unnatural speed, grabbing the old soldier by the left side of his hip. The being's grip was crushing, like a vice closing around the human's bones, intensifying in strength with each passing blink. The force elicited a raspy scream of pain which echoed from inside Edlevin's helmet, overtaking his senses and vibrating the metal around his head.

The knight held the human steady for a few moments, letting the scream play out, before hefting him and launching him with force into the open threshold of the longhouse. Edlevin's hard landing was somewhat softened as he impacted upon the largest pile of corpses near the rear; after a moment to regain his senses, he found himself staring into Sortul's blank eyes. A small trickle of fluid ran down the Marchioness's chin, smelling intensely of sulfur, while his limbs had begun to stiffen in the rigor of death.

The old soldier heaved for a moment before throwing himself back to his feet. He found his sword lying partially impaled in the shoulder of a dead fisherman and retrieved it, forcing himself to pay no thought to the slicing of flesh as it slid out from the posthumous wound. He gripped the weapon tightly and wheeled, hearing the thunder of sabatons upon wood as the knight entered the hall.

The enemy stooped and picked up a corpse nearer to the door, that of Dalvon, juggled it into a more comfortable position with a single hand, and hurled it with force at the old soldier. Edlevin dove to the left, yet still found himself impacted by the leg of the dead Captain, a blow which spun him and forced him to bear witness to the body impacting the wooden throne headfirst with splintering force. A spray of blood and sulfuric purulence erupted from the shattered skull of the deceased human, painting the symbol of Teth's authority and royalty with sickly viscera.

Edlevin was on his feet again in a heartbeat, recovering just as another corpse came sailing at him, followed by another, and another, each of them crunching against the rear wall with bursts of foul fluid. Hardly a thought could be paid to the horrifying display, for the old soldier's focus had to remain on surviving, on avoiding the projectiles that surged towards him at a decidedly terminal velocity. One after the other, man and woman, old and young, whizzed by, the bodies of those passed on treated with as little respect as a stone upon a catapult.

The knight threw two more corpses simultaneously, the last remaining from that side of the room, following them quickly with a booming charge that cracked the floorboards underneath the force of his mighty sabatons.

Edlevin, focused on dodging the cadavers, was caught in the grip of the enemy once more, this time feeling the crushing pressure envelop his right shoulder. The world, in a fraction of a second, became a blur, flying by as the old soldier became the latest projectile, finding himself whipped into the low, thatched ceiling directly above the longhouse's main door. Old iron nails and fresh chips of wood erupted around him, joined by dry leaves and grasses as he tore through the outer layers of the roof. He managed to keep his wits during his prolonged airborne time, hanging onto his sword just long enough to throw it out and to the left, clear of his eventual landing, but still close.

After a few tumbling, sickening rotations in the air, he impacted the ground hard, his armor protecting him well enough from the blunt trauma, but forcing the plates to dig into his flesh at their edges as they caught upon the bumps in the hard, trodden dirt; they drew blood in several places, though the old soldier could hardly notice the pain. Even with the protective shell, his head still snapped to the side inside of his helm, smacking off the inner padding and causing the world to go white for a split second.

He quickly regained his senses and continued his rolling momentum, allowing it to assist in his rise as he planted his left leg into the dirt in an effort to force himself up. Shifting his weight, he came to a stop and steadied himself with the other leg, ending his uncomfortable journey in a standing stance. He looked down, finding Alauren's blade at his feet, and snatched it with his right hand.

"I GOT IT!" Valin screamed from beyond the dock. "LOOSE, BUT DRIFTIN'! RUN, YA OL' BASTARD!"

The sound of the Dwarf's voice brought the old soldier fully back to the present. Feeling no further need for hesitation, he retrieved his sword, which was lying upon the ground to the left, and began to heave his way to the dock, fighting the pain of his injuries all the while. Another sound, far more menacing than the voice of the Priest, echoed through the town and off of the forests surrounding it, steady thumps that soon physically reverberated through the ground, as if a monster of rock and stone had thundered down from the mountains to give chase. Edlevin picked up his pace, desperately filling his lungs and using every spare bit of air that could be sacrificed to drive his steps across the planks of the pier.

A crunching smash resonated from the center of the town; the remains of the market stalls yielded to a force which drove through their blackened structures with hardly an effort, the frames shattered into little more than splinters and ash. The knight emerged from the carnage as if the debris were a portal to another realm, charging through the sooty cloud with a dire vigor in his step. The wood of the dock began to shake and quiver under the human as this beast gained ground behind him, closing in like a twisting, thundering storm.

Edlevin eyed the end of the planks, beyond which the skiff bobbed here and there, only needing its sail dropped to speed away in the increasingly heavy wind. *Far,* thought the old soldier. *Too far? Wearing plate.* The edge of the pier was just upon him now, only two strides away, while the darkness behind had drawn just as close. *Damn it all.*

The human planted both of his feet upon the last board on the dock and threw himself forward with all of his might, sailing over the depths. Time crawled, giving him a good look at the twisting darkness below, the rush of water waiting to drag him under, to use the weight of his plate to give the gods of the ocean a gift of life to be drained away.

He closed his eyes and breathed deeply, feeling the salty air brush across his nose.

Too far, likely. Shit.

Time seemed to have no meaning as the smith drove her pony north. The world around her was blurred and unfamiliar, though she had seen the exact sights of the painted trees and purple mountains just hours ago. She rode hard, kicking the animal in regular intervals to keep it moving, a motion that eventually became automatic.

She found herself lapsing in and out of consciousness, seeing fleeting visions of the past each time the world went dark. She could hear voices, familiar but unknown, echoing from the darkest recesses of her mind. One rang out the loudest, a female voice with a soothing quality.

My dearest, my love, my memory. Always and forever.

It repeated in her mind, dominating her thoughts until the darkness subsided once more. Alauren looked upwards, realizing that the light-filled sky which had seemed to have been there a moment ago was replaced by stars, thousands of them, seeming to shine brighter than ever before, filling the heavens with an ocean of pale light. The moons, both glowing in their full majesty, hung steadily above, illuminating the road in a soft glow that pounded painfully in the smith's head. She closed her eyes, trying to escape the pain.

Another memory was dredged by the dark, a vision of a night sky seen from atop a mountain. She could see a person standing near a cliff edge, silhouetted in soft moonlight and the emerald glow of the northern auroras; both united to cast a blinding backdrop for the solitary figure, any fine details invisible against the brilliant, shifting colors. The being extended a hand, beckoning to her.

The smith woke again, greeted this time by the sun cracking above the horizon to her left. Just ahead lay Nordiska, beginning to stir in the first light of morning.

The pony's body finally fell to exhaustion, willing to continue no further. Every muscle in Alauren's body pained as the animal came to a sudden halt, throwing her to the road in a hard tumble. Tears welled in her eyes as she slapped across the hard ground, and she feebly crawled towards the village, reaching out towards the tents.

"Ronnok!" wailed the smith. "Ronnok!"

A trio of Nort women rushed to her aid, kneeling over her and attempting to speak.

"Eru ia vjell?" one asked, gazing at the distressed arrival with sparkling blue eyes. A small crowd began to form behind her.

"Ronnok," Alauren growled. "Find Ronnok."

"Lìda fá Ronnok," the Nort directed, pointing to a boy.

He quickly obeyed, running off towards the center of camp. A small girl appeared with a horn full of water, which the smith drank in a single gulp, while a vast amount escaped her maw to run unnoticed down her chin.

Ronnok, after a few minutes, appeared from somewhere within the city and hurried to the scene, wearing a face of solemn concern.

"What happened?" asked the Chieftain. "Bandits? Highwaymen? We'll find them."

"No," Alauren hissed in reply, gasping for breath. "Big men.

Bigger than you. Bronze armor. They killed Teth. They killed everyone."

Ronnok sighed heavily as a sorrow overtook his eyes. "A tale that rings familiar to my people." He picked up the smith, carrying her softly in his arms. "You must rest now. We will leave this place, but my people will carry you with us. You are protected, small one."

"Edlev... Ed..." Alauren attempted to say as her consciousness lapsed.

"He will be found," Ronnok replied surely. "I will see to it personally."

PART TWO:

THE WORLD BEYOND

CHAPTER NINE:

SHATTERED

*The Northmen may be the most confusing race to
have ever graced the shores of Odenseye: brutal,
yet organized; wrathful, yet intelligent. Chief
among their traits, though, is the sense of devotion
they carry towards those that they care about,
willing to shed blood (their own and others') in
defense of their family and clan. Many call them
savage, yet would savages sacrifice a dozen
warriors to buy their weak ones a few precious
minutes to run? Would savages give gifts of
carved wood and elegant cloth, their own make, to
fellows in their clan? Our mistake in fighting the
Norts thus far has been a stubborn, prideful
unwillingness to ask ourselves such questions,
assuming that we already know our enemy.*

We do not.

   –   Gauis Truvani, in "Nations of Odenseye"

10th OF THE MORN OF HARVEST
NORTHERN YEAR 715

For a time, Alauren felt only a dark serenity, as if she were drifting along carelessly in a calm, warm ocean. She could hear the waves impact something wooden, which would tilt her back and forth, bobbing her up and down, telling her with surety that she was at sea.

As time wore on, however, she began to hear other sounds; footsteps, creaking wood, and voices rang out, though each was muffled, as if they were being heard through a wall. There was an occasional odor, someone cooking fish or meat, a smell that seemed strikingly bitter and unpleasant in the moment. She was half-aware of cold liquid touching her lips and running down her throat periodically, given by someone with a gentle touch.

Eventually, her sight went from blackness to a slightly lighter blur. She could tell that she was in a small storeroom, alone, in a hammock strung between two walls. She was wearing fresh clothes, a black button-up shirt and a pair of gray trousers. The room swayed this way and that, dark save for a sparse spattering of sunlight which managed to peer through the few gaps in the overlapping boards above. Each beam sent a splitting pain shooting through her head any time they glinted over her eyes, though such an event was mercifully rare. Regardless, she slammed her eyelids shut and returned to her slumber whenever the glowing agony brushed across her face.

She was awoken sometime later by the sound of whispers on either side of her hammock, chittering about something in an indecipherable language. The smith opened her eyes slowly to find Solveig and Alvilda hovering over her, looking on with starry eyes and curious stares, each tilting here and there as they moved expertly with the rolling of the ship around them. They jumped back at the sight of the wakeful guest, but quickly smiled.

"Ia eru vikr!" the blonde-haired Alvilda said. "Lìda Karlmaðr!"

Solveig bounded out of the room, practically bouncing off the walls as she careened through the half-ajar door. Alvilda smiled brightly and handed Alauren a cup of water, which was gratefully accepted and greedily gulped. Moments later, Solveig burst back through the door, followed by a familiar voice.

"What, is she awake?" asked the old soldier, poking his head through the threshold. He looked exhausted, with deep purple bags under his eyes and many a bruise upon his face, but he perked up quickly when he saw the smith's semi-conscious face looking back. He hurried over, rushed the children out of the room, and knelt.

"Still alive, I see," Alauren groaned weakly.

Edlevin smiled, a clear relief in his eyes. "As you should have expected, my friend."

The smith chuckled briefly, a pitiful sound that ended in a far more sorrowful tone than it began. "Valin?"

"Topside, drinking, as he has been since we were found," the old soldier answered with a soothing chuckle. "We're okay, Ally. We're on board Ronnok's ship, the *Skylðrek*."

Alauren rubbed her temple, fighting off a throbbing headache. "Where did they find you?"

"The ocean," Edlevin replied. "The horses were gone. We really only had one method of leaving."

"You took a boat?" Alauren asked.

"Yes, that small skiff near the dock, if you remember," the old soldier explained, drawing a nod from his old friend. "Valin got it ready while I distracted that armored bastard, and I made the leap from the pier to the boat with a thumb's length to spare. We set sail and made it a ways out, against the wind, when Valin said he could enchant the sail to always have wind with one of his runes."

"He has a rune for everything, doesn't he?" the smith observed.

"Nope," Edlevin deadpanned. "He accidentally lit the ship on fire. 'Fergot which rune was which', if his words are to be believed." He huffed a laugh. "The whole thing went up, but we had a small dinghy tied to the back. We were on that, watching the mast of the boat descend below the waves, when we realized that the dinghy oars were going down with it. We drifted a few hours from Teth until the Norts found us."

"Well, at least we know you're still a shitty sailor," quipped the smith, trying to manage a smile.

Edlevin let out a boisterous laugh. "I always will be, too."

Silence between the two old friends ensued for a moment, while the room seemed to be robbed of any warmth, like a door had been flung wide open during a winter of blustery, bitter cold. In a breath, the cracks in their hearts finally gave way, and a spout of sorrow poured forth from the jagged spillway.

The smith's face began to drip with the occasional tear, followed quickly by that of the old soldier. Without a word, he embraced his old friend heavily and buried his face against her shoulder; Alauren did the same, and for a while, all that could be heard were the pitiful sobs of two broken souls, their minds at last catching up to what they had seen.

"My forge, the Inn, my friends…" choked the smith.

"I know," Edlevin said, pulling away and attempting to gather himself with a hard swallow and a deep breath. "I know…"

"They were looking for us, weren't they?" Alauren asked, forcibly grunting out the words between her body's attempts to sob.

Edlevin's eyes turned to the wall and emptied, settling into a blank stare. His mouth opened, as if it was trying to allow for the coming of words, yet no sound escaped save for a deep, rattling rumble.

"Edlevin," demanded the smith. "They were looking for us. Yes?"

A darkness came over the old human in that moment, in the fleeting shadows of the Nort ship. His shoulders sagged heavily, and the lively jump typical of the scruffy old man appeared as if it had been exsanguinated in a mere breath. Despite this, his sunken eyes met Alauren's with a profound sorrow, filled with nothing but a world-weariness that was strikingly new to anyone close to him. "Yes," he stated coldly, before dropping his gaze to the floor.

"If we had been there-" Alauren began, rising slightly.

"Nothing would have changed," Edlevin cut off, quickly returning his eyes to his old friend. "You would just be among the bodies. Lay down."

"There were three of them!" Alauren yelled, ignoring the man's advice and rising further, despite the protests of pain erupting in her head at the movement. "You and Valin killed all three, didn't you? How else would you be here?"

"No," Edlevin replied with clear surety. "One of them couldn't be hurt, and we barely made it away from him alive. Ally, I stabbed a gap in his armor with my sword, and it slid off of whatever was under there like it was another layer of plate. I've never seen anything like it. After I leapt to the skiff, he stalked off to the north on foot, as if the fight with me hadn't exhausted him a bit." His voice was quivering and confused, like he was unwilling to believe his own experience. "The ones we did kill were pure luck. My bracer saved me, and Drell saved Valin, though the Dwarf might be quick to argue." He sighed and rubbed his eyes, responding to the grimace on the face of his old friend. "What I'm trying to say is that our presence wouldn't have made a difference. These men were overwhelmingly skilled and strong, indicative of the same force that drove the Norts out of their homes. The town was doomed the moment those bastards laid eyes on it."

"Violence might not have been necessary," Alauren retorted. "I would have given myself to protect the others, had I been there."

"As would I," the old soldier replied softly. "You know that to be true. What could have been matters little, Ally. We were not there."

"Only because you made me go north," muttered the smith, with more than a little frustration coloring her voice. She fell back into the hammock and buried her head in the Nortish quilts that lined it. "Things could have been different."

"Different isn't always better," Edlevin pointed out, standing. "All of us could have just as easily been killed." He looked at the floor for a moment and shook his head lightly. "Don't worry over what could have been. Get some rest, for your mind as well as your body. We've been through too much. Take the time you need. I'll be up on the deck if you require me."

Alauren simply grunted in reply, the sound muffled under her makeshift cave of quilts.

Edlevin, with a last sigh, took his leave, exiting to find himself in a storeroom packed with grain, having a single door to his left. To the right, a finely crafted staircase rose to the main deck, and a wooden cover bounced on its hinges at the top.

The old soldier hurried up and lifted the hatch, emerging on the center-right of the vessel, where glorious sunlight bathed over his cold, hardened soul. He froze for a moment, feeling the warmth on his skin while salty sea air whipped about around him, tussling his hair. He rocked back and forth along with the ship, bringing himself back to the physical world, centering himself in the present. There was a sense of relief, like the peaceful dawn had just woken him from a lucid nightmare, despite the very real loss he had incurred. The adrenaline and stress melted away, and though sorrow remained, he took comfort in the surviving shards of another shattered life.

Across the wooden deck, Norts worked on various tasks while sails billowed above them, moored upon the *Skylðrek*'s dual masts. The fine canvas of the mainsail was embroidered with the visage of a golden dragon that spewed crimson flames upward, spreading across the top. Golden fringe accentuated the majestic serpent, while the edges of the cloth were adorned with tassels that fluttered in the wind.

Beyond the wooden railing, dozens of ships (identical to their lead save for the varied designs upon their sails) cruised in perfect formation. These vessels were impressive, a clear product of centuries perfecting the traditional Northmen design; they would be best compared to the Fangirmish Barque, multi-decked, squat, and fast, though the latter often possessed three masts, rather than the two of the Nortish former.

Ronnok sat on a box at the bow of his vessel, just behind a carved figurehead of a long-fanged serpent. The Nort was enjoying a freshly tapped keg with Valin; upon noticing the human's arrival on deck, the Chieftain waved him forward eagerly.

"Ah! You missed the best part of the small one's story!" bellowed the Northman. "Did you know there is an annoying man living in his scythe?"

Edlevin nodded, bearing a subdued smirk. "We had ample time to talk on the dinghy, yes. Quite the storyteller, this one."

"The more ale, the better the story!" Valin laughed. "Is the lass awake?"

"Yeah, and already furious," Edlevin sighed. He grabbed a mug from a small crate and filled it, careful not to let any drops escape as the waves lifted and bucked the ship. "I expected her to be silent for a few days before she started looking for explanations." He took a sip and savored the stark bitterness of the brew. "Already, she's asking how and why, and I can't hope to answer."

"She seems to be a fiery one," Ronnok pointed out, taking a tone of ease. "Such feelings are expected."

Edlevin nodded. "I know. I've seen countless soldiers go through this kind of loss. I've watched it destroy and end lives."

"Just watched, eh?" Valin cut in.

The old soldier chuckled darkly. "I lived it, as well, a long time ago." He thought for a moment, letting the crisp ocean breeze caress his skin. "I'm better equipped to handle it this time. I have Alauren to watch over, and I can focus my sadness and anger to that end. Her, though..." He trailed off. "That remains an open book."

"You're afraid for her?" Ronnok asked.

"Yes," Edlevin confirmed quickly. "She's a soul that is easily shaken, even by things as simple as not knowing where her hammer is." He sighed again and took another sip. "She's got a monster of a temper when she's stressed, too. Anger, sorrow and aimlessness make for horrid companions, especially given what she's lost."

"What exactly has she lost?" Ronnok asked, raising an eyebrow.

Edlevin tilted his head in slight confusion. "Her home, her friends, everything but her life," he listed, humoring the Nort.

"Then she is in the right company," proclaimed the Chieftain, meeting Edlevin's eyes.

The old soldier looked to the Nort, then to Valin, then back to the Chieftain, finding a strange comfort in their weary eyes, both glittering in the sunlight. "Yeah," he murmured with a sorrowful smile. "I guess she is."

Alauren could do little but sob pitifully while the boat rocked gently back and forth, the lapping of the waves on the hull drowning out her quiet, solitary agony. So vivid was the memory of the longhouse that she could not hope to close her eyes without seeing the twisted image of her friend's faces staring fearfully into oblivion, without beholding the past as if it were the present once more. Peace had left her, leaving nightmares behind.

For hours, the smith would lay still, willing herself to rouse, to escape from the horror that had become her life. In those moments, she truly believed that she could open her eyes to find herself awake once more in her forge on a sunny day, surrounded by the sweet smells of ale and cooking food from the Inn, all accompanied by the sounds of chattering villagers as they went about their business. She had to believe that if she willed it to be so, it would be so, that the world could be changed by nothing more than her own determination.

Hour after hour, her efforts were met only with footsteps on the wooden deck above and the slosh of the roiling ocean below. The sounds became like thunder, repeated booms that clanged through her head, interrupting her vain pursuit of the unattainable, driving her to the brink of madness and causing her to squirm in her hammock. The sweet smells never manifested, nor did the image of the longhouse leave her mind. Her only respite from the pain was the young Nort girls smiling warmly as they brought her food and drink now and again, before once more leaving her to her suffering.

For a time, the smith fully hid from the world, wrapping herself in her belief that reality was not something set in stone, that the world would change back to its comfortable and happy self at any moment.

She ate little, drank only what was brought to her, and moved only when necessary, preferring the dark abyss of the quilts and hammock to her new reality. Only the crimson sun of her third morning, peering through the deck above, was able to break the illusion and force her to accept the world as it was.

She rose slowly, stumbling here and there as she gained some semblance of balance, before cautiously stepping through the door with a firm hold on the wall all the way. The adjacent room was deserted save for two Nort women, both beautiful and blonde-haired, who gave her warm smiles and words of clear encouragement in a language that the smith could not begin to comprehend; still, she returned them with a polite nod as she made her way up the stairs.

A blast of fresh, salty sea air washed over her as she pushed the small deck hatch upwards and climbed into the shining light of dawn. All around, Norts went about their business working with ropes, rigging and sails, hardly paying a care to the emergence of their guest. She instantly spotted Eira and Thyra to her left, sorting through boxes of supplies; their children sat next to them, braiding the bright blonde hair of another girl.

"The small one lives!" Ronnok bellowed from behind, startling the smith. The final word was followed up by a hearty, friendly clap on the upper back, which tilted her off balance.

Eira and Thyra shot Ronnok a narrow-eyed glare of warning from their seats, causing the Chieftain to sheepishly steady the blacksmith with a few uneasy chuckles. He gave her a tap on the shoulder once she had solid footing, a gesture of a far more reasonable force than the last.

"Is that a typical Nort 'hello'?" Alauren murmured. Though she was feeling steadier by the moment, she still chose to lean on the ship's tall side railing for support.

"Only if we like you," Ronnok chortled in response, wearing a floppy grin. "And if I don't think my wives are looking."

"Lass!" Valin yelled, bounding from the bow of the ship, followed closely by Edlevin. "I was startin' t' think I'd have t' come carry ye out o' that hammock!"

Alauren allowed a small smile to creep onto her face, a feat of clear and visible effort. "Good to see you too, Valin. I thought you would have left by now, given what I've led you to."

"Hah!" exclaimed the Dwarf. "Ye've led me t' ale. Twice! Why would I leave ye?"

"I suppose I'm as adept at finding alcohol as I am at finding trouble," Alauren said with a noticeable weakness, struggling to project her voice over the lapping of the waves and the banging of riggings. She stepped closer to Edlevin and stared out over the vast Nort fleet, and, in turn, the expansive ocean beyond. Any land looked to be long gone, left in the maw of the horizon. "Where are we?"

"The Borean Ocean, some distance west of Teth," answered the old soldier. "We're headed to somewhere beyond the horizon."

"We're leaving Odenseye?" Alauren asked, furrowing her brow.

"It has once again become a dangerous place," Ronnok confirmed. "The Nations stir, as do darker things. The coming bloodshed will be too much, even for us." He erupted into a sly, lopsided smile. "There are far more reasonable places to make a living."

Alauren cocked an eyebrow. "By make a living, you mean...?"

"Raiding," the Chieftain confirmed surely. "The islands west of Odenseye have not seen Nort ships in many a decade. Their purses and storehouses will be quite full."

Alauren nodded, putting aside the frightening thought of a Nort raid for the moment. She looked back across the waves, to the eastern horizon. "We'll be so far from home..."

"And we'll be further still when our boots touch solid ground again," Edlevin added, placing a hand on the woman's shoulder. "Welcome to the wide world, Ally."

CHAPTER TEN:

ADJUSTMENT

12th OF THE MORN OF HARVEST
NORTHERN YEAR 715

Alauren of Teth was a legendary blacksmith among the sailors and fisherman of the rough-and-tumble Brumal Sea, a region within the Borean Ocean that comprised the continental shelf and the beginnings of deeper water to the west of Se'Vikoral. Common to the area were choppy waves, severe weather, and frigid water to embrace you should you have the misfortune to fall victim to either of the former. In a place like this, only the best sufficed when it came to the vessel that separated you from a numb death.

The metalworks of the smith had held against the onslaught of nature for hundreds of sailing ships, whether they be using her nails on the structure or her hinges on the hatches. Her creations were perfectly suited for the job, forged with centuries of experience in whatever the rough Northern seas could conjure.

The experience, however, was not often her own, but rather gathered from the tangled tales of sailors, each drawing from their own applied knowledge to help her innovate and improve. Never had the smith's inexperience on the sea been clearer than now, as she vomited the remains of a pastry over the side of the Nort longship.

"It will pass," Edlevin reassured for the ninth time. "You just have to get your legs under you."

"Easy to say for someone who was able to keep breakfast this morning," Alauren groaned, wiping her mouth on her sleeve. "It doesn't help that my head is pounding, either."

"Both will subside, I assure you," the old soldier soothed. "Focus on your balance for now. Find how to move with the ship."

"The vessel is the master here, indeed," Ronnok affirmed, sauntering up from the central staircase of the *Skylðrek*. "Do not try to conquer it. Ride it."

Alauren's eyes went wide as she heaved again; mercifully, there was nothing left to spew, save for a wretched sound that landed somewhere between a gag and a choke. After a moment, she was able to speak once more. "Might take me a bit."

Ronnok chuckled. "Balance will come when you know the sea. You may be suffering, but only through this sickness will you find an understanding of the giver of life and death that we now sail upon. It will become as a god of its own to you, one worthy of respect and fear. As terrible as you feel, it is an experience shared by all Norts the first time we depart, and it is necessary."

Alauren nodded, but offered no verbal reply.

Ronnok walked to the railing and leaned over, joining the smith. He breathed deeply of the ocean air and rolled his gaze across the Nordiskan fleet. "It has been too long since the Norts have set upon the path of a saga. There are new stories to be made, new tales that will echo through the sands of time in our people's traditions." He smirked, eyeing the sick visitor with an amused glance. "I am glad to have you on this one." He shifted his gaze to Edlevin. "All of you. Your company has been warm and most welcome."

"Likewise," Edlevin said with a nod.

"I am sorry that it could not be under better circumstances," the Chieftain continued. "You have lost much, but I hope that you will find that you've gained a safe place with those who will watch over you."

Edlevin nodded again. "It's appreciated beyond words. Taking us in so readily is something you did not have to do."

Ronnok scoffed and waved his hand dismissively. "Of course I did! You showed the Norts respect in your actions and honesty in your words. These things are increasingly rare among the Nations, and they must be held close when they are found." He turned his gaze to the smith. "We do, however, ask for some things in return."

"Such as?" Alauren asked with a groan.

"I've heard you are quite the blacksmith," said the Chieftain. "We need someone who can work metal to travel with us." He ground his teeth, lost to thought for a single breath before returning to the present. "Our retreat has been costly, and we have precious few with the knowledge to run a forge. If you are as skilled as this one says you are," he said, pointing to Edlevin, "I would have you serve in this capacity."

"I'm better than he says I am," chirped the smith.

Edlevin chortled. "She's probably right. I know a bit, but the deeper lore of the hammer and anvil are lost to me."

"Anything you need," Alauren continued. "Nails, armor, blades. I can make it."

"We'll stick to nails and armor for now," Ronnok replied. "Norts are very attached to our weapons. You will need to prove your works trustworthy before most Northmen will put their lives in your hands in such a way."

"I will," the smith stated confidently, stepping back from the railing. She still wobbled as the large vessel tumbled over the choppy waves, but she was beginning to find a steady enough center to stand and walk unassisted. "I'll need to know what I have to work with."

"We will be resupplying in time," Ronnok said. "For now, what few ingots and pieces of scrap we could carry with us lay below. Come, I can show you to the storeroom."

Alauren, with some difficulty, obliged, following the Chieftain down the main stairs, which lay just in front of the helm. There, they found themselves on the middle of the three decks, in a room packed tightly with supplies that Norts still worked to sort and move to their place. Valin drank and laughed with a group of Northmen in the corner, clearly annoying those who chose to spend their time with labor.

"Behind us lies my room, and the room of my children," Ronnok said. "In front, our destination. Come."

He led the way forward, dodging his fellows and their burdens when necessary. A small oaken door led to a far more well-decorated chamber, with a map table that was covered in a mess of cartography and astronomy equipment. On either side, walls made of curtains separated the intricate rug below their feet with the simple planks of two descending staircases. The twin masts continued down and through the floor at the room's center, anchored on the third deck, while two of the ship's many ribs (the vertical pieces that form the structure of the vessel) terminated in finely carved visages of ancient dragons on either side.

"This is the map room and command center, at the absolute center of the ship," Ronnok explained, moving swiftly through, straight ahead. Another door led to a much narrower room, packed with weapons and armor. "Your chambers lie just to the left of this storage hall," Ronnok said, pointing to the left wall, "and the Karlmaðr's to the right. These can only be accessed through the attached storerooms and the hatch on the top deck." He opened a door on the left wall, showing the grain room and ascending stairs directly adjacent to Alauren's quarters. He shut it without entering, meaning only to help the smith get her bearings, and waved her forward, toward the bow. "At the end of the ship, we store our smithing supplies. They should be among the first things unloaded when we land." Piles of tools and metal lay strewn about a room that inclined and reached a peak as it approached the bow of the ship, the trouble of sorting clearly placed aside for whoever would take on the job of blacksmith. "We will help with this, of course."

"I hope so," Alauren gasped with mouth agape. "This is a mess, Ronnok. It'll be all I have just to sort it." She shook her head. "And we absolutely need to get some of this metal covered before it gets stained and eroded by seawater."

"Hmm," Ronnok grunted, stroking his beard, finding several hairs coming loose with the action, each of them discarded to the deck below without a thought. "We did not consider this."

"You need to," scolded the smith. "If I'm going to craft for you, my materials need to be taken care of. We need to get to work storing all of this stuff properly."

"Do not feel pressured, small one," the Chieftain eased. "You will have ample time to do so in the coming days, and I will have a few of my people wrap the metals and place them in boxes, if any can be found. For now…" He smiled warmly. "You need to get some rest. You have been through much. Understand the sea, get yourself feeling better, and then worry about work. Come on." He beckoned the smith, waving her through the grain room door and leading her up the stairs, where she rejoined her old friend on the deck.

"How's the supplies looking, Ally?" Edlevin asked.

"You'll see for yourself when you help me sort it," replied the smith. "For now, though, I'd like to focus on keeping food down over forge work."

Edlevin chuckled heartily. "Fair enough."

The sunset cast a burgundy and pink light across the Nordiskan fleet, the colors mixing into a soft, otherworldly glow, fluctuating in intensity as the sun slowly but surely dropped below the horizon to the east; though this view had been witnessed by the smith a thousand times before, the darkening eastern sky held an unfamiliar sorrow. The enveloping blanket of its warmth disappeared further with each breath, leaving only the raw cold of the ocean behind.

Alauren sat on the stern railing of the *Skylörek* and stared towards the cascading colors, towards the faces she once knew, towards a lost life and a lost family. Her heart bled more with every wave that was overtaken, for they only solidified the truth.

There, beyond the sinking sun, lay a life that now existed as nothing more than a memory, a time and place that had ceased to exist in the matter of what seemed to be a blink. All of her centuries in Teth now seemed no more than a single moment in time, disappearing before her eyes like a whisper in the wind. The tears poured forth, caught only by the dark waters below.

"You are in pain, little one," Ronnok said softly. His voice crept over her with a comforting warmth, and his feet were impossibly soft upon the deck as he approached. "I am, too."

Alauren sniffled and looked up, finding the slightest twitch in the Chieftain's solid expression as he leaned on the railing. There was a quiver in his lips, subdued, yet unmistakable. "Ronnok…" she gasped, finding just enough time in between sobs for a word.

"You have lost all you know, all you held dear," the Nort continued, placing a hand on her shoulder. "Faces have disappeared into the past, never to return."

The smith could only sob in reply.

"I share this," Ronnok said, his voice trembling lightly. "My adoptive father, Fiske, is dead. My best friend, Kalì, has also gone beyond this realm, joined by hundreds of my people, all of them personally known to me." His eyes glossed over for a moment, looking somewhere far beyond the smith, returning only after a few moments of little but the sloshing of the ocean below to fill the silence. "I know you must wonder, truly, why we took you in. I have given you a reason, but I think you know better than to believe that niceties alone would allow you an invitation to live with the Norts."

Alauren nodded, still unable to speak.

"My people, above all, value two things: strength and compassion," the Chieftain explained. "These are the fortitude to use tragedy to find a stronger soul within, and for that soul to forge a greater world for those around us. Each Northman has this fire within them, fueled by a love for their family and clan." He smiled warmly. "Smith, you have this fire, as do your companions. For a Nort, it is easy to recognize, like we can feel the wafting heat of a hearth that lie deep within you. In your town, you were fueled by the same love of family and clan."

Alauren finally managed to get enough control to speak, choking back tears as best she could. "They're gone now. The fire is out."

Ronnok shook his head. "Perhaps it does not blaze as it once did, lacking the same fuel, but such a thing is impossible to extinguish fully. You are now surrounded by others like you, those who share the crushing sorrow that sends you, and I, into nightmares each time we close our eyes."

Alauren nodded silently.

"If there is something here to help grow that fire beyond the embers that it has become, you are welcome to it," Ronnok said, shifting his gaze out and beyond the horizon, where the last light of the sun fought a dying battle against the passage of time. "We must all find a new path now, a new life away from the places we call home. You are welcome to find it beside us, beside folk who know your nightmares, if you wish."

"Thank you, Ronnok," said the smith, almost in a whisper. "For now, though, I think pain is the only thing I can muster within. The flame will have to wait."

"Of course," Ronnok replied, giving her one last tap on the shoulder. "Be well, and do not hesitate to ask for my ear, should you require it."

Alauren nodded as the Chieftain walked off, beckoned by the call of his wife. The last light of the evening disappeared below the horizon, enveloping the world in a blanket of shadow. The bright stars of the northern sky, however, were finally able to show their full glory, parading across the great dark for any who were willing to cast their gaze upwards to the heavens and bear witness. Constellations twinkled softly as they stretched out; though the lights were pale and cold, they managed (however mysteriously) to bring a warmth to the heart of the sorrowful smith. She always found a comfort in the sparkling majesty above, a calm that seemed to draw her out of her mind and into the vast dark of whatever wonders swam in the black abyss beyond the sky.

"Nilfi, servant of Hläs, cursed to carry oceans across the night sky forever," Edlevin said, approaching and swinging himself upon the railing next to the smith. He let his mind's eye fill in the blanks, seeing the stars above connect into an image of a human carrying two buckets, each suspended by their handles on a rod which ran across the back of the celestial giant. "When the oceans were still fresh as a spring, unpolluted by the salt of the land, it is said that he attempted to steal two of them, meaning to keep all the fresh water for himself, a lifetime's supply, under the nose of his master, telling Hläs that he carried only milk from their livestock. He became used to the purity, the invigoration of the fresh water as he sipped carefully from his hidden stores, day after day, year after year."

Alauren chuckled lightly (and with significant effort). "Stealing oceans? Ambitious."

"An ambition rewarded with an unchanging eternity," Edlevin continued. "Eventually, Nilfi found his stolen oceans to have run dry. Now, every night, he walks across the sky, and every night he will return to do the same again, attempting to find those lost, ancient oceans once again, yet he will come across only salt for his efforts."

Alauren sighed. "If there's a lesson here, I'm not sure I want to hear it right now."

"Ah, maybe it's got some lessons if you dig deep enough, but I just wanted to talk about something that wasn't violent for a while," the old soldier reassured. "The stars are as good a topic as any."

"Go on, then," Alauren said. "What else is up there?"

"Well, look off to the left and you'll see Mi'Ka'Li, the Lotus of the Lunari," Edlevin obliged. He pointed to a series of stars that seemed, from this perspective, to sit in a spiral pattern. "The Lunari believe that, in the earliest days of their people, each was given a magic lotus, white as the purest silk, which would float on the wind and guide their spirits to the afterlife when they passed. In time, the source of the lotus became corrupted, diseased, and it wilted. Ha'Ni'La, their eldest god, sacrificed herself to paint a lotus upon the night sky, so that all Lunari would be guided to their afterlife, so long as the sky was there."

Alauren sniffled lightly. "I hope it helped some of the folk back home, too, when the time came."

Edlevin smiled warmly yet sorrowfully, the pain on his face unmistakable. He wrapped an arm around his old friend and held her tightly. "I know it did. They have found peace, Ally. Now we have to do the same. It won't be easy, but…" He turned his attention to the night sky, allowing himself to be lost in the dark abyss. "We'll find our way. I promise."

"Can you?" asked the smith, drawing a raised eyebrow from her mentor. "Promise me that, I mean."

Edlevin huffed a laugh, never taking his eyes off the sky above. "No, I guess I can't. I can only promise to be there to help, however I can." He breathed deeply, centering himself. "I've discovered, Ally, that finding the way is often secondary in importance to those who walk it with us. Through our friends and allies, new paths will open to us, new ways to carry forward. Just keep your mind sharp and your trusted circle close. The rest comes after."

Alauren looked to the sloshing waves below, rising like tiny mountains before succumbing to the demands of time and crashing down upon themselves with all the force that drove them up in the first place. "Ed," said the smith, "do you trust the Norts?"

The old soldier considered the words for a moment. "I do, to a point. They have been just and honest in their dealings with us, and they've assuredly saved our lives. We shall see, though. I have a feeling that we'll be getting to know each other far better in the coming weeks."

Alauren nodded and looked back up to the night sky, once more finding herself lost in the shimmering abyss, until the bite of the ocean air became too frigid, and there was no longer any choice but to surrender to her body's demand for sleep.

CHAPTER ELEVEN:

HIGH SEAS

The oceans beyond the outer islands are as dangerous as they are mysterious, conquered by none of the vast empires. Few expeditions have returned to share their story, and those handful that managed to limp their vessels to port told of waves that could engulf cities, forming out of seemingly nowhere, unimaginably powerful blows from an angry beast, as frequent as the wind. Islands such as Arvyn and Flokil mark the end of navigable waters and the beginning of those wilds that stretch beyond, while even the nearer, milder seas can have a killer instinct. Of the peoples of Odenseye, only the Norts can say they know what lies across the hungriest depths; even then, only the oldest generation still drawing breath can speak with true experience. We will uncover its secrets someday, but for now, we are happy with what little we can conquer.

– Gauis Truvani, in "Nations of Odenseye"

14th OF THE MORN OF HARVEST
NORTHERN YEAR 715

Alauren spent the dawn basking in the sun, which was quite warm on her skin despite the growing cold of the air. Activity was an everlasting feature on the *Skylörek*, with the daily hustle and bustle of a dozen Northman families taking place on the crowded decks of the vessel around her. Most Norts, lost in busywork, left Alauren to her solitary thoughts as she stared over the bow of the ship, watching the waves roll and crest with white caps. It felt as if becoming lost in the roiling waters below could stave off the darkness that lurked behind her, ever ready to swarm and overtake her mind.

Edlevin would occasionally kneel next to her and say a few words of encouragement before returning to his self-adopted duties of assisting the running of the sail, all while Valin 'critiqued' his performance. Now, though, he plonked an empty barrel down next to his old friend and sat with a loud groan.

"I think I might be getting too old for this kind of work," he huffed, struggling to fully catch his breath. "Actually, it's definitely not the age; I'm as spry as ever, to be honest."

"You're just out of shape," Alauren deadpanned, never breaking her forward gaze. "Too many ales at the Inn, I think."

Edlevin chuckled. "Can you blame me? Martin was the best brewer in the north."

"For me, he was the best in the world," the smith replied with wavering voice. "I'm going to miss him, Edlevin."

"As will I," the old soldier said with a sorrowful half-smile. "But at the very least, he will be remembered. All of them will be, as long as we live."

"If only memory was enough," Alauren said softly.

"Enough?" Edlevin echoed. "Can you give them any more than that, Ally?"

The smith's only reply was a light shake of the head as she stared blankly over the waves.

"Then it is enough," the old soldier continued with a hushed tone. "We're weak beings, powerless save for our perseverance in memory. That perseverance, though, can give meaning to the meaningless. How many more will hear about Martin's incredible talents as we travel the world? I know I won't be shy about spreading his praises."

Alauren lowered her head. "Yet none will ever taste his legendary concoctions again. They will hear his praises, but what good are they without the proof? Without the man himself being alive to benefit?"

"I suppose you'll have to find that out yourself," Edlevin replied with a shrug. "I have been where you are many times, yet I can't direct you to the meaning you seek. I can only assure you that it's there, obscured as it may seem."

Alauren glanced briefly at her old friend, but quickly turned her gaze back to the water. "Is there meaning? In any of it? I keep asking myself why, but I have no answers. I still don't even know who those knights were."

Edlevin shifted in his seat at the comment, inhaling deeply.

Alauren looked to the man and narrowed her eyes slightly. "You know something?"

"Not really, no," Edlevin dismissed. "Nothing of import."

"Speak," the blacksmith ordered gruffly. "You're a bad liar, and you always will be. Spill it."

Edlevin grimaced, looking out over the oceans, but complied. "It's all quite ridiculous, to be honest. Do you recall what the Se'Vikorans believe about the creation of the world?"

Alauren furrowed her brow in confusion, but did her best to answer. "A little. There was a war of the gods. The scars of the conflict created the rivers and the mountains, and the gods disappeared forever, ashamed of what they had done." She shook her head. "What does this have to do with those men?"

"Very little memory remains of the fabled gods," Edlevin elaborated. "What works survived the passing of millennia describe gargantuan men, strong as Northern horses and wise as the oldest historians. They spoke with booming authority, and the few times one of them was said to fall in combat they bled gray, due to their immortal spirit leaving the vessel and taking with it the font of life that existed within."

Alauren's brow further furrowed in befuddlement "We were attacked by gods?"

Edlevin risked a chuckle and shook his head. "I don't believe so. As proficient as I may be in the art of combat, I don't believe I could slay a god. Still, the description is suspiciously accurate, don't you think?"

"It is," the smith affirmed with a nod. "If not the gods of old… Who? And what do they want with me?"

"My guess is as good as yours," Edlevin said amidst a shrug. "I truly wish I had further answers for you, Ally. I do not."

"You have seemed to have quite the lack of them lately, haven't you?" snapped the smith. Her voice was colored by an uncharacteristic venom, a corrosive tone. "You force me out of my home for the first time in centuries, and the village dies for it. It all happened so perfectly, yet you have no answers."

Edlevin recoiled lightly at the barbed comment, yet remained calm, as if the words were expected. "What are you saying, Ally?"

The blacksmith dropped her eyes to the deck and took a moment to recenter. After several blinks and a deep breath, she found words once more. "Nothing. I didn't…" Her shoulders sunk, and she ran her fingers through her hair uneasily. "I didn't mean it that way. I'm sorry. There's just this anger that keeps boiling up now and then, driven by thoughts that just seem to pop into my mind uninvited."

"Trust me, I know," Edlevin said warmly. "You are forgiven. Your search for answers will lead your mind to many places; some will be of anger, some of sorrow, and many more will be of pain. Don't be afraid to explore them, but also be mindful not to lose yourself in them." He wrapped his arm around the woman's shoulder, giving her a small hug. "I've got to get back to work. Holler if you need me." He stood, stretched, and ran off to the aid of a beckoning Nort rigger, who was struggling with a rope.

Alauren turned her attention once again to the ocean, bright and blue in the morning sun, capped by white waves which seagulls sailed over with ease. A small island broke the horizon ahead, and upon the speck of land a towering mountain sailed into the wild blue of the sky. She paid the birds and the land little mind as her thoughts wandered elsewhere, to the ever burning need to know what was happening in the chaotic nightmare that had become her life.

Gods? thought the smith. She was the first to admit that she wasn't a particularly spiritual person, yet in a time of such insanity, it seemed to be as likely as any other theory.

Niralan, perhaps. The Eastern men were certainly violent enough to kill a village, but they bled as red as any other human, and she failed to glean why an empire at war would waste their time and resources on her.

Dwarves? They were an insular race, wholly unknown to many surface dwellers, yet their short stature and (usually) nonviolent nature ruled them out. Besides, if the Dwarves wanted her dead, the blacksmith knew that Valin could have simply left her to Drell's mercy.

She had heard of cryptic beings that lived beyond the impassable open oceans to the east and west of Odenseye, in lands shrouded in mystery. Perhaps they had made the long and arduous journey across the waters to find her, though any reason for doing so was fully lost on their apparent target.

Nothing made sense.

The smith was snapped from her thoughts by a loud clunking noise behind her. She turned to see Valin smirking under his ragged beard and waddling towards her with a powder-blue keg, held aloft with both arms and tapped with an expert hand.

"Drell says ye look too blue," rumbled the Dwarf. He procured the scythe from under his left arm as he plunked the alcohol down, and set the weapon safely to the side. "He says ye need a drink. Fer once, we happen to agree." He chuckled moistly. "I think he respects ye, lassie."

Alauren cracked a small smile. "Or, maybe, he just wants to get me drunk enough to touch the scythe again."

Valin looked at the scythe, then to Alauren, then back to the scythe, before letting out a guffaw. "HA! I think ye guessed right, lass. He's bein' quiet again."

The smith allowed herself a small chuckle. "It's pretty early, still, but…" She tilted her head back and forth in consideration. "Sure."

Valin procured two metal mugs from underneath his right arm. He filled both to their limit, leaving a generous amount of froth that sloshed back and forth along with the boat, and gave one to Alauren.

The blacksmith sipped it slowly at first, savoring the initial fruity sweetness before a pleasantly bitter aftertaste set in. "This is…" She smacked her lips lightly, admiring the flavor. "Really good. What is it?"

"The big man says it's a family recipe," replied the Dwarf, with a point over his shoulder, towards the Chieftain. "Made with some type o' ground fruit that they, eh, 'liberated' from some merchants years ago."

"I continue to be surprised by their varying craftsmanship," Alauren said between sips. "I didn't know the Norts could do things like this."

"Honestly, lass, I might never leave 'em!" Valin exclaimed. "They've got the best food and drink outside Dol Marad, and they're good company t' boot."

Alauren cocked her head inquisitively. "Dol Marad is your Capital, yes? I know your people are quite skilled at smithing. I can't say I've heard of their skill in cooking or brewing, though."

"Well, fer that ye'd have t' visit me city, and that isn't happenin' anytime soon, as the tight arses don't let many outsiders in," the Dwarf enlightened brightly. "The only ones who come up here are the Garradh, the warrior class, and they rarely have any interest in the finer things." He snickered as he took a sip. "Well, unless ye count knockin' heads as a finer thing."

"I mean, I might," Alauren replied with a smirk. "Depends on which heads you're knocking."

"I'll drink t' that!" Valin spewed, taking a large swig of his beverage.

"You said the warriors are a class," the smith said, rubbing her chin. "What do you mean?"

"Ah!" Valin exclaimed, clearly quite happy to elaborate. "Me people are divided into three classes after our tenth year o' life. That's…" He trailed off as he muttered various numbers to himself, twitching his fingers while he ran the calculation in his mind. "Twenty-three years, by yer calendar. We're assigned t' one o' 'em, dependin' on our skills. Ye can be Rìgh, a Noble. They're diplomats and priests."

"I assume you belong to that one?" Alauren asked.

"Used to," the Dwarf flatly replied. "Not anymore."

Alauren recoiled slightly. "Yeah. Sorry."

"Not a problem, lass. They're twits anyway!" Valin soothed, drawing a chuckle from the smith before continuing with his thought. "Anyways, If yer the violent type, Garradh is fer ye. They're guards and soldiers and mercenaries, and ye'll occasionally see 'em up here on the surface. They keep their beards short, though, and most o' 'em are tall, by our standards, at least." He scratched his beard, but shortly continued. "Then there's the Ceàrdach, who do just about everythin' else. Bake, mine, forge. They're the lowest in the hierarchy, but me people are nothin' without their hard work."

"Your kind sound much more orderly than I ever would have guessed," Alauren observed, sipping her drink.

"When we wanna be," Valin quickly replied. "We can be just as messy as ye surface dwellers at times."

Alauren's face turned to one of feigned and exaggerated offense. "You mean to tell me you think we're unorganized?"

"One look at yer arsefaced innkeep would prove that!" bellowed the Dwarf. The words stole any mirth from Alauren's face, causing the stout man to go pale in a horrifying realization. "I'm so sorry, lass, I know that wound is still fresh fer ye. I've just learned t' deal with loss in me own unique way."

"It's all right, Valin," Alauren replied softly, looking out over the waves. "No harm."

Valin glanced at his scythe with an annoyed look. "Shut yer mouth, ye imprisoned windbag."

Alauren smirked once more. "What did he say now?"

"*Smooth*," Valin quoted. "He doesn't hesitate t' remind me that I'm not socially adjusted t' surface life."

"Few of us are," Alauren said softly. She finished her drink with a loud gulp and refilled it with a fervor, eager for the coming conversation and the distraction that it entailed.

The two wayward wanderers sat and drank for a long while, swapping stories about the lives they once knew while tumbling over the waves of the vast Borean Ocean, far from the homes that they spoke so fondly of.

The day reached its midpoint as Valin finished up his last story, involving a stolen horse, two kegs of mead, teleportation, and a particularly perturbed Captain of the Guard.

"Never seen Drell teleport more than just me 'till then. I managed to maneuver meself and the captain over a suitably deep part o' the lake as we fell," bellowed the Dwarf. "The meaty slap t' our left told us the horse wasn't so lucky!"

Alauren snickered and shook her head. "And the kegs of mead you stole?"

"Still at the bottom o' the lake, methinks," Valin replied. "If a jail could hold me, I woulda been in fer a long time."

"Without ale? You would have died!" Edlevin exclaimed, sauntering up beside the two. He was wearing his chestplate, while his helm hung from a leather strip at his side, though he looked to be forgoing the limiting greaves and sabatons for the moment. "By this point, I'm pretty sure you've got it running through your veins."

"Ha!" Valin hollered. "It's about a fifty-fifty mix."

Edlevin grinned and let out a gruff chuckle. He readjusted his chestplate and scabbard, pulling them higher up on his chest.

"Armor? Weapons?" Alauren asked, after a few moments of silence. "You really need that on the sea?"

Edlevin shook his head. "You haven't been paying attention, have you? Look around."

Alauren followed the old man's instructions and let her gaze search the deck of the longship. All around her, Norts were donning their own armor, silvery metal chestplates worn over cloth and leather garments. Each wore a helmet with a metal noseguard that wrapped back up to the main dome on either side, creating two eyeholes, while a slatted plate stretched down to protect the lower jaw and neck.

"I honestly didn't notice," Alauren said. "Too focused on the stories." Her eyes grew heavy, and her face became painted with concern. "Are we expecting a fight?"

"Hopefully not," answered the old soldier. "There's an island up ahead where the Norts mean to resupply before the longer leg of the journey." He pointed off the port bow, towards the formerly distant bit of land. Closer now, it was covered in a vast expanse of yellow, orange, and red-hued trees that were encased in beaches of white sand. A single peak, standing high above the rest of the land, was tipped with a beacon of fire that poured black smoke.

Alauren stood and leaned over the railing, gazing toward the island. "There's people there, I assume?"

"So the Norts say," Edlevin verified, joining her on the railing. "They haven't visited this island in a decade or more, however. While the locals have previously dealt peacefully, our hosts are quite ready to take what they need if required."

"You're going to help them?" Alauren asked, with a point towards the old soldier's scrappy armor and weaponry. "If it gets violent, I mean."

Edlevin furrowed his brow, silently scolding the smith. "They took us in, gave us meals and shelter… They saved our lives, Ally. I will do what they ask of me."

"That's rather dark," Alauren retorted. "They have treated us well, no doubt, but you would already kill for them?"

Edlevin bit his lip and looked out over the waves, like the white crests and dark depths beneath could reveal a clearer answer than the tumultuous abyss of his own mind. "Ally, you knew of a peaceful world, relatively free of the full brunt of the strife of life," he said after a moment. His gaze shifted to the Nort fleet as he truly (and ever so rarely) struggled to find words suitable for his thoughts. "There is a difference between surviving and living. Living means that you can pick and choose your allies, that you can hold yourself to what you believe is a higher standard. Surviving means that you take your best shot at seeing tomorrow and throw yourself fully into it." He sighed. "In Teth, we lived. Here, we survive."

"Again, that's rather dark," replied the smith.

"Such is the way of the world," Edlevin muttered, his voice draped in shadow.

"Well, I hope they don't expect me to-" Alauren began, interrupted by a booming voice from behind.

"We do!" Ronnok bellowed, plonking a large shield onto the deck. It was wooden, green in color, with a large golden eagle design that splayed around the center metal boss. "This is yours. Treat it well."

Alauren looked to the shield uneasily, then to Edlevin. After a curt nod from her old friend, she attempted to lift the large object with its centered metal handle, struggling to heft it above her waist.

"It's too heavy," she huffed, letting the blocker drop back to the deck. "I can't lift it."

"If you need to, you will," the Chieftain remarked with a smirk.

"Reassuring," Alauren quipped sarcastically. "I'll try and stay behind you, so I don't need it."

"Not me!" Ronnok corrected. "You'll be traveling with my wives. For the landing, at least."

"Eira and Thyra?" Alauren asked, visibly confused. "The women will fight?"

"This is why your people were always easy prey!" the Chieftain cackled. "If women don't join in, you're only half as effective. They will fight, and they will fight well." He smirked wickedly. "If needed."

"I suppose I have some warming to do to your culture," the smith replied shakily.

"You will understand, in time," Ronnok assured, clapping her on the shoulder with a gentle force. "Get yourselves ready. We land in one hour." He nodded to the gathered outsiders before turning back to his duties.

"You had better suit up," Edlevin instructed with a rub of his chin. "Though, I'm not sure there's much armor around that can fit you."

"Just let her wear one o' yer bracers," Valin suggested. "Given what I saw of 'em, it's all the lass needs."

Edlevin nodded with a wide grin. "That may be a good idea, actually." He removed his right wrist covering carefully and handed it to his old friend. It was a simple piece of metal, etched with visages of roaring flames, and was secured to the hand with leather straps arranged in a glove-like pattern. "These will block just about anything and absorb the blow with little harm to your wrist. If you wear it on your sword hand, you'll essentially have two shields."

Alauren slid the bracer onto her right wrist, tightened the straps to a snug fit, and nodded. "I've been wondering about that, actually," she said. "The fight at Teth is a bit of a blur, but I remember these holding against a full-power sword blow. How?"

The comment drew a chuckle from the Dwarf and a smile from Edlevin. "Valin figured it out immediately, as I knew he would. It is a product of his people."

"Nasgadh!" Valin exclaimed. "Enchanted at the great forge o' Runegate t' be as strong as solid rock and as light as leather."

"It translates roughly to 'Mountain's Skin' or 'Skin of the Mountain'," Edlevin added. "A gift I acquired on one of my many travels. Turns out getting on the good side of a company of Garradh Warriors has its advantages."

Alauren looked over the bracer carefully and spotted a faded "⚒" Rune near the center. She turned her wrist this way and that, finding the weight and balance to be flawless. "Amazing," she said. "Thank you, Edlevin."

"Anything to keep you from dying on me, Ally," replied the old soldier. "Oh, and you'll find your blade in your quarters, freshly cleaned. Try not to leave it lying around this time!"

CHAPTER TWELVE:

LANDING

...Odenseye is a dangerous, dark forest, ever stalked by hungering phantoms who wish our lives exhausted at their haunting command; one will find no more rapid demise, in my estimation, than if they would choose to forgo the protection of the empires, and thus the combined might that would stand as a bulwark against those who mean harm. In our modern world, there is no choice but to count oneself among the Nations, for the only other option is an assured death.

> – Gauis Truvani, in "Nations of Odenseye"

The cresting waves slapped hard against the side of the small dinghy as it pulled steadily closer to the glistening white sands of the island's beaches. The large longships were left far behind, anchored in neat and organized rows while the shore parties made their landfall. Edlevin, helmeted, knelt atop the bow of the first dinghy to the left of the smith's, cackling with Ronnok and Valin about some violent joke or another as he wobbled here and there in the rough surf.

Alauren sat in a small huddle with her arms hugging her chest tightly. Though the day was quite warm for the season, especially upon the ocean, she still felt a deep cold inside, a frigidity that iced over her extremities and chilled her heart. She was joined, as promised, by Eira and Thyra, who gave the smaller woman an occasional nudge of warm reassurance. Even so, the smith couldn't stop her hands from quaking.

"Calm, small one," Eira said with a heavy Northmen accent. Though it colored her words with a distinctive curtness, rolling to a sudden halt like an out-of-control minecart impacting a rail stop, it remained thoroughly decipherable.

"Easier said than done," Alauren replied. She rubbed her ice-cold hands together as the dinghy sloshed back and forth in the surf, a failed attempt at self-soothing. "If this gets violent…"

"You'll do well," Thyra interjected, speaking with a nearly identical accent, only differentiated by a slightly icier and more reserved tone. "You possess certain advantages on this potential battlefield."

Alauren raised her eyebrow curiously. "Such as?"

"You're a very tiny thing," Eira stated, grinning from ear to ear. "Tiny things can be sneaky."

"Sneaky enough to do some backstabbing," Thyra supported. "*Very* painful backstabbing, indeed."

Alauren looked to the damp boards of the dinghy's deck, toeing at a loose splinter with her boot. "That's if I don't get backstabbed first."

"There's not enough of you to jab!" Eira exclaimed, grabbing Alauren's shoulder and shaking her playfully.

"Move even a hair and they'd miss!" Thyra added.

The smith couldn't help but let out a small smile. "I suppose. For now, I'll just stay behind you."

"Watch and learn," the sisters said in unison, accompanied by simultaneous points towards the shore. The Nort dinghies were mere strides away from the sands now, and they apparently had company.

A group of ten men, clad in chainmail and leather, emerged from the island's treeline and stood stoically on the shore. They kept their posture straight and their eyes locked upon the arriving boats, betraying no fear as the tsunami of colossal Northman approached. All were armed with long and pointed polearms, save for the centermost man's glimmering longsword, which he drove down into the sand with substantial force.

"Well, at least we know his sword is blunted now," mumbled the blacksmith, amidst a shake of the head.

The dinghy impacted the shore with a hard *thump,* followed shortly by rough rocking as Eira jumped into the ankle-high water. Thyra followed suit, and both met quickly with their husband in front of the lapping waves. Alauren was the last out, struggling to lift her large wooden shield over the edge of the boat.

After a few moments of vain hefting (and several amused grins from the disembarking Norts), she gave up the fight, leaving the buckler behind. She hopped over the side and gasped sharply as the glacial water of the Borean Ocean slipped into her boots. The sand wanted to suck her feet down, causing a few light stumbles, but the smith found her way to Edlevin's side in good time. To her right, a final dinghy arrived with its shore party, numbering the visitors at about a dozen altogether.

The smith's eyes were drawn immediately to one of the new arrivals. He was a shirtless, colossal Northman, standing head and shoulders above his already large fellows; he drew nervous glances from the native's welcoming party, the first time that their show of strength had shown a crack. This Nort's massive stature was complemented by a scraggly brown beard and long hair, as well as several intricate dragon tattoos that ran up his back and spiraled down his arms. Even Edlevin, well-traveled as he was, looked to the man with amazement.

"I wonder how many times he's cracked his head on doorways," Valin quipped with a whisper of a chuckle. The comment drew the smallest of smirks from the smith, but she quickly returned her focus to the natives.

"Do your people still speak the trade tongue?" Ronnok asked from the front of the group, his voice gruff and low.

"We do," the centermost man replied elegantly. He stood about as tall as Edlevin, though he had a far less disheveled look about him, and significant gray streaks on his otherwise black hair and beard betrayed his more advanced age. The men flanking him were young, clean-shaven, and more visibly nervous by the second, but this one stood tall.

"I am Ronnok, Chief of Nordiska," the Nort leader said, taking a diplomatic tone. "Do you know of my clan?"

"I know of Nordiska, but not of Ronnok," the man replied. His accent was soft and flowing, and each word rolled exquisitely from his tongue. "What of Chief Erik?"

"Dead," Ronnok stated emotionlessly. "A time ago."

The comment caused the man to shift uncomfortably, but he quickly gathered himself. "I am Roan, Governor of the free peoples." He breathed in heavily, but never let his unblinking gaze leave the Nort Chieftain. Each man stared into the other's eyes with an equal intensity, seeming as if they were studying the very souls of the being that stood at their opposite. Roan was the first to break the silence.

"Do you abide by our covenant, Ronnok of Nordiska?"

The Chieftain remained silent for a time, letting the lapping of the waves become the only sound as the words were considered. A strong ocean wind blew onto the beach, washing over the gathered masses as it hurried into the trees ahead.

"I'm glad you remember," Ronnok said, after some time. "I do. We will stay for a time, take what we need, and leave in peace."

Roan stood silent for a moment in clear contemplation, but nodded without further delay. "Keep your people in order and you will have whatever you desire. I must warn you, however, that any spilling of my people's blood will be answered for."

"Our people will behave," Ronnok assured, beckoning with his right hand.

The gargantuan Nort strode forward confidently, looking down upon Ronnok before shifting his gaze to the Governor, a dark and eager grin painting his face all the while.

"This is Arvid," the Chieftain continued. "He will ensure the good conduct of all parties."

"He had better," Roan rumbled, matching the large Nort's stare with unflinching confidence. He shifted his eyes to Alauren, Valin and Edlevin, and raised one of his bushy eyebrows in curiosity. "What of the outsiders? A Dwarf, an Elf, and…" He trailed off with a vague gesture. "Whatever that armored one is."

"A man," Edlevin clarified, his voice slightly muffled by his helm. He reached up and lifted his faceplate (which squeaked loudly), revealing a disarming smile.

Roan gave the old soldier a curt, respectful nod. "Even so, strange company for a Nort to keep. Do they abide by our covenant, Ronnok of Nordiska?"

The Chieftain turned to his companions, finding his gaze settling on Alauren, who practically shook in her boots. He smiled and winked before looking back toward the cadre of locals. "Though they have only recently joined us, they are of Nordiska all the same," he said surely. "Our promises are theirs, and theirs, ours."

Roan stood silently for a few moments, looking over every one of the foreigners on the beach individually, one after another, from head to toe. A tension hung in the air, as if the waves that lapped the shore were pressing in, forcing a decision.

The Governor abruptly pulled his sword from the sand, which caused a few Norts to tense up noticeably. "Welcome, then, Northmen of Nordiska, to the free island of Alsara," he said with disarming voice, careful to pick a gentle tone. "May our dealings be swift and bloodless."

"As they have been for decades," affirmed the Chieftain, following the Alsarans as they led the way into the glistening forests of their home.

The paths to the Alsaran settlement were largely overgrown, covered with all manner of vines and weeds, yet the cracked and gray rock of a long disused cobblestone road could still be picked out amongst the varying greenery. It would have been quaint, like something out of an old children's tale, were it not for the heavily armed warriors that clomped along its mossy stones.

Painted trees rose all around, swaying gently to and fro in the wind, as if the whistling of the salty air through their branches were soft music accompanying their dance. They formed a shady tunnel over the road, making the hike pleasantly cool and refreshing.

The Alsaran warriors, now jesting and laughing among themselves, led the group forward. Roan, clearly a careful man, stood between his fellows and the Norts, just in front of Ronnok and his entourage. It was curious, the smith thought, that he chose to be closer to the foreigners than the safety of his own people.

"Roan, you do not walk at the head of your men," Ronnok observed after a while, evidently noticing the same. "Why?"

Roan chuckled. "Your first mistake is calling them 'my' men. Our loyalty is to Alsara and our ideals, not to me."

"Those ideals being?" asked the Chieftain, bearing a clear eagerness to be well-informed.

"That none should have to lay down their life for anything but their home," the Governor answered, visibly happy to educate. "That none should suffer and die for the selfish desires of another."

"Honorable," Edlevin said, chiming in. He had removed his

helmet in order to breathe freely of the fresh air, and he seemed to carry himself quite casually, like he was among well-known friends. "Yet, those are ideals that would last all of a minute on the mainland."

Roan chuckled and nodded in wholehearted agreement. "There is a reason we choose to live here. We lack the amenities and the constant supply lines of the great Nations and Kingdoms, but our home has known peace for over two centuries." He carried a clear confidence and pride as he spoke. "The Nort incidents excluded, of course. That peace alone is worth the flaws in our steel and the hardships of winter." He became lost in thought for a moment, before a smirk erupted on his lips. "If we live, we live of our own volition. If we die, we die by our own choices."

"Reasonable, as well," replied the Chieftain. "But my question remains unanswered. If the men serve Alsara and you are the governor, why do you not walk at their head?"

"We're an insular people," the Governor explained. He rubbed several beads of sweat from the ridge of his brow and heaved a few solid breaths, clearly struggling to split his lungful of air between the acts of walking and talking. "Despite our diversity, our social skills aren't always in line with those of transients and traders. Better that my people remain with others like them, with me forming a buffer." He looked at Ronnok with a lopsided smile, matched by the Chieftain. "I, for one, enjoy new company, and am far less likely to be set off by differences in culture."

Ronnok nodded, satisfied with the answer, and gave the man a respite to catch his breath.

Alauren, though she heard the gist of the conversation, took greater interest in the armor and weapons of the locals, which clanked around in loose scabbards and scrappy leather straps. The steel was flawed, indeed, but an impressive craftsmanship more than made up for the faults; where there was a weakness, there would be reinforcement, and where there would be a broken piece, another, similar part would take its place, welded with the deft hand of experience. After a long period of silently trudging up the broken path, the smith gathered the courage to speak.

"Your sword is blunt, you know," she grumbled, stepping up her pace to match that of the Governor.

"What?" Roan mumbled, looking over his shoulder as the small woman approached. "Are you speaking to me?"

"You're the only one who drove his sword into the ground," the blacksmith deadpanned. "Typically, you want to keep your blade out of anything but enemies. You've got to treat your weapons well, you know."

The few Norts who could understand the trade tongue nodded in full agreement and double-checked their own weapons, ensuring that they were safe and at hand.

"Well, uh..." rumbled the Governor. His cheeks flushed and, though he tried to hide his embarrassment, he couldn't help but shrink under the gaze of the judgmental foreigners. "You see, it's more ceremonial than anything. I much prefer the polearm when I need to fight. Longer reach, and usually a bit easier to handle."

"Polearms are good choices for large-scale conventional warfare, when you can just have a quartermaster provide a new one, but for a people like the Alsarans?" Edlevin interjected. "A sword is better. Sturdier." He banged on his armor lightly, which elicited several subdued booms. "With advances in arms and armor, it's getting hard to make spears and polearms that won't break after a few seconds in combat, even for the nations."

"It would be a good blade, if you take care of it," the smith supported with a nod.

Roan chuckled and let his embarrassment turn to amusement. "You sound like Bennis, the town blacksmith. We get a single bit of rust on our armor, and we've failed the ancestors that founded the island."

"Sounds like good company," said the old soldier. "Ally here had her own smith, for a time, and she is quite skilled at the forge."

Roan raised an eyebrow and stole a glance at the small woman, giving her another once-over. "You look a little..."

"Small?" Alauren finished for him.

"Better you say it than I," chortled the Governor. "Most smiths I know of are burly men, packed with muscle."

The comment drew a hearty chuckle from Edlevin. "You'd be surprised. Ally here packs a mean punch, and she's got skill to back it up. She's one of the best I've ever laid eyes on."

"Perhaps you could prove it by fixing up my newly blunted blade," Roan proposed. "Bennis will be perturbed that I didn't bring it to him, but he'll likely want to see your work for himself. He's always looking to one-up competition."

"Five elysium," Alauren replied instantly. "Due up front."

The Governor snickered lightly. "I suppose little in life is free. Deal. We'll go see Bennis when we arrive in town."

The group returned to silence for a long while, sweating in the brisk winds as they climbed their way further into the forest. Though it bore a similarity to the Se'Vikoran woods, there was a distinctive aroma that made the place seem strikingly different from Alauren's home. Salty sea air mixed with the smells of freshwater and the local flora to form a moment that was strikingly different from anything the smith had experienced before. Occasionally, she would cast her eyes upward to peer at the overhanging branches and cascading shadows with a wonder that was not lost upon her old friend.

"I told you there was a world to see, Ally," Edlevin said. There was a chipper cadence about voice, which served to betray his own fascination with this place. "I can see the look in your eyes. Beyond the cold of your sorrow and the despair, there's a spark."

Alauren couldn't help but let a small smirk creep onto her face, unable to contend the point. "Seeing a place like this, appreciating it… It does help numb the pain, somewhat." She turned her eyes to the limbs above once more. "It keeps my mind occupied, at the very least."

"As it did for me, all that time ago," Edlevin replied. "And, as unwelcome as the circumstances are, I am finding that merciful occupation once more." He laced his hands behind his back and swept his eyes over the reaches of the forest. "Back then, it was a far different place, though. I recall laying eyes upon the Arbari lands for the first time, when my soul seemed to be shattered beyond repair."

"The Wood Elves?" asked the smith.

"Oh, indeed," the old soldier replied quickly. "I spent many weeks living among them. Did you know their cities are built inside of gigantic mushrooms that grow on the side of the even larger sapa trees?"

Alauren shook her head. "No, I didn't."

"We'll have to go someday," Edlevin said. A few strands of hair, whipped by the wind, blew across his face, only to be pushed out of the way by a gauntleted hand. "They are quite fine hosts, as long as you respect the nature around you. In their homeland, I saw a world beyond my own grief and pain, and in that world, I found enough relief to get me home."

"So, you think I can find the same here?" asked the smith.

"Perhaps," the old soldier considered, rubbing at his stubble. "But do not be dismayed if you don't. One must bandage their wound before it can heal, and this may well be your cloth rather than your cure."

"I suppose we'll find out," Alauren said softly, focusing back onto the road ahead. "Onward."

CHAPTER THIRTEEN:

ODDITIES

There were few places left in Odenseye's reach that one would consider wholly separate from the world at large. Indeed, even the furthest-flung islands could find themselves answering to a power beyond that of their own isolated reaches, should the circumstances arise.

Alsara, visibly, was not one of those places.

One look at the town's unkempt and winding stone streets would show little influence from what one might call 'trained' planners. The buildings that lined the avenues looked to be the product of a hundred eclectic designs haphazardly mashed into one, each clearly patched and re-patched by inhabitants of wildly varying backgrounds over the long decades; some were jagged and Fangirmish, a few were rounded and Elysian, while still others bore no resemblance to familiar cultures whatsoever.

The group of travelers chose their steps carefully, trudging down a steep path to a lowland that the town had been built within, seeming from a distance as if the streets and buildings were the last bits of stew left in a roughly carved wooden bowl. From their elevated position, they could see all manner of Humans and Elves mill about their usual business in the streets, oblivious to the approaching Nortish warriors as they made steady progress towards the settlement.

"Alsara welcomes you," Roan said as soon as his feet touched the flat thoroughfare of the town, laying at the base of the ridge. "Stay close and try not to look threatening." Though the road grew more developed as it entered the limits of civilization, this section was still rather overgrown, and its beginning was marked only by a small sign to the left of the path, reading: *Alsara: Founded 520.*

The visitors followed closely and, though they could not realistically obey Roan's latter command, they did their best to maintain a peaceable air. Alauren, for her part, found herself having to be towed along by her old friend while her gaze shot rapidly about the streets. There was a deep curiosity in her eyes, and every new sight seemed to serve as tinder for the intensity.

Upon turning a corner, her eyes landed on a purple-skinned trio of short and slender elves, who loitered around the front of a rickety general store. Noticing her stare, they looked back with deep, solid black eyes, and returned her curiosity with polite nods and slim smiles. They broke contact and lost their mirth, however, when the group of Norts thundering behind finally made their way around the bend. The locals quickly shuffled inside of the wooden building, eager to be out of sight.

"Lunari. Moon Elves," Edlevin explained, sensing the smith's curiosity. "Friendly people, but careful ones."

"Are all their eyes…?" asked the blacksmith.

"Yes, they all look like dark voids," chuckled the old soldier. "And yes, it is always unsettling. You get used to it."

"Fascinating," Alauren whispered to herself. "You never know where they're looking, do you?"

Edlevin huffed a laugh. "No. That's why they tend to stay among their own. In a place like this, though-"

"They feel welcome," Roan finished proudly. He had fallen slightly behind his cadre of soldiers, and he obviously felt more comfortable now that he was surrounded by greater numbers of his own people. "As do all who come peacefully."

"It doesn't seem like they're too fond of the Norts, either way," Edlevin observed, noticing the wide berth that was given to their party. Indeed, all around, Humans and Elves alike retreated into back alleys and buildings with unmatched rapidity.

Roan nodded. "For those families who have been here for generations, the memory of rampaging Northmen is still quite vivid. Even if they did not live in the time before our covenant of peace, most have heard stories of the brutal raiding." He shrugged and smirked. "Their trepidation will have to be forgiven."

"I don't think we mind," the smith noted, accompanied by a glance over her shoulder. Just behind, she could see a wide smile painting over Ronnok's face, a look of amusement and pride as the Alsarans scurried away.

"Roan!" A female voice yelled from ahead. A tall, cloaked, and long-coated figure lifted her hood to reveal the golden skin and sandy hair of a Solvari, a Sun Elf. Her face had high cheekbones and a slender, carved jaw, accompanied by a rigid brow and wide brown eyes that stared curiously at the approaching foreigners. "What have you brought to town this time?"

"Old... uh..." the Governor trailed off, thinking. He turned to Ronnok. "Friends?"

"Good enough," replied the Northman. "I am Ronnok, Chieftain of Clan Nordiska."

The Solvari approached without hesitation and extended her hand. Her fingers were long and bony, while her nails were painted a deep black. "I am Xendra, a transient here, but a frequent one."

Ronnok took her hand, smiled, and shook it firmly.

"Bah!" Roan spat with a dismissive wave. "This is your home, Xen. You just don't want to admit it."

"It's not my home until I say it is, old man," the Solvari jabbed with a chuckle. "Tell me, Ronnok, who are the guests you keep?"

"Edlevin is the human," Ronnok introduced with a point towards the old soldier. "Long winded, long-in-the-tooth, but supremely capable."

Edlevin crossed his arms, visibly rankled, yet he seemed appreciative of the praise, nonetheless. He nodded a curt, silent greeting.

"The Dwarf is Valin," Ronnok continued, gesturing to the toothy grin of his bearded fellow. "He's a priest or some such. Someone lives in his scythe. Don't touch it." He tapped the smith lightly on the shoulder. "Alauren is the third, a Half-Elf blacksmith of the finest quality."

Xendra approached Alauren, who could only look up at the much taller woman with starry eyes.

"H-h-Hello," stammered the smith.

"Hello," Xendra echoed. "Which half of you is Elf?"

"Excuse me?" Alauren asked with bewilderment.

"Right or left?" prompted the Solvari.

"Whichever side holds the hammer, I guess?" Alauren blurted, pressured to say *something* by the amused silence that surrounded her.

Xendra chortled heartily. "I've asked several hundred beings that question. You have the best answer." She clapped the shorter woman lightly on the shoulder. "I possess some skill at the forge myself, though likely not as much as you. I have business elsewhere for the moment, but you seem like good company. I'd like to talk to you more, if you don't mind hanging around the tavern tonight."

Alauren glanced at Edlevin, who simply shrugged in return.

"Okay," the smith agreed, unsure of the stranger's demeanor, but happy to find friendly company, nonetheless. "Wherever that is."

"You'll see, eventually," Roan said. "Come, let us continue."

The group bid Xendra farewell and moved on. They found streets that were largely empty, though not deserted in the traditional sense; just like Teth, word of anything unusual spread rapidly among the folk of such a sleepy little town. The residents were clearly meaning to hide and wait out any potential trouble, but window shutters could occasionally still be heard creaking open as children and adults alike dared to sneak a peek from the safety of their little hovels.

The Nortish party came upon the Inn in good time, near the end of the main road and on the right. A wide two-story building, it was constructed of stained white wood, and two massive windows flanked dual oaken doors. Across the street, the blocky blacksmith's shop poured smoke from a single pipe jutting out of its gray and textured stone walls.

Between the two structures, at the final end of the road and up a slope, there was a massive courthouse constructed of deep black wood, which was easily identifiable as shadowbeech. A single tower rose from the front, topped off with a large belfry bearing a flaming sconce on each of its corners. The building was a magnificent Fangirmish masterpiece, one of the few here that did not possess eclectic patches and modifications, a true remnant of the town's original roots.

"You may stay one night at the Inn, free of charge," the Governor stated, stopping well short of the courthouse doors and beckoning Ronnok forward. "You will, however, have to pay for your food and drink."

"Of course," agreed the Chieftain. "As the covenant says."

Roan nodded. "You have your manifest?"

Ronnok was quick to hand a small parchment over, scrawled on with hasty (yet remarkably neat) text in the trade tongue. "Have these things together by morning," the Nort instructed. "This should be everything needed for our journey."

Roan looked over the paper carefully. "A dozen barrels of ale, a ship's worth of salted rations, twenty iron ingots…" He sighed deeply as he read each new item with increasingly weary eyes. "You request much, but you shall have it."

"We are flexible," Ronnok said, his words quite reserved despite the grim authority with which they spilled forth. "Speak to me once you have a better idea of what you can spare. We will arrange our lodging while we wait."

"I'll be at the forge," Alauren barked, moving towards Roan's blade, which was being held in a scabbard by his side. His men tensed up, but the Governor himself gave only an amused smile in reply. "I thought payment was due up front?"

"It is," replied the smith, holding out her hand. "Elysium, let's go."

Roan let out a hearty laugh as he counted five coins from his pocket and dropped them into Alauren's hand. Without another word, he pulled the glimmering blade from its sheath, took a long look at the blunted tip, and handed it over. The smith, reacting instantly, snatched it and bounded towards the forge.

"You don't want a drink first?" Edlevin called after her, raising an eyebrow.

"Later!" the blacksmith yelled. Her reply was accentuated by the banging of the smithy door as it closed shut behind her, enclosing her in a welcoming stuffiness that felt starkly different from the temperate town.

Inside the building, a massive furnace was situated in the center of three separate anvil stations. One was occupied by an ebony-skinned, muscular man who bore a well-worn leather apron, from under which wide, hairy arms streamed forth.

"Huh?" grunted the local. He swept his brow clear of sweat, though he rubbed a large amount of it into his kinked, curly hair. "Can I help you?" His voice was gruff and low, but his tone was one more of curiosity than annoyance.

"I'm with the new folks," Alauren enlightened, holding up the large blade. "Roan wanted me to work on his sword."

"New folks? Roan? Wot?" the man muttered. Each confused query furrowed his brow a bit more while he tried to process the unexpected onslaught of information.

Alauren, enamored by the complexity of the shop, was deaf to the questions, and she stationed herself at an open grinding wheel with hardly a thought paid towards the man's bewildered grumbles. "You must be Bennis."

"I am," the man grumbled. "Why... Why are you touching my forge?"

"Oh, sorry," Alauren said with a sheepish chuckle. "I'm not used to using someone else's equipment. I'll just be a bit, while I fulfill the contract."

Bennis crossed his arms. "Now hold on. You can't just walk in here and-"

"She can!" Roan growled loudly, poking his head through the door. "She's with the Norts, Bennis. Do what she says." The door slammed with the order, leaving only the crackling of the forge to break a silence that lasted several elongated moments.

Bennis' annoyed attitude, after a short time, cooled down. "Well, I suppose in the case of Norts..."

"I'm good?" Alauren prompted.

"Yeah," the man conceded. "You don't look like much of a smith to me, though. Don't break nothin', and don't use up a bunch of my water unless you wanna fetch more."

"Sure," the blacksmith mumbled. She kept starry eyes on the sword while she inspected its blunted end, poring over every bit of the blade's honed edge to determine the damage. It was a simple job, by the looks of it, one that would hardly be worth her time otherwise. Being back in a shop, though, around the bitter, stinging smells and heat that wafted through the air like a windless summer day, gave her a feeling of purpose. An order needed to be fulfilled, and any other thoughts could be put off until another time.

"You know, you kinda remind me of the last one," Bennis said.

"The last one?" Alauren asked, looking up. The silvery metal of the sword glinted off the furnace and painted her face with wild pinpricks of light that danced about, responding to even the slightest movements.

"Yeah," the man confirmed. "She comes through here occasionally. Looks like you, except a bit..." He gestured vaguely into the air. "Taller. Didn't think she'd be much of a smith either, but she held her own."

"Xendra?" Alauren asked.

"Yeah, you've met her then," Bennis said. "I honestly didn't even know she was in town again. She comes and goes."

"What's her deal?" Alauren asked, shifting the bulk of her attention back to the sword. "She seems a bit odd."

"Shit, kid," Bennis said with a rumbling laugh. "It's Alsara. We're all odd."

"Good company, then," Alauren chuckled. "I look forward to swapping some stories with the people here."

"Speaking of…" Bennis began. "What's yours?"

"Well, my name is Alauren, for starters," the woman replied. "I was the town smith of Teth'Nerhol, in Se'Vikoral."

"Teth?" Bennis yelped. "We got a shipment of swords from there not too long ago. Magnificent items! You mean to tell me you made them?"

Alauren suppressed a grin, keeping the pride at the recognition of her works within herself. "If you're talking about the order from the Synda merchants, then yes, that was me."

"Ha!" Bennis laughed, throwing his hands onto his hips. "Some of the best blades I've seen. It's hard to believe, if I'm bein' honest. You'll have to prove it."

Alauren remained silent, but the challenge was accepted without hesitation. She quickly lost herself in the shimmering depths of the sword, any offense she could have taken from the gruff man's words serving as nothing more than kindling for her inner fire. She moved the weapon above the large white grindstone and focused in.

She began spinning the gritty piece of stone toward her with a foot-pedal mechanism and carefully applied a small amount of water (conveniently dispensed from a faucet, using another foot-pedal) to the surface of the device as it rotated. She set the blunted edge of the blade to the tool's exterior, an action which immediately elicited a loud, shrill sound, like the shrieking of a hawk, were it greatly prolonged and unceasing. The smith kept her unflinching focus on the cutting edge of the sword, hardly noticing the awful noise as steel ground against the rough rock.

Bennis watched intently all the while, admiring the small woman's unwavering hand as she moved the sword left and right in perfectly timed intervals, ever focused on the point of contact as it attempted to jump this way and that. Her hands held the blade soundly, though, like her very life depended on whether she could keep its razor edge upon the grindstone. Periodically, she would use her free foot to call forth just the right amount of water, wasting little, if any, from the reservoir of the local smith.

After grinding for a few more minutes, flipping the blade several times to get at both edges, she plunked the sword onto a table near the wheel with a self-satisfied smile. "If you so much as touch this edge, you'll draw blood," she proclaimed confidently.

Bennis walked over with a skeptical smirk upon his craggy face. He pulled an apple from his pocket, set it on the table, and picked up the sword. Using only the natural weight of the weapon, he was able to slide it cleanly through the fruit with a perfectly vertical cut. "Hey kid," he chuckled, popping the slice into his mouth. "You wanna stay and work for me?"

Alauren chuckled lightly and shook her head. "Not unless you can convince the Norts to stick around."

"Given what I just saw, I might have to try," Bennis mused. He recoiled, lightly nipping his finger as he tested the blade's razor edge. "You have a natural talent. This quality of work in such a small amount of time is borderline impossible."

"It's not natural," Alauren corrected. "I've had..." she held her tongue for a moment, catching herself before the intended words could burst forth. "I've had a significant amount of experience."

"In any case, you have some sort of gift," Bennis rumbled, hefting the blade while admiring the smoothness of the edge. "You know, I've been meanin' to make somethin' for myself. Just a knife for butcherin', but if you think you can repeat this quality of work on a harder assignment, I'd pay you well to do it for me."

"Twenty elysium well?" Alauren proposed.

"Worth every piece," Bennis agreed instantly. "Oh, and do me a favor, toss that there amethyst into the pommel." He pointed forcefully toward a glittering indigo gem on a nearby table. "Long as I'm payin' that much gold, I might as well have you make it look pretty!"

The DewDrop Inn was normally a rather cramped place, filled wall-to-wall with joyous patrons who greedily drank their fill amidst a general din that echoed off the walls and fluttered about the cavernous dining hall. Now, with the presence of the large Nort warriors, those who dared remain in the room found themselves shoulder-to-shoulder at the bar as the visitors commandeered the rear section of tables for themselves.

Edlevin sat next to Valin and Ronnok, across from Eira and Thyra, at a square table in the center of the room, just below a sparkling chandelier that the old soldier instantly recognized as a design from the Fangirmish Empire. He watched in awe as the hundreds of individual crystals caught and refracted the light of the hearth, glistening in what seemed to be a thousand different colors.

"Would you like us to add it to our list?" Ronnok offered with a lopsided smile, clearly noticing Edlevin's fascination.

The old soldier snickered, a sound that was barely heard above the chatter of the Inn. "No, though the thought is appreciated. I simply admire the craftsmanship of my homeland."

"Too fragile anyway," Eira said. She sneered at the crystals with an expression that resembled revulsion, only far more subdued. "It wouldn't last a day on a boat."

"Solveig would knock it down almost instantly, as well," agreed the Chieftain. "Probably best that it stays far away from her."

"You know, as much as I admire your lifestyle, you have to admit it doesn't leave much room for the finer things," Edlevin commented, lowering his eyes back to the table and sipping from his mug.

"Good steel, good food, good music…" Ronnok replied. "Those are fine enough for me. Your people hold value in the strangest of things. Tell me, what good is a rock that only glistens?"

Edlevin chuckled and shook his head. "When most of your life revolves around staying in one place, it's nice to keep things that are just nice to look at."

"Oh, shut up!" Valin interjected abruptly, drawing curious looks from around the table. He blushed sheepishly and let out a miniscule, careful chuckle. "Never mind me, the wizard is bein' an arse again."

"What now?" Ronnok asked.

"Well, I'd rather not…" the Dwarf trailed off, quite purposefully.

"Explain!" Ronnok bellowed with a light slap on the wooden table. "If the annoying man has something to say, let it be said!"

"Well... sure," Valin acquiesced hesitantly. "He said yer wives are nice enough t' look at, or somethin' thereabouts."

The Chieftain erupted into a jovial laughter that was swiftly followed by Eira and Thyra. "That they are!" He clapped the Dwarf heartily on the back and followed it up with a reassuring nudge. "There is no harm in his words, short one."

"Just keep in mind," Valin said, "if there ever is, do yer best t' remember which mouth the words actually came from!"

"Of course, Master Dwarf," Ronnok affirmed.

The last of Edlevin's ale swirled down the hatch, accompanied by a amused shake of the head toward the antics. "More?" he asked, displaying his empty cup towards a table of eagerly nodding comrades.

The old soldier swiftly grabbed the five mugs by the handles and, after ensuring his grip was solid, headed towards the front of the Inn. He dodged a few nervous locals as he snaked his way through the crowded hall, before placing the cups down next to an oversized human who hunched heavily over the bar.

The man looked to Edlevin with clear disdain, scratching his balding, graying hair before signaling the bartender for another drink. He wore a green tunic and a pair of black trousers, both of which were stained with wear (and alcoholic beverages). He had a rather sweaty look about him, and his garments were slightly damp at the chest and armpits.

"Yer with the murderers, then?" he asked bluntly, surprising the old soldier.

"Correct me if I'm wrong, but nobody has been killed," Edlevin corrected coldly, accentuated by the clinking of coins as he handed the bartender his payment.

"Not this time," the man said. "But my grandpappy fought them Norts, hundreds of 'em. Watched his friends die face down in the sand trying to drive 'em out."

"Hence why a covenant was formed," Edlevin said dismissively, showing a clear lack of interest in whatever bunk the local was selling.

"Piss on the covenant," the man spat. "They shouldn't be here. You shouldn't be here with 'em."

"But they are, and I am," Edlevin replied calmly. "You'd be best to stay out of their way."

"Ha!" the man bellowed derisively. "We'll do no such thing. My grandpappy didn't run from Norts, and neither does Rhus Haug!"

Edlevin raised an eyebrow. "Your name, I presume?"

"You'll know it well," Rhus replied confidently.

"Is that a threat?" the old soldier growled, allowing any lingering humor to bleed out of his expression. He met the braggart's gaze with a cold, wintry glare, a visage of stone dredged up from a long-dead life. He bore the eyes of a soldier, weary and stricken by the terror of memory, instantly recognizable to any who shared his unenviable experiences. It was, at once, a stark warning and a grave threat, a signal that foolishness would not be tolerated.

"It is what you want it to be," Rhus deadpanned, oblivious to the shift in demeanor.

"Word of advice, Rhus," rumbled the old soldier, leaning on the bar. "Whatever you're brewing, drop it. Folks like you don't fare well against those who make warfare their lives."

"We'll see," Rhus stated, making way for five full mugs as they were delivered to the foreigner.

Edlevin gave the man a final, stern scowl before making off with the cups, filled to the brim with a sweet mead that was as golden as honey and three times as cloudy. He plunked the drinks heavily onto the table, ensured that they reached the right hands, and moved on to more pressing matters. "You'd best come with me for a moment," he whispered into Ronnok's ear, pointing to an unoccupied table in the corner.

The Chieftain, bellowing with laughter at a particularly dubious story from the Dwarf, was resistant at first, but a few pestering nudges brought with them the Nort's full attention. He followed the soldier to the unoccupied table and sat.

Once they had settled in, Edlevin spoke. "You see that man in the front? The large, balding one?"

"The one in the stained tunic," Ronnok confirmed without the need to look. "He's been giving me sideways glances all night."

"He says his name is Rhus Haug," Edlevin said with a deep, exasperated sigh. "A local man, second or third generation by the sounds of it. He's brewing something. He seemed unhappy to have us."

"Most are," Ronnok pointed out. "Could just be drunk bravery, you know."

"Are you willing to take that risk?" Edlevin asked with a raised eyebrow. "Pathetic as he looks, he could still cause damage."

Ronnok considered the words for a moment before nodding. "Indeed. We must respect any potential foe. Sometimes the least imposing end up being the most dangerous."

"Speaking of...," said the old soldier. He pointed towards the table at which Valin and the Nort women were still sitting. A particularly drunk human, plump and red-faced, pawed lightly at Thyra with a hardly alluring, yellow-toothed smile.

Ronnok smirked and waved his hand dismissively. "It will be fine."

The man got progressively more handsy with the two Nort women, wrapping his arm around their shoulders and pulling them uncomfortably close as he (poorly) sang a local tune. Eira and Thyra responded by gently pushing him away.

"We should probably-" Edlevin started.

"It will be fine," Ronnok assured with a reassuring pat on the old soldier's shoulder.

The man tussled Eira's hair and whispered a few words softly into her ear, which drew a grimace from the Nort woman. She pushed him away again. This time, though, the man drew in extremely close to her face and attempted to grab her leg.

Edlevin shot out of his seat, but he felt a heavy hand envelop his wrist with a tight grip. Ronnok roughly pulled the old soldier back into his chair as if the human was a small, misbehaving child.

"It *will* be fine," growled the Chieftain.

Alauren stepped through the smithy doors and out into a night that was colored by the smells of autumn leaves, a salty breeze, and a sweet odor coming from the Inn. A cold air had descended on the island, blowing through the lowlands with a biting chill.

Bennis emerged behind her, gazing at his new blade with wonder. The work of the foreign smith was as refined as it was rapid, and he could do little but inspect the shining steel with bewilderment. With all the materials on hand and a preheated forge, a few hours were all that was needed for Alauren to work her magic, and she did so with an efficiency typical of her experienced hand.

"This is simply astonishing work," Bennis admired, each bewildered word seeming like a deep gasp. He used the blade to cut into another apple, finding a satisfying ease in how smoothly it glided, as if it was carving through air. He gave the slice of fruit to Alauren, which was happily accepted by the weary smith. He flipped the weapon and ran his finger over the ridges of a perfectly set amethyst with a pure, unrivaled joy. "Astonishing!"

"Time and experience, Bennis," Alauren replied with modesty. "Decades do their job."

"I'll say it again: this goes beyond experience," the local blacksmith replied surely. "This is natural, somethin' else entirely."

"That 'somethin'' is all day, every day, spent at work," Alauren said with a chortle. "Practice really does make perfect."

"I do the same!" Bennis bellowed. "I still can't make a blade like this, kid. Well, at least not that fast."

"Bennis," Alauren said with amusement. "I'm not a kid. I'm older than you."

"You-? Wha?" Bennis stammered.

"Yeah," Alauren affirmed. "Significantly, too, most likely. We'll leave it at that, yeah?"

"I guess so," Bennis replied timidly. He sliced another piece of the apple and popped it into his mouth. "Roan should be up in the town hall, if you wanna-"

A large, red-faced man suddenly soared through the leftmost of the Inn's large windows. Shards of glass and splinters of wood exploded around the portly human, accompanying him on his rough tumble to the ground, where he landed with a solid, hollow *thud*. His breath was taken away, and he could do little but wheeze and heave while he writhed on the ground.

The doors of the Inn were forcefully shouldered open as Eira and Thyra stalked through simultaneously. Both of the Nort women had stone-cold looks of hatred on their face, but Thyra stopped short to allow her sister to reach the man first.

Eira hefted him up and slammed him violently against the wall of the Inn, holding him by the neck while his feet hovered a finger's length from the ground.

"You want to get intimate?" Eira growled with a frost-bound fury.

"How's this for intimate?" She punched the man hard in the mouth, sending blood (and a tooth) splattering against the Inn wall. She proceeded to lift and spike him hard onto the road as if he were a mere doll, and any remaining breath was stolen from his lungs as he bounced off the hard stones.

Eira spat upon the man and stormed back into the Inn with her sister, ending the show with as bold of a statement as one could ask for.

"Well..." Bennis quipped after a moment of bewildered silence. "That was amusing."

The smith shook herself from her surprise just as the bloody man was able to rise and scurry off into the dark streets. "He's brave, at least, hitting on Nort women."

Bennis laughed. "Yeah, that's about normal."

"You know him?" Alauren asked.

"It's an island," Bennis chuckled. "Everyone knows everyone. He goes by the name of Ael. Makes his living selling healing salves, and he spends near all of it on women."

"Guess he found out not everyone values money the same," observed the smith. She waved the local man toward the still-ajar doors of the Inn. "Come on, first round is on me."

Bennis happily obliged; they entered the establishment, obtaining two brimming mugs before joining the rest of the group (after some hesitation from the local, who was offput by the sight of the loud and boisterous Norts).

"This is Bennis," Alauren introduced, taking a seat at the center table. "Local blacksmith."

"Edlevin," the old soldier greeted warmly. "Well met, and all that!" A smirk erupted on his face. "I'm surprised you joined us, given what just happened."

"I'm smart enough to know when someone deserves it," Bennis stated amidst a yelping chortle. "Ael is a bit of a moron, but he's mostly harmless, in most cases. Man can't take a light slap without runnin' off."

"Yes, we found out," Ronnok chuckled. "I am Ronnok, Chieftain of Nordiska. They are Eira and Thyra, my wives."

"Well met," the sisters said in unison.

"I'm Valin!" the Dwarf said, though the words were muffled by a hunk of buttered bread being shoved into his maw.

"Such varied folk," Bennis observed. "I've seen a lot of travelers in my time. Dwarves, Elves, all manner of humans… but I've never seen 'em travel together."

"Unlikely allies are often a consequence of circumstance," Alauren spoke, which drew an amused look from the Norts. She shrunk in her seat, quite unsure what had been said to elicit the smiles. "What?"

"You sound like the Karlmaðr," said the Chieftain. "Your words are becoming as overly complicated as his."

"Shit," the smith spat, sinking into her the chair with the wide eyes of realization.

"Just don't inherit the long-windedness, eh?" Valin said with a sharp laugh.

"I fail to see the problem!" Edlevin protested. "I think my manner of speaking is quite elegant, all truth be told, and I do take a good deal of pride in my erudite and well-crafted…" He trailed off, suddenly noticing the entertained expressions watching him prove their point. He cleared his throat. "Anyway…"

The night went on for a while, occupied by loud conversation and thunderous laughs. Eventually, though, the Norts and Edlevin retired to their beds, as did Bennis and Valin. Alauren would have, too, had it not been for the lingering nightmares she knew would greet her in slumber. She had stayed in her place, drinking full, awaiting the promised arrival of the local Solvari.

Only the final hour of the long evening brought Xendra's presence along with it. Rain had been pouring outside for a while, and her flowing brown hair now stuck together under her cloak as she stepped through the door. Undeterred, she made her way to Alauren, removed her dripping covering, and sat down.

"Apologies for my lateness," said the Solvari, brushing her wet hair away from her face. "I often get lost in my thoughts out there." Her voice had shifted in demeanor, the smith noticed; during their first meeting, it had carried a light cadence, one of an affable (if strange) resident of the rural island. Now, though, it was low and grating, coldly serious, but deeply curious.

"Not a problem, Xendra," Alauren said. Her words were half-slurred from her many cups of mead, as well as more than a little drowsiness. "I do the same thing at my forge."

"Call me Xen," the Solvari instructed, eliciting a nod from the blacksmith. "I noticed the blade you carry on your hip. Your own make?"

Alauren nodded proudly. "It was supposed to be a gift for the Norts, but it's a bit undersized for the recipients."

"It is a special sword, you know," Xendra pointed out. "Are all your creations like that one?"

"Mostly," Alauren replied, amidst a few slow blinks. "Depends on how much time you give me. A good edge takes a while for anything bigger than a knife."

The Solvari chuckled. "I'm not just talking about the edge, you know."

Alauren raised an eyebrow. "What do you mean?"

"There is an enchantment upon that blade," Xendra said with a shrewd smile. "By the very nature of enchantments, it is difficult to discern what it does, as the specks of magic are bound deep within the metal. Still, it is there."

"Unless Valin put a rune on it when I wasn't looking, there's nothing magical about it," the smith huffed proudly. "I don't cheat."

"No offense to your craft was meant!" Xendra quickly apologized, throwing up her hands disarmingly. "The metal is a work of art, yet there is absolutely something beneath its surface. Alvari like me, High Elves, are quite good at detecting such things."

"Huh," Alauren grunted. "And here I thought you were Solvari."

"Half and half," Xendra replied. Her voice was strangely dismissive, as if the detail was remarkably unimportant. "Regardless, there is something special about your work, something naturally powerful about how you wield your hammer."

"I have a lot of experience," the smith retorted. "That should explain most everything. I'm sure my Elven half helps, but my works are superb by my own hand."

Xendra leaned forward and studied the visitor intently, her eyes narrow and intense. "You know, I jested earlier, but I did find myself wondering what Elven mix you have in your blood. Your looks seem much alike to a Solvari, but you have the stature of a Lunari. The tone of your muscle says Arbari, and yet the strength of your craftsmanship contradicts that notion by seeming most like an Alvari. You are most confusing."

"Thanks?" Alauren chortled. "I don't know, truth be told. It doesn't really matter to me. I have-" She cut herself off with a wince. "I *had* what I wanted."

Xendra's face grew concerned, though her voice couldn't hide a deep curiosity at the sudden malaise. "What happened?"

"It... It doesn't matter," muttered the smith, waving off the thought. "I'd rather not talk about it."

"It could help," Xendra pushed. "I have known loss, too. Give it a try, at least?"

Alauren shifted for a moment, but obliged, too weak under the weight of the woman's gaze and the fog of the alcohol. "Okay. I was the blacksmith in a town called Teth," she explained. "Valin showed up one day, and we ended up taking this blade out of town to offer to the Norts as a token of peace." Her eyes grew heavy. "When we got back, everyone was dead. Locked in the longhouse. They..." She grimaced and swallowed hard as a wave of memory-driven nausea swept through her stomach. "They were frozen in death. Their eyes were this solid, bloody red color, and they were clutching at their necks like they were being strangled."

Xendra seemed to lean a little further forward with every detail given. Her eyes lit up with a spark of interest, and her words became quite intense. "What happened to them?"

"I don't know," mumbled the blacksmith. "Three men, tall as I've ever seen, showed up. They looked like old, ancient knights. They tried to kill us, saying something about a dream. I got hit on the head, and a lot of it is a blur now." She swallowed hard again, trying to bury the vile disgust that attempted to rise within her. "Edlevin and I were the only natives of the town to make it out. Everyone else was murdered."

A silence, heavy and enduring, hung in the air. Xendra met the smith's eyes, but it seemed that she was looking far beyond the sorrowful gaze that was returned, lost inside of her mind for the moment as the words were considered.

"I'm sorry," Xendra comforted after a few protracted seconds. "You have lost much more than I would have thought." She leaned back in her chair and relaxed, though the act took deliberate and visible effort. "Do you know who these men were?"

"Not a clue," replied the smith. "Xen, can we stop talking about it now? I want to keep my mind in the here and now."

"As you wish," Xendra acquiesced. "Just keep your eyes open and your head up. The world is changing more rapidly than any of us would like, and all we can do is keep on moving to the horizon and beyond." She smiled warmly. "I, for instance, am headed to some outer islands once we are done speaking here. That's why I was out so late, as my craft needed to be readied for the journey. I have some friends out there that I have ignored for some time, and you happened to remind me of them."

"Are they all this sssorrowful?" Alauren slurred. Her eyes grew heavy with exhaustion (as well as the very early beginnings of a hangover).

"You have no idea," Xendra confirmed with surety. "You look like you need a pillow under you. Come on, we'll get you to bed."

Alauren, already half-asleep, obeyed without question.

CHAPTER FOURTEEN:

HUBRIS

15th OF THE MORN OF HARVEST
NORTHERN YEAR 715

Mists surrounded the blacksmith as she strode through darkened forests, listening closely to a soft breeze that whispered past her ears. It seemed to carry thoughts upon it, varied and fleeting, barely having a chance to be deciphered before they drifted away like a feather in the wind. Try as she might to listen closely, the soft murmurs would inevitably remain unheard.

The trees around Alauren suddenly stood and scurried away on their roots, revealing a rolling meadow of ankle-high grass in front of her. Within the clearing, a pond reflected the silvery image of a moon that didn't seem to exist in the sky above, the heavens filled only with darkness. The water stood as still and flat as the glassy surface of a mirror, untouched by the soft winds.

The smith approached the calm pool with curiosity, finding some of the whispers on the wind becoming louder, resolving into something she could decipher. They were a voice, soft and loving, from a source that felt close, yet unfamiliar. *My love,* they said, *my everything. I will not forget you.*

Alauren wanted to hear more, to draw these vague murmurs into something that was more than a sketch in her imagination. She felt as if there was a face to see, or a memory to play out, yet there was little more to be found than the passing of the voice as it continued on its way.

She blinked heavily and snapped into a sudden lucidity. In the matter of a second, she understood that she was within a dream, and that the placid world around her didn't seem to make sense. The surface of the pond began to rumble, followed by the emergence of a robed figure who hastily approached her.

"Drell," Alauren stated coldly. "What is this?"

"A venue to talk," Drell growled. "I want to fill in some blanks. I want to help you."

"Sure you do," the smith grumbled caustically, crossing her arms. "Is this my dream, or some construct of yours?"

"A little of both," the sorcerer replied. "This effort, to project myself here, within your mind's creation, pains me greatly. However, you need knowledge."

Alauren bit her lip and thought for a moment. "As long as it's only knowledge," she growled. "Touch me again, and I'll melt that fucking scythe for scrap."

"Agreed," Drell huffed indignantly. "Xendra knows what happened to your village."

Alauren cocked an eyebrow but remained silent, leaving the field open for the man to continue.

"Did you not feel how her interest burned when you spoke of their fate, how her soul came alight? I did, even from my place in another room," the sorcerer continued. "When she first saw you, on the town road, her eyes lit up with recognition. You were all too enamored of the sights to notice, but I don't watch such things." He took a deep breath that caused the still waters behind him to ripple. "She has departed, but there are answers to be had, and the word that will lead you to her again is Arvyn."

"Sure," the blacksmith stated skeptically. "Is that a name, or…?"

"I have given you all that I am willing," Drell rumbled. "Do with it what you will."

Alauren's brow furrowed. "Now, hold on one-"

The smith's words were interrupted by a distinct sizzling sound as the sorcerer turned to a pillar of ash. A wind, unfelt by the dreamer, carried the last vestiges of the man's presence in her mind off into the shifting forest. A dark fog crept in, and she became lost in the abyss of her slumbering mind.

Alauren awoke with a start, drenched in sweat and lying on a small cot within one of the Inn's rooms. She took a moment to gather herself and ready her soul for the incoming assault of existence. The crushing blows of dread and sorrow were hardest to bear in the minutes following the opening of her eyes, the recollection of where she was and what she had experienced. These were enemies that lay in wait for her weakness to show, and never was there a more vulnerable moment than when she was pulled from her peace to face the fresh realization that there was another day to overcome. The struggle hadn't become any easier, and it took the effort of an empire to see herself through.

The window of her room glinted with light, and the height of the sun informed the smith that it was about mid-morning. Outside her door, loud footsteps echoed through the hall, clomping about like several horses had rented the rooms around her. It was the Norts, of course, but she found her spirits lifted ever so slightly by the mental image of the more absurd explanation.

Alauren dressed herself and tied her hair back before heading to the door. The wooden threshold opened into a hall that smelled strongly of ham and bacon, along with a bitter touch from some hot beverage being brewed in the dining room at the end of the hall.

She wasn't keen to eat, nor was she particularly interested in a hot, black liquid that a few Norts at the bar slurped of gleefully. There was a biting pain in the pit of her stomach, a shaky unease that permeated her senses just as strongly as the odors that brushed lightly by while she made her way out the front door.

"Mornin'." Edlevin warbled as the smith walked onto the street. He had been leaning next to the shattered window (now patched with planks), apparently awaiting the waking of his old friend.

"Yeah, it sure is," Alauren replied flatly.

The old soldier raised an eyebrow. "Hungover, are we?"

"No," the blacksmith mumbled. "Well, yes, but I don't mind that part so much. It was just a bad night, is all."

"Nightmares?" Edlevin asked.

"Yeah," answered the smith.

"You want to talk about them?" Edlevin offered. His tone was gentle and careful to demand nothing.

"Not particularly," Alauren grumbled, heading towards the smithy.

"That's what everyone says," Edlevin countered, following her closely into the dark building. Bennis worked in the opposite corner and gave the new arrivals a curt nod when he looked up.

"I just don't want to think about it right now, Ed," Alauren replied, running her hand through her hair. "Just… just give me some time." She picked up Roan's longsword from a wooden table and blew past the old soldier, back through the small door and onto the street.

Her hustle was stopped a few steps outside the smithy by a hand on her shoulder, gentle, but firm. "Ally, hold on," Edlevin said. He spun her around and smiled. "I just want to know how you're doing. Slow down a bit and put my mind at ease."

Alauren shook off the older man's hand roughly. "I can't," she snapped. Her breath became ragged, and it was clear that she was struggling to constrain a writhing darkness. "I have to keep working. I don't have a choice. I don't want to see them."

"I know," soothed the old soldier. "It is okay, truly, to feel whatever you're feeling right now. Take a moment and let it be."

"It's…" Alauren mumbled. She shook her head and bit her lip, trying to contain a slurry of overflowing sorrow and dark anger. The emotions were like monstrous waves, and the power of her own will served as the only break to shatter them before they engulfed her. "I don't see them when I'm working, Ed."

"The villagers?" asked the old soldier.

"All of it," the smith said with a nod. "The villagers, the fight, the ride north. When I'm focused, though, I can find relief."

Edlevin nodded. "Do what you have to do, but don't run from this for too long, Ally. It *will* catch you, sooner or later, and you will have simply exhausted yourself when it does."

"I suppose you're familiar with the feeling?" Alauren asked, though she already knew the answer quite well.

"Much too familiar," the old soldier stated softly. "You feel like you are outnumbered thousands to one against the nightmares. This feeling is something shared by every widowed old woman, by every surviving soldier of a decimated company, and by nearly everyone that surrounds you now." He smiled warmly. "Thousands to one is a bad bet, thousands to a couple are a little better. Always stand with others, if you can."

Alauren nodded and breathed heavily, closing her eyes and recentering. "I'll keep that in mind." She glanced towards the town hall. "For now, I've got to get Roan his sword. Deadlines to keep and all."

"No need, as providence would have it," Roan said with a cheery smile, sauntering up from an alley behind the smithy. "Let's see the quality of your work."

Alauren handed the man his sword, which he inspected closely, looking intently at every bit of the edge. "Damn good work," he said after a moment of intense focus on the mirror-shined blade. "Impressive, I must admit."

"As always," Alauren said proudly, interlacing her hands behind her back while she stood tall.

"This is why we keep her!" Ronnok chuckled as he emerged from the Inn. He was carrying a number of bulging canvas sacks on his shoulders, the last of the agreed-upon supplies from the Alsarans. He was followed closely by Arvid, for whom the morning crowd parted with impressive haste.

"You don't keep me," the blacksmith riposted with a feigned indignance. "My presence here is held only on my good graces."

The Chieftain chuckled, but appeared ready to move on to business. He did not hesitate to share mirth, Alauren noticed, but his more important duties always seemed to be foremost in his mind.

"We've gotten our supplies from your men, Roan of Alsara," Ronnok said. "Your help, and your respect for the covenant, is appreciated."

Roan nodded with a smile. "Better than being gutted on the beach, by any measure."

"That it is," Ronnok agreed, accompanied by the eruption of a lopsided grin. "Is there anything else we require?"

"An anvil would be nice, I guess," Alauren said. "Mine is still back at Teth."

Arvid replied with a nod and ducked into the smithy. After a brief exchange of colorful words, he emerged with a massive hunk of metal perched upon his shoulder, seeming to have no more trouble with it than one might with a bag of grain.

"You can't just walk out with an anvil!" Bennis protested, trailing after the large Nort with an expression of utter disbelief. "Who does that?"

"Sorry," the smith apologized timidly. "I need one. You have two more, anyway."

Bennis gave Alauren a nasty look, but was quick to contain the emotion. "I really liked that one, though!"

"Is nice," Arvid boomed in agreement. He spoke with a thick Nort accent that was much more noticeable than that of his fellows, tumbling along like a boulder rolling down a hill. "That is why I chose."

Bennis simply sighed and shrugged in exasperated acceptance. "I suppose you'll make good use of it, at least."

"Promise," Alauren replied. "That's all for me, then. Are we ready?"

"Valin and my wives await us on the beach, while others have already embarked," Ronnok replied "Come now, for the sea awaits."

After verifying that no Northmen remained in the town, the last guests of this peaceful place walked quickly out of the village, followed closely by a Governor that was visibly eager to see them off.

The group arrived at the beach in good time, only to find an impressive argument in full swing between Valin and a group of about two-dozen men. The lively debate was watched calmly by Eira and Thyra, while Harald and Bjorn muttered between themselves behind the women. All save the Dwarf had their shields and weapons ready, and they would occasionally glance at the gathered locals with dark sneers.

The gathering of shabby looking (but heavily armed) townsfolk, each wearing gambesons or leather armor, was headed by Rhus, who leered at the Dwarf silently. Ael wasn't far behind his fellow islander, more red-faced, rotund, and ready than he had ever been, despite a bloody and purple bruise between his mouth and left eye. Valin, meanwhile, spewed various intricate profanities that were barely discernable under his accent, and his words sounded more like a moist, inarticulate growl than a coherent stream of thought.

"Yer out o' yer mind, ye reekin' reprobate!" bellowed the Dwarf.

"Me?" Rhus snapped incredulously. "You talk to your scythe!"

"Yeah, 'cause it talks t' me," Valin retorted. An evil smile grew on his face, and he held the weapon with an outstretched hand. "Here laddie, why don't ye let me prove it to y-"

"Valin, no," Edlevin interjected. He donned his helmet, concealing a grim scowl behind the shining metal faceplate. "No need for bloodshed."

"Oh, isn't there?" Rhus replied sarcastically. "Way we look at it, there is a certain lack of justice in our situation."

"Think about your next words carefully," cautioned the old soldier, taking the full attention of the enemy force while Valin and the sisters re-positioned with their fellows. "Heed what I told you last night, Rhus."

"Oh, I have," the Alsaran hummed with a devilish smile. He turned to Ronnok. "This covenant we have… it is between the Alsarans and the Northmen, is it not?"

The Chieftain's face one was of stone, unmoving and calm, but he allowed himself a nod to keep the man talking.

"These few," Rhus continued, with a point to non-Nort guests, "are not in either of those groups. In our eyes, you're an enemy, Northman."

Ronnok said nothing. The heavy load he had been carrying on his shoulders dropped to the sand with a *thud*. Arvid followed suit, tossing the anvil down at his side.

"However, we have a deal, and we respect that," Rhus continued diplomatically. "Those three, though… they travel with you. They share their stories with you." He chuckled darkly. "Shit, they probably help you kill!"

"Enough, Rhus," Roan growled, putting himself between the two groups. "They travel together, and so the covenant includes them."

"Not what the copy of it in the town hall says!" Ael erupted. "You didn't even see me take it, did you?" He held up the document, a small manuscript of parchment, proudly.

"I watched the cultural librarian check it out for you, Ael," the Governor replied with a bewildered shake of the head.

"Beside the point," Rhus interjected. "It says, and I shall quote: 'This covenant, which is to be held between those who are of Nordiska and the free peoples of Alsara'."

"Nothin' about anybody else!" Ael affirmed.

"They are of Nordiska," Ronnok replied calmly, focusing in on the brash local with an unblinking stare.

"Oh, are they?" Rhus asked smarmily. "What are their marks?"

Ronnok's only response was the furrowing of his brow.

The local's grin only grew at the silence. "I know the Northmen, Ronnok of Nordiska. Maybe better than anyone else who is not one of you. In any case, they cannot be considered one of your clan without the prop-"

"They are of Nordiska the same," the Chieftain interrupted. His eyes began to gloss over, and they peered to something far beyond the horizon. A smile surged to his face, standing at odds with a demeanor that had shifted instantly from a reasonable leader to a savage and menacing warrior. He squared his shoulders and stood to his full height, towering over the human locals.

"You have your options, Norts," Rhus growled obliviously. "Leave the outsiders or leave with blood."

"Rhus!" Roan howled furiously. The icy gravity of the words drew in every gaze save for the Chieftain's, and the Governor peered on with a clear and visible fear in his widened eyes. "If it comes to it, this is your fight. The people of Alsara do not choose war! We do not choose to die!"

"You don't speak for us!" Ael retorted. "You are an ineffective old man!"

"You don't speak for them!" Roan snapped back, with a point to the direction of the town. "They will not bleed because of your stupidity, Rhus. The Norts could kill them a-"

"Your people will not be harmed," Ronnok cut off, his voice still and calm as a pond in summer, "if this one chooses the wrong path."

"*You* have the choice, Ronnok of Nordiska," Rhus replied, letting every syllable of the Nort's name slither off his tongue, venomous and hateful.

Ronnok nodded solemnly, as his decision had been made long before the seemingly decisive moment.

The Chieftain casually drew his axes from his back, twin, single-edged blades etched with fires and serpents, and huddled close to his allies. The rest of the Norts did the same, forming a shield wall, while Arvid knelt and disappeared as the blockers came together.

"Rhus!" Edlevin yelped, trying one last attempt to cool tensions.

The gesture was too late, however. Ael, as prepared and riotous as he had ever been, let out a great bellow and charged spear-first toward the enemy line. He made it far for his peculiar size, heaving across the sand with strides that carried him an impressive distance in just a few moments.

The zealous local might have made it to the shield wall, in fact, had it not opened ever so slightly to let an anvil (gliding quite gently for *its* size) soar through the gap. The pointed end impacted Ael hard in the face with a pronounced *ping-crack*, clotheslining him, and he dropped with the full weight of the hunk of metal that was now embedded in his skull.

"Down!" Edlevin screamed, pulling Alauren close behind the defensive line. They hugged the Norts tightly and braced against the shield wall.

A single, unified roar of the town militiamen signaled the beginning of their charge, and the thunder against shields that rang in Alauren's ears confirmed the arrival of the attacking force in full. Bangs and bloodthirsty battle cries erupted from the other side of the blockers while the locals tried to find openings.

The Norts held strong against the force, outnumbered as they were. Occasionally, the sisters would open their shields enough for a single Alsaran to slip through while he was off-balance, allowing their husband a chance to dispatch him cleanly with his dual axes.

This orderly fighting fashion lasted for only a precious few moments; for as strong as the Norts were, numbers are an inevitable, heavy weight on the scales of battle. Chaos erupted as the shield wall gave way and the fighting became one-on-one.

Edlevin immediately engaged with a target, a man in a gambeson who stabbed and swiped frantically with a spear. The more seasoned warrior danced around as if it was a choreographed routine, bobbing left and right, frustrating his opponent with a deceptive speed.

Alauren, after a moment, was forced to fend for herself. She carefully weaved in and out of the fray, doing her best to use her small form to stay unnoticed in the melee. Screams and clanks erupted in the chaos around her, which seemed to stretch as far as she could see, from the ocean to the forest. The world grew tight and cluttered, as if the cacophony of the battle only grew stronger at her attempts to escape. For a time, all she could do was react, rolling herself through the gaps in the violence like a dinghy on a stormy sea.

The strategy worked, to her credit, guiding her past the soaring arms of a freshly cleaved local and allowing her a chance to hustle to the edge of the woods, where she could get her bearings. She stood tall and risked a look around.

To her left, Edlevin was finishing off his foe with a ruthless efficiency. He plunged his sword through the now-prone man's gambeson like it was a woolen sweater, ending the life of the bearer without a moment of hesitation. After a quick glance to ensure his old friend's safety, he engaged another target, striding forward to the Alsaran with a steady, aggressive stance, like a crotchety noble who had places to be.

She found Ronnok and the sisters in the crowd, fighting with glee; each of them bore wicked smiles, accompanying the splatters of blood across their faces. Despite the violence erupting around them, they seemed quite unafraid, and the smith had not yet witnessed the wild eyes of these exotic warriors look quite so alive.

The Chieftain chopped at one enemy, hitting the human's left shoulder and sending him tumbling to the ground. Another Alsaran took his place instantly, trying to keep the Northmen pinned down in their position. The trio of Norts stayed in a defensive formation, forming a small triangle, with each warrior at the tips, ensuring that their flanks were covered.

Eira, though, was falling behind. Her focus was intently on her target, a large man with a gambeson and pike. He kept his distance and used his longer weapon to a distinct advantage, poking and prodding around the Nort woman's shield.

In a moment, the man Ronnok had injured appeared in Alauren's vision, rising from a bloody pool in the sand. He was brandishing a dagger and lurching toward the distracted Nort woman with a burning hatred in his eyes. He closed fast, and the blacksmith had little but the passing of a blink to react.

Alauren's world became a blur. She felt her legs move under her, though the command to do so did not feel as if it was her own. Nevertheless, she found herself sprinting fearlessly through the fray, not daring to take a breath while she navigated the pandemonium of the battlefield.

An Alsaran, lifted from his feet by the blow of Harald's axe, began to tumble backwards in front of the smith. She ducked and lunged under the aerial corpse before letting her momentum carry her back to her feet. She closed in on her target, unseen and unheard.

A single moment before the man could plunge his blade into Eira's back, Alauren plunged her own through his belly, exhaling as the blade slipped in with fascinating ease.

The sword squelched within the Alsaran's guts, and he could do little but retch as the razor edge ripped through his organs and poked out the other side. He dropped slowly to his knees, convulsing in pain all the while.

Alauren dropped with him, staring on with wide eyes as the weapon within her hands seemed to siphon the life away from the human. Blood crept up the hilt of her sword, finding its way onto her palms. It was disturbingly warm, smelling strongly of metal, and a rattling sound began to escape from the mortally wounded man's mouth, a failed attempt at a groan. The experience of her senses in these moments, the revolting act of her own hand, seared into her mind, and even the finest details would remain there forevermore.

Eira, who had used the time to cleave her distractor's chest open, wheeled on the gravely wounded fighter. She looked past him, to the smith. "Well done," chortled the Nort, wearing a wicked grin. Without further hesitation, she cleanly removed the would-be attacker's head with a well-placed cleave.

The blacksmith felt a warm mist impact her face, sending her reeling backwards onto the sand. She maintained her grip on her sword, which slid out of the newly headless Alsaran with a disturbing ease and little but the sound of squishing flesh to go along with it. Blood ran down her cheeks, the warmth of life within fading as the drips beaded and dried under her horrified eyes.

The world turned heavily inward; it felt as if a wool bag were over her head, obscuring all but a fleeting few details while muffling the sounds around her to a dull roar. She blinked the haze away, urgently regaining her senses, realizing suddenly that she was surrounded by violence and completely helpless. A terror welled inside her, deep and primal, making her feel as if death was a heartbeat away.

In the few moments she had been involved, though, the rest of the Norts had left the beach painted with the blood of Alsara. Over two-dozen bodies lay among the seafoam, with not a Northmen to be found among them. Slowly, the world became more detailed, and the muffled sounds turned sharp.

Screams, loud and piercing, echoed over the battlefield, only to be silenced with the evident *thud* of an axe. Harald was moving from corpse to corpse, ripping golden molars from their mouths with pliers, while Bjorn and Arvid helped their Chieftain to secure the beach.

Alauren found Edlevin in the crowd, surveying the scene with his helmet off, casting a disgusted glare over the blood-soaked sands. He stood tall among the bodies, and he hardly seemed fazed by the viscera that surrounded him.

Alauren scrambled to her feet and enveloped her old friend in a heavy embrace, which was reciprocated in kind. Edlevin's armor was covered in viscera, yet the smith found herself bothered little by the rapidly drying blood.

The soldier hugged his old friend tightly while crimson rivers of blood and seawater trickled around their feet, making for the hungry tides beyond. The smith could do little but stare into nothing; her breath was ragged, and her mind was well beyond its limit, unable to process the violence of the world around her.

Arvid threw Rhus, still very much alive (and quite upset), onto the ground in front of Ronnok. "Hiding in trees," the large Nort rumbled, only just intelligible under his accent.

"You... My people...!" Rhus stammered.

"*Not* your people, Rhus!" Roan roared, emerging from behind the tree line. Tears streamed down a face of agonized disgust, though the early beginnings of a potent fury were beginning to peek through. "Not anymore! Now, they're twenty-eight dead men. Fathers, sons, gone!" He walked to the man silently, his gaze so focused, so furious, that even Ronnok stepped back respectfully. The Governor knelt next to Rhus and moved close. "*You* killed them."

"They stood in defiance of those who dishonor our people!" Rhus spat. "Their sacrifice... is not in vain!"

"And how about *yours*?" Roan growled with a gritty, barely-controlled fury overtaking his voice.

"W-what...?" Rhus stammered, shifting uneasily.

"You heard me," Roan grumbled coldly, rising from the sand.

Terror grew on Rhus' face, a deep and unmistakable fear. He eyed his surroundings, looking for any method of escape. "According to

Alsaran law," he barked desperately, "any who surrender after a military engagemen-"

"Will stand trial, I know," Roan finished for him. He huffed a single laugh, entertained in the darkest of ways by the younger man's naivety. "Did you really expect to walk away from this, Rhus?"

Rhus, for the first time, went white with fear. "But the law-"

"Is only the law when it's enforced," Roan stated with a maddened cackle. "Look around you. Who will enforce it?"

Rhus began to rise to his feet, meaning to run, but Arvid violently kicked the much smaller human back to his knees. Roan shook his head a final time and stepped back, disgust overtaking him.

"The people... the people will revolt when they hear of this!" Rhus shrieked. "You have a responsibility!"

"I do," Roan agreed. "First and foremost, to my people's safety. You have been a threat to that for a time, Rhus. No more."

"No, no, NO!" Rhus wailed. His voice strained and cracked more with every word. "You can't-"

A heavy backhand slap and a distinct, meaty *crunch* showed that Ronnok, in fact, could. Rhus' lifeless body fell to the sand, among his brothers.

"My apologies," Roan muttered after a moment of silence. All who fought were spattered (or, like Ronnok, drenched) in blood, a sight that brought a clear spark of memory into the man's aging eyes. His breath was ragged and uneven, and he rubbed his temple intensely, as if he could physically push this newly crafted memory away. "Never thought I'd have to see this again."

"Perhaps this is the last time, then," Ronnok grumbled in reply. He attempted to wipe the blood from his face, but the action did little save for spreading the gore around. "Perhaps this is a lesson."

"I have a feeling it will be," Roan deadpanned with a final glance across the grisly scene. "You lot best move on. I have work to do here."

CHAPTER FIFTEEN:

A PATH UNCHARTED

"What a sore few days we've had, eh?" quipped the old soldier. He lifted his chestplate off of his torso with a groan and set it on the floor next to him, beside the smith's hammock. The rocking of the ship made the task difficult, but he had certainly armored both up and down in far worse predicaments.

Alauren didn't answer. She seemed to hear nothing of her friend's words, in fact, and she stared at her quivering hands with empty, lost eyes. Her only movements were a light swaying as the hammock tilted in response to the waves, as well as the slightest of twitches that had erupted on her left eyelid.

"Hey," Edlevin said quietly. "You saved a life back there."

Alauren, again, didn't answer, still staring intently into nothing at all.

"Ally, are you-" Edlevin inquired, placing his hand on her shoulder.

Alauren jumped and gasped at the touch, recoiling heavily, like it was an icicle brushing against her skin.

"...alright?" the old soldier finished, mercifully ignoring the obvious answer.

"Yeah, I'm good," Alauren said shakily, and after a long pause. "Just shocked, is all. What the fuck did we just go through, Ed?"

"A rather unfortunate experience, the shock of which will pass," Edlevin assured softly. "Like dizziness after a shot to the head, which you're already familiar with."

Alauren nodded somberly. "You know... it doesn't feel like I thought it would."

"Killing?" Edlevin asked. He took a seat on a box next to her and began untying his boots. "Technically, you didn't-"

"I know," the smith cut off. "But helping, hearing the sickly sounds of it, with the smell of blood as it splattered across my face..." She took a deep breath and attempted to gather herself. "I've been expecting it to be more like what I felt after the longhouse, like a darkness looming over me."

"…And yet you feel nothing," Edlevin finished, a frigid familiarity in his voice.

"Cold," Alauren corrected. "Just… cold."

Edlevin stopped working on his boots for a moment and hunched over, resting his elbows upon his knees. "I know the feeling. However, it's one that I can't truthfully say that I relate to. Fully, at least."

"That's rare," Alauren quipped.

"It is," the old soldier affirmed with a sorrowful smile. "You know, through all the stories we've shared, I don't think I've ever told you of home."

"Fangirm?" Alauren posited. "You've told me a little."

"Just that it was my home, really," Edlevin replied. "We were a very practical people, you know, never shying away from the necessary parts of life. I knew my path, and even in my earliest memories, I recall playing with sticks and wooden swords, beating on some poor, downtrodden bush as if it were trying to invade."

Alauren smiled slightly at the thought and allowed her old friend to continue.

"I grew up prepared for the day you just experienced, Ally," Edlevin said with a voice as soft as the summer wind. "I ran through it time and time again in my head, imagining what I would feel and what I would do on the day I finally took my first life." He removed the first of his boots with a rough grunt, but soon picked up his thought. "While I cannot say that it was easy for me in the aftermath, my world prepared me for what we all knew was inevitable. I was trained, and I was able to properly prepare. I had an advantage."

"You're my advantage," Alauren said quietly. She scooted closer, laid her head on Edlevin's shoulder, and attempted to smile. "If there's a path through all this, you're the one who would know. You'll put me on the right road."

"I will," murmured the old soldier, hugging his old friend close. "Though I'm sorry I have to."

Alauren awoke with a start, feeling groggy and confused while her vision slowly blurred in. As was now common, waking from the rare bits of peaceful sleep she could find was an unending struggle. Even here, in a place she had come to know, she felt a pit in her stomach grow with every blink, and her nerves fluttered with every breath.

She forced herself up and out of the hammock. Going back to sleep now would do her more harm than good, she knew, even if her now-racing mind could find the quiet necessary to lull herself back into anything resembling slumber.

There were voices, faint and buried beneath the groaning of the hull, but the smith could recognize them as belonging to Edlevin and Ronnok. She took a moment to tidy herself up, grabbing fresh clothes procured from the Alsaran supplies. Again, she wore a button-up shirt of a dark blue hue, which was accompanied by simple, black trousers. After gathering herself, she followed the voices, which emanated from the luxurious map room.

"Ah!" Ronnok beamed, waving the blacksmith forward as she crept into the light. He was flanked by Eira and Thyra, who beckoned to their visitor with a similar warmth. Below the gestures of the Norts, there was a large piece of parchment affixed to the map table with flat-topped pins, one on each corner. "Come in, small one. We could use another pair of eyes."

"We're trying to figure out where to go," Edlevin added, leaning over the map like a lord studying the ever-moving boundaries of his domain. "Come on, take a look."

"Ay, lass!" Valin yelped. He was hardly noticeable, standing just over the tall table, and his large nose was practically lying at rest upon the fine wooden surface. "Find me alcohol!"

Alauren chuckled and stepped forward. She took a place next to Edlevin and silently inspected the map; it was a hand-copied drawing in black ink, with color thrown in sparingly on top of the sepia-colored parchment. There were a great many islands splayed on the further reaches of the Borean Ocean to the left side, while the right was dominated by the Brumal Sea and the Se'Vikoran coast. A large, uncharted mass laid between the Norts' current position (marked by a small wooden ship) and the possible destinations beyond.

"What is that?" Alauren asked, pointing to the gap, which was dyed with a notably darker blue color.

"A place called Leviath," replied the Chieftain. "Open ocean for many days, even with the wind at our back. To be beyond Odenseye, we will need to cross it."

"After that?" queried the smith. "It seems like there's a lot of island chains out there."

"Many of them uninhabited," Edlevin said with a remarkably chipper voice. He was clearly proud of his knowledge on the niche subject, and even happier at his opportunity to show it off. "However, there are a good many places that have built their own civilizations, with everything from mines to lumber yards."

"Many of them are wealthy, having trade with the nations," Ronnok added. "Our ancestors plundered those lands in years past, taking many things that could be sold and traded once we returned to our homes."

Edlevin nodded along and, once the Chieftain had finished his thought, eagerly continued. "The question now is: which one will hold the most riches? Which one will be the most interesting?"

"I don't know if I can help much," Alauren replied with a shrug. "I have no clue what's out there."

"You can throw in a vote, at least," Edlevin said. "We've been caught between Barina, in the south, or Flokil, in the north."

Alauren looked at the map once more, trying to locate Barina first. It was an easy task, as the island was rather large, and it looked to have many coves and bays that could help to hide the Nort fleet.

There, thought the smith, placing her finger on the island. She promptly slid her fingertip north on the map in an attempt to locate Flokil, finding the texture of the parchment to be rough and heavy. She passed many smaller archipelagos as she searched, which she read the names of silently. *Cligsgandr. Leniken. Arvyn.*

Arvyn?

Her finger halted and rested upon a relatively small island, near the exact center of the map's left side. It was vaguely crescent-shaped, and was surrounded by a few sand bars and habitable patches of land off the main coast. While it was a good deal larger than the Free Island of Alsara, it was dwarfed by the other isles and chains within the further reaches of the ocean.

Ronnok raised an eyebrow. "Arvyn?"

"No," Alauren said, waving the idea away quickly. "That name is just familiar to me, is all."

Edlevin furrowed his brow. "Ally, even I don't know of that one. Where did you hear of it?"

"I'm… not sure," Alauren muttered, returning her eyes to the map. "It's just familiar, is all."

Edlevin looked at his old friend with a furrowed brow and a doubtful glare, quite like a father being assured by his child that the drawings on the wall were a product of the family dog. "Ally," the old soldier demanded. "Where did you hear it?"

Alauren sighed and ran a hand through her hair. "Fine, Karlmaðr. Drell."

"Eh?" Valin grunted. "Did ye-"

"No, Valin," the smith answered gently. "I saw him in a dream, back on Alsara. He reached out to me. Maybe it wasn't even really him."

"Now, hold on," Edlevin grumbled, ever skeptical. "Drell is from the storyboo-"

"He's not, Ed," Alauren cut off. "I've spoken to him. I touched the scythe."

"You *what*?" the old soldier snapped angrily. "Ally, that was an incredibly dim thing to do! Sorcerer or not, that weapon is magic. You must be more cautious!"

"Take it down a few notches, Ed," the smith growled, feeling her own chest come alight with indignation. "It was a mistake, but it happened, and no harm was done."

"Lass," Valin stated loudly, unwilling to let the conversation veer too far off topic. "Tell me about this dream."

"Yeah, alright," Alauren said with a sigh and a rub of the temple. "My apologies, I find talking about things like this to be quite difficult."

"It's alright, lass," soothed the Dwarf. "Go on."

"I was next to a calm pond, with a cold breeze blowing around me and a bright moon shining off the water, but not hanging in the sky," the smith recounted slowly, trying her best to paint the memory with some level of detail. "He came out of the lake and told me something. Does everyone remember Xendra? The Solvari from Alsara?"

A number of heads nodded in confirmation, signaling her to go ahead.

"She came to talk to me in the Inn after all of you went to sleep,"

Alauren continued. "She was acting strange, very intently asking questions about who I was and where I came from. I thought her peculiarity was just my drunken state clouding my mind, at first, but something about her seemed truly off." She tapped the table a few times. "She mentioned going to see some friends on some far-flung islands. Drell, apparently, told me those islands were Arvyn, though I hadn't figured that out until now."

"Ye absolute bitchfist!" Valin growled, followed instantly by his eyes enlarging in horror. "Oh, uh… not you, lass. The twitwit in me scythe. He told me the whole story before ye even spoke, and every detail matches up."

"How did he manage to reach out?" Edlevin asked worriedly. "Is he a danger?"

"I don't rightly know," the Dwarf answered, after some consideration. "Some o' his magics even I don't fully understand. If he tries t' do any damage, though, I'll catch it."

"In any case, Drell said that Xendra had answers," Alauren continued. "I'm starting to believe him. Something about her wasn't right. It seemed like the sight of me triggered something in her, a curious determination."

"If she has knowledge, we will follow," Ronnok said. "To Arvyn."

Edlevin wheeled on the Chieftain. "Now, hold on, you're actually going to listen to that sorcerer? That's a bad idea."

Ronnok sighed deeply. He was obviously annoyed, but there was still an appreciation of the counsel in his weary expression. "You are not the only one to need answers. Our people were slaughtered during our escape from Odenseye, cut down with a brutality that you cannot fully understand, even given your own experience." He leaned forward, resting his hands on the table while the soft flickering of the hanging lanterns became the only light left upon his face. "Until now, we've had little idea of who they are or what they want. If there are answers on Arvyn, we go to Arvyn. Our spilled blood must be repaid."

Nearly on cue, a small hatch tucked away in a corner of the room opened, and a Nort Alauren recognized as Bjorn lowered himself from the top deck using the small port.

"Heyl," the young Northman said with a sheepish half-bow before his Chieftain. "Orr Svölt kölmen. Svatr sìvl höls hija."

Ronnok rubbed his beard, clearly troubled.

"What did he say?" Edlevin asked.

"Our scouts saw a few vessels at Alsara," the Chieftain replied, staring at the map thoughtfully. "Crimson sails. They shadowed us until they could see our fleet, and then backed off and sailed on. They are ahead of us now."

"Any idea who they are?" inquired the old soldier, trying to dig further. "Niralan?"

Ronnok shook his head. "I don't know. They seem uneager to engage, but we must be cautious. Enemies still stir in the dark."

"So, they do," Edlevin said, looking down at the map. "Well… Arvyn it is, then."

All around the table nodded in unison. The small speck of an island on the map seemed to call out to them in the dim glow, its mysteries foremost in their thoughts.

CHAPTER SIXTEEN:

PLANS

17th OF THE MORN OF HARVEST
NORTHERN YEAR 715

Alauren sighed in exasperation as her pencil, once again, veered off course, turning what was meant to be a straight line into a curving half-circle of failure. Even from her seat in the middle of the ship, at the bolted-down map table, she struggled to find solid enough ground to make any sort of headway.

"Damn it, Ed!" yelped the smith. "I wish the ocean wasn't such an asshole. Every time I go to make a stroke, it decides that it needs to roll us."

"You have to learn to roll with it, Ally," Edlevin replied through a half-mouthful of an exotic fruit. It was a crimson red orb with tan splotches here and there, and fiery-colored flesh poked out from where the old soldier's bite had broken the thin skin. His feet were kicked up on the map table as he relaxed, enjoying the snack from his comfortable seat in a padded chair. "No other way."

"Easy to say for someone who doesn't have to draw blueprints," Alauren chirped, shoving his feet down and out of the way. "Some of us have jobs here, you know."

Edlevin threw his arms up quizzically, while a smarmy smirk emerged on his face. "I have spent the entire morning fighting with rope and rigging! I have risen to the challenge of the sea and the sky, and I have found them kneeling before me!" His grin only grew at the sight of the smith's absent, unamused blinking. "I am the grand champion, and I think I deserve a break."

"Sounds like you made some manner of headway with the riggings," Alauren said after a moment, careful to distance herself from the bravado before speaking. "I've made three decent lines. Our frustration levels are quite different."

"What are you doing, anyway?" Edlevin asked. "And before you say that you already told me, an indecipherable grunt and a low utterance of 'plate' does not count as an answer."

The smith chortled lightly. "No, I suppose it doesn't. I'm working on some armor designs now that I've seen the Norts fight." She held the blueprint up, showing the beginnings of what looked like a chestplate. "They tend to use heavy, longer strokes, throwing their bodies into blows. I think I can design something around that."

"Let me know if I can be of assistance," Edlevin said, shortly before taking a noticeably moist bite of the fruit, slurping away at the juices to stop them running down his chin.

"You can start by eating that somewhere where I don't have to focus," Alauren grumbled once the noise had passed.

"Ah, fair enough," the old soldier replied. "Though…" He sprung to his feet and procured another small orb of the fruit from his pocket. "It's Fangirmish kolla fruit, rare in the north. Try it."

The smith sighed deeply. "I don't know, Ed. I'm still having trouble keeping food down."

"Still seasick?" Edlevin asked. "Or…?"

"The latter," Alauren replied amidst a particularly deep sigh. "Remember how I told you about those thoughts that just pop into my mind uninvited?"

The old soldier nodded silently.

"It seems like they've turned their anger inward," Alauren continued in a subdued murmur. "They attack me now, showing me things that…" She choked on her words for a single moment before regaining her steely demeanor. "Things I'd rather not see again. I feel like I'm constantly on the defensive, and I'm exhausted."

"I understand," Edlevin replied quietly. He extended the fruit towards the woman once more. "Have a bite, at least, and let it remind you of where you are now."

Alauren nodded, accepted the fruit, and bit into it ever so slightly, just enough that the juices could disperse in her mouth. The flavor was equal parts tart and sweet, mixing well with a texture that was balanced perfectly between chewy and firm. It sent a shock through her taste buds, not unpleasant, but strong and invigorating.

Edlevin raised an eyebrow. "Well?"

The smith nodded and took another bite. "It'll work."

"In times like these, that's all we can ask for," the old soldier affirmed with a nod. "Something that can keep us in the here and now."

Alauren glanced back down at her blueprints. "Speaking of, the sea is a bit too rough to sketch anything today, I think. Would you help me sort some of the smithing equipment up front instead?"

"Only if you make Valin help, too," Edlevin replied. "He spent the entire morning on the sidelines being wrong about how to run a sailing vessel. He needs something to keep him busy."

"Sounds like a plan," said the smith. "Fetch him, and I'll meet you up front."

Edlevin nodded and headed off to the main stairs in search of his charge.

After carefully rolling up her blueprints and depositing a few in a box below the table, Alauren stepped through the map room's door and toward the bow of the ship, where fresh equipment (including an anvil, lightly dented) lay in front of the old mess. Alsara had been able to spare a good amount of materials, though they only added to the gathered disaster that lay before her now. The smith took a deep breath and a final bite of the kolla fruit, savoring the morsel and the moment.

"I was drinkin'!" Valin bellowed as he approached from behind. "Ye coulda at least let me finish!"

"You never finish drinking, Valin," Edlevin growled derisively. He looked at his old friend with exasperation. "Did you know that it is scientifically proven that Dwarves bitch more than any other peoples on Odenseye?"

"Did ye know that yer a scientifically proven elk testicle?" retorted the Dwarf.

"Hey, that's just a theory!" countered the old soldier, gravely serious.

Alauren chortled and allowed a small smile to peek through her focused demeanor. "Now, there's no fighting when there's work to do, children."

Edlevin let out a deep, exaggerated sigh. "Fine! Where should we start?"

"Valin, clamber up over those boxes toward the bow and see if you can find any flux," the smith instructed. She paused for a moment before speaking further. "You know what flux is, right?"

"I'm a Dwarf," Valin deadpanned.

"Right, forge god and all that," Alauren replied. "There's got to be some around, and given the look of some of these ingots..." She picked up a slab of solid iron that was speckled with amber flakes of some impurity or another. "Further refinement will be necessary."

"Aye, on it!" cried the Dwarf. He sailed past the blacksmith in an admittedly impressive lunge, quickly disappearing into the clustered piles of equipment and material.

"Ed, try and sort these ingots out," the smith continued. "It should be easy to see their purity well enough to group them." She scratched her head, looking over the piles of equipment (and the rummaging Dwarf now somewhere within). "I'm going to try to look for coal and a crucible. We find this stuff, and I'll least have the basics."

"Aye," Edlevin concurred, tossing one last bit of fruit in his mouth. "I'll try to get you more than the basics, if its here."

"Let's hope," Alauren affirmed. She grabbed a long, flat tool and used it to crack open a wooden box. "Without my forge, I feel like I've lost a part of my soul. Like something is missing."

Edlevin gave no reply, though his eyes became noticeably heavier and more sorrowful. He buried them in the deep box of ingots, focusing on his work.

Rain slapped upon the deck of the *Skylðrek*, sending a steady roar through the bowels of the vessel. Though a few drips would occasionally find their way through the overlapping boards and into the smith's quarters, they would be swiftly carried away from her hammock by a taut tarp, which guided them harmlessly into a collection cup in the corner of the room. She took comfort in the sound of the thundering water, as it tended to drown out her darker thoughts.

Her eyes were heavy after a day of digging through dusty equipment, some clearly having been in its place for decades. There was enough, though, and dry land would bring with it the scorching heat of the forge once more. For now, she could do little but wait and pore over her rough blueprints by whatever meager light a hanging lantern could provide. A few more lines had been added to the drawings, a few more labels, and these most recent designs were beginning to take shape as something more than a piece of her imagination.

A knock came at her door, light and barely noticeable over the pounding rain above. She swung herself up in her hammock and set the print aside. "Come in."

The door cracked open slowly, with a loud creak. A single eye, highlighted by crimson threads of flowing hair, peeked out from behind.

Alauren giggled, which was immediately mimicked by the visitor. "Come on, then," snickered the smith, beckoning.

The Nort girl skipped inside without further hesitation. She held her hands behind her back and wore a grin whose warmth seemed to radiate throughout the room. Her hair drooped beautifully over her dress, the soft strands glinting now and again in the soft light.

"Solveig, yes?" Alauren asked.

"Jað, öa Solveig," the girl replied with a point to herself. "Eru ia Al…" Her face scrunched up, searching her memory. "Alouran?"

"Alauren," the smith stated, slowly and clearly. "Al-ore-ehn."

"Alauren!" Solveig repeated, quite accurately.

"Indeed!" beamed the blacksmith. "What can I do for you?"

The girl returned with the question with puzzled, starry eyes. "Uh… Eru…" She sputtered. "Ah! Löda svija!" She bounded towards the door and beckoned heavily. "Lö! Lö!"

Alauren obeyed, curious at the girl's fervor (and quite amused at her energy). Solveig led the way into the map room, where she practically dove under the table to root around in a box filled with scrolls and books.

"What is it?" asked the smith. "What are you after?"

"Iar fróð!" Solveig exclaimed. Her head was buried in the dusty box, and her voice was quite muffled; still, she rumbled and fumbled in the depths of the old crate with a vigorous determination. After a few more moments, she sprung backward and held out a piece of badly stained parchment, along with a rolled-up piece of more recently deposited work. "Fróð!"

Alauren took both with a raised eyebrow and looked over them carefully. The older parchment was in bad shape; the ink was bleeding, and several rips threatened to tear the scraggly pieces asunder. Still, she could make out plans for a Nort chestplate, drawn by the hand of someone unknown, likely decades ago. The blueprint she had drawn herself seemed to mirror the older design, differing only in the levels of completion.

"This is…" Alauren muttered, astonished at the similarity of the works. "This will save me some time, I think." She smiled warmly at the Nort girl. "Thank you!"

"Vjeði!" Solveig exclaimed exuberantly. She suddenly bounded off past her father, who hastily made way in the door for the barreling ball of energy that was his daughter.

"You seem to have excited her," Ronnok observed. "I hope this does not cause her to be restless tonight."

"Well, if she is, it can at least be worth it," replied the smith, still looking over the blueprints intently. "I even looked through those boxes and missed this one. How did she know it was in there?"

Ronnok chuckled, a low rumble that seemed to vibrate the wood around him, adding to the roar of the rain that still fell upon the deck above. "Children and boredom lead to them getting to know every detail of their surroundings." He erupted into a lopsided smile. "They stick their noses into *everything*."

"I'm glad she did," Alauren said. "I've been working on something, Ronnok, some plans for armor. My goal is to hit the ground running as soon as my feet can touch it again." She smirked. "Gotta prove my works to you, after all."

"That you do!" Ronnok exclaimed. "How much does that parchment help?"

"Well, it fills in some gaps, for one," the smith replied. "I've seen you fight, but not in the greatest of detail, and I'm not much of fighter myself. However, I understand a few things about how all this works." She laid the parchment down on the table and tapped it. "When a blade strikes plate, the armor is typically designed to deal with that in one of two ways: by locking it into place, allowing for a closure of distance and a disarm, or by deflecting it off to somewhere that would allow a counter strike. I want to make something that can do both interchangeably."

"Ambitious," Ronnok mused. "Though, I feel that armor such as this would be nearly impossible to make. There is a balance between hardiness and limberness that does not seem achievable. You cannot have flexibility without seams, can you?"

"Not at first glance," Alauren replied, never taking her eyes off the table and the designs that lie upon it. "I don't think any but the Norts, with their size and speed combined, could make this work, but your people are unique in how they fight." She looked up and smiled wickedly. "I'm going to be honest, it will be heavy and intricate, but once it's on, I bet you'll make good use of it."

"We will see, once it is reality," the Chieftain replied with a lopsided smile. "For now, focus on making it one."

"Aye," Alauren concurred, losing herself in the sketches once again. "I will."

"Ay, lass!" Valin's voice carried across the deck as the smith ascended into the midday sun. He was sitting across from Bjorn, who was busy counting out a number of flat marbles and placing them into a series of twelve concave pits, carved into a plank of wood that extended vertically in front of him. There were two side-by-side lines of six pits each, with two additional cavities on each end being doubly as large as the others. "Ye gotta play this game!"

"As long as it's not gambling, I'm interested," the Alauren replied.

"I'll second that!" Edlevin cried. He was standing on the ship's railing, holding a rope fast while Harald worked to repair a rigging on the mast above. "She's never angrier than when she loses something tangible!"

"Hah!" the Dwarf bellowed. "Naw, it's, uh... what's is called again, laddie?"

"Manakala," Bjorn replied with a heavy accent; though he could apparently understand the trade tongue, it clearly took effort for the man to parse what was being said, a fact evident given the pause and furrowed brow after the Dwarf's words. He placed the last of the marbles within the smaller pits, four marbles for each. "Starfall."

"Right!" Valin exclaimed. "Ye pick one of the holes on yer side, then drop the marbles one by one in the holes until yer out of 'em, and if ye land the last one o' yer hand in an empty hole, ye get to keep all the ones in the hole on yer opponent's side. The longer pit on the end here is yer reserve, and whoever ends up with more 'stars' in there wins." He chuckled. "Bjorn here is cheatin', swear on me mum!"

"Let me try, then," Alauren said, shooing away the Dwarf with a wave.

Bjorn obliged. Choosing to go first, he picked a pit four down from his reserve, managing to land his last marble within the longer cavity on Alauren's end. "This is called Mana," he explained, still navigating the trade tongue with some difficulty. "If you get last star in hand to go here, you go again." He chose the furthest cup to his right this time, dropping one marble in his reserve and laying the rest on Alauren's side.

Understanding immediately that she could not mirror Bjorn's opening moves, the blacksmith picked the second cup on her left, and the five marbles within allowed a free turn. A battle of wits and wills ensued as the combatants considered their every decision, trying to think as many steps ahead as was reasonable. Eventually, there were no marbles left in the smaller pits, and a final count had begun.

"Twenty-three." Alauren beamed as she dropped the last of her marbles back into the reserve. "That was a hard-fought battle, but I think I did pretty well."

"Not be hasty," Bjorn cautioned smarmily, trying his best to find the words of the trade tongue while he grinned widely. "I have twenty-five."

The words had hardly left his mouth before a handful of marbles impacted his chest. "Bullshit!" cried the smith. "You had some up your sleeve, didn't you?"

"Come now," Bjorn droned with a tone of melancholy. "Is only game. Why mad?"

"Uh huh," Alauren grunted. She narrowed her eyes. "A likely deflection."

"HAHAHA!" Valin bellowed. "I told ye he wasn't on the up and up!"

"Again," the blacksmith demanded. "I'll get you this time."

"Just, no hit with star again," Bjorn rumbled, picking up the loose pieces that had been whipped at him. "Stings."

"She can't make that promise!" Edlevin exclaimed with a laugh, still holding fast to the rope. "Proceed with caution!"

"Again," Alauren repeated. "Don't cheat and there will be no sting, I promise."

Bjorn obliged, though he was clearly skeptical, and the two combatants lost themselves in the depths of strategy once more.

CHAPTER SEVENTEEN:

THUNDER

*There is only one rule in close naval combat with
Norts: **Do not** engage in close naval combat with
Norts.*

– Nirali Field Manual, Section 2, p. 45

20th OF THE MORN OF HARVEST
NORTHERN YEAR 715

For those who made their way over the vast oceans that surrounded
Odenseye, fog was an ancient and well-known enemy. The bane of
even the most experienced captains, it blinded any caught within the
heavy mists to anything save for the lapping waves next to their vessel.
By the demand of nature herself, a frigid blanket would be pulled over
the heads of any that transited her waters, and she would simply laugh
at any who vainly tried to resist.

This foe, unlike many others, could not be injured nor killed, and
acceptance of its danger and a leaning towards caution were the only
ways to lessen the sting of defeat. Even with the challenges, the
Northmen navigated within the icy, gripping clouds with seemingly
no thought to the dangers it imposed. For, Ronnok had said, there was
little to fear from this foe in an open place like Leviath.

Alauren still found herself cursing the wretched existence of the
vile fog. For the smith, the resentment did not lie in the perils of
blindly stumbling around the waves; rather, it was in the effects that
it had on the mind. The mist seemed to penetrate into her skull and
cloud her thoughts just as much as it obscured the grand fleet of the
Nordiskan people.

For a day prior, the blacksmith had stared across the vast Northern armada with absent eyes and matching thoughts. She was able to let her mind drift away with the salty gust of the ocean winds, which billowed in the sail of the *Skylðrek* before storming back to the freedom of open water. The horizon captured her mind, and seldom were her eyes not gazing far beyond the thin line that separated sky and ocean. Her spot on a barrel near the bow was solitary, but quiet, something that she needed more than anything else while she was lost upon the numb waves of another sea, her seat often serving as her only attachment to the physical world.

Now, though, she peered out into the mists to be met with a reflection of the terrors that had come to pass. Like staring into a wall, the fog forced her mind to remain present, alert, and thoughtful. Screams careened through her head, and the physical memory of her own face caked in the warm, metallic spray of another life caused her cheeks to twitch in revulsion.

She relived the moments of battle time and again, lost to a vain search for some solace in the fact that she only did what was required of her. She tried with any might she had left to stir up feelings of acceptance, only to find a cold void of nothing at all; like staring into a dark well, there was no comfort found in the darkness.

Edlevin had warned her of as much. '*The coming days will be difficult*', he told his dear friend soon after the initial shock had passed. '*You may feel a true dread, or you may feel nothing at all. Be mindful, for it will pass in good time.*'

Alauren crossed her arms, the first of her movements in several hours. The autumn fog was borne within a biting air, and only now did the lingering cold penetrate her turbulent thoughts. She wore little but her typical shirt and trousers, and the consequences of that choice were becoming clear as tremors began to run through her extremities.

"You look cold," Ronnok observed, approaching from behind. He carried a large coat made of snowy, soft fur, a material which matched his own garment. "It may be a bit large, but it's the smallest we have. A child's size."

Alauren accepted the jacket gratefully, and with a nod. She wrapped it around her shoulders, and found it to be a near-perfect fit for her lithe form, even if it was a bit on the short side for her height. The soft leather of the inside was comfortable, and the fur genuinely helped to ward of the assault of the icy air.

"Did you sleep?" asked the Chieftain.

"No," the smith replied quietly. "My dreams aren't friendly at the moment."

"They rarely are, for us," Ronnok chortled half-heartedly. "Why do you think Norts drink so much?"

Alauren nodded in reply.

"The keg is open, if you need," the Chieftain continued. "It does wonders to get you rested. We're a good distance out from Arvyn, so be sure to take advantage."

"Thank you," replied the blacksmith. "I will."

"You and me both," Edlevin added, appearing from the clouds of fog at the far end of the ship. He wore a padded coat and gripped a mug tightly with both hands. "The damn creaking of the boat keeps me up otherwise."

"You've been spoiled by southern vessels," Ronnok grunted. "A real ship speaks to you. *Skylðrek* is a wise teacher, and you should listen to her words."

"Speaking would be fine," Edlevin retorted. "This ship shrieks! And I've got to listen to it for another week?"

"I've got to listen to you for another week," Ronnok riposted instantly. "We'll call it even."

The old soldier guffawed, quite unable to retort. Ronnok opened his mouth to speak on the matter further, but found himself interrupted by Eira's beckoning call. Though annoyed, he gave the guests a nod and wisely obeyed his wife's command.

"I'm fine, if that's what you're here to ask," Alauren said after a moment of silence.

"Well, yes, partly," Edlevin replied. "But I'm also quite bored. With Valin passed out below and an unchanging wind, there's little for me to do but keep what company I can."

"Mine isn't the greatest to keep right now," sighed the smith. "I keep looking into the fog, trying to peer through it. Seeing the horizon brings me small comfort."

"Those are the best kinds of comforts," replied the old soldier. "The kind that give you the will to see one more moment."

Alauren nodded in agreement. "Now, though…"

"Nothing to occupy you but the past," Edlevin finished with surety. "The pauses and the silence were always the worst part for me, too."

"Of war?" Alauren asked.

"Yes," Edlevin confirmed. He kicked at the deck with his boot, rolling a loose splinter around as he spoke. "When we would be moving around or fighting, even working the mess, life was alright. But in those quiet moments, where we had nothing to do but hurry up and wait, the agony of our idleness would drive us mad." He paused to shake his head. "You can't help but feel your mind drift back, like you've been set afloat on a river with only your hands to paddle against the current."

"It's more like a riptide than any normal current," Alauren said. "Even with oars, I could row and row, but it would just keep pulling at me, dragging me back."

Edlevin nodded. "There's little you can do against it but occupy yourself while it plays out. Even a riptide isn't so terrifying when you know it will subside."

The blacksmith nodded and took another look across the waves, hoping for a respite. Her feeble wishes were dashed, yet again, by the white wall that greeted her, and a clear look of distress found its way onto her face.

"Come on, then," Edlevin said with a pat on his old friend's back. "It's long past time that I teach you how to use that blade."

A bruise erupted on the smith's shoulder, radiating pain from a single epicenter where an impact had landed a mere second before. Sweat dripped from her brow as she collapsed to her knees, and her face was twisted into a gritty grimace while the sting cascaded through her back.

"You're nimbler than that!" Edlevin taunted. "Watch my overhead strikes. You can counter effectively, especially given your size."

The hours spent sparring with the old soldier had taken a toll physically, but they had done wonders to ease her mind. Each new ache in a muscle or sting on her skin brought with it a respite from a dread that creeped like a hungering shadow, ever waiting for the right moment to engulf her once more. Alauren was focused on combat, tactics, and exercise, and found herself mercifully free of that clawing embrace for the moment.

In terms of stemming the tides of despair, she had done well. Less successful were the attacks she drove at her old friend; though she threw the full weight of her determination behind every attempted strike, it only ever seemed to guide her hands toward thin air and another clean miss. Her blade was light and well-balanced, feeling like a feather that could slice the wind itself asunder, yet time and again she struggled to bring it anywhere near her instructor. Over and over, Edlevin would strike her with a bulky, wooden training sword, and he seemed to be willing to show little mercy in his lessons. So great was the old soldier's confidence that his skin was protected only by a North Elysian kaftan, a long-sleeved jacket of wool that draped to the knees. He was evidently unconcerned with the thought of being stabbed or sliced; even the tendons and flesh of his legs were entrusted to a simple pair of cloth pants and his own self-measured skill.

"Up, on your feet," Edlevin ordered confidently, clearly in his element. "Try again."

Alauren, keeping a stone-cold visage despite the pain, rose and planted herself in a wide stance. She bobbed here and there with the ship; her sea legs had developed well, and the rough waves of the Borean Ocean seemed far less daunting than they had just days ago. The smith narrowed her eyes and breathed in, apparently centering herself. Halfway through the breath, though, she snapped her back straight and jabbed out heavily, moving as fast as her body would carry her.

Edlevin casually batted the strike to his left and angled his wooden blade vertically, which caused the smith's sword to slip off the edge and towards the deck. In a single moment, her momentum and weight were directed awkwardly downward. It was a perfect counter, despite the woman's attempt to hide her coming assault. His reaction to the attack was instant, as if he had read her mind, and it even gave him a generous window in which to strike out at the now-tumbling blacksmith. He moved to stab downwards without delay, for he knew that a connection was all but assured.

Alauren was able to shift her weight at the last second and throw herself backwards in desperation. She expected to hit the deck on her back, helpless, yet only air rose up to meet her. The *Skylǒrek* had begun to ascend a wave, giving the smith just enough time to throw her body weight forward and right herself. She landed deftly on her feet and stood tall as the vessel came back up to meet her feet.

Wasting no time, she moved in once more and struck out with a few quick blows, twice high and once low, all delivered in less than a breath. Each attack was blocked by the wooden sword, but the deceptive strength behind the smaller woman's strikes sent the surprised soldier back on his heels.

Alauren sliced inward, coming to within a hair's length of Edlevin's arm, but found herself over-committing and losing her balance to forward momentum. The ship rolled again, rising behind her this time as the *Skylǒrek* began its descent on the same wave which had assisted her. She sailed forward with wide eyes, finding a fist rocketing towards her face.

"Watch out for that one, too," cackled the old soldier, uncoiling his grip just before it struck true. He used the hand to help balance his student, rather than to punish her, and he gave her a smile of warm amusement. "You don't want another knock to the head, right?"

"I can't get my balance because of the damn waves!" Alauren spat with visible frustration. She took a step back and threw her arms out in exasperation. "How am I supposed to do this right when I'm being rocked around?"

"Time and practice," Edlevin replied confidently. "If you can learn to control your center while at sea, fighting on a still surface will be as easy as dancing."

"You know I can't dance, Ed," jabbed the smith. "Pick better metaphors."

"I don't need to change perfection," Edlevin chuckled. "My words are worth more than gold, and you know it."

"Uh-huh," Alauren grunted condescendingly. She cast a glance across the deck towards Ronnok, who was hurrying towards the bow with an atypical urgency. After a worried look between them, the sparring partners followed the Nort with nervous springs in their step.

The Chieftain stood on the bow of the ship, holding on to the vertical figurehead. He was still as a stone and quiet as the fog that surrounded his vessel, and he had tilted his right ear towards the open waters off the prow.

"Is something wrong?" asked the smith.

Ronnok, though silent, held up a balled fist, beckoning silence.

Alauren, despite the ignition of her nerves, obeyed. She followed the Northman's action, listening closely to the sea as it churned against the ship. It was only now that she noticed how the general din of the Nort fleet had died to nothing but the creaking of the boats, and how quiet the tumultuous ocean could really be.

Edlevin, ever ready to help, moved to Ronnok's side.

"Do you hear it?" Ronnok whispered as the old soldier approached.

Silence returned as those present listened ever closer. There wasn't much, save for the lapping of waves and the 'speech' of the vessels to color the air. After a while, though, the faintest of voices could be heard carrying across the water, barely audible, but most definitely present. Accentuating the muffled speech were the sound of loud clunks, signifying a fully rigged ship.

"Se'Vikorans?" Edlevin asked in a subdued whisper, running through the possibilities in his mind.

"No," Ronnok answered with confidence. "Even now, they do not approach these waters. There is nothing of value to be found here."

Edlevin looked inquisitively at the Nort. "Not even fishing vessels?"

The Chieftain nodded. "This is a desolate, cursed place, wandered only by those with ill intent or little choice in the matter. Whoever is out there likely does not share the Se'Vikoran's kind dispositions."

"I suppose we had better ready for the worst-case scenario, then," the old soldier said with a nod. "I'll get suited up."

"There is no time," Ronnok replied. "They are close." He wheeled around and signaled an alert to his crew by opening and closing his fist several times. "Arm yourself and prepare."

Edlevin nodded, turned, and gave the blacksmith a pat on the shoulder. "Ally, there is a citadel on the third deck, at the aft of the ship. Stay there and stay safe."

"You can't go without armor," Alauren protested. "It's too dangerous."

"Less dangerous than being half-suited when they arrive," countered the old soldier. "Before you hunker down, go and fetch Valin. We may need him."

Alauren did so dutifully, plunging below the deck without further delay.

Men and women alike hurried to their duties, securing the young ones and setting the sails to a position where any potential damage would be most mitigated. Edlevin pulled his sword from a long box on the deck and unfurled it from a protective cloth wrapping. The blade was visibly blunted on the edges, owing to the combat it had seen over the past few days, but the point was as sharp and ready as ever. Just as in decades past, as in wars past, it would serve him with the same reliability and fortitude that it had shown throughout his life. He ran his fingers across the steel, breathing deeply as he noted his own grizzled reflection within the silvery sheen.

"Ugh, me head," a rattling voice erupted, sounding quite annoyed. "Feels like it was hit with a pickaxe, lassie."

"Yeah, yeah," Alauren muttered, similarly irritated. "Get topside."

Edlevin turned to see the disheveled Dwarf ascend into the cold fog with a scraggly beard and a pronounced grimace. He immediately shivered and glared towards the human.

"Good morning," the old soldier chirped cheerily. "Ally, go ahead and hole up. Stay safe!"

"You too," Alauren murmured. She spun and headed down into the bowels of the ship without further delay.

"Welcome back to the world of the living, Priest," Edlevin continued. "Get yourself ready. Someone is coming."

"Not some friendly folk, I take it?" Valin asked.

"If only we were so lucky," Edlevin replied flatly. "I don't know who they are for certain, but Ronnok is rousing his warriors. Sounds like the crimson sails his scouts spotted."

"Ye look rather under-armored for a fight," observed the Dwarf, with a point to Edlevin's fur garments. "Lotsa soft parts that can get poked."

"No other options," Edlevin curtly replied. "No time."

"Eh?" Valin grunted indignantly. "Hold still."

"What are you-" Edlevin attempted to say, but was cut off as Valin rushed zealously towards him.

The Dwarf moved quickly to pull a piece of charcoal from one of his many pockets. Picking a bare spot on the kaftan, he drew a "Y" symbol upon the wool and began to chant. "Creag!" he squawked, once, then twice, before the garment solidified into stone and wrapped itself tightly around Edlevin's torso with a third, final bellow from the stout Priest.

"There," said the Dwarf, quite proud of his work. "No more squishy spots."

"Much obliged," Edlevin mumbled with a nod, inspecting and adjusting the stiff stone coat to test its flexibility. The joints of the garment crunched as if they were pebbles loosely held together, and they provided just enough free movement to be practical. "Glad there was no fire this time."

"Karlmaðr!" Ronnok called from the bow of the boat, as quietly as he could. "With me!"

"Is that my name now, or...?" Edlevin began. He pushed the thought out of his mind with a shake of his head and joined his Nort host without further delay, ready to serve.

"You are not to leave this ship," Ronnok ordered. "Keep to the deck if you can, but guard the weak ones below if needed."

"With my life," the old soldier affirmed amidst a grim nod.

For a time, there was little more than the sound of riggings and voices growing ever louder to break the eerie silence in the dense fog. The Northmen could do nothing but wait silently, attempting to still their ragged breath while the cacophony of the enemy ships grew louder, each sound filling the warriors with eager excitement for the coming storm.

The Chieftain savored these few moments before a battle, when the air seemed to be at its most fresh, like he was standing in an untouched meadow, or next to a mossy stream deep within a hollow. The salty breeze of the moment gave him life, a purpose, a righteous cause with which to fight. Nordiska was all he had, and he would dive into the depths of Leviath itself to keep it safe. When it came to life and death, clan was all that mattered, and any who sought to endanger them would meet the latter fate.

The clunks and voices went silent, responding to the growling call of an authoritative voice. The enemy had caught on, understanding too late the extent of their drift upon these choppy waters. Ronnok, from his place near the bow, gripped his axe handles tightly and readied, steeling himself for what was to come. A dark silhouette came into view, seeming like a shadowy monster upon the waves of the ocean, shrouded and hungering.

The vessel grew close, its details becoming clear as it lumbered through the fog like a lost giant; it was a southern carrack, tall and imposing, and its lifted deck easily overtook that of the squat longship by the measure of two average Norts, were they stacked on each other's shoulders. The southern ship was elegantly decorated, covered in red and black paint in a tiger-striped pattern, further adorned with crimson sails and a figurehead of a green-eyed needlefish whose single, short tooth jutted out from the front of its head.

The carrack ran along the starboard side of the longship, close enough to make brief contact and facilitate the trading of paint. Men jumped from the higher deck, each of them adorned in scrappy but well-built plate armor that covered their most vulnerable points. While the hard steel and chain mail was clearly a patchwork, they were held together by the bonds of experience, and each piece was well chosen for strength and flexibility.

The assailants fell fully into their assault, thundering onto the deck before tucking into heavy forward rolls. They used their momentum to spring up like grasshoppers, instantly squaring into a ready fighting stance.

Ronnok engaged the closest, a man noticeably shorter than he. The Chieftain rained down blows upon the heavy armor with both axes; each strike was a dose of pure Nort fury, denting and sundering the plate. The human's defense held, though, allowing the man to duck one of Ronnok's hits and deliver a high slash, which bit into the left arm of the Northman, drawing blood.

Ronnok, quite perturbed, endured the pain, swiping low and hard to the left with both axes. The strike took one of the armored man's legs out from under him and sent him tumbling to the deck in a heap, where he was unable to regain his footing. The enemy could do little but writhe about like a turtle as he was bucked about by the choppy waves.

The Chieftain smirked wickedly, quite happy to assist the pathetic creature. He roughly kicked away the human's weapon and gripped the man by the back of the collar, lifting him by the scruff like a kitten. His smirk erupting into a full grin, the Northman deposited the man into the small gap between the two vessels. A yelp and a splash were the last sounds of the invader, for the weight of his plate dragged him down, into the cold and unending abyss of Leviath.

Ronnok turned to survey the scene. Edlevin was at work running his sword through a gap in another opponent's armor, while the rest of the Norts similarly found their own creative methods of attack. Eira, for instance, used the curve on the rear of her axe to hook an opponent's chest armor on the side before slamming him down with force. The sick *crack* of the man's skull and neck on the deck ended the conversation without further argument.

The corpses of the rest of the armored attackers were concentrated around the main stairs, as if they had been trying to establish a pocket of resistance within the bowels of the *Skylðrek*. A common tactic in the south, Ronnok noted, but one most unsuitable against the Northmen, for even those below were ready to fight with bestial vigor in defense of their own. The carrack, realizing the failure of their boarding party, attempted to turn away and break off, likely wanting to regroup.

Thyra, for her part, was hard at work ensuring that the southern vessel would not escape their punishment so easily. Joined by a few others, she procured a thick woven netting from a box and hurled it over the side of the carrack, where metal claws found their hold and bit into the wood. A heavy, sturdy ladder was formed, and moors on the longship's deck ensured that the *Skylðrek* remained alongside their quarry for as long as the Northmen deemed necessary.

The Nort counterattack was as organized as it was overwhelming, carried out with the efficiency of well-practiced warriors. They scaled the netting in a mere breath, brandishing their weapons all the while, and the few humans who stood at the summit to meet them quickly found demise, whether it be at the end of an axe or after a short trip to the waiting blades of the defenders below.

Ronnok and his clanmates stormed forward onto the deck, creating a salient and driving their wide-eyed enemies back on their heels. The fighters here were unarmored, he noticed, wearing a gambeson at most, but they fought just as fiercely as their counterparts;

like all southerners, they were quite unwilling to suffer barbarian feet upon their 'civilized' vessel of war. A small number battled bravely to hold back the storm, allowing their comrades a chance to regroup and rally.

The Chieftain engaged the last of the zealous defenders, batting away the woman's downward-swinging sword hard to the left. A vertical drop of his axes relieved her of her arms, and a single sideways swipe removed her fully from the equation.

Two freshly rallied opponents engaged him a single breath later, one on each side, both armed with long polearms. They stabbed in, one high and one low, which forced Ronnok to contort his body wildly in an attempt to avoid the blows. Still, one of the blades caught him on the lower ribs and lacerated a muscle near his belly. The attackers backed off, smirking while their enemy bled and groaned in pain.

Again, the humans drove the attack, and again, Ronnok was forced to contort and dodge, unable to close the distance to the enemy without risking further injury. One of the men cackled as he backed off again, preparing to jab out from a safe distance once more. Ronnok, however, had grown quite sick of the games; he launched one of his axes at the jovial attacker, where it struck deep into his chest cavity with a pronounced crunch.

The Chieftain dodged another polearm stab by the remaining man, ducking down and left before swinging his axe to the right, cleaving the wooden shaft of the longer weapon. He abruptly pivoted and shifted his momentum back to the left, burying his weapon in the human's skull and ripping it out before the corpse hit the deck, convulsing heavily.

Ronnok retrieved his other ax, finding a moment of difficulty as he tried to pry it out of the man's cloven and twisted ribcage. "Istumaji!" he snapped, cursing the oversized gut of the corpse as the axe finally broke loose. He stepped back, took a breath, and looked around.

Blood covered the dark wooden deck of the carrack, the Chieftain's own included as it dripped off of his side. The Southerners, for their part, seemed to be retreating, meaning to guard the helm's steep stairs with a wall of bodies. Two Norts, meanwhile, were badly wounded, covered in the blood of their foes, as well as ample amounts of their own.

"Protect the Nirali!" a voice screamed, gruff and old, coming from a man dressed in a brilliant blue naval coat atop the helm. "Now!"

Ronnok furrowed his brow. Nirali, seemingly, had no place on a southern vessel, nor would they have good reason to be in a place like Leviath.

Rarely did one have time for such thoughts in a battle, and one of the humans took full advantage of the Nort Chieftain's momentary distraction. He charged fully and quickly, slipping between Eira and Harald's relentless assaults on the enemy battle line before slamming into Ronnok's lower chest with a metal shield. Both combatants were knocked off balance, but the Chieftain was able to keep his wits and grab onto the edges of the buckler. He carried it backwards with him as he stumbled, using the momentum to throw both man and blocker hard over the carrack's railing. A loud *thump* confirmed that the enemy had hit the longship deck below, and the Northman heaved himself back to his feet.

Ronnok grunted in annoyance as a new wave of southern warriors, suited in armor, emerged from the vessel's rear hatch. Though bloodthirsty and furious, he realized the folly of fighting this opponent on their terms, and on their own territory. The Norts had secured only a small portion of the upper deck, and dozens of men and women stood between them and whatever could be considered victory. Unorthodox tactics were needed.

"Víkva!" Ronnok called to his fighters. "Víkva!"

Fast as lightning, the Norts leaped back from their respective engagements, ripped out the moors of the netting which they had used to ensnare the carrack, and jumped back to the longship. The southern vessel, finally, was able to pull away, and it made a hard turn to port without further delay before disappearing frantically into the fog.

Ronnok breathed heavily and regained his bearings. The Norts were either scrambling to ready for another attack or attending to the wounded, while Edlevin held the man that had been thrown overboard at the point of his blade.

"We need the short one!" Ronnok growled, grabbing some curled rope. He strode to the terrified prisoner and began tying him tightly.

"Valin?" Edlevin asked incredulously. "He ran down the stairs when the first wave hit the deck."

"Get him, Karlmaðr!" ordered the Chieftain. He kneed the squirming captive in the back, bringing about enough stillness to finish the knots.

Edlevin nodded and disappeared below deck before emerging with an annoyed Dwarf in tow.

"What the shite do ye need me fer?" Valin yelped. "All I got t' fight with are runes, ye madman!"

"Short one!" Ronnok bellowed, silencing the Dwarf instantly. "Can you disperse this fog? We must be able to see our foe."

"That's like askin' me if I can make it stop rainin'!" Valin replied gruffly. "Nature doesn't obey me, no matter what kinda magic I've got!"

"What about the annoying man?" pushed the Chieftain, his voice strained with irritation. "You said he has magic you do not understand. We must end this quickly. If they get away unscathed, it is likely that they will return reinforced."

"That's a dangerous road to venture down, ladd-" Valin began.

"Yes or no?" Ronnok barked. "Can he help?"

Valin cocked an eyebrow at the scythe, listening for a moment. After a skeptical glare and a subdued scoff towards the blade, he lifted it high.

The pointed end began to pour smoke, far more than usual, emitting a sizzling sound that could be heard across the ship, like bacon frying in a pan. The blade glowed a crimson red, blinding to any who looked directly into it. Crackling bolts of static reached out and snapped at the fog, the heat condensing the mists into drops which fell heavily to the deck. The thorns that wrapped around the hilt crawled and creeped, as if they had a life of their own, snaking around the shaft and coiling closely to the metal.

Nothing happened.

"Come on ye arse, stop bein' a tool!" growled the Dwarf. A grimace erupted on his face. "Call me that again and I'll throw ye t' the bottom o' the ocean, ye crushin' wank! Do the damned thing!"

Drell, evidently not willing to take the risk, complied. The scythe whined for a moment before sending out a thin shockwave, like a blurred distortion above a campfire, burning away the fog as it soared outward, yet doing seemingly nothing to the delicate sails of the longship or the living beings on board.

The fog condensed into drops and fell to the sea, forming a massive cube-shaped gap that stretched the entire Nort fleet. The carrack, revealed as the fog dispersed, was rapidly retreating just ahead of Ronnok's vessel, putting distance between the two combatants. Behind the *Skylðrek*, four other carracks had entangled in combat with the armada, each of them embroiled in their own desperate struggle to escape the grasp of the Northmen.

In the distance, well beyond the ships, towering walls of dense fog rose vertically before falling into rain when they touched the now-stationary shockwave. Above the crackling field of magic, a darkened sky threatened with a low rumble, like the clouds themselves had become a combatant, grim, and ready to die. An easterly wind began to blow, intense and unrelenting, bitingly frigid and heavy with the smell of the sea.

Ronnok smiled devilishly. "It is time. We take them now."

"That ship is too fast with the wind!" Edlevin yelled above the roaring gusts. "We'll get bucked around too much in the chop to catch up!"

"So, they think!" Ronnok yelled back with confidence. His hair began to become soaked with rain, and the drops from above only grew larger in size as the moments went on. "Northmen! Þrymja!" bellowed the Chieftain, to which the Norts roared in agreement.

"Thunder?" Edlevin translated, confused.

"Thunder!" Ronnok confirmed with a vicious smile. "A rare occurrence, dangerous, powerful, and used most sparingly. Go, fetch the little one! All of us must participate."

"In what?" thundered the old soldier, struggling to lift his voice above the sounds of the weather and the sea.

"You'll see," Ronnok growled, annoyed at the delay. "Just do as we do!"

"This oughta be fun, eh?" Valin quipped, holding the scythe high while the old soldier obeyed the command.

Edlevin did not have to move, for the smith (urged along by Alvilda) made her way with the mass of Norts pouring from the ship's hatches. The deck became shoulder-to-shoulder with men, women, and children, all swaying with their vessel as it tilted here and there, each of them hardly noticing the falling rain. They brought with them large oars which were affixed to the ship's railing; two operators manned each of the eight stations, with four stations on each side. Ronnok stood at the bow, peering at the fleeing southern ship with a wicked grin as the rain ran from his braided beard.

"What's going on?" Alauren queried, quite confused. Her hair whipped in the wind, and she stared in amazement at the mountain-sized walls of fog that surrounded them.

"I honestly don't know, Ally," Edlevin yelled with a shrug. "Thunder, apparently."

"Thund-?" Alauren began to ask. Her words, though, were cut off by loud grunts from the Northmen as they began to row.

"HUH!" bellowed the Norts, loud and guttural, repeating once and again, in a perfect rhythm with the movement of the oars.

"HUH!" Even the children's voices seemed to be low and vicious.

With each chant, the clouds above seemed to grow darker and more menacing, as if a deep night was summoned by the rowing and the cries of the Northmen. Flashes from within the black sky signaled the coming of lighting; bright cracks in the heavens jumped from cloud to cloud, and each of their leaps were followed by thunder that rumbled throughout the bowels of the *Skylõrek*.

A glance over the Nort fleet showed the smith that many of the other ships had fallen into formation, mimicking the lead vessel perfectly in their rowing rhythm, as if they could feel and follow the beating of a single heart.

"HUH!" continued the Norts, this time joined by the old soldier. He nudged Alauren, who shivered uncomfortably.

"Edlevin, I don't understand," she grumbled. "What's going on?"

"You ask me like I have an answer!" Edlevin said with an exasperated cackle. Rain rolled across his face and dripped heavily from the stubble on his chin as a smile came about. "Just do as they do, and we'll see!"

Alauren thought for a moment, before nodding and grunting along with the Norts.

"HUH!"

Strangely, the low, primal sound brought with it an instant feeling of unity, as if her voice blended with the many to form a single call to something beyond the clouds. The blacksmith felt a rush of strength in the harmony, emboldening her to be louder and more forceful as her spirit seemed to rise to the heavens. The water upon her head began to sizzle and pop, evaporating harmlessly while strands of her now-dry hair rose of their own accord.

"HUH!"

The Northmen cried out in unison as the clouds began to coalesce and crawl towards the carrack, stalking it across the dark waters. Each aboard the Nordiskan fleet could feel a crackle in their spine and a buzz in their teeth, as if they had been run through with a strike from the tempest above. The lightning grew brighter and more intense, cascading towards the center of an ever-growing vortex of black thunderclouds. They twirled like a maelstrom of myth, reaching forth from the heavens as if they were the finger of a god, seeking out the unworthy.

"HUH!"

With a final call, each soul on the vessel felt a shiver run down their spines, like they had suddenly dipped into a frigid pond in winter. It was unlike anything the smith had ever felt, a powerful wakefulness that lifted her heart and steeled her mind. The world, in that single, fleeting moment, felt as if it was a milky glass marble, all the problems and ambitions within nothing more than a small bother in the palm of her hand.

She felt invincible.

Within a breath of the thought a single, massive pillar of lighting, crackling with energy, formed in the exact middle of the cyclone, borne from a spiderweb of coalescing bolts before rushing forth as a united power. The flash lasted a mere instant, yet it provided ample lighting for the show.

The carrack charged with energy as it was struck by the buzzing sword of the heavens, the wooden hull glowing in a luminescent white for a breath while it tumbled upon the waves. With a great flash, the southern vessel suddenly splintered outwards in a magnificent explosion, sending pieces of hull, sail, and living beings soaring across the waves, while small tendrils of lightning jumped back into the clouds from whence they came. A shockwave hit the *Skylðrek* hard and rumbled heavily along the vessel, stumbling Alauren backwards. Thunder sundered the air, vibrating even the choppy waters of the ocean.

"Þrymja!" The Norts cheered in unison, raising their arms to the skies above in praise. The violent cyclone, content with its bloodshed and its thanks, returned to the sky and quickly dissipated.

"Amazing," Edlevin said with a fascinated grin. "I get the feeling our problems with whoever was on those ships are over."

"Glad I'm on this side of the fight," Valin agreed with wide eyes. He finally lowered his scythe and allowed the fog to begin to creep back in.

"Bask in this, guests of Nordiska," Ronnok bellowed with a wicked, lopsided grin upon his face. "For even the Norts rarely see the will of the gods unleashed. It will be many a morn before it happens again."

The four remaining carracks, now freed from their bindings, sped away from the Nort fleet and into the encroaching fog as fast as their heavy vessels would take them, wanting no further part in this fight.

CHAPTER EIGHTEEN:

MERCY

It is unlike a Fangirman to be open-minded, just as it is unlike a Nirali to be at peace. They are a proud empire, older than Elysia, yet the goals and morals they obstinately cling to are becoming less relevant with each passing morn. The future of Odenseye cannot be a stubborn attempt to ignore the coming of darker days, nor can it be a shocking complacency towards meeting the momentous moments of the next dawn. We have moved on, yet they live as normal, working, sailing, drinking, blind to anything aside from their musty sense of honor while the world crumbles around them. Fangirm may be the largest and oldest empire on this continent, yet size will only hasten their downfall, should the time come. They live in what is nothing more than a dream, and so the sands of time will consume them all.

– Gauis Truvani, in "Nations of Odenseye"

21st OF THE MORN OF HARVEST
NORTHERN YEAR 715

The young man lay bound in the deepest recess of the longship, sequestered within a dark storage hold at the valley of the vessel's bilge, spending his miserable hours being bucked hard against the wooden hull with every wave, unable to protect or right himself in the incessant churn. Warm, salty water sloshed against his skin, while a stuffy, blanketing heat caused him to sweat out whatever fresh water was left in his body. The darkness penetrated his mind, and he was left only with the images of his experience.

He had taken a level of punishment that impressed even the barbaric Northmen, beaten and lacerated by many members of this ship's savage crew, each of them united in their pleasure at his suffering. Fitting behavior, in his mind, for their unwashed, uncivilized type. Even through his grievous (yet carefully inflicted) injuries, he revealed nothing.

A hatch above him opened once again; he flinched instinctively, the rush of relatively fresh air typically a portent of pain. A small man, clearly not a Nort, descended into the humid, stuffy depths of the longship, bearing a small lantern. The flickering light was like a burning sun to the prisoner's eyes, causing him to slam them shut as he recoiled in clear discomfort. After a moment, he hazarded a peek, and recognized the grim face that had held him at the point of a sword a day earlier.

The visitor was covered in a beading, fresh sweat, while his hair crisscrossed his face wildly. Despite this disheveled look, he carried himself with an unfamiliar air of respect and confidence, an unexpected sight on this ship of beasts.

"I must admit, your resilience impresses me," the visitor said. He moved close, untied the bonds of the prisoner, and took a seat on a box near the entryway. He set the lantern upon a hanging hook, where it swayed here and there. "Few others could endure such pain for so long without even revealing a name."

"They don't deserve it," the younger man snapped weakly, rubbing swollen skin where the ropes had ground against his skin. He risked a few momentary blinks, allowing his eyes to adjust to the light. "Savages."

"Spoken like a true Fangirmish warrior," the man chuckled through a weary voice, one colored by age and experience. He procured a flask of water and handed it over. "I fought with a lot of your folk; you know. Hearty and strong, the lot. But, stubborn most of all."

"We didn't build an empire by giving in," the prisoner gasped after several large gulps from the container. He could focus his vision now, and he eyed the visitor warily.

"No, you didn't," the older man agreed. "Stubbornness won't help you here, lad. What can I call you?"

"Syla," sighed the prisoner, a matching weariness draping over his voice. He cleared the sweat from his brow with a shaky swipe of the hand. "My name is Syla."

"That wasn't so hard," the older man said. "You could have been saved many bruises."

"I gladly give it to a human," Syla snarled, his voice alight with a sudden, righteous fury. "Those savages? They don't deserve to look a civilized man in the eye."

"There's more to them than you would like to think," the older man pointed out. "They are artists, for instance."

Syla scoffed. "Artists? They look like they haven't experienced a bath in weeks! How could they have a mind for the finer things?"

The older man smirked. "They express their creative pursuits in their own way, of course." A full grin erupted on his face. "Tell me, have you ever heard of the blood eagle?"

Syla's brow furrowed. "No."

The older man huffed in self-affirming delight, clearly pleased to have already guessed the answer. "I thought not. You see, when the Norts have grown sufficiently angry with a particular guest, they put their skills in the macabre to good use." He pulled a small knife and a piece of fruit from a pouch near his waist before continuing. "They lay the man or woman in question down upon an altar, usually to one god or another."

Syla chuckled derisively. "You mean to tell me they have gods?"

The older man chortled while he sliced away at the snack. "Of course. Many, or so I hear." He waved away the thought, returning to the point at hand. "The Norts then take a curved blade, usually covered in a hot oil, and remove the skin from the back of the sacrifice. From there, they separate the ribs from the spine using a hammer and a sharp tool. The sound is quite gut-wrenching for any Southerner, of course, but the Norts tend to find it soothing."

The man took a bit of cut fruit and offered it to Syla, which was gratefully (but carefully) accepted. The prisoner held the slice in his mouth, savoring the sweetness, the rush of flavor that interrupted the stale, musty agony that he had known for many hours.

"The ribs are set to the side, so as not to be in the way for the next step," continued the older man. "You see, this is when their grand vision comes together, when the true beauty of their art is exposed.

They hook the lungs, each with a small, curved knife, and pull them through the new openings. From there, they are strung up upon poles, and they appear as wings upon the subject, who is still very much alive."

"Horrific," Syla stated coldly, shaking his head in disgust. Another swipe of the hand cleared the fresh sweat from his forehead before continuing upwards to run his fingers through his hair. "An act of barbary."

"To most. To the Norts, it is a thing of beauty," the older man replied, chuckling darkly. "I look forward to seeing it."

Syla stared at the floor for a moment and swallowed hard. He picked at the skin around his thumbnails, an instinctive action as his thoughts raced within his mind. He suddenly shook his head and scrunched his face in a furious disgust. "You can't just watch them do that to me!" His voice, though urgent, was soft and fleeting, resembling a desperate plea more than a demand. "It isn't a fitting death for a civilized man."

The older man leaned in, coming close enough that the prisoner could feel the warmth of his breath, even in the moist conditions of the bilge. "I'm not just going to watch, Syla," he growled, revealing a hooked knife hidden within a fold in his clothes. "You have a choice to make."

"I… I can't," Syla stammered, his skin white as the lightning that had detonated his ship. "My honor dictates-"

"Your honor?" the older man cut off angrily. "Will it be honorable to die helpless by the hands of those you consider savage?" His voice grew darker with each passing word, the last of them delivered with a menacing, protracted growl. "Do not think me unfamiliar of your customs, boy."

"I… I-" Syla stammered, half-sobbing and overwhelmed, having only a pained dread in glossy eyes that grew increasingly rapid in their movements.

"I can give you a death required of the Enduring Empire: quick, and at the hands of one worthy to deal it out," the older man continued, returning to a gentler tone as he leaned back. He twirled the fruit knife in his hand and eyed it with a dreadful gaze that matched that of the prisoner. "The choice for me would be easy, but I would not think to rob you of your own destiny by making it for you."

Syla shrunk back for a moment, feeling his chest heave. This choice, momentary life or immediate darkness, seeing another dawn or fulfilling a duty, was one that every Fangirman had prepared for, at length. Death was familiar to them, and so they ever spent their lives making ready to greet the dark with a smile.

All those years of preparation, yet the choice was made no easier.

After a moment, Syla took a single, heavy breath and steadied himself. "At least let me know your name first, so I may know who sends me beyond."

"Edlevin," the older man stated without emotion.

"Edlevin of?" Syla asked, meeting the soldier's gaze. "From what nation do you hail?"

Edlevin sat silently for a moment and began to bounce his knee, like a passenger impatiently awaiting their scheduled carriage. "Edlevin the wanderer," he said after a while, "for I know no nation." He leaned forward and took a deep breath. "It is irrelevant. Will you answer the questions or not?"

The man's eyes sank for a moment, yet he acquiesced with a nod. "What do you wish to know?"

"Who you are, first off," Edlevin said. "You and your crew."

"Privateers," answered the prisoner. "I'm from Fangirm, of course, but we come from all corners of Odenseye."

"Hm," Edlevin grunted. "Why are you attacking Norts? There's a war going on. War means refugees, which means profit for your type. Why go after the dangerous prey?"

"We're not common scoundrels," Syla snapped pridefully. "We are the best for-hire group upon the Borean Ocean."

"Were," Edlevin corrected coldly.

"Were, yes," the prisoner conceded with a dejected nod, rubbing his hands together nervously. "We miscalculated, lost our position in the fog. We drifted right into you."

"Unfortunate for you," Edlevin replied coldly. "Was the Nirali there for the usual reasons?"

"Wha-?" Syla grunted with a half shake of the head.

"When Niralan hires privateers, they always send a junior officer to supervise," Edlevin said. "He was there to watch you?"

"Oh! Oh, yes," the prisoner quickly replied. "We were hired to strike out at the Nort fleet, preferably in ship-to-ship combat. We wanted to keep quiet behind you and wait for favorable conditions for a hit-and-run attack, swarming one or two ships before speeding off."

"What went wrong?" Edlevin asked, now bouncing his leg casually.

"You stopped," Syla stated matter-of-factly. "We were unprepared for that, and we were spotted. The Nirali commanded us to sail on as if we had no business with you, then wait for the opportunity we needed from ahead."

"To what end?" Edlevin queried. "Why were you following us?"

"Don't know," muttered the prisoner. "I know Niralan wanted something you have, but that's the most I ever gathered."

Edlevin sighed deeply. "I feared as much. Continue."

Syla obliged, visibly eager to speed the end of these final, excruciating moments. "We first picked up the Nirali at the Arvyn Archipelago a few morns back, where our boss was invited to a dinner to get to know his new crewmate." He huffed with a laugh as his eyes glossed over. "Captain Tanis had seen through battle after battle, war after war, with a stone gaze and unending courage. That night, he came back scared *shitless*."

Edlevin's eyebrow raised with curiosity. "By what?"

"Damned if I know," Syla answered absently. "Tanis didn't say a word. The dockworkers, though, seemed as strange as Lunari to me. Could have had something to do with it."

Edlevin scratched at his stubble and leaned a bit further forward. "Strange? How so?"

"Ghost white, more so than I've ever seen in a human," Syla replied. He bit his lower lip, as the memory seemed to make him quite unsettled. "They had these bloodshot eyes, with matted up hair and an unsure manner of speaking." He eyed the straight knife, still fluttering about in Edlevin's hand. "Just... strange folk."

The old soldier nodded silently. "Anything else?"

"No," Syla said. "I was a professional. I didn't ask questions. I did my job."

Edlevin nodded solemnly and sighed deeply; dread once again began to surface in his eyes while his teeth ground below them. He cut another piece of fruit with his knife and offered it, holding it out to the prisoner. The young man gratefully accepted, reaching for what he knew to be his last meal.

Edlevin's blade abruptly shot forward and punctured the young man's chest at the heart. Syla met the soldier's gaze with one of great fear, fighting against a tide tugging him away. His eyes darted rapidly this way and that before slowing and, eventually, succumbing to the dark. He slumped backwards, and the standing seawater at the bottom of the Skylðrek became heavy with cloudy, crimson streaks.

Edlevin stood, wiped the viscera from his knife on a box, and used the blade to cut another piece of fruit. "Honorable, they call it," he murmured, the words dripping in an ichor of caustic acidity. Biting the morsel away from the razor edge, he hefted himself up and through the hatch once more, eager to be away from the grim sight.

"He's dead," Edlevin stated flatly as he climbed the main stairs of the *Skylðrek*. The words drew a curious stare from the trio of Valin, Alauren, and Ronnok, who were seated on barrels near the railing. Each held a mug that sloshed along with the choppy seas, making their best effort to contain their drink within their cups.

"Did you...?" Alauren trailed off, unsure of whether she wanted an answer.

It came, regardless, in the form of Bjorn launching Syla's body out of the main stairway and over the railing, producing a loud *gloop-splash* sound from somewhere within the churning waters.

"I did," Edlevin confirmed, grabbing his own mug from a box and filling it from a newly tapped keg. He downed the hoppy, bitter beer rapidly and, after a gasp for breath, reached for a refill. "I gave him a choice, and he made it."

Alauren didn't react with the shock that was expected by her old friend, instead choosing to simply nod before returning her eyes to her cup.

"I hope you didn't end him before he could be of use," Ronnok grumbled. He pawed at a bandage on his lower torso, trying to scratch an itch beneath. "I could have done so easily enough."

"I got him to speak, yes," the old soldier reassured. "By promising him death, oddly enough."

"Shame," Valin chuckled. "I wanted t' see what the big man could do with him."

"Next time, short one," Ronnok promised, returning the chuckle. "What did he say, Karlmaðr?"

"Niralan has a presence on Arvyn," Edlevin stated somberly. "Where they go, ill winds blow."

"Hm," Ronnok grunted, musing for a moment. "What are they doing on such a remote island?"

"The machinations of the Nirali people, and their military, are often indecipherable," the old soldier said with a sigh.

The comment drew an eye roll from the smith. "You try too hard to sound deep, old man."

Edlevin shrugged and smiled smarmily, quite like a father who had just delivered history's worst joke. "Are you truly questioning the operation of my varied, colorful, intricate, principled, exemplary, and well-seasoned vocabulary?" He chuckled at his own jest, which, to his delight, drew a half-smile from the blacksmith. "I digress. The kid didn't know much, beyond that we were to be attacked. In any case, we should avoid Arvyn for the time being."

"No," Ronnok rumbled with a shake of the head and a scratch of the beard.

"No?" Edlevin echoed, taken off guard.

"Karlmaðr, think," urged the Chieftain. "Niralan has a presence in the west. They are attacking us. Why?"

"You've often fought against them," the old soldier pointed out. "They could just want you gone. Permanently, this time."

Ronnok shook his head, practically begging the man to accept the true answer. "When Niralan wants something of violence done, they do it themselves. When have you known the Nirali to use privateers?"

Edlevin closed his eyes, nodded, and breathed heavily. "When the fight is not their own. When someone else needs something done."

"The threads are there, Karlmaðr," the Chieftain pushed. "It must be the answer."

"Niralan is working with the men who attacked Teth," Edlevin relented, each word a struggle. He turned to Alauren and ran his fingers nervously through his hair. "Ally, I think they're after you, as well."

Alauren caught her rapidly sinking head in her mugless hand and rubbed her temple. "For what *fucking* reason, Edlevin?" snarled the smith, the sharp strain of her voice betraying the fear behind the backhanded comment. "I hit metal with a hammer. Nothing more, nothing less."

Ronnok nodded. "This is why we continue to Arvyn. Norts do not wait for answers, we find them."

"As you command, I will follow," Edlevin conceded. "I owe you that."

The group remained silent for a long while, thinking over the mystery and trying desperately to dredge up anything that could be of use from the depths of their memory. Answers were as rare as a favorable wind, however, and so no headway was made.

"I remember readin' a little about these islanders during me priestly studies," Valin commented, breaking the silence. "They've got a couple o' churches they take a pilgrimage to about once a year. Should be comin' up shortly."

"Indeed," Ronnok said with a nod. "They will carry with them offerings: food, drink, and many shiny things. While answers are our primary goal, they cannot be eaten or traded for goods. We will raid as necessary, taking from monks and priests on the paths of their god."

"Sounds rather…" Alauren hesitated, trying to find the right word.

"Savage?" the Chieftain finished with a knowing, lopsided smile.

"Something like that," the blacksmith confirmed.

"Such tactics lead to the least bloodshed, for both parties," Ronnok explained, followed by a small sip of his drink. "We intimidate, and they give up without a fight. If they do not, every Nort stands ready and eager to embrace the glory of combat. We will remain swift and firmly ahead of our foes while we make our way."

Edlevin rested his chin upon a balled fist. "Sounds like a plan. I will warn you, though, if Niralan can locate us…" His voice tapered off in a groaning stutter. "It will be bloody."

"We will deal with that tribulation if it comes, Karlmaðr," Ronnok replied, standing tall. "For now, enjoy your peaceful days upon the sea. It will be over a week's time before we reach the shores of Arvyn. Until then, I must see to the preparations. On that thought…" He trailed off and finished his drink. "I've been relaxing for too long, I think. I should return to my duties." With a respectful nod, he took his leave.

A moment of silence ensued as all drank from their cups and stared across the vast Nort flotilla, to the open water beyond.

Alauren was the first to break the silence. "How did you do it, Ed?"

Edlevin tilted his head in slight confusion.

"The prisoner," the smith clarified. "You slice his throat?"

"No, too slow, too cruel," Edlevin replied somberly. "A clean cut to the heart was the best death I could hope to give him. Quick and easy, for all involved."

Alauren shifted in her seat. "Honestly, Ed, quick and with ease seems to be how you handle all of this." She paused for a moment after the words, noting a raised eyebrow from her mentor, beckoning elaboration. "The way you fight and the way you kill, I mean. You make it seem easy."

"It is not," Edlevin stated instantly, in a flat deadpan, letting a momentary weariness surface in his eyes. "I remember every single one."

A silence ensued for a few moments as the blacksmith digested the words. Wisely, she decided to move the conversation along. "How about the choice you gave him?" she asked. "Seems like he had only one, in actuality."

"It would seem," Edlevin said with a light shrug. "Things are different in Fangirm. Death is not something feared and detested, but is, rather, accepted and celebrated, so long as it comes on the terms of the victim. If the howling dark is to come, we must enter it with bravery and honor, and of our own accord whenever possible."

"Seems like it would be a depressing life," Alauren observed. "Thinking so deeply about death so often."

"That's the thing, Ally," Edlevin replied, peering into a memory through his mind's eye. "Once we accept it, we are free of the burden. We lose the need to think about death itself, and we can instead focus on making sure the event itself is honorable. It is, in a way, freeing, and it gives us a clear path to acceptance of the inevitable." He chortled darkly. "That's what they told us at training, anyway."

Alauren nodded. "So, the man died honorably?"

"Syla," Edlevin corrected. "His name was Syla, and his choice was to die to a human or to die to a Nort. He died on his terms." He took a long sip of ale. "He died properly."

Alauren nodded. "I guess I understand."

"No, you don't," Edlevin was quick to correct. "Even I don't. Well, not fully, at least. I'm beginning to suspect that the 'acceptance' Fangirm preaches only comes when the blade is finally in your chest, and you have no other choice. Until then, it is simply ignoring the rising waters around you."

The blacksmith nodded quietly, thinking on the words.

"How are you feeling about your skills with the blade?" Edlevin asked, awkwardly changing the subject.

"Shaky," Alauren answered quickly. She held up a hand, which quivered wildly. "Very much so."

"Bah!" Valin spat, venturing a comment after listening quietly for some time. "It's just the ship that's shaky, lass. Yer doin' fine, all things considered."

"How would you know?" Edlevin jabbed with a grin. "Do priests often engage in the sharp arts?"

"One o' me best friends was Garradh!" Valin replied. "Came up here t' earn gold, and he returned a madman. Wore barrels on his feet!"

Edlevin and Alauren exchanged amused glances before furrowing their brows at the stout Priest.

"Got sick o' bein' called short, so he fixed it. HA!" bellowed the Dwarf. "Anyhows, I spent a long time watchin' him spar with the other Garradhs while I ate me lunches. Picked up some things, ye know?"

"Ah, so you are obviously quite skilled," the old soldier quipped. "Given that watching is equal to doing, and all."

"I'm just tryin' t' encourage the lass, ye crotchety ol' hog log!" Valin exclaimed.

Edlevin blurted a howl of laughter. "That's a new insult."

Valin rumbled with a chuckle. "Credit where credit is due, that one came from Drell."

"I guess even ancient jackasses can innovate," Alauren noted with a smirk and a sip.

"You'd have to. Just think…" Edlevin illustrated, waving his hands about majestically and beckoning imagination. "All day. Every day. Nothing but Valin. You look up, Valin. Down, more Valin. You drink an ale, and it's made of Valin."

Alauren snickered. "I don't like where this is going."

"Oh, I do, lassie," Valin rumbled with wide, eager eyes. "Ye may wanna write this down, sounds like the next great stage show in the south!"

The trio shared a bit more mirth, but soon returned to a subdued and somber silence. Alauren, clearly growing more and more tormented by the idleness, broke the pause.

"I'd like to train more," said the smith. "As much as we can, in fact, before we hit the shore. I'm tired of being defenseless."

Edlevin nodded proudly. "We will remedy that, I promise."

PART THREE:

THE COMING STORM

CHAPTER NINETEEN:

LOGISTICS

Niralan are marauders, murderers, thieves, and every other moniker you would think to place upon a most hated foe. We have fought against the tyranny of the east for centuries, economically and physically, yet they have come, again and again, feebly attempting to topple Elysia's rightful place as the greatest empire of the north. It is a pity, then, that the traits of madness afflicting the Nirali are accompanied by a surprising competence, an orderliness that drives a thundering machine of war. They will dominate, given the chance, and any who rise in defense of truth and justice will find themselves dangling from the gallows within a morn. Their way of life cannot be allowed to expand.

– Gauis Truvani, in "Nations of Odenseye"

Vulmoor, Elysian Province

14th OF THE MORN OF HARVEST
NORTHERN YEAR 715

In western Elysia, some distance east of the great shadowbeech forest of Mayahina (and the de-facto border of Se'Vikoral), there was a town called Vulmoor, a veritable oasis of civilization among a rural wilderness that well characterized the vast lands of the imperial west. Despite its seemingly remote location, commerce was the backbone of this place (due to having direct routes to the rest of the empire), and the riches that flowed through its well-kept streets were known to be second only to the Elysian capital itself. However, while the City of Elysia dealt in the wealth of gold coins and finely cut gems, Vulmoor's prosperity was in its raw materials; those of ore, lumber, crops and furs.

Just off the center crossroads of the town, next to an apothecary, there was an establishment known as Inn the Shadows, an eatery and watering hole for locals as well as the myriads of merchants that transited their regular routes upon the cobblestones of the four streets. The Inn was a rather large place, constantly expanding as Vulmoor grew in prominence, and both the town and the business found themselves becoming ever more critical to the flow of the empire's riches as the seasons passed.

The dim light and gloomy corners of the Inn were intensified by dark and knotted shadowbeech wood which made up every chair, table, and wall within. Light danced from a single, massive chandelier that hung from the high roof, dangling directly in the center of the establishment's dining room while it fought a pitched battle against the dark. The bar, located in the far-left corner, was isolated and perpetually cloaked in a dull glow, a perfect place for private conversations. A small balcony leading to second-story rooms rose above it, connected with the lower floor by a set of curving stairs to the immediate left of the main door.

Morvin sat upon one of the wooden stools at the bar, sloshing his drink about in a mug as he waited for his Lieutenant to join him. The road to subduing Elysia had been long and bloody, a war of its own horrors, but the assimilation of Vulmoor would signal a final end to the death throes of the once-great empire. Centuries had led to this, the victory that the Nirali had sought since the unification of their feudal Korals under a single crown.

Morvin sipped from the cup, savoring the flavor of a local ale that was bitter and hoppy, stinging his taste buds pleasantly as it washed over them. The bite of the alcohol on his tongue was a much-needed break from the constant barking of orders and hanging of those with more ambition than sense, and so the wearied General of the Nirali was sure to enjoy every second of this momentary peace. Forgoing his limiting armor for a traditional Nirali greatcoat, he was able to sink into his seat and relax, with the added bonus of looking markedly less threatening to his new people.

Behind the General, a crowd had gathered, standing shoulder to shoulder to hear the words of the Nirali conquerors who had marched into their town days earlier. Resistance here had been light, and most of the locals showed more fear toward their new rulers than they did anger or resentment. There was a dose of curiosity within the people's eyes, too, something that Niralan would be sure to take full advantage of.

Skarde flew through the door with a thundering zeal, sending a wave cascading through the crowd as the people parted before him, quite like tides being pushed about by the movement of the moons. His greatcoat billowed behind him as he rapidly crossed the distance to the bar, where he sat down next to his superior with a huff.

"They had better listen to me this time," growled the Lieutenant. He waved for a drink and plunked a coin down. "I'm getting sick of having to find and dispose of the willfully deaf."

"I don't know that they'll be a problem," Morvin observed, sipping from his mug. "This crowd is bigger than the last few. Afraid, but ready to hear what we offer."

"Crowds are dangerous," Skarde countered, accepting the mug that was delivered to him by a noticeably nervous bartender. "They can turn on you in heartbeat, all at once."

"Well, you had better put the charm on, then," Morvin said in the midst of a gruff chuckle. "Remember what we talked about. Don't demand respect, command it. If you find that control, the crowd will be right there with you."

"I hope so," grumbled the younger officer, casting a wary glance across the gathered locals. "We can't afford any more delays in our campaign."

"We will stay on schedule," assured the General, giving Skarde's shoulder a hefty pat. "I've seen your speeches. You'll be fine."

"To soldiers, yes," Skarde replied, his voice straining in a clear and uncharacteristic anxiety. "Talking about how we are going to die gloriously is less effective on civilians." He shifted in his seat. "Sir, permission to speak freely?"

Morvin chuckled and shook his head. "You know you don't need permission."

Skarde nodded and, after a moment of grinding his teeth, spoke. "We need to finish the Elysian campaign soon. Winter will be harsh.

If I cock this up, we might not reach Se'Vikoral on time. It's not often that an entire campaign schedule can be set back by one man. I'd rather not be that man."

"Have some faith, Skarde," Morvin soothed. "Should the worst come to pass, Se'Vikorans are little more than fisherman and farmers." His voice was respectful, not being dismissive of the threats that lie ahead, but careful to keep them in a realistic context. "They've been protected by Elysia for their entire existence. We'll manage."

"They've fought the Norts," Skarde rebutted.

"Centuries ago, before Elysia stepped in," Morvin quickly replied. "They will be unprepared. We will keep to our schedule. Focus on Vulmoor for now."

"I suppose you're right," Skarde conceded with a sigh, followed by a sip of his drink.

"Remember, let them ask their own questions about their current situation," instructed the General. "Focus on showing them the way, rather than dragging them along."

"As you command, sir," Skarde said with a nod. The Lieutenant rapped his knuckles on the wooden bar a few times before rising and pushing through the crowd, all of whom parted dutifully the moment they noticed his billowing, long coat heading towards them.

Skarde leaped onto a raised platform and took a moment to survey the crowd, a number so great that it stretched to the far wall of the cavernous Inn, where a fire burned intensely within a large hearth. Their eyes were wide, focusing in on the foreign conqueror; Skarde's gaze, however, looked over many a citizen, picking out the minute details in the mass of townspeople, noting every speck of dirt (or lack thereof) on their clothes.

Most of them were simple farmers or villagers, wearing ragged tunics and muddy pants upon skin that was rough and worn, while their eyes were ragged and weary. For Skarde, there was little but pity and a subdued anger welling up within him at the indications of their poor treatment, at the lack of respect shown to those commoners who made the wheels of this place turn. This was a common sight in every town from one side of the 'great' empire to another; despite Elysia's riches, poverty was no stranger to the simple folk of this storied nation.

"Listen to my words and heed them well!" Skarde bellowed suddenly, his deep voice reverberating from the walls and bringing the Inn to an absolute silence. The eyes of the people locked with his own, and he was careful to meet them as an equal, projecting little emotion save a calm empathy. "The Emperor is dead. Elysia is dead." His words were icy and matter of fact, holding no anger or hatred within. "Where once the shining Gem of the North stood, a testament to material corruption, there is now a new way of life. A life as equals under a single banner, never again to slave in servitude for a fraction of your labor's worth." His face hardened. "You may have heard of Niralan's ways, how we hang dissenters in the town squares."

The crowd murmured in cautious agreement, shrinking back from the man's voice all the while.

"The truth, however, is that these 'dissenters' are those who once stood on the foundations of power that we have turned to dust," Skarde continued. "They are men who fight to keep our ways from changing their world." He took a moment to make certain that he had the crowd's attention, and was sure to meet the occasional farmer or beggar's eyes as he swept his gaze over them. One and all stood wide-eyed, listening intently.

"You!" Skarde barked, pointing to a skinny farmer with only a ragged pair of green overalls for clothes. "What is your name?"

"M-my name is Kly," the man stammered with a heavily wavering voice.

"Tell me, Kly: how is your farm doing?" asked the Lieutenant.

"Pardon?" Kly replied in confusion.

"My apologies for assuming your line of work if I am incorrect," Skarde said diplomatically.

"No," the man replied, coming to his senses quickly. "You were correct. I'm a farmer. Just not used to bein' asked that, is all." He hesitated for a moment, only continuing after a nod from the imposing Nirali. "We've been survivin', growin' all we can. Of course, we pay out a good deal to the farm's owners."

"So, you just work on a farm?" Skarde asked. "You don't own it?"

"No, M'Lord," the farmer replied. "Well, I own the cabin, but Mr. Kurne bought the land from my father. Helped us survive a cold winter, he did."

"Call me Skarde, Kly," the Lieutenant instructed. "There are no lords here anymore." After a nod of affirmation from the farmer, he continued. "Who is Mr. Kurne?"

"Runs a whole bunch of farms 'round here," Kly said. "Well, he lets us run 'em for pay."

An old, well-dressed man stirred in the back of the Inn near the fireplace, a slight motion that was noticed instantly by the wary vision of the Nirali. Skarde narrowed his eyes, but quickly shifted his attention back to the conversation at hand. "So, Mr. Kurne bought your farm. That must have been a lot of money."

"Eight hundred elysium!" Kly exclaimed proudly.

"That's a good deal," Skarde said with an impressed nod. "You must be doing better than ever."

"Well..." Kly hesitated, having a slight waver in his voice. "Gold gets spent pretty quickly around here, is the thing, and we give most of our produce to Kurne. Used the eight hundred on repairs to the cabin and some clothes. What we grow now works out to about twenty-five elysium a morn for us."

"How much would you make per morn before Kurne?" Skarde asked, seizing on a clear opportunity.

"Sixty-five," the farmer answered sheepishly.

"So, that adds up to a loss of forty elysium per morn, yes?" the Nirali posited.

Kly nodded. "Yeah, I guess you could look at it that ways. Y'know, thinkin' on it, I've probably paid Mr. Kurne about triple what he bought the farm for since then."

Skarde smirked, knowing the man's mind had found the path laid out for him. "That seems unfair."

"I guess it is, kinda," Kly grumbled with a scratch of the head.

"They must treat you pretty well for you to accept such a loss," the Lieutenant continued, guiding the man along. "Good clothes, good tools, care when you're sick."

"No, Skarde, not so much," muttered the farmer. "We have to buy our own clothes and tools. Our families give us care."

Skarde crossed his arms and raised an incredulous eyebrow. "Kly, are you happy with that deal?"

The farmer stirred in an uncomfortable silence for a single, elongated moment, casting a glance about, but was compelled to speak by the dominating presence of the Nirali. "Now that I'm thinkin' about it... no, sir."

"Familiar words," Skarde proclaimed loudly, turning his eyes back to the people as a whole. "Ones that we have heard from one side of Elysia to another, without fail. I would not think of this as a conquering, dear people, but as a liberation." He smiled warmly and splayed out his arms. "Niralan will provide you, each and every one, with clothes and with seed. With us, your people will not grow hungry, nor will they die from lack of proper care for ailments. You will be entitled to what you produce, with our nation taking only what we need to continue in spreading our ways in the north." He folded his hands behind his back. "We offer you a better way, a future where we thrive together instead of suffering alone."

"You'll want something in return!" a voice huffed from the back of the room. "You always do!"

Skarde searched for a moment, but was unable to pick out the source of the comment. "Indeed," affirmed the Nirali, "we ask for loyalty to Grand Marshal Karsus and to Niralan. We would also require each of you to follow our laws."

"What laws are those?" yelled another voice. Curiosity had clearly prevailed over fear, it seemed, and the crowd listened intently for an answer.

The Nirali General nodded, happy to explain. "First and foremost, you are to treat others with the respect you show yourselves. In Niralan, there is no difference between a human or one of the elvish kin. You may be a man or woman, a wizened elder or plucky youngster; regardless, you are equals, and you must treat each other as such." His demeanor grew dark, and his tone became grave. "If any are caught breaking this respect by acts of murder, assault, rape, theft, deceptive practices, or exploitation, they will be tried by a jury of their peers. If convicted, they will be executed."

The final word brought about a collective gasp; the people murmured disapprovingly among themselves, the thought of such punishment clearly a source of great fear.

"I know the weight that word carries here in Elysia," Skarde continued calmly. "People have been beheaded or quartered for unjust reasons, by nobles with too much power." He stood tall and proud, keeping his hands folded behind his back, taking confidence in the justice of his nation's ways. "I can promise you this: the men and women at the top of Niralan's government do not make the decision on who lives and who dies, nor do we practice such barbary as tortuous deaths." He took a moment to let the words sink in before continuing. "In Niralan, you die by the rope, with dignity, as deemed proper by the people. Punishment, wholly, is left to unbiased members of the community. Additionally," he added after a quick breath and a swallow, "you will be able to appeal any judgement stemming from one of the severe crimes I spoke of to an arbitrator, who will travel from the Capital."

"I understand, sir," Kly said. "You mentioned a jury, though. Who picks them?"

Skarde smiled and nodded approvingly at the man, impressed at the perception of the simple farmer. "Vulmoor will be assigned a local Magistrate," explained the Nirali, eager to allay concern. "It will be one of you, elected by the community. They should be one of respect and honor within your town, someone who will regularly communicate with our Magistrates in the east."

The crowd seemed more content, but concerns remained, as evidenced by the continued grumbling of some within the gathered masses.

"Will yah force us into military service?" A woman asked. "I hear yah got a war to finish out there."

"Conscription of non-Nirali soldiers is limited to defensive action," Skarde replied brightly, clearly much more confident in his ability to explain military strategy. "However, we offer several benefits for willingly joining our campaign. Foremost among them, my people, are grants of land on which to farm, accompanied by an immediate payment of one hundred elysium. While the claimant must leave to fight, their family will be given all enlistment benefits at the first available opportunity."

The crowd erupted into excited chatter at the idea. The room seemed to have come alight with excitement in a single breath, for those under Elysia's rule had long lived in resignation of their destitute lot. Skarde shot Morvin a smile, to which the General replied with a proud smirk and a raised mug.

"In conclusion," continued the Lieutenant, his booming voice quickly regaining the attention of the shuffling crowd. "You have a choice to make. You may be one of us, equal and unified, or you may hold on to a dead empire who lashed you into serfdom. Recruiters are ready at the town hall; clothes and food will be handed out tomorrow at midday. Make your choice."

Skarde bowed to his new people and stepped down from the stage. No more did the folk of Vulmoor part in a vast wave before him; instead, they gave him a pathway where he could rub shoulders with them and share in their joy. There were smiles all around, and the young Nirali officer found himself the recipient of many warm greetings and friendly introductions. After a small while, he was able to break free and rejoin his superior.

"Not bad," Morvin praised, keeping his voice low so as not to be heard above the general din. "You had all of them hanging off of every word."

"Nearly all of them," Skarde corrected, taking a swig of his drink. "I believe Mr. Kurne was unhappy with my line of questioning, though I could not pick him out."

"I saw him," Morvin said. "He was dressed in fine silks and gold fringe. He didn't seem to like our suggestions."

"As it's been in every town," sighed the Lieutenant, his tone venomous and contemptuous. "The... *elite* of Elysia are a poison."

Morvin nodded. "For the masses, equality elevates. But for power..."

"It brings them low," Skarde finished.

"Exactly," affirmed the General. "We should be watchful."

"Perhaps we should be more proactive this time," Skarde said. "When we allow them room to work, we risk allowing the seeds of rebellion to be planted. For smaller towns, that wasn't a problem. Vulmoor is a much bigger chance to take."

"The seeds of loyalty grow tall and strong," Morvin countered. "We cannot risk trampling them with rash measures. Let the Nobles play their games, and let the people see them exposed to the full light of day."

"As Karsus decreed," conceded the Lieutenant. "You have my full support."

The nights in the forests to the west of Vulmoor were especially dark, owing their starless abyss to the great trunks and branches of sprawling shadowbeech groves which lay in pockets across the western lands of Elysia. Black, viscous sap ran like living shadows down the dark purple bark, while the wide leaves above absorbed any celestial light that would seek to reach the well-cobbled path below.

It was here that the Noble families had built their homes and businesses, their centers of both luxury and power. Like the Inn, these structures were made from the shadowbeeches that surrounded them; the dangerous sap had to be carefully drained from the hollow veins that ran the length of their trunks, an arduous and expensive process that only the richest could hope to afford. The homesteads had been constructed as large cabins, initially, but had found themselves gradually expanded by generation after generation of Elysian royalty, whose elegant lifestyles would often require more and more indoor space. Gargoyles jutted off the steep roofs wherever practical, carrying rainwater away from the structures in a stunningly superfluous process.

The interior walls on the north wing of this particular manor were dominated by the shelves of a cavernous, two-tiered library that contained texts from across the continent. So large was the collection of the gilded Remure family that a rolling ladder would often be required to reach the highest ledges, where dust-covered masterworks were displayed solely for posterity by the well-off family.

In the center of the room, all manner of maps and letters lay strewn haphazardly on a shadowbeech table, which itself lay on a bright yellow rug from the Sun Elf lands far to the south. In the corner, meanwhile, a servant reset the pendulum on a grandfather clock, fully occupied with his sole duty of keeping the many devices within the property ticking.

"It's absurd!" Alistair Remure, the head of his family, grumbled. He was a middle-aged man with a clean-cut white beard and green, intense eyes that could stare fear into any man in Elysia. His nine fingers (missing one from an unfortunate hunting accident) were each adorned with a ring, and the metal loops were, in turn, topped with their own unique gemstone, from the shimmering of diamonds to the milky blue of an opal. The Remure family (or rather, their workers) had mined the nearby mountains for decades, sending their goods across Odenseye while amassing a respectable horde of wealth.

Across the table, three men thought on his words; youngest among them was Ven Moryn, a purple-skinned Lunari who had come to prominence by exporting shadowbeech wood across the continent. Ven was a small, unimposing figure with thinning white hair, yet his devious mind had led him to an absolute monopoly in the business of lumber. Impeccable black robes concealed all manner of weapons, and there was ever a sinister air around the shifty Elf.

Algernon Kurne, a human, was much older. The patriarch of his family, he occupied a venerated position as the richest of the Vulmoor Nobles. His withered, long beard was a snow-white color, perfectly matching his short and tangled hair. He always seemed to have bags under his brown eyes, even as a younger man, and there was seldom a moment when he was not occupied with his work. Addled by old age, he would now forgo the typical trappings of luxury for loose garments (barring any special occasions), and he often had a disheveled look about him. He had made his fortune from the backs of farmers, running a single dominating trading company that sold Vulmoor's goods across the north.

Ingvald Skjorn was the last and most physically threatening of the group; a man of North Elysian descent, his were a people easily identified by brown skin, rigid cheeks, and wide, imposing eyes. A hulk of a human, Skjorn easily towered above anyone in Vulmoor, be they man or Elf. His early years were spent as a woodsman in the north, living off the vibrant fur trade, and his business had grown to immense levels due to both his savviness and his bloodthirst. His success culminated, eventually, in a move south and the joining of the venerated Noble class.

Skjorn was the first to reply to Remure, as was often the case. "If it were up to me, we woulda just killed the generals at the bar. Cut the head off and all that." His voice was deep and thundering, like a distant avalanche.

Moryn laughed at the comment openly, erupting in a throaty cackle that drew deadly looks from his gathered peers. "We'd all be hung, and they'd have replacements take command tomorrow," he snapped. "If we could even succeed, which I doubt."

"I certainly couldn't hope to kill either of them," Kurne supported with a grinding tone that ever carried a demand for respect within. "You're the only one that might be able to, Skjorn. I doubt it, though, given your disposition for foolish anger."

"Keep talking, old man," Skjorn growled. "See where it leads."

"Enough!" Remure snapped, banging on the table violently with his four-fingered hand. "We must not kid ourselves, gentleman. Elysia is dead. We must focus on staying alive and keeping what we have. We can do that only together." He was careful to meet the eyes of his peers, granting each a moment of the molten determination that poured from his hazel gaze. "We cannot let ourselves fall to infighting. We will all die."

"Agreed," Moryn slithered. "Niralan sent me a letter, told me they would be seizing my lumber yards for the people and the war effort. This cannot happen."

"They said the same of my farms," Kurne added.

"And my fur trade," Skjorn said. "They want control of commerce completely, I think."

"Well look at that, he *can* think!" Moryn jabbed, bearing a particularly annoying grin.

"Stop prodding the bear, you idiot!" Remure growled with another bang on the table. "We have had our troubles in the past, I know. Conflicts between us." His eyes still shifted to each of his peers in regular intervals, ensuring that their attention remained upon him. "Today, though, we must be unified to face this new threat to our livelihood and to our legacy. If they take our industries now, we will not see them returned. We have everything to lose. We have to hold on."

The heads of the gathered Nobles nodded up and down in agreement. Remure briefly shuffled a few scrolls around the table before unfurling one in the center. At the top, the words *Vulmoor Trade Routes* had been written in painstakingly clean penmanship.

"I have a plan," Remure said with an insidious smile. "Let us not deceive ourselves: our peers nearer to the capital rarely had to fight for what they had. Talisia ensured his favored ones stayed in power. Niralan will be expecting a bold and foolish move against them, not a calculated strategy."

The other Nobles concurred with several more nods.

"We need to play this quietly," Remure continued. "If we do this right, we can put Niralan in a position where we have leverage. It will require each of us." He breathed deeply. "Are you with me?"

"Aye," Skjorn replied immediately, a word quickly echoed by Kurne and Moryn.

"Good," Remure thrummed. "Listen close, and listen well."

CHAPTER TWENTY:

COMPROMISE

16th OF THE MORN OF HARVEST
NORTHERN YEAR 715

A creak erupted in the dim interior of a shadowy shed, drawn out from a wobbly leg that precariously assisted in propping up a wooden table. This was a place both damp and cold, ever having an air of mild discomfort, and the smell of mildew could regularly be caught wafting through Morvin's nostrils as he attended to his duties. The General paid little mind to the minor flaws of this hastily constructed hovel; as was the Nirali way, practicality won out, for his place the center of the soggiest field he could find would prove unequal in both personal safety and the security of his battle plans.

He studied maps of Se'Vikoral in the flickering light of a hanging lantern, finding his thoughts resting firmly on the road ahead. Niralan could see a united north by year's end, should they keep to their timetable. Centuries of war for the Nirali people and the decades he had personally spent waging that infernal struggle could come to a final, thundering conclusion, a lasting victory that had seemed to be nothing more than a dream even just a year ago.

Peace, Morvin mused to himself. *For the first time in my life.*

He pushed the thought away and tried to refocus. Requests from the four Noble house heads, all for a personal audience, lay strewn about the floor, coldly forgotten amidst the administration of an army. The Nirali had little patience for people like them, men who stole the sweat of their people from the very brow on their heads while returning to them only the wages of a bare, unfulfilling survival. The rich royalty of Elysia were sick, and Morvin thought it a pity that the disease was not fatal.

The General's thoughts were interrupted by two quick bangs on the door, followed by the entrance of his Lieutenant, who ripped off his helmet before slamming the rickety wooden threshold shut behind him. He was once again donning his shining silver armor, his hair drenched in sweat, and he appeared to be quite visibly upset.

"There's been an attack on the farm traders," Skarde panted, slamming a small map down on the table. "Here, near the old Landen Fort ruins."

Morvin cleared some space on the surface and splayed out the parchment. "What was taken?"

"Everything," Skarde heaved gravely. "Meat, potatoes, seeds... We may not have the resources to feed the people today."

"Calm yourself," the General ordered in a stern growl. "Take a moment to get your breath."

"My apologies, sir," Skarde said. He leaned against the wall for a moment and, after a small bout of coughing, continued on. "I ran directly here after some arguments with the town hall over my right to take maps."

"You ran here from the town hall?" Morvin queried incredulously.

"Yes," the Lieutenant replied evenly.

The General's eyes glowed with amazement (and more than a little horror). "In full plate mail? That's impressive."

"Thank you, sir," Skarde said, waving the compliment away while he fully filled his lungs. "On to business."

"Right," Morvin said with a nod. "Are the Nobles moving on us?"

"I'm not sure, honestly," replied the younger officer. "There were survivors, but our scouts reported that the farmers and wagon drivers could only identify the assailants as some bandits from the hills. The Beechbloods, they call themselves."

"Dramatic," Morvin grumbled. "Childish names aside, it makes sense. They would want to feel out how difficult of a mark we'll be."

"I'll make sure Intelligence has their ears out," Skarde said, leaning forward. "We should make sure our flanks are covered in case the Nobles have their fingers in this."

"Very good," Morvin concurred. "However, what gives me pause is, and correct me if I'm wrong, those wagons would be owned by the Kurne family, yes?"

"They were," confirmed the Lieutenant.

"I wonder if they'd really attack one of their own," Morvin mulled, scratching at the surprisingly lengthy stubble on his chin. Se'Vikoral had dominated his thoughts, occupying so much of his focus that it had caused him to forget something as simple as shaving. He filed the reflection for later consideration and brought his mind back to the topic at hand. "You said there were survivors?"

"Yes," Skarde replied. "All of them, actually. They were beaten, but alive. Only material goods were stolen."

"What do you know about..." Morvin said, trailing off for a moment. "What was it, the Beechbloods?"

Skarde nodded. "Yes sir. Big, North Elysian men that wear masks made from shadowbeech bark. They use the sap of the tree for torches and torture."

"Manual entry sixty-seven," Morvin affirmed, finding his memory jogged by the younger officer's words. "The sap needs to be refined, usually, but can cause severe burns even in raw form when ignited."

"Aye," Skarde replied. "These criminals paint people's skin with it. So I hear, anyway."

"Well, this all does sound like common outlaws," Morvin said. He tapped his fingers on the table a few times, assisting him in shuffling through his thoughts. "They want to see our response, but they're not willing to brave the consequences of murder yet, brutal as they may have been in Elysia." He ground his teeth and took a moment to gather himself. "Our focus must be on Se'Vikoral, but we'll keep a close eye on this matter. Take action as you see fit."

The younger officer saluted. "As you command."

"Oh!" Morvin exclaimed. "Before you go, have our forces begun to make camp at the border?"

"We are sending more and more soldiers on the road by the hour," Skarde replied proudly. "We'll be ready when the time comes."

"Very good," Morvin said. "Was there anything else?"

"News from the east, actually," Skarde said. "Karsus has begun sending ambassadors for the new government. Vulmoor will need a Magistrate soon."

Any potential reply was interrupted by a rapping at the door, a metallic sound that signified the hand of a plated guard. Morvin exchanged a glance with Skarde before rising and stepping out into the sunlight.

A runner, clad in newly provided Nirali clothes (a simple black tunic, trousers, and leather-soled shoes), caught his breath a few strides from the shack. Morvin blew past the soldiers guarding the door and closed the distance quickly, standing tall above the simple villager.

"Speak," the General snapped with a clear air of authority.

"Apologies for interrupting you, M'Lord," the man whimpered.

"*Sir* is fine," Morvin corrected. "I'm not your lord."

"Of course, M'-" The man began, before cutting himself off with a wince. "I mean, of course, sir. Alistair of House Remure requests your presence at the private room at the Inn."

"On what grounds am I summoned?" Morvin demanded, his voice still cold and serious. "I have much to attend to."

"To discuss matters involving industry, sir," the man explained sheepishly, blurting the words as quickly as his mouth would carry them. "That's all I know."

"Very well," Morvin said, after a deep sigh. "Tell Remure we will meet in two hours' time."

The runner nodded and darted off without wasting a second, hardly seeming to notice the mud clinging to his shoes as he tore away from the imposing Nirali soldiers.

"Interesting," Skarde said. "Would you like me to attend, as well?"

Morvin nodded. "I'll meet you there. For now, dismissed."

Skarde saluted dutifully and ran off to his tasks, while Morvin retreated once more to the quiet of his sanctuary. He took a seat and studied the trading map for any details that could prove to be a value.

A quiet fell over the shack as the General's focus fell inward. For a great while, there was little but the sound of his breathing to accompany his contemplation, his visions of a future that seemed, for the first time in his lengthy experience of life, to be brighter than days past. His heart, at once, soared with confidence and fluttered with nerves, for the finish was firmly in sight.

Another knock came at the door after some time, repeating in a *thump-thump, thump-thump-thump* pattern. Morvin, roughly pulled from his peace, sighed and steeled himself for what was to come. "Enter."

A black-robed woman stepped through the door. Though she kept her hood pulled tightly around her head, like a partial shroud, her lower jaw was visible and painted in a deep hue of indigo. Her breath misted as it emerged from obsidian lips, making it appear as if the cold bite of winter had already fallen upon the land, and her bony hands tremored profoundly in the nonexistent chill. "Morvin," she said, speaking with a soft venom in her voice. "We are displeased."

Morvin grimaced and turned his attention back to his maps. He had been ordered to show these beings respect, but he could conjure up little but a vile revulsion at their presence. "That's too bad."

"Our pact is clear," the woman spat. She stared unflinchingly ahead, through her hood and towards the back wall. "You must give us our recompense. The Northmen have been removed, as we promised, but we have received little of your payment in recent days." She sucked in an unsettling, rattling breath. "You march in a military campaign, and yet our Dreamer still has so few instruments to conduct. There must be death. We must have our prizes."

Morvin was still, but glared from under his downturned brow. "They are not prizes, worm. They are people."

"They are hers," the woman countered. "You must provide. The pact is clear."

"We won't see combat for another morn, at least, so she'll have to make do," Morvin replied coldly, leaving no room for argument. "Was there anything else?"

"Combat is not necessary," the woman said in a strange, warbling cadence. "Any can serve her. Any can rise to life, to see the great breaking of the Dawn. This town is full, and there are many who are ripe for the harvest."

Morvin stood and squared his shoulders, moving close to the woman and towering over her. "No, as you well know that is against our pact. Leave, and tell the Dreamer that she can be disappointed."

"You-" the woman began.

"Get out, before I send you to see your prophesized Dawn," growled the General, pointing heavily towards the door.

The unsettling visitor grimaced, but obliged, gliding out of the shack. A guard shut the door behind her, leaving the General alone with his thoughts once more.

He focused in again, attempting (however vainly) to swallow the lingering bitterness of disgust which held in his mouth like a teaspoon of bile.

The single private room at the Inn was cavernous enough to hold an entire convoy, animals and all, though it was usually occupied by just a few of those with the wealth to afford the cushy beds and wide tables. With just Morvin, Skarde, and Remure, the dim chamber was little more than a cavernous waste of space to the sensibility of a Nirali. The center table was covered in elegantly prepared foods from cultures across the empire, and a noticeable draft wafted throughout the room, sending the occasional shiver down the neck of the General.

Morvin, despite the varied delicacies, ate nothing. Any Nirali would have found their stomachs turned by the Nobleman's well-fitted tunic and jeweled buttons; his uniquely sickening trait, though, was the air of pride he carried with him, as if he deserved all that he had taken from his people.

In his time in Vulmoor, the General had borne witness to the full brunt of the Elysian Empire's truth. The poorest here were emaciated, nearly skeletal, and they had little to hope for beyond an endless struggle to avoid a starved death in the gutter. Small girls wore sacks of grain as dresses, and women resorted to patching together ragged, reeking horse blankets to try to fend off the growing cold. Though the reality of Elysia was not new to him, the emotional bite of what he had seen was enduring, and it would thrive in his mind until these old ways finally became nothing more than a reviled piece of history.

"Alright, Remure, you've provided quite enough food and ale," Morvin growled, quite sick of the Noble's pleasantries. Skarde seemed to disagree with the final point, sipping from a flagon (though he had also found his stomach too turned to eat).

"As you command," Remure said warmly. His words were delivered with a royal elegance; each was chosen carefully and spoken perfectly, signifying a personal education. "Should we get down to business?"

"I'm curious what business you think we have," countered the General, crossing his arms. "We've already notified you of the next steps."

"Steps which will take time," Remure pointed out. "You can't march into and take over a town of this size and importance without certain issues arising, you know."

"Tread carefully, Remure," Morvin rumbled. "That sounded like a threat."

The Noble waved his hands disarmingly. "Oh my goodness, no! It wasn't meant that way. My apologies." He cleared his throat in a moment of clearly awkward discomfort. "Our town runs on an impeccable schedule, relying on constantly active supply routes for everything from food to international commerce. If this process gets interrupted, even for a few days, we will experience shortages of necessary goods and income." He managed to regain his steely demeanor, evidently confident enough in his explanation to risk taking a breath. "Simply put, not much is produced in the area of the town proper, and we absolutely must ensure that everything runs on schedule."

"A Nirali specialty," Skarde chimed in. "We'll keep things flowing."

"Oh, I believe you," Remure assured. "However, I do have a suggestion that might make your life easier in this regard."

"This should be good," Morvin derided.

Remure, at great (and visibly apparent) effort, ignored the snide comment. "As it is, we rely on imports as much as we do exports, and we cannot wait for supply lines to the capital to be secured. This town's ability to sustain itself is built upon a foundation of the deals that I and the other families have managed to secure abroad. Our wheat supply, for instance, is largely sourced from Fangirm, while our oats come from farms near Khal'Dorpane, in Se'Vikoral. All that we produce locally are greens, small amounts of barley, and varying legumes, as well as some beef and pork."

Morvin nodded. "Continue."

"The names and faces of this town's Nobles are known in the other nations," Remure obliged. "We can continue to keep up commerce and trade. Where southern businesses would be hesitant to deal with Niralan, they would likely be open to us. Vulmoor could continue as usual."

Morvin tapped on the table with his fingers. "What do you get out of this? I do not believe that your purpose here is benevolent."

"We want to help our people," the Noble answered with a deadly conviction. "I will admit to some selfishness in this, General Morvin, for I wish to see the prosperity of my family. I understand that the old empire is dead, but I also know that my loved ones are not. I, and the other Nobles here, are willing to work with you." He smiled confidently. "You can keep on marching."

"Hm," Morvin grunted, tapping on the table with a little more intensity. His ideas made sense, even if they came from a place of self-preservation. "Can you promise you can keep your businesses running?"

Remure returned the comment with a confused furrowing of his brow. "I'm not sure I follow."

"One of Kurne's farm wagons was attacked by bandits," Morvin elaborated. "A small attack, but enough to put us behind schedule on deliveries."

"News had not reached me, no," the Noble muttered, rubbing his beard. "Troubling. Though, if Elysia cannot stand against Niralan, bandits won't be much trouble." He stood. "I will draw from my personal meat stores to ensure that your soldiers remain fed, as a gesture of goodwill. I do hope you will consider all that I've said here."

Morvin narrowed his eyes and tossed the topic about in his head. For rich men, there was always another angle, something to gain that those mixed up in the web of their machinations were never privy to. The Nirali Intelligence Service had uncovered plot after plot from nobles across the rotting corpse of this empire, little more than maggots that desperately wished to feed on the last morsels left before bare bone. Fortunately for Niralan, old money always seemed to be poor in sense.

The General finally surfaced from thought and met Remure's eyes. "Give us time for consideration."

"Of course," said the Noble, nodding in understanding. "The room is paid through the night. You are welcome to ruminate here, if you wish. I will await your decision." With the words, the man bowed and took his leave, closing the door behind him.

"Cunt," Skarde blurted with considerable contempt. "His people live in squalor and all he can think about is how he's going to keep the gold flowing for himself."

"I expect no less," Morvin said amidst a sigh. "Still, this might be the smartest thing a former man of power has done, throughout the entire campaign. If they can keep everyone supplied, we can move on as soon as the first wave of our ambassadors gets here. It would be a lot of leeway."

"I don't believe it," Skarde countered. "He knows what we stand for. He knows that our occupation garrison will rip his precious gems from his buttons when they arrive. He's just delaying the inevitable."

"Is he, though?" Morvin posited, leaning back in the chair. "Most nobles end up getting themselves executed because they can't let go of what they once had. These men might see a different path. Jewels and gold aren't power." He smirked proudly. "Not anymore. Remember, there are few who do not deserve a chance to unite with our ways. Despite their sins, I would give them the opportunity to rise from the mud and be one of us, if they desired it so."

"Perhaps," replied the Lieutenant. "I hesitate to believe they're that smart, though. Caution is warranted."

Morvin nodded. "You're probably right. Still, if this deal can keep us marching, it might be worth it. Let's let this play out and see what shakes loose."

"As you command," Skarde affirmed dutifully. After a look over the table, which was still stuffed with food, he nabbed a few bowls, filled them, and headed towards the door. "Grab a few as well," he suggested. "If the Nobles of Vulmoor won't help the poorest here, we can do it for them."

"Aye," Morvin replied instantly, snapping to his feet to follow the younger officer's fine example.

CHAPTER TWENTY-ONE:

CONSPIRACY

I, as a royal historian of the highest order, have visited every corner of our great continent. In the darkest gutters of the most unkempt streets, there ever lies a puddle of shifting dregs, a writhing mass of poverty and crime that clings to the bottom of our coats like mud. I have seen the darkest depths of what this world has to offer, and each day of my journeys seemed to hold a new revelation of the evil that can be held in a person's heart.

Let it emphasize my word, then, that the worst man I have ever met was a member of the Elysian nobility.

For all the strengths of our great empire, we are weak in men of courage. A ruler should only live as well as their poorest countryman, yet many governors and magistrates have twice as many rings as they do fingers. They must be hypnotized by the sparkling of their jewels, I think, to be so pleasantly ignorant to the world as it is. If the Empire of the Elysian Fields is ever to wilt, there is no doubt in my mind that they would be the cause.

– Gauis Truvani, in "Nations of Odenseye"

23rd OF THE MORN OF HARVEST
NORTHERN YEAR 715

Everything was falling apart.

Requests and angry diatribes had poured in, piling into Morvin's command center like snow through an open door on a blustery winter night, overtaking what little space he had to work on military concerns in the small shack. Despite his efforts to rid himself of the letters, he often found himself picking a gold-fringed leaflet out of the nooks of his coat before furiously throwing it away in a heap that only seemed to grow with each passing hour. The shed was crushing and choked at every moment, as if he were trapped in a poorly ventilated closet, and he ever felt an itch in his spine at the disorganization of his command space.

Morvin, needing to leave the stuffy building for a few moments, opted to take a walk into town, one that he hoped would provide some peace under the assault of stress. He had donned his armor and cloak, preferring preparedness while he tried to escape the ever-growing problems of Vulmoor. Unfortunately, his thoughts had followed him, and he would find no respite.

Niralan had underestimated the bandits. They were cunning enough to get in, do their jobs, and get out before any help could be summoned. Their targets had been expanded as of late, hitting the few imports from abroad that still made their way to the town as much as they did local shipping. Though they only took a small amount each time, even drips can add up to a lake, especially when the lake is critical food stores for an oncoming winter.

Nirali patrols, meanwhile, could hardly keep up; the officers that would have normally led campaigns against civil unrest were hard at work training Elysian recruits and inducting them into the ways of the east. Simply put, the forces here were stretched too thin by staging and military logistics to give proper chase or, as the Nobles vehemently requested, to post soldiers with every wagon. The war effort, as it always had, came first.

A mere week after arriving, the new military government found that they could not reliably supply the village with the food they had been promised. Remure's statements had rung true; Vulmoor's economy had not been able to keep up with even a momentary interruption in imports and exports. Many families were beginning to go without meals until dinner to stave off a famine that seemed all but inevitable. For the orderly and practical Nirali, they could feel little but shock at how quickly the foundation under this town had crumbled.

The people were unhappy. Careful and respectful, but angry, nonetheless. The General was met with many sour glances as he made his way into the town square, though his bowed head and inward thoughts kept him from fully noticing the grimaces.

"They promise you meals, clothing, wealth," an old, wavering voice cried, pulling Morvin from his haze. "Yet they do not provide!".

Morvin looked up to find and elderly man sitting upon a chair at the front-and-center of the newly constructed gallows, identifiable as Kurne, one of the Nobles. The mid-morning sun crossed warmly across his white robes, and the hoarse call of his voice had begun to assemble a crowd. Kurne wasn't authorized to climb the structure, certainly, but Morvin dared not remove such a respected man in so dire of a time. The General opted to stop and listen, leaning his clanking armor against a small shop across the street.

Kurne yelled as loudly as his feeble voice would carry. "My family is suffering as you are, my friends! How ironic is it that the mighty conquerors of Elysia cannot even provide us with protection from simple mountain bandits?"

The crowd murmured a tepid agreement.

Kurne stopped for a moment to catch his breath and examine the crowd. His eyes landed on Morvin, and they became alight with anger and resentment at the sight of the Nirali. "My stores grow low," the old man continued, turning his gaze back to the commoners. "How can we expect to survive the winter when we have to draw from reserves now? Niralan's incompetence will starve us!"

"It's not so easy dealing with a guerilla force," Morvin chimed in. The crowd, finally noticing his presence, shrunk before his thundering voice, looking on timidly. "Nobody ever seems to see a thing. These bandits, the Beechbloods, are in and out before we can respond." He crossed his arms. "Tell me, were you ever militarily trained?"

"In tactics, yes," Kurne bragged, glowing with pride. "From my time at the University in the Capital."

"Then you know that you cannot win a guerilla war by force alone," Morvin stated. "One must have information."

Kurne nodded, but remained silent.

"We need to know more about who we face, clearly," Morvin continued. "Perhaps you can provide me some enlightenment on our enemy."

"Of course, General," Kurne said. "I will get us a private room to-"

"No," Morvin growled with a few slow, plodding steps forward. "We'll do it here, among the people. I want them to hear your answers, too." He breathed deeply, centering himself before speaking. "I'm curious as to why this didn't happen before we arrived. Elysia had very little problem with them, but Niralan is suddenly a target. These are your farm routes, Kurne. Any insight?"

Kurne pursed his lips and shook his head. "No, not so much. I only know that the Beechbloods were petrified of Elysia."

"Does that not give them all the more reason to fear Niralan?" Morvin posited. "Have we not felled that mighty tree? What could Elysia boast that their killer does not?"

Kurne rumbled in a smarmy, derisive chuckle. "You think you're terrifying, don't you, General?" He leaned forward with a toothy, yellowed grin. "You think that Niralan's rope is the greatest fear that has ever touched this world. There are worse things than dying."

"Such as?" asked the General.

"Flaying. Amputations. Castration. Brands. Quartering," Kurne listed coldly. "All punishments laid out by the former empire against thieves and murderers like this, a fact that I think you well know. Compared to that, your threats of hanging may as well be an invitation to die peacefully in bed."

"Such barbaric punishments are facets of the old world," Morvin riposted. "Sadistic fantasies dreamed up by demented men. Our way is right."

"Right as it may be, it only emboldens the wicked," Kurne contended. "Fear is required in a place like this."

The people murmured in wary agreement.

"You must commit forces to weed them out and deal this just punishment," continued the Noble. "You claim to be the saviors of the Elysian people. Prove it with your actions."

"When we can," Morvin replied. "For now, we are overstretched."

The crowd grumbled in disagreement, casting many a frustrated glance toward their conqueror.

Kurne was quick to utilize the unrest. "By what, I wonder?" His eyes blazed with a furious determination. "Some damn conquering romp into Se'Vikoral, perhaps? More mass murder to gain land that you do not need? You would let people starve to spill more blood?"

"It's more than that," Morvin snapped. "It's a better world, an idea of peace."

"I'm sure," the Noble replied, his voice encrusted in a viscous, flowing sarcasm. "How many people will this peaceful idea kill?"

"Those deserving, and them alone," answered the General, a stoic confidence emboldening his words. "This problem will be addressed. You have my word."

The gathered crowd grumbled in unsurety as the Nirali strode off, amidst a billowing cloak and the metallic thunder of armor.

The door to the command center flew open and banged against the wall, making way for an armored being of pure frustration. The threshold was slammed back shut with equal force, and a small crack began to run across its shabby wooden planks.

Morvin violently shoved a freshly delivered pile of letters from the table. He could barely see his invasion maps beneath the glittery parchments and ornate gold letterheads of the cretinous wastrels, and shiny specks of glitter had managed to find their way onto every river and mountain drawn on the sepia-colored paper below.

"I take it the walk didn't go well," Skarde observed, waiting in the corner patiently for his commander. "What happened?"

"Kurne was whipping up the people," Morvin said, finally taking a moment to slow his rage. "According to him, these bandits don't fear us."

"He called us weak?" Skarde asked.

"In a word," grumbled the General. He rapped his knuckles on the table, mulling a thought. "The people of Vulmoor seem to agree. From the sound of it, this part of Elysia was much more used to tortuous punishments for criminal activity. Uncivilized and unspeakable acts." He shook his head. "One can't help but wonder if they might have been necessary ones. What do you think, Skarde?"

The Lieutenant smiled, maintaining a calm and sure demeanor in the face of his superior's frustration. "General, what is Karsus' first command?"

Morvin looked to the floor and sighed, but obliged. "Preserve the people."

"I've heard some whispers of what used to happen in the dungeons of this part of the world," Skarde said softly. "East Elysia fell because we showed the people a better way. We will do the same in the west."

"I hope so," Morvin rumbled, closing his eyes. "I can see it, Skarde, like it's right there." He smiled and subconsciously reached out his hand, as if he could grab hold of the thought. "A north where everyone can prosper. An enviable, unified nation standing in defiance of a cold and uncaring continent."

"I can too, sir," replied the Lieutenant, placing a hand on the General's shoulder. "We will take Se'Vikoral by year's end, but we will not do so at the expense of our creed. We will follow Karsus' commands."

"We will," Morvin affirmed, opening his eyes. "Thank you, Skarde."

The young man nodded with a smile. "Of course. There's one more thing, though." He pointed to a trade route map on the table. "Moryn got hit. There wasn't much lumber stolen, but a lot of it was burned, and it was bound to be traded for wheat."

Morvin sighed deeply, an involuntary act that was becoming uncomfortably commonplace. "We should expect the same to happen to Remure and Skjorn, then."

"Yessir," Skarde affirmed. "We can send a few mounted scouts to watch over the roads and see what they can shake loose."

"Do so," instructed the General. "We need all the troops we can spare to deal with this."

Skarde nodded. "I'll send them out at first light."

"Very good," Morvin said. "How goes the staging?"

Skarde smiled brightly. "Better news. The armies are massing and preparing operating bases neat the Se'Vikoran border. Silena has already arrived, and Tarkus isn't far behind." He shifted uncomfortably and furrowed his brow. "We'll be the last to arrive, though."

"The superior General being late will hurt morale," Morvin observed with a scratch at his stubble.

"They had easier routes," soothed the Lieutenant. "We'll get there, sir."

Morvin nodded solemnly, a feat of effort, like the heaviness on his face had a measurable weight to it. "Military strategy always came easily to me, Skarde. Moving troops, picking points of attack, setting up defenses…" He tapped the table lightly. "I'm the man who can take territory, and the man who can hold it. I'm not sure I'm the man who can stick around afterwards to pick up the pieces."

Skarde chuckled. "Few of us are. Politics are for the more even minded." He slapped his superior officer on the shoulder and grinned widely. "People like us don't feel that kind of calm peace unless we've been stabbed."

Morvin chortled at the jest, but he quickly moved on, as his mind had little room for such small pleasures. "What do you think of Remure's deal?"

The question gave Skarde pause, but an answer soon came. "It makes sense. We could continue our march as soon as our criminal element has been dealt with. No sense in waiting for supplies from the capital if we don't have to."

"*If* we can get control of the bandits," Morvin pointed out. "We need to focus in and get this done. Keep your eyes and ears open and wait for a mistake."

Skarde nodded, saluted, and strode out the door, leaving Morvin alone to contemplate past, present, and future in the quiet shack.

CHAPTER TWENTY-TWO:

UNRAVELED

26th OF THE MORN OF HARVEST
NORTHERN YEAR 715

"You march into our town with your armies, you great conquerors of the gilded Empire of Elysia!" Remure spat, his voice echoing about the walls of the private room at the Inn. This time, the Noble was not alone, but was flanked by two furious faces, those of Ingvald Skjorn and Ven Moryn. "But bandits?" the man continued, his face as red as a ripe tomato while spittle soared across the table with every word. "No, they cannot stop bandits! Five full shipments from the three of us *in one day*, Morvin. An absurdity!"

"We want them dealt with as much as you do, Remure," Morvin replied with a deep sigh. He glanced at Skarde with exasperation (returned by a shrug), but he quickly snapped his eyes back to the Noblemen. "We can't exactly go out and run them down. These forests are vast."

"Elysia did," Skjorn said coldly, his voice a low, subdued rumble, like distant thunder. "Every five years or so, when they got bold. We'd get a whole battalion of conscripts to comb the woods, root 'em out."

"For morns on end, I hear," Skarde said. "You know such resources are beyond us."

"Because you want Se'Vikoral," Remure snarled, pointing accusatorily while the shadows of the room danced over a face of disgust. "You want to conquer."

"We want to unite," corrected the General. "It is irrelevant. We cannot spare the troops."

"I've had enough, Morvin!" Remure thundered. His crimson face seemed to grow ever brighter with fury, and each moment brought with it less restraint from the contempt he clearly felt welling within. "Your inaction is going to cost lives."

"Falling even further behind on schedule may cost many more,"

Morvin countered. "There are certain obstacles in the west that we'd rather not face."

"Soldiers," Moryn quickly rebutted. His voice was clammy and coarse, each word seeming to hang like an acrid vapor in the still air of the room. "They would be people who signed up to die. Here, innocent people will starve. Children."

Morvin rubbed his temple and shot his subordinate another glance. The younger officer shared the General's zealous drive to continue, but his mind was calmer, not plagued by the past failures and nightmares of an old soldier. His mind stayed with the people, where it belonged, and a single look at the fervor on Skarde's face was all it took for Morvin's mind to be made up.

"We will stay," conceded the General. "The people must be preserved, at all costs."

Remure recoiled lightly and smiled in genuine surprise. "The mighty General of Niralan relents!" he nodded in calm acceptance. "Your aid is appreciated, but that is only one half of the whole issue." He leaned heavily against the table. "What of the deal I proposed? It will be needed now more than ever."

"We would be inclined to take it," Morvin said. "Our ways would be implemented fully with the coming of our garrison, but you would run things economically until then." He waved a hand. "Anything that gets us moving quicker."

"I may have a solution that would benefit all parties," Skjorn rumbled.

Remure furrowed his brow, casting a sideways glance towards the North Elysian. "You didn't tell us."

"No reason," Skjorn shrugged. "Nothin' you could do. Wanted to see how it all played out first."

"On with it, then!" Morvin snapped with impatience.

"I know a coupla boys," Skjorn obliged calmly. "Northern, like me. Old soldiers. They formed a merc band a few years back, call themselves the 'darkness' or some dumb thing like that. Take payment for just about anything."

"You think they can deal with the bandits?" Morvin asked.

Skjorn nodded. "They can stick around a hell of a lot longer than you can, and they're brutal to boot." He crossed his arms. "Given our losses in goods, our pockets are gonna be tied up with imports to help survive the winter. Niralan would need to pay for their services, but we could handle the coordination."

"I see," Morvin said, tapping his fingers on the table. "Sounds expensive."

"I may have another solution, if we're discussing hiring outside security forces," Moryn purred, drawing inquisitive looks all around. "I know a group. Made up of white-and-golds that owe me a favor, true professionals."

"*White-and-golds*?" Remure repeated incredulously. His tone was of a genuine, unsettled surprise. "What are you on about?"

"Elysian Royal Swordsmen," Moryn explained. "They owe me a favor."

Morvin's eyelids quivered as he met the Lunari's stare, finding a rapidly sinking abyss looking back. Moryn's obsidian eyes poured a cold and calculating glare toward the Nirali, containing an unmistakable intelligence and unfaltering confidence within. In little more than a moment, the Elf had shifted his demeanor from insolence and hubris to determination and respect, an unsettling metamorphosis that did not go unnoticed by the perceptive Nirali.

"Out," Morvin ordered, his eyes suddenly alight. "All of you. Now."

"Morvin-" Remure attempted to protest.

"OUT!" Morvin boomed, his voice shaking the table. "This meeting has concluded. Return to your homes."

The Nobles, after a few nasty glares at Moryn, indignantly obeyed, filing out the door.

The General collapsed his head into his hands the moment the threshold swung shut. He rubbed his temple and let out a groan.

"Sir?" Skarde asked. "We should seriously think about hiring the mercenaries. Se'Vikoral can't wai-"

"We made a mistake," growled the General.

"Pardon, sir?" Skarde said.

"Recite the Nirali military intelligence field manual entry on the Elysian Royal Swordsmen," Morvin ordered.

Skarde hesitated, but did so dutifully after a moment. "The Elysian Royal Swordsmen, also known informally as the white-and-golds, are special forces units of the Elysian military. They often operate behind enemy lines, willing to sacrifice anything for their empire." His eyes finally ignited, coming to an understanding. "Elysia believes that every citizen owes the Swordsmen their lives, and that any who served honorably in that capacity owe nothing further to their nation or those in it."

"We made a mistake, Skarde," Morvin grumbled, lost deep in a fury that was directed fully at himself. "We underestimated the intelligence of desperate men."

Skarde nodded silently.

Morvin sighed, rubbing his temple. "The Swordsmen didn't often serve in the imperial west, or even near the Capital. Remure and Skjorn had no idea what Moryn was talking about, but he had to know that one of us would understand. He signaled us."

"For what reason?" Skarde asked, rubbing his chin.

"I'm not sure," Morvin muttered. "We've dealt with creatures of emotion until now, predictable men whose effort to work against us was plain to the eye." He sighed again. "When one is so focused on the road ahead, plenty can occur unnoticed behind his back. They used our determination against us."

"I still hesitate to believe they could orchestrate anything greater than a pile of coins," Skarde said, a clear hatred seeping through his voice. "I don't know that those men have a full brain cell between them. They're just like the others."

"Therein lies the problem," Morvin rumbled with a growing hoarseness in his voice. "Skarde, how often have we met with these men?"

"Not much," replied the Lieutenant, running his hand through his hair. "We've been operating independently as much as we can."

"We've claimed to know them, Skarde," Morvin continued. "We *knew* they wouldn't hurt another respected family; we *knew* that they couldn't plan more than a meal; we *knew* that they were pompous, bumbling fools like the others." He ground his teeth while he suppressed a self-disgusted grimace. "Skarde, *how did we know?*"

Skarde bit his lip and lowered his head, breathing quickly and heavily. "A lot of recent experience dealing with their kind."

"Too much," the General growled in agreement. "Moryn dropped his act for barely a moment, yet it was enough to remind me just how little we know of these men. For an instant, I saw who he truly was." He stirred, rising from his seat. "Skarde, we may have been played into humoring a deal that leaves them with their wealth and influence while our ambassadors make the trek from the Capital. All the while, we're so blinded by our ambitions in the west that we considered paying for their own personal army. We need to make a move, and we need to do it now."

"House Moryn?" Skarde asked.

"House Moryn," Morvin confirmed, stalking out the door.

The glow from the small lantern barely lit the way through the paths to Moryn's lodge, despite fighting a full-hearted campaign against the encroaching darkness of the shadowbeech forest. Morvin hefted the dim light aloft, focusing it on the path ahead as he trudged along in his plate. Behind, Skarde and two of his most trusted soldiers listened and watched for anything out of the usual.

A soft glow emanated from somewhere ahead, flickering in the shadows. Eventually, the source became clear, a series of torches on either side of the path. They were placed between the road's edge and towering rows of well-kept hedges on either side, and, though the light was welcome, the sight of such a narrow corridor was unnerving for those who meant to walk within its walls.

"Nice place for an ambush," Skarde said, sizing up the square, perfectly trimmed bushes.

"It is," Morvin replied quietly. "He's smart."

The General halted at the torches' edge and inspected them closely. They glowed a hot red at the center and orange at the fringe, letting off a thick black smoke that was mostly odorless, having only a small twinge of bitterness to the aroma. Morvin, satisfied after a few moments of investigation, moved on.

The cresting of a small hill a short distance up the path brought with it the sight of the Moryn lodge, lying behind a tall, iron gate. Contrary to the other Noble homesteads, this was a simple structure, two-storied, not more than two decades old. The only superfluous adornment were two statues of armored, well-armed men that flanked the sides of the main passage. The tree line had been cut back across the property, leaving space for tables and outdoor activities (such as a horseshoe pit near the left wing).

"Looks like Moryn has the life out here," Skarde derided with a scoff. "He lives in a place like this while people starve."

The final word found itself overtaken by a gust of wind from the lodge, heavy and strong, blowing out the flames of torch and lantern alike as if they were wax candles. The lodge's lighting went dark at the same time, causing the Nirali to find themselves enveloped in a pressing gloom. They formed a defensive circle instinctively, attempting to gain their bearings in the crushing darkness.

"Moryn!" Morvin yelled toward the house. His voice echoed through a silent forest, with nary the skitter of a squirrel to be heard. "We are not here for violence. We wish to speak."

"So, speak!" the Noble's voice called from somewhere near the house.

"It is regarding your offer," Morvin explained. "Please, let us have a moment for discussion!"

Silence ensued for a few seconds, leaving only the whistling of the wind.

"Just you!" Moryn finally yelled. "Leave your men where they are and walk forward. Slowly."

"Sir?" Skarde asked unsurely.

"It's alright, Lieutenant," assured the General amidst his first step forward. "Stay on guard."

Morvin inched along, careful to stay on the road in the blinding darkness. Mercifully, a light came about ahead, held by one of Moryn's guards, a portly man wearing a gambeson. He met the Nirali halfway, guiding him through the impeccably kept front yard and, subsequently, to the wooden doors of the home.

The foyer was smaller than expected, with a simple coatrack and footlocker on either side of the entryway. This place had an overall rustic look to it; it wasn't an expression of wealth, but rather one of comfort, like a mountain inn during winter. Even the wood of the floor and the walls were of merely acceptable quality, a statement of frugality that seemed to be uncommon to the Nobles of Elysia.

In front of Morvin, through an archway, there was a sitting room where two padded chairs flanked a shadowbeech table. Moryn sat in the chair to the right and quickly motioned for the General to take a place opposite him.

Morvin moved towards the seat, but stopped short. "I'll stand. Hard to sit in plate, you know."

"Of course!" Moryn said warmly. "My apologies for the suspicion; the world is changing rapidly, and one can never be too careful."

"On that, we agree," Morvin said. "I wanted to talk to you about something you said, back at the Inn."

"Oh, I'm sure you do!" the Noble exclaimed with a smirk. "The white-and-golds would be happy to serve."

"I'm sure," Morvin said, humoring the deception. "If you don't mind my asking, though, how did they become indebted to you?"

"It wasn't easy to get them to owe me a favor," Moryn replied eagerly, smirking in amusement. "It never is, with their type."

The General scoffed and chortled, unable to continue with the charade. "Who are you, Moryn?" he asked bluntly. "You're not some smarmy, royal-born idiot like the others, are you?"

"No longer blinded by ambition, I see," Moryn commended with a thin smile. "You're starting to see reality. To discern the false from the true."

"You and your peers have done well to blind me to the truth, surely," said Morvin, "but Moryn, once that truth is exposed, all bets are off. The Nirali will find you."

"Oh, indeed, General," Moryn agreed, interlacing his fingers upon his belly and leaning forward. "You see, my peers do not understand the fire that they play with. They do not understand the destructive power behind Niralan." Even through the solid black of his eyes, Morvin was able to glean a palpable air of sorrow that held the weight of memory within, and the Lunari found himself momentarily lost within the torment of the past. "I do."

"You know of us?" the General asked, cocking an eyebrow.

"I was a child in Eastern Elysia during the last war," Moryn replied softly. "I know your kind, and your ways. These other men think that, just because you do not make brutal examples of your enemies, you are a safe target. They do not know the reach of your vision, nor the effectiveness with which you use it. Eventually, Niralan will find and purge the cancers that infect them. They will find the truth."

"What is that truth, Moryn?" Morvin asked.

"Not yet!" the Noble quickly retorted. "I must know that my neck will not be in a noose once I give it to you."

"If you allow me to purge the corruption here, I will ensure that you and your family prosper," the Nirali assured. "We must continue with the campaign. If you facilitate that…"

"Of course," Moryn said with a chuckle. "If I support your war, you support me."

"Exactly," Morvin stated. "The truth. Now."

The Noble only extended his hand, beckoning a shake. "I have your word that I will not be harmed?"

Morvin stared for a moment, thinking deeply. He accepted the offer after a few breaths of consideration, finding the Lunari's grip to be surprisingly strong as the deal was sealed. "You have my word."

"Very well," Moryn warbled. His eyes drifted to the floor for a moment as he gathered his words. "General, have you ever seen a Dwarven mining machine?"

"Once, yes," answered the Nirali.

"You've seen the numerous gears and pistons then?" the Noble continued, finding the pace of his speech wavering under the iron gaze of the Nirali. "Each performs its individual function as steam flows through the whole device, powering it."

Morvin nodded.

"All it takes for the entire contraption to come to a grinding halt, General, is for a single piece to fail," Moryn said. "One gear cracks, and the whole machine becomes a paperweight until it's replaced." He smiled wickedly. "Moving parts are unreliable, yet critical."

Morvin nodded silently once again.

"What my peers do not understand is that sometime, someplace…" He trailed off while a clear gratification painted his face, as if these precious few moments of treachery were the finest of his life. "A piece of their little conspiracy will break. A farmer will see too much, or a captured bandit will speak."

"You wanted to get out before the piece broke?" Morvin asked.

"No," Moryn corrected. "I simply wanted to be the first piece to break. If I'm the gear that cracks…"

"Ah," Morvin replied with a smirk. He was coming to respect the man more with every word, and this turn of events was a pleasant, if unexpected, surprise. "You can take the rest of the machine down on your terms."

"Precisely," Moryn hissed with a frigidness that ran a tingle up Morvin's spine. "You see, I have accepted the inevitable. My business is no longer my business, nor will it ever be again. We both know this."

"Your possessions belong to Niralan now," confirmed the Nirali.

Moryn nodded. "Gold and wealth are the pillars of the old world. I see the new one that you're building, and I know my place within it."

Morvin shook his head and smiled as relief (and more than a little amusement) washed over his face. "You want to be Magistrate."

"I do," Moryn affirmed, standing. "I could make Vulmoor into a city as great as Elysia. This could be your capital in the Imperial West, but only if there is a unity behind one man. This cannot happen while the other families still draw breath." His voice became icy cold, dripping in resentment. "It is time for their kind to fade into history."

Morvin tossed the idea around in his head, chewing on his lower lip. "You are unlike any noble we've met," he said after a while. "While the rest squabble to keep what they have, you have moved on, haven't you?"

"As I said, I know your people," Moryn replied. "I can see beyond my fortune, to far greater days. For Vulmoor, and for my new home and empire. For those like me, the only thing left is to become one with the ways of the Nirali."

"Agreed," Morvin said. "You've proven to be quite the valuable mind, Moryn. Fitting for the leader of this town."

The Noble smiled again, this time with a clear pride. "Thank you, General. Now, shall we begin dismantling the rest of the machine?"

Morvin nodded and listened intently while the Nobleman spooled out the twisting threads of treachery and resistance before his eyes.

CHAPTER TWENTY-THREE:

A NEW DAWN

27th OF THE MORN OF HARVEST
NORTHERN YEAR 715

A rumble of thunder shook the roof of the Inn, sending vibrations through the wooden walls and floors of the establishment. The roar of the sky seemed to bolster the assault of a frigid wind which slammed rain against the windows and rattled their frames. The massive fireplace roared in the corner, burning with a black plume of smoke that ascended a large iron chimney to the roof above. All the while, shadows flickered in the gloomy dining hall, fighting a warm glow from the chandelier that hung peacefully above a growing mob of farmers and workmen.

"Barely got in the door without being noticed," Skarde murmured, slipping into a seat next to Morvin at the bar. He was dressed in a chestnut brown cloak and matching hood, plain-looking garments that served to mask his face from prying eyes. Morvin wore the same, keeping the cloth wrapped tightly around his head while he hunched in his seat.

"As did I," rumbled the General. "The crowd was big then. It's been growing. Moryn was right. They mean to make their move."

"Indeed," Skarde agreed contemptuously. "The last day must have been unnerving for them." He shot a glance towards the fireplace, where the three Nobles talked and gathered their people.

They stood tall in front of the roaring flames, rallying more to their cause with each passing moment. All were dressed in their finest clothes; Remure in a bright red tunic with gold fringe, Kurne in a purple jacket studded down the middle with precious gems, while Skjorn stood out in a traditional northern cloak of snow-white fur.

"Again and again, they promised us wealth and prosperity, yet they do not deliver their promises," Remure growled loudly. "We have given from our own stores to help feed their soldiers so that you may eat. We have asked Niralan time and again to work with the people who actually know this town, yet they refuse!"

"My farms produce, yet their fruits never reach you, nor do any of the goods I import," Kurne chimed in. "In the time before Niralan, you could be sure that food and supplies would arrive in good time. Now, new rulers arrive, and that surety disappears. Not a single wagon has gone without being waylaid in three days."

The crowd responded with a unified growl of anger. "My family hasn't had a full meal in four!" a farmer screamed.

"Not for lack of our trying, that I assure you!" Remure pointed out. "It has become clear to us that Niralan has no interest in our people. Tell me, how many of your family have joined their army?"

Various numbers rang out from the crowd, from one to six.

"Our people agree to lay down their lives for this nation," the Nobleman continued. "How can they expect their promised reward of land if Niralan will not even provide food for their current subjects? Why won't Niralan use their vaunted military force to protect us? To make sure that even a single wagon gets through these relentless assaults?"

"We've offered them solutions, as well," Skjorn boomed. "We have many forces that can act as security for us, if only Niralan would provide the coin. These *liberators* could continue marauding, having only to ensure that the proper payment is made on time. They refused."

The crowd's anger grew to a boiling point as the Nobles continued, and each word served as a rod that stoked the embers of rebellion.

"Our only hope is ensuring that Niralan allows us to protect ourselves," Remure growled. "My people, we have accepted their conditions without question. We have trusted them to fulfill a great many promises. It is now time to put our foot down and force them to do so!"

"We ask you to march with us to meet General Morvin and his toady Lieutenant," Kurne cried, which caused Skarde to shift angrily in his seat. "We must ensure that our voices are heard by the elite of Niralan. We are with you!"

"Are you with us?" Remure bellowed.

"For Vulmoor!" a farmer shouted from the crowd, which drew an echoing cheer from the rest.

"Good!" Remure shouted with an unparalleled energy. "Let us

make our voice heard!"

"It already has been," Morvin thundered. His voice projected across the room with a frigid anger behind it, silencing the Inn to nothing but the dull roar of rain and thunder, joined only by the crackling of the fire.

"Gen-... Morvin?" Remure stammered.

"Indeed," the General confirmed, removing his hood. Skarde followed suit, pulling back his cowl with a smirk. The crowd grew visibly frightened at the sight of the invaders, but Morvin was careful to keep his gaze focused solely on the Noble lords.

"I see you've finally decided to face your people directly," Remure spat. "You have heard our arguments, clearly. What is your response?"

Morvin took a deep breath. "Well, it's all a very nice story," he said calmly. "The murderous, lying new government, the old nobles who care about their people standing as a bulwark to defend against injustice." He chuckled. "You've got one thing wrong, though."

"Is that so?" Remure shot back incredulously. "What?"

Morvin allowed a smarmy grin to cross his face. "These complaints have already been addressed."

Again, silence overtook the Inn, leaving the forceful pounding of the rain upon the roof and the dull sloshing of overfilled gutters outside to dominate the moment.

"Is... Is that so?" Remure sputtered, after a moment of recovery from a clear confusion.

"Oh yes," Morvin confirmed. "You see, my soldiers came across a storehouse in the mountains. Quite well hidden, I must say, below a bunch of brush and built into the side of a hill. Lots of booby traps leading up to it." The Nobles' faces seemed to go whiter with each word. "Do you know what we found there?"

"I... I haven't a clue," Remure muttered shakily, struggling to keep his composure.

"Shipments from Kurne's farms. Furs from Skjorn's traders..." Morvin listed, savoring the fear that was betrayed in the eyes of these infernal men. "Ore from your mines. The bandits had been stockpiling every bit in safe locations."

"So, the bandit problem is solved?" Kurne asked, markedly calmer than his younger fellows.

"Not quite," answered the General. "We killed every Beechblood we could get our hands on, but one…" He chortled. "He had some interesting things to say. We were eager to have him meet you."

The people of Vulmoor wore looks of utter confusion at the Nirali's words. The anger and resentment seemed to have vanished, to be replaced only by curiosity.

"Come on out!" Skarde yelled over bar.

A large, North Elysian man crept cautiously through the kitchen door, pushed along by the blade of a lightly armored Nirali scout. He was mostly unharmed (save for a few bruises on his face), and he wore tattered, sweaty clothes upon his discolored skin. His wooden mask hung at his side, caked in blood.

"Tell them who you are," Morvin instructed.

Skjorn met the bandit's eyes with a glare whose intensity could have killed the man on the spot. Morvin, watching the hatred pour forth like molten metal from the Noble's eyes, felt a subdued joy welling within. They were cornered, and they knew it.

The bandit took a moment to gather himself before speaking. "My name is Fyn. I'm a member of the Beechbloods," he said with a gritty voice, wavering in fear. "I was hired by Ingvald Skjorn."

The room itself seemed to gasp, and the people whispered amongst themselves intently.

"To do what, exactly?" Skarde asked.

"To waylay wagons on the way to Vulmoor," Fyn replied. "Niralan doesn't know these lands, and we knew we could steal and flee to our heart's content without bein' found. It was supposed to be an easy job."

"Were you hired to hurt any of the Nobles?" Morvin interrogated. "To hurt Kurne, for instance?"

"No," Fyn answered, practically wilting under the weight of Skjorn's eyes. Still, he managed to continue. "We were told not to hurt nobody. Just steal from the wagons and bring 'em up into mountains to hide. Skjorn said he'd get *real* angry if we killed anyone or destroyed anything without orders to do that. He didn't want to hurt the old timer, especially."

"This is preposterous!" Remure exclaimed, his face still white as a ghost. "You've obviously forced this poor man into saying what you want him to."

"Tell me, Fyn, what purpose did these raids serve?" Morvin posited, ignoring the Noble entirely.

"They didn't say much about why," Fyn obeyed shakily. "But eventually we figured it out. We were hittin' wagons to stop supplies from reachin' Vulmoor, and to keep 'em from bein' traded for goods and such."

"How exactly did you figure it out?" Morvin said, continuing on with the line of thought.

"Well, the people was starvin' for one," the bandit replied. "Only reason that they were is 'cause Skjorn, Kurne and Remure hired us to make it so. Me and Dray, our leader, figured that they wouldn't let that happen less they were up to somethin'."

"This is all very entertaining," Kurne said calmly. After his initial surprise, he continued to retain a cool head. "What does any of this serve? Who is to say that this isn't some man you found on the street?"

"Me," a cold, slimy voice replied, echoing throughout the cavernous Inn. Moryn leaned upon the railing of the second floor's balcony, unseen by his former comrades and content to watch until now.

"Ven?" Kurne growled. Though he clearly meant the sound to be low and threatening, there was a palpable dread held within.

"My people," Moryn boomed, "Niralan brings you the truth. These men attempted to recruit me into their little scheme."

"Could you identify who you mean by 'these men'?" Morvin prompted.

"Alistair Remure, Algernon Kurne and Ingvald Skjorn, General," Moryn replied calmly, staring at the Nobles. "They desire the power of the old world above all else, because they know nothing more. They starved the people of this town and interrupted their own trade, all to force Niralan into concessions."

"I would apologize for our conduct," Morvin quickly added. "Our eyes were too focused on a future that hasn't yet arrived. We want to offer Se'Vikoral the same things we did Vulmoor, but our idealism got the better of us. Our people are our priority." He gave Moryn a go-ahead nod.

"Niralan had a lapse in judgement," Moryn continued. "These men sought to take advantage of that. They offered the Nirali a deal: Let them keep their trade routes and their unfair contracts with you, provide them with a personal army, and let them manage Vulmoor as they always have. For them, nothing would have fundamentally changed." His eyes turned downward. "I realize that my treatment of all of you, my people, hasn't exactly been an example to the world. Unlike these others, though, I can understand my mistakes and move on." He sighed and shook his head in disgust. "They would rather see you die than give up their gold and power. I had a problem with that."

The people slowly turned to the Nobles. Their eyes burned with the rage of the sun, blazing a palpable fear into the tremoring lords of Vulmoor.

"You will let Niralan and their stooges feed you lies?" Remure screamed in desperation, a crimson red hue creeping out from his cheeks. "This is a preposterous claim! We provided for Niralan from our own storehouses so that our people could eat their own hard-grown food, or is that fact forgotten so suddenly?"

"It makes sense now!" a voice yelled from the crowd. They pushed their way through the cluster of bodies and into the clearing between Morvin and the Nobles. It was Kly, the farmer Skarde had singled out during his first speech here. "They said they donated a bunch, yeah?"

Morvin nodded and grunted an affirmative.

"I was up there at Kurne's delivering some barley the other day," Kly said. "Last harvest of the year. Mr. Kurne's storehouses were burstin'. He was well stocked for the winter, I remember thinkin'."

"Yeah!" Another farmer yelled. "He had heaps of grain piled and there was some meats hangin' from the rafters. Didn't look like he gave much away, if anything."

"Curious," Skarde said with a grin. "The Beechblood storehouse was conspicuously missing a fair bit of supplies, according to the ledgers the bandits kept. The amount was consistent with what our soldiers would need for a few days." He met Remure's eyes. "You didn't give a damn thing up, did you?"

The dark room grew pitch black as the crowd looked back and forth between the foreigners and the Nobles. The Nirali, for their part, simply stood silent and let the people make their decision.

"They are fooling you!" Remure yelped with a voice both terrified and shrill. "They would tell you anything to-"

The Noble's words were interrupted by Skjorn flinging a small knife from out of the sleeves of his robes. It sailed through the crowd with pinpoint accuracy, slicing the fringes of clothes and cloaks as it whistled through the miniscule gaps, before impacting Fyn with a wet slap. It cut into his heart, killing him instantly and sending him crumpling to the floor.

Skjorn whipped another knife, causing the gathered crowd to reel away and try to shelter. This blade soared upwards, however, and sliced into Moryn's shoulder, which sent him spinning backwards.

"See to him!" Morvin ordered, prompting an immediate response from the younger Nirali.

The General charged and leaped over a table, grabbing a mug as he went. The whistling of a third knife appeared, careening through a crowd that tried madly to part before harm could befall them. Morvin, spotting the blade hurtling towards him, hurled the tankard with all of his might. It intercepted the projectile, and both dagger and cup went tumbling harmlessly away.

The crowd finally managed to part fully, revealing Skjorn's imposing figure standing tall. His shoulders were squared, and the roaring fireplace silhouetted the fibers of his fur cloak in an intense glow as he began his charge. He thundered forward, throwing all of his rage into his strides.

Morvin obliged the man's anger, meeting him head-on with a hard impact. An unstoppable force met an immovable object, and so both bounced backwards onto the floor with a thundering *crash-crack* as the boards splintered beneath tumbling titans.

Morvin, being no stranger to hard hits, was upon his feet without delay, having endured far worse in the last few morns. Skjorn, meanwhile, was disoriented, being unused to combat, and he had only made it to his knees when his face met the sole of the Nirali's boot. He went tumbling backwards, landing between Remure and Kurne, who could only look on in horror.

Skjorn tried to rise again, heaving with breath. Morvin was quite happy to assist; he grabbed the Noble by the front of the collar and hefted him up. The North Elysian, half conscious, glared at his enemy with defiance.

"Had to take a few with me before I went out," Skjorn grumbled weakly. "Knew we lost the moment you showed up here. Hang me and get it over with."

Morvin smirked wickedly, letting darkness overtake his heart. "No."

He tossed the large man forcefully forward, directly into the center of the roaring fire beyond. Shadowbeech had been used for warmth that freezing night, wood which would bleed its sap and create a long-smoldering heat source during the long winters. As Skjorn was finding out, though, it was quite unpleasant when the liquid stuck to your flesh.

The Noble rolled out from the pit, slathered in red embers which crept over his skin like the magma of a volcano. The blaze steadily intensified as the viscous sap ran like honey over his flesh and clothing. Skjorn screamed, an unnaturally high-pitched sound, the pain forcing him back to his full wits. He scrambled madly to his feet and danced around in place, just for a moment, before grabbing hold of Kurne's wrist. "Help me, old man!"

The older Noble could offer no assistance against the running of the flame. Skjorn's grip, in fact, served only to cause some of the embering sap to bleed onto the old man, transferring from skin to skin. Kurne screamed in agony, only for a moment, before his North Elysian fellow succumbed to the pain and collapsed forward. The large man's smoldering corpse shifted and bumped while the elder attempted to escape his similarly fiery fate, all in vain.

Morvin's chest heaved. He suddenly realized that there was blood upon his nose, feeling a tickle as it dripped off the end. He felt his forehead, finding a large gash from the impact of the Nobleman. Men, meanwhile, arrived with buckets of water, eager to put out the blaze before it spread to something of value.

Remure stared wide eyed at Morvin, finding no words strong enough to push through his terror. His skin looked as if it was a dead man's, pale, with a slight touch of sickly green.

"Skarde?" Morvin called, keeping his eye on the Noble.

"He's fine," Skarde reported. "Just a laceration!"

The crowd gathered around the scene, gawking at the two burned bodies while the farmers struggled to extinguish the flames that painted their blackened skin. Morvin was quick to ensnare attention and pull the people's eyes away from the brutality.

"Vulmoor!" bellowed the Nirali General, locking eyes with Remure. "You've been used as a pawn and left to starve by those who called you their own. You suffered while they attempted to retain riches and power for families who have no regard for the common people. The last of them stands before you now." He smiled widely. "What justice do the people of Niralan desire for Alistair Remure?"

Remure shrunk into the corner as the crowd's decision was rendered: "Death!"

Morvin sat in the grand library of Alistair Remure (now converted to a command center), listening to the steady *click-clack* of a grandfather clock as its pendulum swung back and forth, breaking an otherwise silent room. The device had to be reset often, yet the General had no issues doing so himself, for the rhythmic sound brought him comfort and focus, the first he had been able to attain since his arrival in this town.

Remure had been hung days earlier. It was a simple ceremony that, in traditional Nirali fashion, got the job done quickly and without fanfare. A magisterial election had been held, finding Moryn to have cleanly won against his only challenger, an older farmer previously indentured to Kurne. Meanwhile, with the meddling nobility out of the way, southern traders had been remarkably open to dealing with the Eastmen, finding the alluring glitter of gold a fine counterbalance to the anxiety typical of partnerships with Niralan.

Vulmoor, at last, was secured.

Niralan's attention could finally turn toward the great forests and fortresses of Se'Vikoral, the last step to a united north. Their armies massed on the border, a march of about a week from Vulmoor. All that was left to do was to finalize the recruitment of Elysians willing to fight, mustering them to arms under the doctrine of Niralan. It would take time, but the new blood would make fine soldiers, the General knew.

A knock came at the door. *thump-thump, thump-thump-thump.*

Morvin sighed deeply and tensed. "Enter."

An iron banded door at the far side of the room slowly creaked open, revealing the hooded, indigo-chinned woman who had visited his shack weeks earlier. "Morvin."

"I don't care what the Dreamer wants," Morvin growled. "She has to wait."

"Do I?" the woman asked. Her voice was noticeably different, in both pitch and cadence, being more confident and more drawn out. "I don't recall that being a part of our deal, General. I was there when it was reached, remember."

Morvin eyed the woman warily. "You weren't."

The woman sighed. She pulled off her hood, revealing a bald head and blackened eyes that swirled with a silvery, milky color within. Creeping tendrils of shadow escaped from those glimmering depths and crawled upon her face, probing around like worms searching for rot. "You do not speak with one of our anointed at this moment, Nirali, for through her my voice can reach you." She smirked and stood tall. "I am the Dreamer, Morvin, and I signed the pact with a shimmering red ink."

"Hm," Morvin grunted. Searching his memory, he found the small detail to be correct. "Good. I can tell you this to your face, then: I will not give you non-combatants. You have to wait."

"I am not here for that," the woman replied calmly. "I am only here to inform you personally of our standing. There has been a development."

Morvin's eyes narrowed, ever suspicious of his nation's enigmatic benefactors. "What?"

"My Dream, General, and the herald of a world that will grow tall." She took a deep, uneven breath. "I finally have proof that what I have told my people is true, and that my waking is not needed. I am on the trail of a quarry that we have sought for centuries, the last piece of our long-held plans. Our focus will remain on this until it is dealt with."

"What about Se'Vikoral?" Morvin asked, having little patience for anything beyond what benefited his nation. "Our pact?"

"My people will fulfill that obligation, I assure you," the woman soothed. "Stay on your course and let us see this through. The final fragment of our new world is at hand, and we will help to deliver that which was earned."

"See that you do," growled the General. "You will be needed."

"In due time, Morvin," the woman replied. "I will reach out again when we've reached a resolution."

Morvin nodded in reply, watching warily as the woman shuffled through the door and closed it behind her. He looked down at his maps once more, seeing the blood and glory of a dozen battles looming in the fog of the future. The *click-clack* of the clock again became the dominant sound in the room, and the General of Niralan fell deep into his thoughts.

PART FOUR:

THE VISION OF REDJA

CHAPTER TWENTY-FOUR:

IMPROVED SKILLS

Nordiskan Fleet, Borean Ocean

25th OF THE MORN OF HARVEST
NORTHERN YEAR 715

He was fast, deceptively so. Despite a convincing show of being aged and slow, Edlevin's hands moved in a blur and found openings, once and again, slapping with wet *thwacks*, leaving behind purple and black bruises that ached with every move. In turn, Alauren's metal blade touched nothing, though an increasing determination was built within her with every failed strike and new injury.

Regardless of success, the smith persisted. She arced her blade, feigning a centered overhead strike with both hands. At the last second, she swept her torso hard to the left and down, going for a low blow on the leg.

Thwack!

The wooden sword impacted her hard on the neck, drawing a grunt. Her weapon, as it had for days, connected only with the deck, shaving off a few splinters effortlessly.

"You're overcommitting," Edlevin critiqued gruffly, adjusting his stiff, stone kaftan. "When you throw your body forward into a low blow like that, your entire upper side is open to me, provided I'm fast enough. Most combatants worth their salt will be."

"Noted," said the blacksmith, rubbing the back her neck; a small indigo splotch had erupted from an earlier blow and, though little more than a thumbprint in size, it still made its presence clearly known. "You know, you don't have to hit so hard, old man."

"How else will you learn, Ally?" Edlevin cackled, throwing out his arms. "Be glad you're not in Fangirm. They used iron rods!"

Alauren cricked her neck, eliciting a loud pop before taking her ready stance once again. She bobbed along with the longship, feeling it rise and fall under her feet. For a time, the vessel's heavy heaving seemed abrupt and unpredictable, like the ocean itself was a great beast slamming upon the hull, trying to knock her over the side and into the hungry depths below. This monster was intractable, wild and furious, yet there was a rhythm to its rage, a balance that lay deep within the well of time and experience. Like a great stag of the Arbari, it could be ridden, if one had the sense for it.

The blacksmith took a deep breath and centered herself. "Again."

The old soldier was happy to oblige. He went on the offensive first, raining down three overhead strikes in rapid succession, driving Alauren back on her heels. She blocked each in turn with quick, heavy swipes that deflected the wooden sword to her right, displaying a skill that had seemed beyond her capability just a week ago. Sensing an opening at the end of the third of Edlevin's failed attacks, she stabbed out forwards, a blow which was batted to the left with little trouble. Knowing that there was enough room behind her, she broke off and jumped backwards in a contortion, just before a quick midsection riposte could connect with her belly.

The smith went on the offensive again, striking left-right-left in careful succession, sure to keep her stance narrow and ready to defend, if need be. Edlevin batted away each attempt easily with his wooden sword, but found himself having to jump backwards to dodge as Alauren concluded her flurry with an unexpected jab towards his chest.

The blacksmith kept her blade pointing towards Edlevin and lunged, carrying forward with three quick steps. In the same motion, she threw her offhand out behind her and spun her torso sideways to minimize her vulnerable points; stabbing out hard, she aimed for the center of the stone jacket and kept her eyes on the old soldier's movements.

Edlevin reacted, throwing himself backward by a step and falling for Alauren's feint. She abruptly whipped her blade hard to the left and instantly back to the right, sending a slash low. The wooden sword appeared just in time, intercepting the assault and holding firm against the pressure.

Alauren's blade dug into the timber, finding a firm hold on a deep notch near the center. The weapons locked into place, caught quite firmly upon each other, allowing her to push the attack, pressing with all her might and forcing Edlevin's weapon to a vertical position at chest level.

The struggle was one of pure might for a few precious moments as both combatants could do little but push and heave, trying desperately to gain the upper hand. They grunted and growled, and Edlevin even found time to shoot his old friend a proud, amused smile in the midst of their deadlock.

The blacksmith, noticing the moment of distraction, suddenly rolled her wrist and carried forward, letting her sword slide off the wood, into a stabbing motion. Edlevin's sword, in turn, shot forward between her chin and shoulder, where it rested softly against her neck.

"Fffffffuck!" Alauren growled in frustration. "I almost had you."

"Almost?" Edlevin replied with a nervous chuckle. Indeed, on the left side of his neck, the blacksmith's blade had also found a resting place, little more than a stubble's length from touching flesh.

"Did I just...?" Alauren said, trailing off with a proud, unbelieving chortle.

"We'll call that one a draw, then," chuckled the old soldier. He disengaged his sword with an unnecessarily elaborate twirl and carefully backed away from the edge of Alauren's blade. "The ship hit a wave right as you rolled your wrist, sent me off balance."

"There wash no damned wave, ye senile blowhard!" Valin slurred from his seat near the railing, where he enjoyed the show with a sloshing cup of mead. "She'sh gettin' better!"

"Says the drunkard," Edlevin snapped facetiously. "You wouldn't know a wave from your arse, in your state."

"Drell agreesh with me!" protested the Dwarf, carrying along a light burp with the last word. "And don't ye undereshtimate me ability t' know whatsh a wave and whatsh not! Some o' me besht friends are shea Dwarvesh!"

"Sounds good to me," Alauren agreed with a chuckle. "I tied you fair and square, Karlmaðr."

"Oh, now you've started with the nickname?" Edlevin grumbled with a deep sigh. "I'm not that old!"

"I like it," the smith replied. "It has a very Edlevin-y feel about it. Rolls off the tongue."

Edlevin crossed his arms and huffed petulantly. "Well, I disagree."

"Then it's a good thing I rarely ask for your opinion on these things, isn't it?" Alauren jabbed with a smirk. "Now, shall I give you a real bruise to match the one on your ego, then?"

The old soldier chuckled, dropping his offended demeanor in the matter of a second. "Just watch your strikes, Ally. That one came close to giving me a crimson shave."

The smith stepped back and squared herself once more, taking a few deep breaths to steady her balance upon the rolling waves. The sword had felt progressively better in her hands over the hours and days, going from an unfamiliar weight she could only begin to control to something that began to feel more like an extension of her physical form. Edlevin had told her that dueling with a blade could be quite like a dance, but she found it to be much more akin to working at her forge, striking carefully and with precision, all while keeping careful watch over her surroundings. Regardless of the metaphor, it had grown on her.

She took the lead in attacking this time, striking twice from the left, horizontally, before bringing her blade up with both hands and arcing it downward, like a lumberjack hacking at a log. Edlevin blocked the first two blows and knocked the third to the side, opening the smith's defensive stance to attacks. She jumped backwards as the ship rolled over a wave, giving her more height on her leap and allowing for an easy reset.

After a protracted moment in the air, Alauren landed hard on her feet and ducked into a forward roll; carried by the now-rising ship below, the momentum delivered her to within striking distance of her mentor in less than a blink.

The blacksmith sprung to her feet and pressed the attack, raining blow after blow upon the wooden sword and its swift wielder. She struck high, aiming for the head, then low, going for the hips, then back to high at neck-height. The plan was to force Edlevin into exposing an opening, but the old soldier was careful to remain in a defensive stance, weathering the storm upon a solid foundation of experience.

There was a consistent weakness in the man's form, however. When the smith sent an assault high, there was a split second where his left leg, holding his weight as he pivoted, was exposed. If she were swift enough, she knew, she might be able to exploit the subtle mistake.

She broke off, preferring caution to another bruise, and used the opportunity to wipe sweat-drenched hair away from her face with her sleeve. With a devilish smile, she charged in again, going for three high strikes.

Just as she anticipated, Edlevin fully committed to blocking them – one, two – his focus remained entirely on her blade. On the third strike, she forcefully kicked out her leg and hit Edlevin's shin hard with her boot. His weight had been, however momentarily, supported by the limb, and he could do little but flail wildly as he fell into an unrecoverable plummet. He hit the deck chest-first with a pronounced *thunk* that echoed through the bowels of the vessel below.

Alauren wasted no time in pressing her sword up to the prone man's back, tapping the stone jacket three times, eliciting a series of clicks. She chuckled heartily. "No wave that time."

"HAHA!" Valin bellowed drunkenly. "WELL DONE, LASH!"

"Clever," Edlevin murmured, rising to his feet with a groan. He brushed an accretion of salt from the ever-soaked deck off of his pants and shook off the lingering shakiness from his rapid descent. "I'm not used to having to defend there."

"Don't have to with Nashgadh," slurred the Dwarf.

"It does tend to absorb the blow," the old soldier concurred. "In any case, you seem to be getting more comfortable with this, Ally."

"Somewhat," Alauren replied. A genuine smile managed to crack her face, the first in many days. "Now I just have to do it consistently."

"Good luck with that," Edlevin said with a laugh. "Don't expect me to make the same mistake twice."

"No, I'll find entirely new ones to take advantage of," replied the blacksmith, a steely confidence in her voice. She planted herself upon the deck and held her blade in front of her, ready to begin a new trial.

The sun set again on the vast ocean, sending crimson light cascading over the massive Nordiskan fleet, painting over the fluttering sails of the longships with a pleasant glow. Alauren, though she had seen largely the same view for the past few nights, never tired of the moment before the sun finally found its way to rest below the water, when the gloaming of the night began to send its creeping tendrils over the bright eastern horizon. She had made a habit of sharing a drink with Edlevin before nightfall, reflecting on the day's activities.

"I should have taught you all of this sooner," mused the old soldier, after a period of silence. "You catch on quick."

"It's quite enjoyable," Alauren agreed. "I'm surprised I never asked."

"There never was a reason to, I suppose," her old friend said, taking a sip. "Life in Teth was quiet enough."

"Beer and smithing," the woman sighed. "A simple existence."

Edlevin nodded. "I was going to teach you when I finally got you to come south with me, to be honest. Until then, I figured..." He trailed off. "What use did any others have for such a skill?"

"Martin probably could have used it to deal with Varuk," Alauren pointed out with a fond smile.

Edlevin chuckled and nodded. "Maybe, but his fists always seemed to be enough. Do you remember when that Warden came through town and gave him a hard time about his prices?"

"I remember the guy leaving with two black eyes," the smith said amidst a deep chortle. "Martin was lucky that Warden was one of the more restrained ones. What was his name?"

Both fell silent in thought, smiling warmly as their minds watched memories go by, searching for an answer in the warm waters of a life passed on.

"Fal?" Edlevin asked. "Or was that the Solvari trader he bum-rushed from the bar?"

Alauren chortled. "No, Fal was the Warden, for sure. Do you remember what Dalvon said to him when he was leaving?"

Edlevin suddenly burst into laughter. "*What happened, Warden, did you take a Fal?*" The laugh turned into a sigh, and he shook his head. "Damn, I miss that smartass guardsman."

"Yeah," Alauren murmured, looking out over the ocean. "They were damn good people." She paused for a moment, rubbing the mug in contemplation. "You know, I've been thinking about what you said to me. About memory."

"Oh?" Edlevin replied, a clear encouragement in his tone.

"We've already been through so much since we've left, countless deaths and violence that burn into my mind," said the blacksmith, poking at her temple with her finger as if it would drill through and ventilate the nightmares. "Despite all of it, I find the most sadness when remembering the simple things. The taste of ale on my tongue, the sweet smells of the inn, the heat from my forge. How can good memories inflict more pain than horrific ones, Ed?"

Edlevin looked over the sunset, considering the words with heavy eyes. "It's not pain," he answered after a while, visibly surprising his old friend. "As absurd as it may seem, it's the memory of happiness. Knowing that you can't go back, that you can't feel that way again… It creates a longing in you. A longing for home, for the good times, for the world you knew which has passed on from this life. The memory will always be there, and all we can hope to do is find a place that can recapture the best parts of what we once knew, while accepting the differences that are, in the end, inevitable." He paused to sip his ale. "Many lose themselves trying to make their future identical to their past, to define their lives by memories gone by. Not us, Ally." He smiled warmly, though sorrow clearly crept in. "We simply need to find another place in this world that feels like home."

"Do you think that's here, with the Norts?" Alauren asked quietly. "Among so much violence, can we really hope to capture what we felt in Teth?"

"Maybe, maybe not," Edlevin replied with a shrug. "A true home, though, is rarely more than welcoming smiles and an unconditional acceptance. I believe both of those lie here, under the rough exterior. They have shown us nothing but love and care since the moment we first entered their city."

Alauren sighed and nodded. "I don't want to think about what could have been had they not found us. Despite all the bloodshed, I do feel peaceful here. It's peculiar, but I'm not arguing with it."

The old soldier gave her another warm smile. "Neither am I. Nordiska isn't Teth, but it could be…"

"Home," finished the smith.

Edlevin nodded. "We'll see, in time."

CHAPTER TWENTY-FIVE:

ANOTHER SIDE

27th OF THE MORN OF HARVEST
NORTHERN YEAR 715

Alauren stumbled down the steep stairs of the longship, trying to hold herself upright amidst the never-ending rolling of the *Skylörek*. She found some difficulty in the task; her legs were weak from the stress of a day of training (and a remarkable amount of sweet ale that had gone down the hatch in the waning hours of the night), yet she conquered the challenge, nonetheless. The smith wanted nothing more than to collapse in her hammock and fall once again into the peaceful darkness of sleep, yet she found pause.

The doors to the storeroom that bordered her makeshift cabin were open, and a soft sound carried through the relative silence of the map room and the hall beyond. It was sweet, like a voice in an Elysian choir, blending each note effortlessly into the next, as if it were a steady stream of flowing mead.

Alauren followed the melody past the map room and beyond the main stairs, hearing the pleasant sound grow stronger with each step. It was coming, she surmised, from the half-open wooden door at the end of a dimly lit passage, and so she found herself approaching silently to steal a curious peek.

Niðr hetch,

niðr hetch,

feur aleinn niðr hetch

ok vérr'll gerannarrr bet,

annarr bet,

annarr bet,

fyrir oneanvérr louv.

Much to Alauren's surprise, the voice came not from Eira or Thyra, who crouched over the small beds of their daughters, but Ronnok, who knelt between them. The girls were already away in sleep when the blacksmith peeked in, and her gaze was quickly met with a raised eyebrow from the Chieftain, finished with his song.

Alauren opened her mouth to apologize but was silently (yet forcefully) shushed by the Nort parents before any words could escape. They shuffled out of the room and into the hallway, where they closed the door and beckoned Alauren into the larger central chamber.

"I'm sorry, I didn't mean to spy," Alauren said, once they were safely out of earshot from the slumbering girls.

"It's quite alright," Ronnok soothed with a smile. "After all, who could not be lured by the glistening sounds of my voice?"

The comment drew a simultaneous eye roll from Eira and Thyra, while Ronnok's grin only grew.

"You sang it well," Alauren complimented. "Well, I think you did, at least. It was new to me."

"A Northmen lullaby, unique to Nordiska," Eira explained. "We've been singing it to the girls since they were born."

Thyra nodded. "It's about ale."

"Your lullaby is about ale?" Alauren said with a subdued chortle, which drew nods from the trio of her hosts. "Well, it was nice. I'm tone deaf, myself, unless it's the sound of metal on metal. If I wasn't, it sounds like the type of song I'd like to learn." She paused for a moment, thinking. "For a lullaby, the melody carries a great deal of power."

"Thanks to yours truly," Ronnok beamed.

Eira smiled and hugged her husband. "At least he can back up his bluster on this matter. It's one of the reasons we married him." The comment drew a concurring nod from her sister, who likewise embraced the Chieftain with an arm over his shoulder.

Alauren mulled over a thought in her head, biting her lip, unsure of whether or not it would be appropriate to voice such a query.

Ronnok, however, was remarkably quick to notice such things, catching her drifting eyes and focusing upon them. "You have a question," he stated flatly. "Ask it."

Alauren nodded. "I'm just... I'm wondering how this came about," she said with awkward point to both women. "Polygamy is… well, it's frowned upon back home."

Ronnok let out a restrained laugh. "I'm sure it is, in your tidy little homes where men and women sit draped in fine cloth and useless gems. We, though, do not hold fast to such traditions that wall off our heart's desires. You've no doubt wondered why we seem to be such a simple folk, needing only our furs and weapons to find happiness."

Alauren nodded silently, letting the man continue.

"Your people take solace from their aching hearts in shiny jewels and glittering gold," Ronnok continued. "We need no such solace, because we know ourselves from the beginning, and we do not deny that which our hearts demand. I've loved Eira and Thyra for as long as I can remember, and life without either would be unthinkable."

"We grew up together," Thyra added with a nod. "We used to fight over who would get to marry him, quite viciously at times."

Eira chuckled. "Ronnok, of course, was oblivious to it all. In fact, when the time came to marry…"

"I couldn't make a decision," Ronnok finished.

"You weren't allowed to," Thyra corrected, raising an annoyed eyebrow.

"We eventually decided to tell him that if he chose one over the other, the rejected would kill him," Eira stated.

"They jested, of course," Ronnok hastily explained.

"…Did they?" queried the smith, wearing a wry smirk.

Ronnok did his best to contain his laughter at the remark, but let out a loud yelp that drew glares from both of the women flanking him. He shrunk away sheepishly, fortunate that the girls didn't wake.

"Eventually," Eira continued with exaggerated exasperation, "he agreed to marry both of us. For Thyra and I, there is no hesitation in sharing one true love, for in him we both find a happiness that many of your *civilized* people only dream of."

"I think I understand," Alauren said after a moment of contemplation. "Is this practice, having two wives, common for the Norts? Or are you more unique?"

"You will find many others in Nordiska like us," Ronnok answered happily. "Many men have multiple wives, many women have multiple husbands, and every combination in between. It's as common as our people desire it to be. We place few fences on the path to happiness, and we are better for it. For us, if a party is adult and agreeable, we only cause pain and division by stopping it, weakening ourselves."

Eira nodded. "Norts think of helping others to see the next sunrise, not of how we can deny them the will to see the new dawn."

"I knew a great deal of folk that would have killed for such honesty in who they were," Alauren said quietly. "People who wasted their lives away in misery because they thought they had no other choice."

"And you?" Ronnok asked, drawing a look of slight confusion from the smith. "Did you find happiness in anyone, or did you waste?"

Alauren chuckled. "No, not unless you count my forge as 'anyone', anyway. Turns out, when you outlive everyone around you, relationships like yours are either doomed to heartbreak or entirely meaningless."

Ronnok, Eira and Thyra cocked their heads simultaneously in confusion.

Alauren winced at her loose lips and, upon realizing the hole she had dug for herself was too deep to escape, sighed heavily. "Yeah, alright," she said, rubbing the back of her neck nervously. "I guess I can tell you. I'm older than any of you. Older than Edlevin and Valin, too."

Ronnok's brow furrowed in further confusion. "You look young," he stated.

"So do most half-elves, up until their final decade or so," Alauren pointed out. "Even then, I've lived more than double the normal Half-Elf lifespan."

"Well, how old are-" Ronnok began, but cut himself off abruptly as the admonishing glares of his wives burned towards him. He pursed lips and shrunk away awkwardly again, squeaking out a few timid words. "Never mind."

Alauren chuckled. "It's alright, I don't mind. Four-hundred and twenty-seven or so, by my very rough count."

"You've been in Teth that long?" Ronnok asked incredulously, cocking his head in disbelief.

"For the majority of it, anyway," Alauren affirmed. "It's funny, how the locals never seemed to care. I was simply a constant to them, always there, but hardly noticed beyond my craft."

"You must have many stories to tell," observed the Chieftain. "Such a long life would bring with it many tales."

"Not really," Alauren refuted, waving off the thought with a shake of her head. "My life was pleasantly boring." She bit her lip, considering her words before she let them loose. "Besides, interacting with new folk, getting close, tends to create a rather strange situation that I'd rather not approach. Too many questions on my age and heritage that I don't know the answer to, and too much sorrow when I inevitably outlive them. For the most part, I kept to myself. In Teth I knew many, but only a precious few knew me."

"Keeping to oneself is strange to us," Eira pointed out. "Perhaps your tales would be more interesting to an audience so different from yourself."

Alauren laughed quietly. "Yeah, maybe."

"Tell me a few in the morning, at least," the Nort woman requested with a smile. "I promise not to ask any questions that have no answers."

Alauren nodded in agreement, stretched, and yawned, an action which was mimicked by the trio of Nort parents. Eira and Thyra lightly touched Ronnok on the shoulder and returned to their bedroom with nods of farewell towards their visitor. The smith held off on her own goodbye, searching for the will to speak while the Chieftain was still around.

"You have something else to ask," the Northman observed. "I can see it in your eyes, glistening like lightning that awaits its escape. Please, know that you may ask anything of me, without offense."

Alauren smirked and let out a light chuckle. "That sentence was a great example of my question, actually." She rubbed her fingers together, thinking over her words. "You are articulate, more so than the vast majority of people in Teth."

Ronnok nodded and met her gaze with a knowing smile. Alauren had seen those sky-blue eyes show the greatest furies in the frenzy of battle, a bloodlust that seemed to turn him into the vessel of a greater being, unstoppable and iron-willed. Now, though, they radiated only warmth, above a lopsided smile that Alauren was noticing to be a common occurrence.

"Your wives speak the tongue with a heavy accent," the smith continued. "Harald, Arvid, and Bjorn seem to barely speak it at all.

How did you learn?"

Ronnok took a breath and gathered himself. The question didn't seem to bother him, but it was clearly reaching into long-passed memories of a better time, a painful shard safely locked away. The blacksmith, experienced as she had become in the matter, recognized the emotion instantly.

"Marcus," answered the Chieftain, cutting off Alauren before any attempted apology could materialize. "He was a Fangir Guardsman, retired with honors and sent north as an envoy to *civilize* the Northmen." He chuckled heartily, yet solemnly, at the thought. "We civilized *him*."

"How long ago was this?" Alauren asked. "I haven't heard of the Fangir in decades, it seems. Usually, with a prolific group like that, you'd hear rumblings around town when they went north."

"I was a child," Ronnok replied. "Twenty-five Northern years ago, before the world went mad and the days began to feel as years."

Alauren nodded silently in wholehearted agreement.

"He saw something in me, I think," continued the Chieftain, an uncharacteristic softness to his voice. "Something like your Karlmaðr feels for you, but for a different reason."

"I can understand why," Alauren whispered with a light nod. "You're unlike anyone I've ever met. Violent but varied, dangerous but calm."

Ronnok accepted the compliments with a smile, but chose to continue his thought. "Marcus brought many books with him, on language and history, on cultures and creatures. He didn't want the Norts to be 'integrated' into the empires of the world, as he once said, but to be accepted as ourselves, and so he took great care to ensure we knew the ways and language of the Nations. I have instructed many in Nordiska in the trade tongue, Eira and Thyra most of all." His eyes glossed over in memory, staring beyond Alauren for the briefest of moments. "Many of my people are alive today because of the things he taught me, about language, battle, and the sickening politics of the south."

Alauren asked her next question carefully and quietly, ensuring the utmost respect in her words. "How did he die?"

"Disease," Ronnok answered as a new weariness dawned on him. "A fever, bred midst the Norts, too strong for his smaller form to overcome, given his age."

"I'm sorry," Alauren said.

"Don't be," the Chieftain quickly assuaged. "He died a happy man, fulfilled in helping his newfound family. His memory is a good one."

"Yeah," Alauren softly spoke, her attention falling within her own mind. "It is."

"You need to learn to fight with a shield," stated the Chieftain, who was watching Edlevin and Alauren's training session closely from his place near the stern. The sun had risen mere minutes ago, yet the two outsiders had already spent several hours sparring on the deck.

"I'm fast enough that I shouldn't need one," Alauren panted, backing away from Edlevin to catch her breath. She signaled her teacher off with a floppy wave, and so both laid down their weapons. "Besides, the things are heavy as shit."

"If you say so," Ronnok articulated with a notable flatness. "I'll have Eira and Thyra be ready with bandages when we hit Arvyn."

Edlevin chortled heartily. "I'd agree, if only your shields didn't weigh as much as a particularly stocky Dwarf."

The comment drew a faint laugh from Valin, who had been passing the time by climbing the riggings far above, his scythe tied to his back haphazardly with moldy rope.

"Better to be heavy and strong than light and weak," Ronnok countered.

"Strength doesn't mean much when she can't lift the damned thing!" Edlevin retorted gruffly. "She has my bracer, anyway."

"Fine, fine!" relented the Chieftain, throwing up his arms dramatically. "But just remember, we can't sew heads back on."

"That's a bit unlikely," Alauren droned. "Clearly, it would be Ed who meets that fate."

Edlevin sneered at his old friend. "After all I've taught you, this is how you repay me? I see how it is."

"Yes, yes you do," said the smith. "Go repair your hurt feelings with a drink or five."

"I think I will!" Edlevin exclaimed, walking off towards the bow of the ship. After a moment, he wheeled around and pointed vigorously towards his old friend. "And not because you told me to!"

"Sure, Karlmaðr, whatever you say," Alauren dismissed with a chortle, waving the man off.

The Chieftain eyed Edlevin with an interested smile as the old soldier sunk below deck, seeking a keg. "I thought you said that you didn't find love in anyone?" Ronnok asked, once he was confident their conversation would be private. "Seems like you've found it in full in the Karlmaðr."

Alauren recoiled in surprise for a moment as her cheeks flushed red. "Wha- No!" She stammered her words, very evidently taken off guard. "Edlevin... It's not like that." With the embarrassment dealt with, she continued with a subdued smile. "He's a good man. Someone with a dark past, most of which even I don't know." She paused for a moment, choosing her words carefully. "None of it matters. In centuries of living in that town, he's the only one who ever cared for me as he cared for himself."

"Why?" Ronnok posited.

"I'm not sure," Alauren replied with a shake of the head. "I've never gotten up the nerve to ask him, honestly. I've thought about it a lot, and the best thing I can come up with is that, through me, he can find a window into a life he was never allowed to have. A peaceful life without the past tormenting him."

The Northman rubbed his beard in thought. "So, he uses you?"

The thought was quickly waved away by the blacksmith. "Hardly. He gives far more than he gets from me. When I needed help with an order, he was there. When I had a troublesome customer yelling at me, he'd don his sword and pay the shop a visit." She chuckled quietly. "When my problems seemed to be world-ending, he didn't counter my anxiety with the mountainous mistakes of his past, but rather saw my distress through my eyes."

"So, you love him," Ronnok stated confidently.

"With some caveats on the definition of love," Alauren noted.

"I was just teasing, little one," the Northman clarified with a disarming chuckle. "However, there are many in Nordiska who possess a strong bond with those who do not share their blood. One's mother may not be the one who brought them into this world, nor is a sibling necessarily one that you grew up beside." He paused again for a moment, scratching his beard. "Tell me: if a bond brings happiness, is it not love? Is love itself anything more than trust and support, in the end?"

Alauren nodded. "I see what you're saying, and I can't argue. Ever since he arrived in Teth, he's been the only one that I felt I could speak to. He always says the right thing, it seems, though I don't always respond in kind."

"Here in Nordiska, there would be little difference than if he was your true parent," Ronnok stated proudly, letting out the warmest of smiles. "Patience, care, tolerance – if you show these things to another, you are family. If you do not, you are not." His chest rumbled with a low chuckle. "Your people care too much for meaningless bloodlines."

Alauren smiled and returned the mirth. "No, 'civilized' people *must* endure their family's wrath, or else. Suffering is a time-honored tradition, you know!"

Ronnok snorted heartily. "If you say so." His attention quickly turned to Eira, who was ascending the main stairs. He beckoned her over and shot Alauren a smile. "I think it's time for us to hear one of those tales of monotony."

Alauren huffed a laugh and waved her hand dismissively. "I was honest last night. There's not much to tell."

"We'll find out," Eira decided. "Let's hear something!"

"Alright, alright," relented the smith. "Let's see… Oh! There was this one time, when Sortul - he was our Marchioness, kind of like a king, but for the town."

Both the Norts nodded in unison.

"He was typically calm and collected, never one to let himself get pissy beyond his normal state of mild annoyance," Alauren recounted with light voice, seeming to float along from word to word like a feather in the breeze. "That changed when Varuk came to town."

"Troublemaker?" asked the Chieftain.

"That's an understatement," the blacksmith corrected with a half-scoff. "He was a good kid, really, an Arbari immigrant from Fangirm."

"An Elf of the forest?" Eira inquired, which drew a nod from the smith. "I've never met one."

"They're peaceful folk, mostly, but always eccentric," Alauren explained. "In their lands, there is little regard for the personal, as they tend to share most parts of their lives with their fellows. If Ed is to be believed, anyway, which one can never really be sure of." The comment brought a duet of chortles, but they soon parted to make way for more of the story as the smith continued. "Varuk was particularly interesting. He was light skinned with darker splotches, like a plank of pine wood. He had sandy hair and bright green eyes, very recognizable. Even so, this crafty twit could hide just about anywhere." She laughed lightly at the memory, though she had to choke back a burst of sorrow that came along for the ride. "The little bastard would steal the Leviathan totems – Leviathan is the Se'Vikoran god of gods, you know," she noted, which drew another nod from the Norts. "He'd hide them all over the damned place… under the longhouse, in the bushes, even in one of our Innkeeper's brewing vats, once. Nobody ever caught him; they'd just see a blur disappearing into the distance, at most."

"I assume that changed?" Eira asked.

"Damn right it did!" bellowed the smith. "The little wanker wasn't happy with totems after a while, and he tried to steal my good hammer. Must have not known – or cared – that I slept in my smith."

"Stealing from the town blacksmith," said the Chieftain. "He must have been truly dim."

"If he had a sane thought in his head, it was surely knocked out of him by my fist!" Alauren thundered, punching the air mockingly with a forceful bravado. "I brought him before Sortul, and he confessed to everything. Wore a shit eating grin the entire time, too. The Marchioness personally kicked his ass up and down the main road before we called it done."

"And what further punishment did such crimes entail?" Eira asked.

"We got drunk together and forgot about it by the next day," Alauren answered with a thin, somber smile. "We didn't take much pleasure in the suffering of folk for the superficial. There were too few of us, and we knew each other far too well. Varuk's quirks were a drop of mild annoyance in the lake of smiles he brought with his antics."

"You miss them," Ronnok stated, looking deep into Alauren's eyes. "More than anything."

Her gaze could not hold, and she felt it drop to the creaking deck like a sinking stone. "Yeah, I do. More than my forge, and more than the warm hearth of the Inn. Shit, I'd gladly let it all go for one more beer with Martin. They were…"

"Family," Eira finished for her.

The comment brought another thin smile to the smith's face, driven by a warmth that she could feel radiating from the Norts. "Yeah," she said, forcing the word through a sorrow-choked throat. "There was never a day when I felt anything less than welcomed by them, even in my worst fits of frustration." She sniffed hard and attempted to gather herself. "I hope they've found peace, wherever they may be."

"Oh, I know where they are," the Chieftain thrummed with a reassuring smile. "They lived honorably, yes?"

"Each one," Alauren confirmed. "They each practiced what they preached: honesty, kindness, and community above all else."

"They dine, then, with the Great Father!" Ronnok declared. "All who live honorably may do so, if they choose."

"The Great Father?" Alauren asked.

"The one and the only!" Eira confirmed intensely. "The God of Gods, the conqueror of the serpents! The greatest warrior to have ever touched the soil of this world, the one who brought life to the Norts, and now, the one who watches over those who have passed on."

"If they've lived honorably, of course," Ronnok added. "When one dies, they go to greet him in a new life."

"He would not force them to do so, of course, but if they had lived well, the choice is theirs," Eira confirmed.

"This goes for anyone, not just Norts?" asked the smith. "I thought most Gods only cared about their own subjects."

"Oh, he prefers us, of that we are certain," the Chieftain chuckled. "We're better company for a being who prefers honesty and simplicity, but any who he feels to be worthy are invited."

Eira nodded. "This is why so many of us meet death with a smile on our face. We do not fear what comes after, because a hard and honorable life can mean only happiness in the end. This is why we so eagerly do battle."

"But even the villagers in Teth, who had hardly picked up a sword in their lives, could be deemed worthy?" Alauren questioned. "Isn't combat how your people find honor?"

"Honor comes from many places," Ronnok corrected. "It can

come from fighting, yes, but it can also just as easily come from ensuring that you remain true to your pacts, or that you watch over your family and your people with pure intent. Honor is not defined by bloodshed, but rather, the strength of our hearts."

"Tell me," Eira added, "if fighting is the only way to find honor, what hope would there be for ones like your Karlmaðr, who may pass on before a sword can strike them?"

Alauren cackled. "He's old, but not that old! I see what you're saying, though. A good life… that's all it takes?"

"That's all it takes," Ronnok confirmed with absolute certainty.

"I hope that's true, then," the blacksmith murmured with a somber smile. "Varuk has probably already managed to make the Great Father hate him, if that's where he is."

"He wouldn't have it any other way," Eira assured with a smile.

The three sat in silence for a time, looking out over the vast ocean, where a small speck on the horizon had appeared. They paid little mind to the distant land, preferring to enjoy the silence of the moment rather than looking to the future.

That changed when Valin, from his perch atop the main mast, missed a jump and tumbled chest-first into the main sail's yard (the crossbar that holds the cloth aloft) with a booming *thump* before landing hard upon his back on the main deck.

He quickly sprung up from his prone position, quite embarrassed, and met eyes with the trio. "Land ho!" he bellowed, pointing to the distance.

CHAPTER TWENTY-SIX:

A NEW WORLD

29th OF THE MORN OF HARVEST
NORTHERN YEAR 715

"We begin moving supplies uphill as soon as we make landfall," instructed the Chieftain. The light of the rising sun on the western horizon silhouetted him in a dim burgundy glow, making the already intimidating warrior seem as if he had been anointed to his position by the dawn itself. "It is imperative that we get off of the beach as soon as possible."

The group of Northmen and guests nodded their heads groggily. Alauren, still having a headache from heavy drinking the night before, gave the much-cheerier Edlevin side-eyes as he eagerly piped up.

"Do we fear being detected?" asked the old soldier. "I thought you said we were landing on an uninhabited island, to the south of the big one."

"It is not the locals we fear at this time," Ronnok said. He glanced over his shoulder, towards a massive peak whose snowy top rose over great swaths of land and ocean, looking like a fang that had broken through the skin of the choppy waters around it. "The local wildlife is far more dangerous."

Thyra, hands interlaced neatly behind her back, nodded. "This side of the Borean Ocean is home to a unique creature, one deserving of respect."

"The Billhook Crab," affirmed the Chieftain. "They are fast, and their claws can shred armor as if it were parchment. I have seen them remove limbs from the strongest men with ease."

"I haven't heard of them," Edlevin replied, scratching his head as if he were searching within for memories. "They must be a rare commodity."

"They are only found here, near the steaming vents that litter the divide," Ronnok explained. "Below us, deep within the depths, there is a trench that many say is bottomless. It marks the final end of Odenseye, and the beginning of a world unknown to much of the mainland."

"Unknown to me, too," said the old soldier, musing over the information. "This cannot stand."

Ronnok grinned widely and nodded. "Hìrvna!"

The crew obeyed instantly, procuring oars from the deck before taking their stations near the railings. Hard they rowed, all in unison, using their might to push the massive longboat ever forward, against the wind, to the shores beyond the choppy waves. For a while, the island seemed to remain just out of reach, as if the Northmen were surging towards a mirage that would never truly arrive.

Alauren felt as if time itself were swirling and bending around her, like she stood in a mystical gateway to another realm, though in reality, she was as bound to flesh and blood as she had ever been. Still, there was a surreal, dream-like quality in these moments of calm; the wind and the sun were like an enveloping blanket, immersing her in a comfortable focus that centered in on the road ahead. This was a new world to explore, new experiences to be had, and she found a determination welling within her at the thought of what her next steps would bring.

From her place on the bow, clutching the figurehead, the blacksmith marveled at the many rocky tide pools that littered the thin, golden sands of the shoreline. A stark contrast to the dull gray color of Teth's coast, these beaches looked to be rather welcoming, though specks of black ash could be seen within the shifting grains as the *Skylðrek* closed in. Dunes stretched beyond the beaches, towards rolling hills of forest and meadow beyond.

Though the physical beauty was refreshing, Alauren also looked to something far deeper, seeing in the Arvyn shorelines the first glimpses of a new life rife with possibilities. For the first time in weeks, the future was something more than a muddled and depressed jumble of worries; rather, it was right in front of her, staring her in the face. All the death, suffering, and grief had led her to this point, a single moment when the old world began to pass away, having no choice but to make way for the new.

For the first time in weeks, she felt genuinely well.

She didn't notice the palm on her shoulder until it was

accompanied by a voice. "We could use a hand getting things on deck, Ally."

Alauren snapped out of her tunnel vision. The shoreline was much closer now, and she could see the white crests of waves splash upon the jagged tidal pools in much greater detail, carrying along foam and seaweed as they churned against the rocks. She shook her head, bringing herself back into the current moment. "I'm sorry. I got lost in thought."

"About?" Edlevin asked curiously.

"What comes next," the smith replied, smiling fully. The expression was quickly suppressed, however, melting away as fast as it had come, surfacing for a single breath from under an ocean of sorrow before once more sinking into the deep.

Her old friend gave her a proud smile in response. "I'm happy for you, Ally. It's nice to see thoughts of the future bring a smile to your face again, even for a moment."

"I don't dare give it more than that," Alauren murmured with a waver, attempting a half-hearted chuckle that failed to clear even the low bar she had set for it. "I feel good, determined, but I have this feeling that if I start to find my place, to find happiness, it'll just get ripped away." She shook her head and looked to her mentor with heavy eyes. "That can't happen again, Ed."

Edlevin crossed his arms and blinked twice, slowly. "It can."

"Thanks," Alauren muttered sarcastically. "Reassuring."

"I don't dare lie to you," the old soldier thrummed with an unsettling chill in his throat. "Anything can be lost at any time, Ally. The world we build for ourselves is more fragile than any of us want to admit, and every detail of that life is subject to its own impermanence. It could take years, or it could take seconds." He sighed and let his arms fall back to his side, while his normally curt posture was visibly weighed upon by his thoughts. "Pieces will fail and fall away, followed shortly by the entire structure, surely."

Alauren raised her eyebrows and cocked her head. "Are you okay, Ed?"

Edlevin bit his lower lip and chuckled darkly. He shook his head. "Sometimes yes, sometimes no."

"Should I be worried?" asked the blacksmith.

The old soldier was lost in thought, giving no answer as he gazed absently across the waves.

"Ed," Alauren pushed. "You rarely get that dark on me. Talk."

Edlevin's attention snapped back to reality. He rubbed his temple and furrowed his brow. "Ally, my life has been spent reeling from one loss after another," he muttered. "Family, friends, leaders; no matter what I sew, I always seem to reap tragedy." He took a deep breath, found his center, and stood tall, returning to the strong rock of a man that his old friend knew well. "I've learned to steady myself, to forget about the past." He shot his old friend a reassuring smile. "I'll be fine, really."

Alauren ground her teeth for a moment. "If you say so. You needed my help?"

"Indeed," Edlevin confirmed, visibly eager to move on. "We'll need to work quickly once we arrive. Come, help get the supplies on deck."

The smith gave a curt nod and followed the old soldier to assist in any way she could.

"Kyfir!" Ronnok shouted, looking across the beach, surveying dozens of Northmen while they feverishly skittered about their duties on the soft sands.

They had laid feet upon shore just moments ago, yet there was already a procession making their way hurriedly up the dunes, pouring from dozens of loaded dinghies that rested just behind the lapping surf. The Nort laborers fell into single file lines that kept them together as they carried their equipment to better ground, while the supply corridors were protected by a half-circle umbrella of armed vanguards who formed a defensive line beyond the hills of sand.

The smith did her part eagerly, handing leather-wrapped bundles of gear off to strong and quick Norts, who diligently ran them up, over the dunes, and out of sight. Though tedious, there was a strange enjoyment in the process, and the task seemed to flow as effortlessly and as quickly as a night at the Inn. Alauren felt the sands of a new world move below her and took heart, for her mind was occupied just enough to think of the possibilities without room to fit the worries in by their side.

Edlevin, working on distributing his own pile of supplies, was quick to notice her demeanor. "How does it feel, Ally? Setting foot here?" He hefted a bundle of swords to a young Nort woman. "For me, it's invigorating."

Alauren nodded, tying up a sack of furs more securely before handing them off. "It feels... refreshing, I guess? It makes me feel healed, if only a little."

"It's only the beginning," assured the old soldier. He returned to his dinghy, grabbed the next set of weapons, and hurried back to hand them off. "I get the feeling there's much more in store."

"Hopefully good answers and better friends," replied the blacksmith. She looked over her shoulder, catching a glance of Solveig playing in a rocky tidal pool a few dozen strides away. The Nort girl's hair floated softly in the wind, catching the rays of the sun while the crimson strands flittered about in the breeze. "There is so much more to see and do with them."

"Indeed!" Edlevin affirmed. "I feel alive!"

Alauren hefted another bundle of furs up, meaning to carry them up the beach, but stole one more glance at Solveig, one more look to remind her of what she had found among the Norts.

Where once the girl splashed around in the pools, there was now only the white crashing of the waves.

Alauren narrowed her eyes and let her burden drop to the sand. She moved forward quickly, curiously, hopping up on the pool's rocks to get a better look around. Even with the point of vantage, the Nort girl was nowhere to be found, disappearing completely in little more than few moments. A wave, holding streaks of red within its white foam, barreled into the stones.

Alauren's eyes went wide as her breath was stolen away from her lungs. She flew forward without another thought, drawing her sword while plunging into the waist-deep saltwater, finding a steady place upon the slippery stones beneath the surf. The waves of the high tide wanted to knock her backwards, to send her tumbling against the rocks, but the blacksmith held strong against the thundering will of the ocean, driving toward the source of the red streaks in the water: what looked to be a barnacle-encrusted hunk of stone, laying still and unmoving just ahead.

The effort, as it so happened, wasn't necessary; the rock rose from the depths and barreled towards her, carving through the powerful surf with ease.

The blacksmith was left with a few precious breaths to inspect her enemy. Four eyes protruded on stalks from a central, armored head, underneath which dripping, hook-like mandibles twitched wildly. Its massive body was divided into two sections of heavy carapace, a torso and a tail which were connected via a center joint. Dual pincers, massive and intimidating, protruded from the upper segment, just in front of the legs; one was thick and blunt, while the other was thin and hooked. In the latter laid Solveig, pinched by the leg, sputtering and screaming as she frantically caught her breath.

The crab assaulted its new prey without further hesitation, emitting shrill chitters as it rapidly closed the distance, its legs thundering upon the choppy waves. It snapped its unoccupied pincer forward and seized hold of Alauren's bracer, gripping the armor tightly, as if it the claw was a massive vice. It kept its hold on Solveig all the while, unintentionally allowing the Nort girl to grab the occasional, vital breath as the waves tilted her captor around.

Even with the Dwarven-enchanted armor protecting her fragile bones, the pressure applied by the gargantuan creature sent an intense pain shooting up the smith's arm. She let out a scream, equal parts agony and anger, but the wailing cry gave way to a gurgling garble as the crab forced her under the water.

Though terror seeped through her every nerve, Alauren found herself in a state of surprising calm, able to push away the panic and find focus. Despite being held down, she managed to swap her sword to her offhand and stab upwards at the creature's carapace.

The blow caught the outer shell and ground against it harmlessly, doing little but angering the animal. In response, one of its many legs shot forward, striking the blacksmith in the torso and knocking the breath from her lungs. Knowing now that the armor was impenetrable, she instead stabbed outward (as much in desperation as in strategy) and connected the tip of her sword with the small joint that held the pincer to the animal's torso.

The pressure on the bracer was instantly relieved as the crushing claw went limp. The creature reared backwards, waving its now-armless stump around wildly.

Alauren rose from the water, grabbed a waterlogged breath between coughs, and focused her glare on the ghastly crustacean. A shriek pierced through the air as Solveig's head surfaced again; the cry of agony from the little girl sliced into the smith's soul, sending rage spiraling through her chest. Another strike, this time at the remaining claw joint, freed the child from the infernal grasp.

Overtaken by a surge of pure fury, a barreling avalanche that focused on the disgusting, chittering abomination before her, Alauren gripped her sword tightly and ground her teeth, planning out her attacks with every heavy beat of her heart. She sliced at the crab's eyes first, blinding them one after another, finding a sinister pleasure in the act. Once finished, she sought a weak point, eager to finalize this creature's last mistake.

The carapace proved to be like layered steel against the blacksmith's blade, her repeated blows serving only to make the creature rear up in fear. It spat seawater and a sickly green mucus towards her in the midst of its wild frenzy, the last resort of a confused and frightened animal to save itself from what had proven to be a much more dangerous predator than itself. Alauren wiped her face clear of the spittle and smiled, finding her solution.

As the creature came heavily back down, the smith dove forward and drove her sword up and into its mouth, penetrating the soft roof of the palate while drawing an ear-shattering, gurgling squeal from deeper within its body.

Alauren showed no mercy, forcing the blade further and further in, taking pleasure in the black-red blood that poured over her head and through her hair. The crab's brains were violently sundered into pieces, forcing it to convulse heavily in the rapidly darkening waters. The carapace was quite soft inside, as had become abundantly clear, and every thrash of the maddened creature only shredded more of its cerebrum against the razor edge.

In the matter of a moment, the crab's wild movements weakened to nothing, and it surrendered to the call of death, its body moved only by the will of the waves. Alauren withdrew her sword and gained her footing upon the floor of the tidal pool once more.

A single breath passed before Ronnok sloshed to the crab, frenzied and wild-eyed. He lifted the heavy corpse and easily hurled it far out into deeper water, as if it was a mere pebble. Without a word, he picked up Alauren and Solveig, one in each arm, and ran them to the safety of the shoreline.

The smith managed to wriggle her way free of the Northman's embrace as Edlevin and Valin arrived, each bearing wide, yet focused, eyes. Alauren followed their gaze to Solveig, who whimpered weakly in her father's arms. Upon the girl's leg was a wide and nasty gash, bleeding profusely, the rent flesh of the wound running horizontally across the midpoint of her calf.

"I need a knife!" Valin bellowed, motioning for the Chieftain to lay the girl down. "Gotta stop the bleedin'!"

Ronnok laid his daughter on the sand with visible tremors in his muscular form. The enraged frenzy in his eyes had been rapidly replaced by an insulating shock and a clear fear which caused his eyelids to quiver. Solveig's blood ran over his quaking hands, and he moved no further.

"A BLADE!" the Dwarf yelled frantically, waving away curious crowds that were drawn in by the commotion. He procured a small leather strip from one of his pockets and placed it in the girl's mouth. "Today, big man!"

Edlevin spoke up. "You're going to cauterize the wound?"

"Damned straight I am!" Valin growled in reply. He looked to Ronnok, who was still frozen in shock save for the continued, involuntary shaking of his body. "Big. Man," droned the Dwarf, slowly and clearly, putting a hand on the Nort's arm. "A blade. Now!"

Ronnok snapped out of his seized-up state, nodded, and procured a curved knife from his waist sheath, snatched from his hands by the Priest with little hesitation and a surprising speed.

"The gash will have to be cleaned, first, if we want to do it right," Edlevin said. "The infection could end up being a lot worse than the wound." He rose to his feet. "Get the blade hot, but hold off until I get back!" He sprinted towards the very tidal pools where Solveig had been snatched, rooting around madly in the surging waves.

Valin, still kneeling, pulled a piece of charcoal from his pocket and drew a "⚱" symbol upon the shining edge of the weapon. "Teine!" squawked the Dwarf, determined and unshakable. "Teine!"

The charcoal symbol began to glow white, then red, followed shortly by the rest of the blade.

"Got one!" Edlevin yelled from his place in the pools. He was quite wet, crowned by a halo of seaweed and algae, the slimy tendrils of the plants hardly a bother as he sprinted back to the scene carrying a small pickle-like creature in his hands.

"What-?" Ronnok began to ask, but the older man waved him off.

"Old Fangirmish Navy trick, works as an antiseptic," panted the old soldier, drawing his sword a small distance out of its sheath before using it to cut the creature open. Immediately, the animal began spewing a slimy, white substance, which Edlevin diligently poured over the wound.

Solveig squirmed violently and let out a muffled scream as the fluid seeped down into the gash, stinging the exposed flesh. The man threw himself over the girl, using a gentle elbow to keep her down while he continued dumping the mysterious substance forth, letting a small amount of it build up against the exposed muscle. The moment he had exhausted the creature of its insides, he nodded to the Dwarf.

There was no hesitation. Valin plunged the white-hot blade into the wound, sending a sickly sizzling sound crackling through the air. A horrible, bitter smell wafted over the gathered observers while Solveig wailed and writhed about, biting heavily on the leather, held firmly into to place by the much larger human.

After a few moments, Valin removed the blade and carefully inspected the wound, running his eyes up and down the seared flesh multiple times before he spoke. "Nasty and deep, but no broke bones and the bleedin' stopped, so she'll be fine," he said, finally letting himself take a calm (but still ragged) breath. "Anyone up fer a drink?"

Alauren, gawking until now, looked down to find that her hands were shaking uncontrollably. "That was…"

"Amazing," Ronnok finished for her, his skin still pale as the snow upon the tip of the great mountain above. "You're sure she'll be alright?"

"Bet me beard on it, big man," Valin replied. "Me people's Priests are as much healers as we are religious figures. This ol' cut is nothin' compared t' what we'd see down in the mines." A chuckle rumbled through his chest. "She's a strong one, too. She'll be fine, long as we keep that wound clean, and long as she avoids any more encounters with the local fauna."

"She shouldn't have encountered this one," growled the Chieftain, stooping to pick up the barely conscious child. She was asleep now, passed out from the pain, and Ronnok brushed her sand-covered hair from her face. "I told her more than once that the sea here is dangerous."

"If children simply listened to us, life would be a great deal easier," Edlevin commented, rising to his feet with a groan while removing the crown of kelp from his head. "However, they would learn far fewer life lessons. I'll bet you my armor she won't forget this one."

Ronnok nodded in agreement, even as he scowled at Solveig with equal parts anger and relief. "You have my gratitude," he thundered, suddenly aware of the crowd of Northmen brothers and sisters that had gathered to bear witness. "All three of you, for this defense of my clan is among the greatest gifts ever given to me." After a look around, noting the gawking stares of his people, he nodded once more. "Some in Nordiska, I will admit, have questioned why I have allowed you to stay. Let this day, this feat, be my answer." Without another word, he strode through the crowds, getting his daughter to higher ground and the care of her mothers.

A few moments of solemn silence ensued while the crowd dispersed; each empty stare of the gathered trio was an individual reflection on the blood and violence they had just seen, the adrenaline bleeding from their veins all the while. For a time, they had little but the sound of the surf and the tatters of their own breath to fill their ears.

This silence was eventually broken by Arvid, however, who thundered past with the dead crab upon his shoulder, its legs draped over his chest and back. He chuckled heartily, with a wide grin. "Food!"

"Indeed," Edlevin confirmed matter-of-factly, reverting from his alert state to one far wearier and more typically disheveled. "Well, I think I'll take Valin up on that drink," he rumbled, eyeing the gigantic Northman as he ambled off on his route. "Let's get this job done so we can make that happen, eh?"

The others wholeheartedly agreed, and so they returned in silence to their duties.

CHAPTER TWENTY-SEVEN:

TENTS AND ANVILS

"Yeah, just set it down anywhere. I'm not picky," Alauren directed. Arvid nodded in response and let the massive Alsaran anvil fall from his shoulder onto the ground, where it stuck fast into the soil. "Thanks, big man," said the blacksmith.

The Nort grunted and gave a curt nod before walking off in search of more heavy things to carry.

"I don't understand how these poles are supposed to work," Edlevin whined. He sat cross-legged just beside Alauren, under the shade of an oak tree, where he struggled to erect a series of wooden posts, each meticulously crafted, and each interlocking neatly with each other to form a structure.

At least, they were *supposed* to. Three hours of work by the old soldier had led to the parts and tools lying strewn about, with only one joint locked together properly. Even then, it looked like it could slip at any moment.

"Just get one o' the biggins t' help ye," Valin rumbled, carefully supervising the work from his place upon a small stump. "They carved these things, after all."

"Bah!" Edlevin spat, waving off the comment. "I can do it. Do you know how many tents-"

"Yes, Edlevin, you were a soldier," Alauren cut off with a roll of the eyes. "You were the best at setting up shelters, and everyone else had to ask for your help." She smirked at the old man mockingly. "Or were you going to say something humble for once?"

"No, that's about right," Edlevin said with a nod. "Right indeed."

"I might as well be able to read your mind with how predictable you've become," jabbed the blacksmith. Her eyes stayed focused on an elk skin bag, and she looked over the tools within it carefully. "Some new boasts would be nice."

"I'm allowed to be proud!" Edlevin yelped with a fake offense in his voice. "I earned that right, back when-"

"Back when you fought off twenty men with only your armor and a small hammer," Alauren finished for him, chuckling, her eyes still locked within the bag. "At least you'll have some new stories after this is all over."

"You're damn right!" Edlevin chirped. His face lit up with the final word, for two of the poles, each in a hand, suddenly connected perfectly to each other with a pronounced *clack*. The slats disappeared as the two pieces locked in, making them seem as if they were carved as one, seamless and perfect. Edlevin beamed a smug look toward the smith, grinning widely. "Told you!"

"Yep," Alauren deadpanned. "Now do it eight more times, and you're done."

Edlevin's face, after a look over the remaining poles, sank heavily into a humbler demeanor. "You know," he said, "maybe I will ask that fellow Bjorn for help, after all…"

Alauren chuckled. "Good luck. He speaks about five full phrases of the trade tongue. Two of which, by the way, are threats."

"I think a point of the finger would suffice here," countered the soldier.

"He's occupied anyway," the smith pointed out. "Getting stone for my furnace."

Edlevin sighed and nodded. "I suppose this challenge needs to be mine to conquer, anyway. After all, I-"

"Always say to never give up easily, even faced with the toughest of problems," Alauren finished for him. "Back to it then, Karlmaðr."

Edlevin sighed once more, before returning to his dutiful struggle.

Crimson runefire, warm and inviting, painted the sagging faces of the three weary companions with flickering shadows, while the last light of day gave way to the march of the evening's gloam. Each was seated upon a cut log, and each possessed a foaming mug of ale that sloshed back and forth with every movement. Behind them, barely visible in the darkness, a half-finished tent and workspace waited patiently for the coming of a dawn that would see its full completion.

"I'm not eating it, end of story!" Alauren yelped. "I'd rather go hungry."

Edlevin shrugged, cracked a massive crab leg over his knee, and procured a dripping slab of perfectly steamed meat. "More for me."

"Couldn't agree more!" Valin said, keeping a careful vigil over the last few legs as they sizzled above the fire, steaming the meat within the hard carapace. The Dwarf was lost in their juicy depths, like a hound staring down a steak, and it seemed as if all of the stars of the sky twinkled in his glossy eyes. "Shellfish are some tashty beashties, they are."

"I guess it's different when they've tried to drown you," Alauren replied after a sip of ale.

"Just makes it sweeter, in my mind," Edlevin articulated moistly, with a mouthful of crab. "Victory is a fine seasoning!"

"Fair enough, Karlmaðr, but I'll still pass on eating anything that tried to kill me," chuckled the smith. "Hey, speaking of, look at this." She held her bracer up to display a small dent in the side. "Those crabs are strong bastards. Didn't this come out unscathed from a full sword cleave?"

"It did," Edlevin confirmed. "That's the thing about Nasgadh: It can survive hard and fast blows quite well, but it doesn't work so well under sustained pressure."

"My arshe it doeshn't!" Valin struggled, ripping his eyes from the crab legs, clearly three sheets to the wind. He pointed at the ground dramatically, accentuating his words as he swayed to and fro. "I've sheen a boulder fall upon a Garradh warrior. Took ush a day and night t' get him out, and hish armor was unshcathed!"

He looked towards his scythe, placed carefully beside him, and rolled his eyes.

"Nobody asked about the condishon o' the warrior, now did they, ye foshilized shitshtain?" slurred the Dwarf, kicking the weapon lightly.

"Dwarven pride," Edlevin mused goadingly. "Or, as I like to call it, denial."

In a single swift motion, impressive for his drunken state, Valin snatched his scythe and rapped the old warrior across the legs with the blunt end, causing the human to nearly stumble from his seat in cackling laughter.

"Ye shite," growled the Dwarf.

"Careful!" Edlevin shrieked, scooting his log away from the smoldering weapon and its crotchety bearer. "I'm not thrilled at the prospect of being disintegrated!"

"Bah!" Valin spat. "Drell shays you'd hardly be worth the effort."

"I agree with the scythe," said the smith after another sip of her mead. A smirk dawned on her face. "Never thought I'd have the occasion to string those words together."

"Indeed," Edlevin mused. He shuffled to his feet and scooted his seat even further from Valin's reach, preferring caution in the presence of the Dwarf. "The strange roads life leads us down. At least they always seem to take us to warm company." He raised his mug towards the Priest. "To the entertaining bastards in our life."

"Hear hear," Valin said, scratching at his beard. "You know, ever since bein' exiled, I've found nothin' but curioush shtares and cold mistrust. I suppose all I needed t' find good company was company as strange as meshelf."

"You think I'm strange?" Alauren jabbed. "How dare you!"

"Yer older than shite," countered the Dwarf. "'Course I do, lassie."

"Well, you'd be right, I suppose!" the woman said with a hearty chuckle. "I suppose I'm even stranger now. I'm a blacksmith, a few centuries old, the killer of both men *and* crabs." She smirked for a moment. "And somehow the crab deserved it less. Truly strange."

Edlevin leaned forward intently. "That's rather dark, Ally," he growled, feigning deep offense while trying to hold back a smile. "Too soon."

"Quiet down, Karlmaðr," the smith shot back. "I won't let someone who told the same joke every night at the Inn lecture me on humor."

"It was only every other night!" Edlevin quickly corrected, a cold and serious gravity about his voice.

"Ye know, I'd quite like t' hear thish joke," Valin thrummed, drawing an exasperated groan from the blacksmith.

"Don't encourage-" Alauren had begun to say, but Edlevin had already launched into his delivery.

"Tell me, O well-traveled Dwarf, what might one call a Se'Vikoran beach at the edge of a great forest?"

Valin tilted his head in confusion, giving Edlevin the signal to finish.

"A shadowbeach!"

Valin leaped from his seat, practically flying, and rapped the old soldier on the shins once more. Edlevin stumbled off his seat this time, laughing all the way and spilling his drink on the ground as the mug tilted over.

"Look what you made me do!" the old soldier cackled, writhing in exaggerated agony. He gestured intensely to the now-empty mug. "A damned shame!"

"Bah!" Valin said, waving off the offense. "Get off yer arshe and get another."

"If I must bear such indignity," Edlevin huffed, hefting himself up walking off into the darkness, towards the mess tent.

The two remaining travelers sat in silence for a while, sipping peacefully. Alauren ground her teeth, finding her curiosity welling up once more. Valin had been with them every step of the way, yet she knew remarkably little of what lay under his boisterous, loud exterior, being so lost in her own mind that his continued presence seemed to be little more than a particularly obvious given. "What do you think of all this, Valin?" the smith asked after a while, shifting in her seat with the words.

"Eh?" grunted the Dwarf.

"This journey, this place, this... new world, I guess," Alauren clarified, waving her arms around the quaint forest they had found themselves in. "For someone who can be so loud, you are remarkably quiet on such things."

"Ah," Valin said with a nod. "Ye'll have t' fergive me, lass. Not many care t' hear my opinionsh."

"Well, I do," Alauren encouraged. "You've been here every step of the way, through the violence and the horror, through the darkness that chases us at every waking moment. I can't help but wonder why? Why stay?"

"Ale," enlightened the Dwarf, holding up his cup with a smirk.

"That can't be the only reason," Alauren pressed, knowing better. "You can find ale anywhere, and you don't have to have your life in mortal danger to do it."

Valin nodded, seeming to sober abruptly while he carefully considered the words. "Yer right, lass," he relented with a sigh and a scratch of his large nose. "Tell ye the truth, it's just a feelin' I got. A feelin' I haven't had since a couple o' Elysian magicians approached me about fixin' the great evil that plagued me city. A feelin' that it's just…" He trailed off. "That it's just the right thing t' do."

"Tell us about these magicians, and that feeling," Alauren said. She glanced at Edlevin, who emerged from the darkness with a full cup and took his seat once more.

"Nothin' much to tell that ye don't know already," Valin said with a shrug. "They knew Drell was down under me city somewhere, blockin' our magic. Me people wouldn't listen t' 'em."

"Save for you," observed the smith.

"Save for me, lass," Valin confirmed. "When I looked around and saw the sufferin' that me people were going through, I had but one choice, and I knew in me heart that it was the right one, consequences be damned. I lost everything fer it, but I helped t' save me home and the people in it."

"You told me that the Elysians had died?" Alauren asked. "How?"

Valin nodded somberly. "Pounded t' mush by stone golems or turned t' stone themselves." He sighed, a deep, rumbling, and moist sound. "Grisly deaths, the stuff of old scary stories and myths, but ones I made worthwhile."

"I'm sorry," murmured the smith.

"They knew what they were walkin' into, lass," Valin soothed. "They knew what could happen, and they did it all fer a people that would have just o' soon cast 'em out fer doin' it. Good men and women, that bunch, ones that I dearly miss."

"It sounds like they had quite the profound impact on you," Edlevin observed.

"Aye, they did," confirmed the Dwarf. "I pledged, after it had all been said and done, t' follow their lead, t' do what needed doin', wherever I went, and at whatever cost was deemed fit."

"That led here," Alauren stated. "What do you think needs doing here, Valin?"

"Like I said, lassie, just a feelin'," Valin muttered. "Just a feelin' that I can finally pay back what I owe t' this world fer puttin' up with me fer so long. There is good t' be done, I know that in me heart, I'm just awaitin' the chance t' do it." He sighed and gestured vaguely towards the smith. "I can't explain it any more than you can explain why yer hair's brown, lass."

Alauren nodded. "Fair enough. I hope that chance comes. Though, helping the Norts…" She trailed off, picking the right words. "Helping the Norts do their thing probably isn't considered assistance by most of the world."

Valin chuckled heartily. "I didn't pledge not to have a wee bit o' fun along the way, now did I?" He scratched his beard, glancing at the scythe for a moment. "Yer right fer once, Drell. Even what the Norts do can have a greater purpose."

"He's just saying that because he enjoys watching them work," Edlevin chuckled.

"Yer not wrong," Valin concurred. "But even I can't disagree with the shitwit on this one."

Edlevin nodded. "I've been to every corner of Odenseye. I've seen everyone from the Solvari to the Dwarves fight. These Northern folks have been impressive, indeed."

"I mean, I would have to think half of that is because of their size," Alauren pointed out. "When you're a head taller than even the biggest Elf, you have a sort of built-in advantage."

"True," Edlevin agreed, "yet there is something else to them. A mind for battle, for tactics both as an individual and as a group. Their intellect is not to be underestimated."

"I'll take your word for it, o master of war," Alauren quipped with a smirk and a nod. "We'll see in the coming days, in any case."

"Speaking of," Edlevin said, "while I was filling my cup, Ronnok mentioned that they're planning an early morning raid at a monastery called Redjadia early tomorrow. It's on a small island not far from here, he says, and it is guarded only by the monks who inhabit it."

"Priests?" Valin asked. "Sounds easy."

"I said the same thing and got laughed at," replied the old soldier. "He says they can be quite violent for religious folk."

"Sounds like a fun time," Alauren yawned. "Wake me for it, Ed. I'd like to see what Arvyn has in store for us."

"Of course," Edlevin affirmed. "On that topic…" He trailed off and downed the rest of his mug before he stood. "I want to make sure I'm awake for it, myself. If you have need of me, I'll be rolled up in some furs enjoying a slumber on dry land."

Alauren yawned again at the thought, watching with amusement while Valin messily devoured the last of the crab legs, practically inhaling the tubular strip of meat as if it were an oversized noodle before discarding the gnawed, cavernous husk of the limb to the ground.

"Not a bad idea, Karlmaðr. Let's see what the next dawn holds," said the smith, grabbing the tossed-aside chitin shell and gazing intently at the few tendrils of meat left within.

CHAPTER TWENTY-EIGHT:

RAID

Redja, mightiest of all men, shall be the edge of our blade and the banding of our buckler. Let him be the truth and the light, the mercy and the justice. Let him guide our hands in all ways, from the pat on the back to the striking of the jaw. His will is like the strongest plate and his vision ever seeks the imperfections of our heart, yearning to redeem us. He does not demand worship, but rather service to his right and true way, that of purity and of courage. Anger does not carry in his hand, only determination, forceful and zealous, towards a better home for his people.

- From "The Sermon of the Five Fires", given by Pontiff Harka of Arvyn in 701.

30th OF THE MORN OF HARVEST
NORTHERN YEAR 715

Ronnok stood over his slumbering (and still very drunk) guests, quite amused at their nasally snores. How they had wanted to come along for the raid, to seek the glory of battle, to get their first taste of a new world with the Norts!

Ale had other ideas, he supposed.

The Chieftain opted not to disturb them. They had been through much, none of it asked for, and they would be through much more by the time their days on Arvyn were done. A day of rest, he decided, separated from violence and on dry land, would be quite good for the inexperienced visitors. He turned away and left them to their sleep.

Eira and Thyra were joined on the beach by a trio of Arvid, Bjorn, and Harald, who were busy preparing a small skiff that could cut across the waves stealthily and with haste. Ronnok followed a narrow path down a dry dune, carefully picking his steps to avoid disturbing the fragile plant and animal life that inhabited the small hills.

"Our guests have opted to stay behind?" Bjorn asked, using the Nort tongue.

Ronnok nodded as his boots met the level sand of the beach. "They are happier asleep, I can tell." He chuckled, the mirth drawn from a blazing excitement within. "Besides, the opening of a raiding campaign is for Norts. They wouldn't appreciate it as we do."

"As you say, my Chieftain," Bjorn replied, throwing a length of rope into the skiff, which was already bobbing in the surf. "The sun ascends. We should move."

Ronnok concurred, helping Arvid to push the craft into the choppy sea while the others boarded. With a few more heavy tilts to the sides, the vessel was fully manned, and the Northmen set out upon the sloshing waves of a foreign domain. The crimson Arvyn sunrise, rising at their back, painted a matching sail as it was unfurled, propelling the skiff with the full force of the wind. They kept an easterly course, careful not to stray too close to the shores of the main island, which dominated their left side.

The churning water grew calm mere minutes into the journey, leaving the party with an eerie silence, little but the clanking of sail riggings to fill the void. No words escaped from upon the tongues of the raiders; all were too eager to experience the coming moments, too anxious to make their first mark in generations upon the shores of this remote treasury. The Northmen had likely become legends in these lands, Ronnok surmised, a long dormant threat that only remained in the minds of those who had the bloody duty of entering combat with them in decades gone by. There would be a reputation to live up to, and the Chieftain looked forward to putting on a show that would stand among the greatest of their stories. A grim, lopsided smile erupted on his face, for the first words of a new saga were at hand.

The ashy beaches of their destination grew near, not a soul stirring on the placid coastline save for the seagulls that hunted for food in the tide. The skiff hit the shore in good time, and the boots of the Norts impacted the sand with squishing splashes, in turn. Their weapons and chain mail clinked lightly, barely loud enough to be heard over the surf despite the heavy movements of their bearers. Arvid moored the skiff to the land with a great iron spike, which he drove into the sand as if it were a nail on wet paper.

"There should be a small temple or church here, likely filled with treasure, though the scouts didn't say how much," Ronnok briefed, savoring every word as they rolled out of his mouth. "I will go in first. Eira, Thyra, watch behind for any attacks, then join us. Harald, you will stay outside and alert us of any ambushes or attacks."

The four Norts nodded.

"Bjorn, stay here with the boat and guard our escape," finished the Chieftain.

Bjorn nodded, though a clear anger flashed onto his face, present only for a single moment before being rapidly suppressed. "It is my honor to do so," he said, returning to the vessel.

Ronnok smirked, watching the young man's lanky gait as he saw to his duty. It was disappointing to be left out of the day's festivities, the Chieftain knew; no greater glory could be found than the wild chaos of battle, and missing the chance to shed blood was a certain blow to the young man's ego. Still, the task of defense was one accepted honorably, as a raiding party with no escape was little more than a mass grave on legs.

With a raised hand, Ronnok beckoned the rest to follow and stepped carefully up a relatively clear path in the dunes. In the distance, a single bell rung out, echoing through the lush forests and ringing in the ears of the annoyed Northmen like the wailing of a petulant child. Irritating as the sound was, the Chieftain found it comforting to know that the locals were agreeable to beckoning everyone and anyone to their location.

After a short hike through a quiet, green forest, the party found a small stone building situated in the center of a clearing, with a single tower rising above its thatched roof. The bell sat at the highest point, clanging away in a repeating tune, though many notes were slightly off key. Colorful stained-glass windows lined the walls, depicting some deity or another, clad in flowing white robes and bearing an amulet of Etia, the greater moon. Gravestones littered the yard, some more impressive than others.

The Northmen crossed the distance in a few strides and hopped over the stone fence with ease. Closing in on the church walls, they could hear a man's voice echoing inside, muffled, but clearly speaking in the trade tongue with a notable fervor.

"He is the one who watches over us," it boomed, "the one who delivers the right-minded and punishes those who do not obey his wise words! Remember how he finds evil, how he roots out our disease!"

The Norts shifted towards the main door, eager to move, but Ronnok calmed them with a wave. This needed to be heard, as knowing the beliefs of an enemy could often be the key to their defeat.

"For, do we not see his vision among us, always seeking out the bloodied wool of the heretics?" the voice continued. "I have heard of your fears, my people, of how seeing his vision in the bushes and in the forest frightens you, how it makes you feel as if there is ever an evil eye upon you. Truly, though, there is no evil! Redja watches over us and protects us, so that those who have faith in his power and his name may shine, white and unstained by the filth of the world! He does these things so that his Redjavik need never worry of tribulations, and so that we may walk free as ascended beings among the mere insects that live beyond his shores. He removes only the necrotic diseases among us, those who would betray his word and his people. If you are righteous in your resolve to act only in his name, you have little to fear!"

Ronnok, with a final deep breath, decided that enough had been heard. He guided his company to the front doors, finding the fine wood to be decorated with carvings of a single man perched atop a mountain, conquering a great winged serpent while lightning erupted around him.

"Arvid, break through the door," the Chieftain ordered in a soft murmur.

"It's probably unlocked," Thyra pointed out.

Ronnok gave his wife a jesting glare. "But that would be quite the mundane entrance, wouldn't it?" He grinned wickedly. "Arvid!"

Dozens of splinters promptly flew into a great hall lined with wooden pews, while the crowds seated on the benches gasped in unison. An ornately robed man stood at an altar in the rear of the building, shocked beyond words as he recoiled in disgust.

Ronnok sauntered through the remains of the threshold with a casual smile and a floppy wave. He held a friendly demeanor, almost as if he were an expected guest of the congregation. With a light groan, he slumped comfortably in the rearmost pew and planted his feet upon the back of the next row, where an older woman wrinkled her nose in disgust and shuffled further away. Eira and Thyra stood ready at either side of the entrance, and Arvid ducked through to block any who tried to escape.

Ronnok furrowed his brow as all eyes turned to him. The people were stunned into silence at the sight of the exotic visitor, unable to do anything save stare on with palpable dread. The Chieftain looked around for a moment and raised his hands in exasperation. "Well, continue!" he bellowed, using the trade tongue.

"You..." the robed man at the altar stammered. "You speak our language?"

"Observant," Ronnok quipped, shooting the disgusted congregant in the seat next to him a smirk before returning his attention to the front. "You were saying something about Redja protecting you, or something to that effect. Please, do not think to stop on my account!"

"Why have you come?" the robed man demanded with an insidious calm. "Who are you?"

Ronnok let out an exaggerated sigh. "The questions can wait. Continue!"

A few men, bald and clothed in plain brown robes, rose from their seats. They had gotten over their shock, it seemed, and they began procuring blades from their sleeves with hateful grimaces.

"I'll ask again," the robed man growled menacingly. "Why does your filth dare defile this sacred place?"

Ronnok sighed once again and rose. "Come now, that's no way to treat a prospective convert."

The brown-robed men crept forward, bearing increasingly venomous scowls upon their faces. Their blades, straight and thin, glinted in red, blue, and yellow as the edges passed beams of sunlight that shone through the painted windows.

"Hmm," grunted the Chieftain, drawing one of his axes. "Fine. I'm happy with my own religion, anyway."

The moment the final word left the mouth of the Northman, the first of the brown-robed men charged towards him with a guttural growl. Ronnok simply stepped aside and tripped the assailant as he passed.

The first man's face had not yet impacted the stone floor when the second began an assault of his own, stabbing out frantically. Ronnok dodged the first two blows (both aimed at his midsection) with a jump back and redirected the third away with a rapid (but remarkably casual) slap from his unoccupied offhand. He pinned the assailant's arm back as the weapon flew aside and quickly guided his axe into the human's ribcage, which cracked and splintered under the might of the strike.

Despite the warm spray that painted his face, the Chieftain noticed that the congregation, save for the brown-robed men, had their heads bowed while the Priest led them in a prayer, like they were attempting to ignore away the threat in their midst.

"Give unto us your spirit, Redja, and allow us victory this day," he chanted, in a voice of quivering vigor. "Deliver us from this evil, so that we may persevere!"

Ronnok grunted in annoyance as the third man pushed the attack. The Northman refocused and stood ready, picking out a hundred flaws in the fighting form of this lumbering foe. He would have cleaved the small, bald man easily, were it not for Arvid's voice calling out behind him.

"Duck!"

The Chieftain calmly dropped to one knee and felt a gust of wind as the first of the robed men went soaring over his head, tumbling like a ragdoll and emitting a warbling yelp all the while.

The airborne enemy impacted his charging ally with a hollow, moist slap, and both tumbled to the ground with a myriad of swears erupting from the tangled pile. Ronnok stood, strode forward stoically, and sliced his axe through the torso of both humans with a single blow before they could untangle.

No more stood to face the invaders. Ronnok looked to the altar, his face dripping in blood, and grinned wildly. "Deliverance?" derided the Northman. "Gods do not deliver you. Weapons do."

"You are nothing to the will of a god!" the priest shrieked. He drew a jagged dagger from the recesses of his robes, an obviously ceremonial piece, and let the blade shimmer in the light. "If Redja's lesser servants cannot rid us of this evil, then one of the greater ones will."

Ronnok looked on with amusement as the slender Priest rushed forward on the wings of faith. He was zealous, to his credit, yet ideas of divine justice do little to stop a blade in the moments of real combat.

The human threw himself forward and stabbed out as soon as he was close enough, an attack which was easily countered by a backhand blow to the wrist, sending the knife soaring vertically into the air.

Ronnok dropped his axe, caught the knife with his right hand, and kicked the Priest's knees out, all in a flurry of motion that took little more than a single, ragged breath. With his unoccupied paw, the Chieftain caught the falling human by the neck and held him aloft.

The Northman placed the tip of the blade at a rest upon the Priest's forehead and bellowed a laugh. "A greater servant, indeed."

"If not me, then another!" spat the human, struggling to speak through the grip of the Northman. His face was flush with fury, and every word was accompanied by the flying of spittle. "Do you really think you can defile the house of God in such a manner? His great Augurs will root you out, just as they root out the impure among us!"

Ronnok pressed the tip of the knife against the Priest's forehead, drawing a small trickle of blood. "These Augurs sound interesting. Where can I find them?"

The Priest cackled madly, his face turning red as a beet. "They will find you. They will kill you."

"As you say," the Chieftain stated, letting go of the man's neck to let him rest on his knees. "Let's ensure that they do so, shall we?"

Stretching his left hand out flat, the Nort smacked the pommel of the jagged blade as hard as he could, sending it sliding through the Priest's skull like butter. The man toppled to the ground in a seizing heap, dead in an instant.

A disgusted gasp echoed throughout the hall; the people shrank away from the invaders in a clear and visible fear, many of them quaking in their places as blood crept across the floor. This was the time to strike, the Chieftain knew, in the moment of most distress.

"Here's how this will proceed," Ronnok said calmly, sending his gaze sailing across the petrified faces of the congregation. "You have food, ale and treasures. You will give them to us, and there will be no more bloodshed. If you are agreeable to our demands, you will have nothing to fear."

"From you," an old, bearded man whimpered as he rose sheepishly.

Ronnok cocked his head in confusion and gestured for the man to continue.

"The vision of Redja has surely seen you defile his house," the local elaborated. "We are supposed to defend his property with our lives. If we give you these things, he will take us." He winced at the thought. "The Augurs will take us."

"Who are these Augurs?" Ronnok asked. "Why do you fear them?"

"They are strong men, the Augurs, stronger individually than our entire homeland put together, knights of old that know all," the man said, bearing a tremble in his voice whose cause was clearly more than age. "They will find us, spirit us away to the mainland." He ground his teeth for a moment. "They will, in their words, 'make us more perfect'. They will kill us." He swept his arms around. "Look around you. We are old folks, frail."

Ronnok nodded. Indeed, most of the congregation looked as if they could hardly wield a butter knife.

"We cannot fight," the man continued. "You have given us a choice between death and death. The moment you stepped foot among us, we were damned. So, take what you will. There is little to think on when the choice is dying now or later."

Ronnok, though unsettled, nodded and directed his party to begin their harvest.

"I have seen them once more," Bjorn said, meeting the treasure laden Norts halfway up the beach with a look of concern upon his face. "The black sails and big ships. Watching us, taking note of our movements."

"Still no further contact?" Ronnok mused. "They are quite antisocial."

"I wonder why?" Harald quipped, striding by with a hearty laugh.

"In any case, they have kept close to shore," Bjorn continued, showing no emotion beyond mild annoyance at his father. "I believe they are harbored on the main island."

"Must be a safe port," Eira mused. "If they sailed close, they couldn't have cared about being spotted."

"Indeed," Ronnok concurred. "As we have found our destination, so they have found theirs. Every road on our journey leads to Arvyn."

"We must prepare," Thyra said. "We cannot count on them to sit back and wait. They will attack."

"Attack all of Nordiska?" Ronnok replied, scratching his beard. "That would be ill-advised."

"As I have told you before, husband, we must be alert," Thyra scolded. "This is no ordinary raiding campaign. Caution is warranted."

Ronnok nodded, having no further retort. Thyra's mind was far less tempestuous than his own, more apt to seeing the entire scale of a given situation. Her counsel on this matter was wise, and the Chieftain knew well to value that wisdom properly.

"They will want the smith," Thyra continued gravely. "They will come."

"How do you think the girl will handle this, if it comes to war?" Harald asked. "She is a small, frail thing, still bleeding from many wounds, both inside and out."

"She is strong," Eira pointed out. "When she is knocked down, there is little hesitation within her to rise. She will stand firm in the face of whatever comes."

"Perhaps," mused the Chieftain. "I see the strength in her, but are there not limits to such a thing? Even the strongest of armor will bend and break under continuing assaults."

Thyra nodded. "She still carries the death of her home with her, the death of all she loved. She has survived a battle, but what of a war?"

"Perhaps the Karlmaðr can enlighten us further," Eira suggested. "He understands the weight of such things."

Ronnok nodded. "I will speak to him and let the task be his. We must focus and prepare our own people."

"I will begin moving the fleet into a defensive position as soon as we return," Thyra said. "We will show them that we are ready."

"No," Ronnok said with a shake of the head. "We must show them neither fear nor confidence. We must remain as mysterious to them as they are to us." He scratched his beard once more. "Unburden the ships and be ready to make away, but show no other action. We will make the first incursion and set them on their heels. More importantly, we will gain final confirmation of our suspicions."

The gathered Norts nodded in agreement before tossing their

plunder into the boat and embarking once more. The wind blew at their backs, and they sliced easily through the calm waters of this seemingly peaceful archipelago.

"That was rude, you know," Alauren quipped as Ronnok strode by, carrying a keg on his shoulder. "Leaving us behind."

"You looked like you needed sleep," Ronnok replied with a shrug and a lopsided smile. He gingerly set his burden down. "Besides, we need your forge up and running."

"Well, you're in luck there, then," Alauren beamed cheerily, waving her hand with pride across her completed setup. A single stone furnace, made of hastily masoned blocks, stood beneath a white Northmen tent; within the forge an intense, white flame sizzled and crackled. Her anvil lay conveniently next to her workbench, at which she had clearly been mixing flux, while a sharpening stone had been set up on an impromptu (yet remarkably well-crafted) wooden structure just outside.

"Hard at work already," Ronnok observed. "Perhaps you can make yourself a shield."

Alauren chuckled, holding up her bracer-clad wrist. "I have this, remember? Besides, I'm busy making those sketches reality."

"If you so choose, wise battlemaster," jabbed the Chieftain. "Tell me, where is the Karlmaðr?"

"He went on a walk with Valin," Alauren replied. "Something about stretching his old bones on dry land. I don't think they left camp."

Ronnok nodded. "I will find them. In the meantime, do you know where to get supplies?"

"Arvid filled me in last night," Alauren confirmed. "Well, as much as he could, anyway. The brown tent next to yours."

"Good," Ronnok rumbled. He turned to step away, but caught himself mid-stride. "Oh, the people of Arvyn graciously gave us some gifts. Here." He tossed a solid, rusty-brown ingot of Ghaldevhal metal to the ground next to the tent, where it embedded solidly with a *thump!*

"Craft yourself something nice."

Alauren's eyes lit up. She shuffled over and snatched the gift without hesitation before carting the ingot to her workbench, oblivious to the Chieftain walking off with his keg and a smirk.

The old man and the Dwarf weren't difficult to find, as they were being told a (quite loud and enunciated) story in the native Northmen tongue by an old woman. The foreign words bounced off their scrunched-up faces like arrows on a metal shield, finding hardly a surface to stick fast.

The Chieftain smiled amusedly. "At er œrinn, Karlvíf," he instructed. The woman looked indignant for a moment, but shuffled off to her duties without another word.

"That sounded interesting," Edlevin said with an affable chortle. "Wish I caught more of it than her calling me a youngster."

"At least someone does," Valin quipped.

Ronnok chuckled, yet was clearly preoccupied with another thought. "Karlmaðr, there is something you should know."

Edlevin's smile died down at the seriousness of the words, his face becoming grave and troubled. After a quick glance at the ground, he nodded at the Chieftain to go ahead.

"Just the Karlmaðr, please," Ronnok requested, looking to Valin.

"Oh, sure, don't tell the short one yer big secret," bellowed the Dwarf, with a mightily exaggerated offense. He moped off, hunched dramatically. "I'll go find some trouble, then."

"The men who killed your people, and mine, are here," Ronnok said, his tone low and quiet, once the Dwarf was out of earshot. "I know it. They are called the Augurs by the people here."

Edlevin's shoulders sagged further. "I was hoping Drell would be full of shit." He groaned, rubbing his temple. "Damnit all."

Ronnok nodded. "We have been driven from our homes, just as you have, Karlmaðr." He rumbled a deep, primal growl, not angry, but colored with a clear lust for recompense. "Now we rest on the home shores of the enemy, clawing at their gates. The Northmen will not miss the opportunity for blood repaid."

"Neither will I," Edlevin replied with a cold fury. "I wanted to avoid this life, one of bloodshed and battle, but if these gargantuan bastards want to pull me back in, I'm going to give them fury for it."

Ronnok took a deep breath and crossed his arms, looking

intensely down at the human. "Allow me to ask you something."

"Of course," the old soldier replied quickly.

"Are you who you say you are?" the Chieftain posited.

Edlevin's eyebrows raised in equal parts shock and confusion. "Before I answer," he said, "tell me why you feel the need to ask such a thing. Do you believe I've been dishonest?"

"I do not know what I believe about you," Ronnok elaborated. "You have a truly impressive knowledge of the world. Certainly more than I would expect from a simple Fangirmish soldier. I believe that there is something dark that lurks deep within you, well-hidden and dangerous."

Edlevin nodded, glancing anxiously at the forests and beyond. "I have told you that I'm an old soldier who has seen and done much in my time, most of which I truly regret," he murmured softly. "I have not told you of the people I've personally hurt or the myriad of lives I have taken. I have not told you of the pain I have helped spread upon innocent lives, nor the guilt that weighs in my mind every day that I draw breath." He paused for a moment, careful to choose the right words. "Ronnok, there is much you do not know about me, and much more that you will never know. I do not wish these things, these echoes of a nightmarish memory gone by, to define who I am to you, or to Ally, or to anyone else. I have left those memories where they belong, and I wish to prove to the world – and to you – that I am far more than my mistakes."

Ronnok rubbed his chin and thought for a moment before speaking further. "You are a changed man, you say, but how can I accept this without knowing who you were? Am I to believe someone who admits, however vaguely, to spreading such pain on his word alone?"

"I do not expect you to accept my silence on the matter of my past simply because I ask it of you," Edlevin corrected firmly. "I expect you to accept it because I have proven, and I will continue to prove, that I am no longer that man."

Ronnok scratched his beard and sighed. "Alright, Karlmaðr," he conceded after a moment. "For helping to save my daughter, you have earned that, at least. Forgive my wariness, but if I am to make you one of Nordiska, such precautions are required."

Edlevin smiled lightly. "One of Nordiska, huh?"

"After our more pressing matter is dealt with," Ronnok nodded with a warm grin. "We will announce ourselves to our hosts soon enough. We want the blacksmith to be there, to confirm our suspicions."

Edlevin bit his lip, thinking for a moment. "When?"

"After a few days, when the fleet is light enough to outrun our enemy should the need arise," answered the Chieftain. "There will be time to prepare."

Edlevin nodded. "Perhaps I will wait a day to tell her about all this, then. She seems quite happy in the moment, and I do not wish to rob her of it."

Ronnok nodded. "Inform her at your discretion, but do not wait too long, Karlmaðr. Do not protect her too much."

"I won't," Edlevin muttered. "If even I could."

CHAPTER TWENTY-NINE:

FINDING TROUBLE

33rd OF THE MORN OF HARVEST
NORTHERN YEAR 715

"How's the work coming?" asked the old soldier, ducking under the white flap of the makeshift smithy.

Alauren was drenched in sweat, pounding a piece of metal into shape with a bestial vigor. She had tied a piece of blue cloth around her forehead and rolled her sleeves up past her elbows, combating the salt of the sweat and the heat from the furnace, respectively.

"Ten prototype chestplates," grunted the strained blacksmith. "In three days. Plus sharpening your sword. How do you think?"

"Thought so," Edlevin replied amidst a chuckle. He set a large skin bottle down upon her workbench. "Just filled it. Hopefully it's still cold for you."

Alauren popped the lid and downed several large, noisy, and particularly messy gulps before using some of the water to rinse her head. She threw the skin back and began banging away again without another word.

"He's testing you, you know," said the old soldier. "You've been talked up quite a bit over the past few weeks, mostly by me."

"So, you're to blame for this untenable workload," Alauren chided, wiping her brow with her forearm. "Good to know."

Edlevin shrugged. "Well, you should like me better after you hear the news. Take a break and listen up." He paused, watching the smith set her tools down. "We're going to the mainland. Today."

Alauren shook her head. "Too much work to do here. Need to have this done by the afternoon to stay on schedule."

"I would say the same, had Ronnok not specifically tasked me with dragging you along," Edlevin replied. "You're coming with."

Alauren shook her head again. "Why does he want me? The last time I was in a fight it took all my focus just to avoid getting skewered." She bit her lip and paused for a moment, looking aimlessly around the tent. "I assume this will be bloody, anyway?"

"It's the Norts," Edlevin stated flatly.

"Yeah," Alauren murmured. "I can't see why I would be of use."

Edlevin shrugged. "Perhaps he's still trying to get a feel for you, Ally. Or, perhaps, he just enjoys having you around. Either way, you're leaving your work for now."

Alauren sighed and looked over her cluttered workbench. "Yeah. I suppose getting some fresh air could do me some good. The fumes of the forge are making my breath ragged." She leaned backwards, resting on her table. "The bad ventilation is making me crazy."

Edlevin smiled smarmily, determined to fish the desired response out of the smith. "You can fix bad ventilation. Admit it, that craziness is driven by something else. You finally understand why I've always wanted you to come south with me."

"Bastard," Alauren spat with a heavily suppressed smile. "Yes, Karlmaðr, I would rather like to see this new world up close, too. Curiosity does get the better of me."

"Don't be afraid to accept that," the old soldier encouraged. "This is what we have, now. Enjoy it."

"I will," Alauren affirmed. "Who else is coming?"

"Ronnok, of course, Eira and Thyra, Harald, and about a dozen other warriors," Edlevin answered. "Young ones, looking to make their mark."

"No Valin?" Alauren asked, raising an eyebrow.

"Says he prefers to stay here and *get t' know the local populace*," the old soldier quoted, followed with a hearty chuckle and a roll of the eyes. "We'll see how far he gets without a translator."

"Ten elysium that he pisses off the wrong old lady," offered the smith.

"Oh, you have a deal," Edlevin said with a robust chuckle. "I say he'll get treed by someone far younger." He crossed his arms. "Ready?"

"Ready as I'll ever be," Alauren replied.

"Good," Edlevin said, followed by a deep breath. "Before we go, Ally... There's one more thing we have to discuss."

"Let me guess, bad news?" the smith asked with a sigh. "Seems like that's all we get lately."

The man sighed and looked to the ground for a moment, grinding his teeth as he mulled over his words. The delay felt painful to the blacksmith, as if each passing second worsened the coming news.

"They are here," Edlevin finally murmured, snapping his eyes back up to meet the smith's. "The men from Teth."

Alauren recoiled visibly. "Drell was right, then?"

"He was," the old soldier confirmed with a sagging shake of the head. "They are called the Augurs, according to Ronnok."

"Augurs?" Alauren asked. "Fortune tellers?"

"Diviners, or some other such thing," Edlevin said, waving his hand dismissively. "Such titles don't fit them, as they are more than a simple side show to separate gullible nobles from their coin." He leaned heavily against one of the wooden posts that made up the doorway. "The Norts have seen certain things over the last few days as they scouted, disturbing signs of something dark inhabiting this small archipelago."

Alauren cocked an eyebrow. "Things like lights in the woods?"

Edlevin snapped up straight. "What?"

"Here and there, staying to the edge of the camp," Alauren continued. "I've seen them a couple times, but I was only sure that my eyes weren't playing tricks on me with the one last night." She tossed her head, mulling over a thought. "I stayed still and watched for a while, but didn't catch much else. It seemed to leave after a while, but there was definitely something there."

"Huh," Edlevin huffed, filing the matter for later consideration. "Interesting. But, no, what the Norts have seen is far worse. It is a population that looks as downtrodden as they do paranoid, behaving extremely antisocially at all times." He was careful to meet the smith's gaze with an expression of utter solemnity. "The site of Ronnok's first raid, a small congregation on an exterior island, has disappeared into the night, like they simply got up and left during dinner. Gone, all of them, with hardly a trace."

"Best we find answers quickly, then," Alauren said, removing her apron. "I've seen quite enough of this type of thing."

Edlevin nodded. "As have I. Come on, we need to get to the mainland."

A smooth ride upon a skiff led the party to the shore, where they were dropped off by a skeleton crew of two Northmen that steered the boat back out to sea, bearing in the direction of the exfiltration point. The smith's eyes were locked on the world rather than the Norts, however; this was a seeming paradise of nature and peace, and she felt an invigoration run through her veins as the warmth of the sun brushed over her skin.

The roads of Arvyn were predictably rough and trodden, climbing many small hills and dipping into a number of ravines, but they provided an easy reference point to the surprisingly detailed map Ronnok had procured from a sealed storage barrel in the lower hold of the *Skylðrek*. The dry parchment was, likely, far older than the Northman who pored over its details, but it had held well against the onslaught of years in the hold of a seagoing vessel. After some distance, the party had stopped for the moment, allowing the Chieftain to study the strokes of ink carefully, trying to figure out what marked routes had fallen out of favor with the local patrols, as well as which ones still existed at all.

Alauren didn't mind the delay. She sat on a large, mossy boulder under a grove of great oaks and evergreens whose arms ran smoothly through the crystal blue of the sky above. Like Alsara, there was a unique color to the air here, though Arvyn's large forests and rippling creeks dulled the smell of the ocean to something additive, rather than a main ingredient as it was on the free island. There was no place, she surmised, like Arvyn, just as there was no place like Alsara, or like Teth. She savored every moment, wholly oblivious the cackling laughter of Edlevin as Eira, Thyra and Harald tried unsuccessfully to teach him the Nort language.

"Loada saviya, oad jodir vìfika?" attempted the old soldier, to which all gathered Norts shook their heads in exasperation.

"Your words need to roll," Eira grumbled. "Like a boat."

"I suppose they're more like a rolling boulder right now, huh?" Edlevin conceded with a chortle. "Your language is beautiful, but hard on the tongue. Reminds me of a particularly glowing barmaid from back when I was traveling through South Fang-"

"Akranúr," Ronnok interrupted, finally breaking his focused silence and drawing all eyes. "A town, just ahead. We should find it in good time. From there, we must go into the forests."

"I look forward to being sociable," chuckled the old soldier. "Perhaps I can serve as translator."

"Not while you still confuse 'maiden' and 'whore'," Harald thundered, drawing a wholehearted laugh from the old human.

"No talking," Ronnok instructed, utterly humorless. "We enter, we investigate, we leave."

Edlevin sobered dutifully and practically stood at attention in front of the Chieftain. "As you command. Lead on!"

The group moved quickly along the road, keeping alert to their surroundings. Save for the occasional rustle of leaves in the woods, produced by a small squirrel or bird, it seemed that they were isolated and alone, far from any who would care to stand against them. Their road was easy, and so they made haste.

Akranúr was little more than a collection of small wooden hovels, built along the side of the main road and in front of what looked to be a logging operation. Great saws were spun by a large creek which crept under a well-worn bridge on the other side of the town, though any industry seemed to have halted for the day.

"Go away!" a voice yelped as the Nort party crossed the town's threshold. A golden goblet came spiraling out of a window on the first hovel to their left and landed in the dry dirt road with a *ping!*

"Take it and go, and don't let them see you!" the voice yelled again, accompanied by a silver platter clanging onto the path.

The other hovels seemed to like the idea, throwing their gold and silver into the streets as if it was morn-old bread in an effort to hasten the departure of their apparently unwelcome guests. Never were the inhabitants seen, yet still their fear was palpable.

"What is going on?" asked the old soldier, unable to stop his searing curiosity from burning through. "Who are you afraid of?"

"Redja!" the voice snapped caustically, as if the foreign visitor had just been crowned the king of all idiots for not immediately knowing the answer. "Get out!"

Edlevin opened his mouth to speak again, but was silenced by a glare from the Chieftain. He (quite sheepishly) helped the party gather the valuables into sacks, not hazarding another word until they were well beyond the town and into the gulley of the creek.

"What just happened?" Edlevin asked, after shuffling carefully down an embankment and onto the round stones of the waterway's bank.

"Something rather annoying," Ronnok growled in reply. "I told you not to speak."

Edlevin sighed. "I know. I'm sorry."

"Don't be sorry," Ronnok chided. "Be mindful. These people are scared for a reason. Questions endanger them."

"Of course," conceded the old soldier with a bow of the head. A thought dawned on him, and he cocked an eyebrow as he considered the idea. "Still, if they can give us anything to help them…"

Alauren lost track of the lively debate as it went on; the polite and utterly respectful exchange of ideas between Edlevin's hard head and Ronnok's iron will proved far less interesting than the new world that engulfed her. The bubbling of the creek's rapids was a soothing hiss in her ears, drawing her further into the wonder of the paradise-like nature all around. Even the rocks here had their own twists and turns within, likely different minerals pushed together and fused over eons. Fossils of snails and other shelled creatures could be seen easily and abundantly on the larger stones, each having its own history to tell.

She looked up and brushed a few gnats from their dance in front of her face. A great, steep bank rose on her left and a wet lowland spread out on the other side of the creek to the right, where her eyes became caught up on something out of place. At a close distance, not more than ten seconds' jog from the smith, laid a perfectly still ball of light.

The orb shone a light blue, the color pulsating in rhythm as if it were breathing, slowly and steadily. Fog rose from the center of the glow, but dissipated quickly as it was caught in the gentle breeze. It seemed as if a part of the sky above had come to life, taken form, and descended to the land, hovering over the rolling waters with hardly a movement.

Alauren froze, finding a single word welling up. "Wisp!"

The orb recoiled, as if it were physically taken aback by the blacksmith's comment, and sped off beyond a distant tree line with nary a wasted second.

"I saw it!" Edlevin confirmed with a childlike wonder. "I thought they were extinct!"

"Yeah," Alauren nodded. "It's been a few decades since I've seen one. That's what I've been seeing in the forest, then."

Ronnok spoke in his native tongue with Harald and Eira, their voices fast and low. After a moment, the Chieftain grew tense. "We must move quickly," he growled. "Leave the gold and silver and keep pace."

A light fog rose above the rippling creek while the scent of the pine trees, whose branches soared out over the water, lightly colored the unseasonably warm air. Alauren breathed deeply, feeling a tingling sensation run up her spine. Every second here was another memory, another experience that quickly settled into a permanent residence within her mind.

The natural beauty of this island went on and on, as far as they could travel. Thousands of trees would stretch unbroken, save for the occasional grassy clearing, bathed in pleasant sunlight. Fresh water was everywhere, provided by the snow-capped peak of the distant mountain, and the sounds of nature permeated every inch of the living forest floor as the party hiked quickly over rock and log.

"Vér res hí," Ronnok said abruptly, halting the group. "Rest and drink," he clarified, nodding to his non-Northmen comrades. The Norts, save for Eira, gladly took the opportunity to plunge into the cool depths of a crystal-clear pool in the creek, washing sweat and pollen from their skin.

"How much further?" Edlevin asked, sipping from a freshly refilled water skin.

"I don't know, Karlmaðr," Ronnok replied, laying down his axes before plunging into the frigid waters of the creek and surfacing after a moment. "Our maps are old, and this island has changed. Perhaps an hour. Perhaps a day."

Edlevin grinned. "I want it to be a day. It has been a long while since a walk has left me this refreshed."

"A long while since you've done it sober, you mean," Alauren corrected.

Edlevin waved the comment away with a chuckle. "We all have our preferred terminology. Right, big man?"

Ronnok gave no answer. He rose slowly from the water, staring stone-faced towards a patch of thick brush near the tree line, his gaze focused and intense.

In front of the bushes stood three men, each taller than any of the Norts and clad in an all-too familiar plate armor. They leaned forward on their glistening swords, peering on from underneath their helmets. Edlevin's face ran white, and Alauren's stomach turned sour.

These were the knights of old, the men from Teth, seemingly appearing out of the air.

"You have come to our doorstep," said the knight in the middle. His voice was familiar, sending the same tingle through the blacksmith's spine as it had weeks ago, yet a cold bloodlust found itself along for the ride this time, a growing anger serving as its kindling within her. "How kind."

"Can't kill you from afar," Ronnok growled.

Edlevin put a hand on his sword. "Who are you? What do you want with us?"

"Not with you," the knight was quick to correct. "You are dust." His helmet twitched ever so slightly as he cocked his head toward the smith. "Her. There must be an awakening."

"What are you talking about?" Alauren attempted to growl, only to find a quivering warble.

"The Dreamer has lost herself to a nightmare," the knight rumbled. "You will wake her."

"I have no idea what you're on about," snapped the smith. "Who are you? What do you want with me?"

"Death," the man stated coldly. "I am Koro, and I am the Dawn."

Without another word, the man hefted his sword and strode forward, a move echoed by his fellows. Their footsteps thundered the ground and shattered the fragile rocks of sand and sediment below their colossal sabatons, cleaving them or crushing them to dust.

Eira hooked her boots under Ronnok's axes and kicked them to the Chieftain, drawing her own weapon at the same time. Both Norts

THE SAGAS OF ODENSEYE: CONQUERING AUTUMN

solidified in a defensive stance, while Edlevin shoved Alauren behind him and did the same.

Abruptly, Koro halted, letting the other two knights charge past him. One tangled immediately with Ronnok, becoming locked in a clear stalemate, while the other pivoted and charged at Edlevin.

The knight raised his sword high and brought a thunderous blow down upon the old soldier. Edlevin snapped his remaining bracer over his head, intercepting the strike and redirecting it towards the ground.

The enemy seemed unbothered by the deflection, bearing no hesitation in his response; the old human found himself kneed hard in the chest, sending him tumbling on to his back, while the knight paused to pull his blade from the solid log that it had impaled cleanly.

Taking advantage of the moment (and his chestplate's absorption of the blow), Edlevin attempted to roll forward and leap to his feet. Instead of springing up as he would have many winters ago, he found his back locked in place, unable to bend enough to allow his momentum to carry him forward. Any further movement brought only a worsening tightness at the base of his spine and a pronounced pain, a creeping, stabbing agony, like a thousand needles were piercing his flesh and bones. He looked up to see the knight raising his sword high again. The old soldier breathed in heavily, helpless, looking at the blade of the enemy as it glinted in the sun.

The sword came down hard. Each heartbeat felt as if it was an eternity and a second at the same time, flitting by while lasting a lifetime. He closed his eyes and prepared as the weapon's edge plummeted, attempting to embrace the coming peace that he had prepared for all of his life; instead, only a striking fear flowed through his heart. A ghastly scream erupted, accompanying the squelch of a blade through flesh.

Edlevin, mysteriously still breathing, opened his eyes to see Alauren standing between him and his doom. The enemy's sword lay on the ground, dropped in surprise, while the smith's blade had slid through his chest armor as if the heavy, angular plate was wet parchment, causing a gray and sickly-looking blood to seep from the seams around the shining edges of her sword.

The wounded enemy roared in pain and anger, punching out hard toward his attacker. The smith was forced to intercept the blow with her bracer, snapping her wrist up and in front of the rapidly approaching gauntlet. Her armor absorbed the strike well, but caused her own hand to snap back and impact hard with her jaw. She reeled backwards as a spray of blood trickled from her mouth, and she fell heavily to the rocks.

The enemy retrieved his blade and limped off, rejoining Koro with hardly a groan. The second combatant had fallen to numbers, finally succumbing when his head and helm were lopped off by an axe, whatever lay underneath the metal dome still hidden fully behind the faceplate. The Chieftain (and his entertained warriors) looked to the enemy leader with matching, wicked grins, proud of their violent feat.

"Ally!" Edlevin screamed, crawling stiffly to the smith. "Ally, are you alright?

"Yeah… Yeah, I'm good," said the woman, scrambling to her knees. Her lip was cut quite horribly, but no other damage seemed to have been inflicted. Her sword was, thankfully, still in her hand, and the bracer was no worse for wear. She positioned herself under the old soldier's arm and lifted with all of her might.

Edlevin struggled to his feet, taking a hunched, pained posture. "Come on, behind the Norts. Go!"

"You are hardy," Koro complimented, his voice booming across the creek and eliciting ripples which cascaded across the surface of the water. He whistled loudly, an impossibly shrill note which crawled through the heads of the Northmen, the sound drawing out four more knights from the thick brush. Each brandished their weapons, and Koro's armor creaked as he hefted his own blade. "Yet, death still comes."

The enemy charged forward again. Each Nort picked a target from among the newly revealed foes, while Ronnok's sole focus was on the leader, who he engaged without hesitation.

Far more skilled than the last knight, Koro moved his heavy frame with an unnatural speed, like his armor weighed little more than a light jacket. Three of the enemy's blows were sent high, three left, then right. Each had to be intercepted and batted away with both axes, while Ronnok found hardly an opening for any attacks of his own.

The Chieftain heard one of his warriors cry out in pain, a young woman by the name of Hyrvi, before being silenced with a gurgle.

Then another, and another. Skadin. Froli. Mata. Young lives were extinguished in a matter of moments as their Chief was locked in a frustrating stalemate, unable to help.

Enraged, Ronnok tried an offensive push, striking out hard with his left axe. He attempted to cleave the man's shoulder plate with a blow at the seam, meaning to get enough leverage to rip it off or crack it.

In a single motion, Koro deflected the attack away with his sword, hooked his blade under Ronnok's axe curve, and removed the weapon from play with single tug.

Ronnok tried again with his right axe, attempting to take advantage of the man's uneven stance. He struck a clear gap in the armor, only to find it colliding with an unyielding substance beneath, as if the knight's flesh was covered over in rock. Koro simply grabbed the weapon and cast it aside, ripping it from the Chieftain's hand as if its hilt was slathered in grease. Seeing no other option, the Nort struck out with a fist, impacting Koro's faceplate with a booming, echoing *crack*.

Seemingly unfazed by the blow, Koro brought his helm forward and smashed Ronnok's face, sending the Nort to his knees, bloodied and woozy. "Strong," hissed the knight, "yet you break."

Edlevin and Alauren could do little but watch the massacre with horror. Eira and Thyra stood watch over their comrades, yet they could only look on as they were surrounded by numbers that grew increasingly lopsided, the other Nortish warriors mercilessly sent to the halls of the Great Father with a ruthless efficiency.

Ronnok, defiant, spat blood at Koro's helmet, eliciting no reaction from the stoic enemy. After a moment, the knight returned the favor with a backhand that sent the Chieftain twirling to the ground, unconscious.

"It is time," Koro stated, turning his expressionless faceplate to the blacksmith. "Time to end the struggle, to wake from the nightmare."

Eira and Thyra attacked at once, attempting to drive the man's arms apart with their shields, meaning to strike a blow to the chest. Koro simply impacted their blockers hard, splintering them into many pieces and sending the women tumbling to the side while he thundered to his true prey without further inhibition.

Alauren could do little but huddle by Edlevin, who, even in his stiff and pained state, made every effort to shield his old friend, standing as tall as he could while searing agony bit the muscles of his back. Koro simply picked the human up with one arm and threw him aside like a child, the gaze of the armored titan never leaving his true prize. Dodging a swipe from her sword, he shoved the smith down roughly and knelt, his armor creaking all the way. He moved close, peering at her from within the infinite shadows of his helm.

"Dawn," whispered the knight, barely audible through his helm. Alauren could feel his breath on her face, cold and wet, smelling of molten nickel. "At last."

Alauren flipped to her belly and tried to skitter away, taking advantage of the enemy's clear fascination. Instead, she found a heavy boot planted on her back, pinning her down. Her head was violently yanked back by the hair, drawing out tears of pain and terror that ran down her cheekbones. She heard a knife unsheathe behind her and quickly found the cold steel glinting below her neck, hovering a hair's length from flesh.

Koro breathed in heavily, raggedly, clearly finding a perverse pleasure in the smith's suffering. "Dawn!"

Alauren's eyes welled with tears. She had come to terms with her eventual demise years ago, an acceptance of the cold inevitability that even she would have to face one day. But, like this? Pinned and crying in a creekbed so far from home?

No, her mind thundered, refusing despair and welling up a primal courage within. She pawed about, finding her sword lying next to her on the ground. Snatching the weapon with an impressive rapidity, the smith drove the blade into the leg that pinned her down, slicing through armor and flesh like it was jelly.

Koro didn't react, save for an involuntary twitch that ran the length of his body.

"Your blade wounds the unwoundable, yet it matters little," the knight muttered, removing the knife from upon her neck and using the hand to slide the sword from his calf gingerly, with abundant caution. He let the blade clatter on the rocks. "Pain will pass, just as the seasons, and I shall endure both."

Alauren looked to Edlevin, her friend and mentor, one last time. While she expected to a find an expression of horror and despair, there was only a confused furrowing of his brow. A voice rang out across the rippling water and the bloodied stones, low and grating.

"To your knees, curs!"

The crushing force on her back was lifted, and the looming presence of her would-be killer stood tall above her. Alauren, thinking no further about the matter, rose, retrieved her sword, and rushed to her old friend. "Ed, I'm alright. Are you...?"

His gaze was still fixed beyond her, and he found no words.

"Eldari!" Koro hissed, moving quickly to brandish his weapon.

His motion was cut off; he erupted in a scream, sharp and blood curdling, like the wailing of a mythical banshee. The knight fell to his knees in anguish, followed by his compatriots, each gripping their helms helplessly as they howled.

Beyond Koro stood a tall, slender figure holding a small metal object. "Go!" it yelled, the voice remarkably familiar to the blacksmith.

"Xen?" Alauren called. "Is-"

"GO!" Xendra screamed, waving them off.

Alauren, without further hesitation, helped to heft Edlevin to his feet, while Eira and Thyra carried a half-conscious Ronnok between them. Behind, Harald slipped from out of the confused fray, taking the opportunity to retrieve his Chieftain's weapons and rally with the few of his clanmates who still drew breath.

Alauren hobbled away with as much haste as she could muster. A thousand questions ran through her mind and a million possible answers presented themselves in turn. There wasn't time to sift through them. For now, there was only one foot in front of another, one more step.

CHAPTER THIRTY:

ALLIES

*Though I am hardly an archaeologist, I find the
study of ancient bones and relics quite intriguing,
as they often hold secrets to our mysterious origin.
The Solvari and the Alvari, for instance, trace
their existence to a single ethnicity that last
existed some five-thousand years ago, confirmed
by the discovery of an ancient burial vault in 601.
The specimens within possessed skeletal features
of both races, unmistakably. Most interesting,
however, is respected archaeologist Glavius
Marus' observation in 659, after seeing the bones
in person:*

*"It is clear, in my mind, that the skeletal structure
of these beings was formed to support the muscle
structure of an Arbari. Many bones are shaped in
such a way that they would easily flex at extreme
angles, anchored only by soft tissue and a loose
fitting at the joint. It is my hypothesis, then, that
these beings were the genesis of three races, and
not two."*

*In any case, we still have much to learn, as we
have only just scratched the surface of the
darkness we emerged from.*

–   Gauis Truvani, in "Nations of Odenseye"

The skiff impacted hard upon the sandy shore, driven to its rough
landing by a most inexperienced (and injured) crew. The remaining
Northmen did what they could, but with the loss of the others, Alauren
and Edlevin were left to assist in keeping the vessel pumping along
the open water as fast as it realistically could. Thankfully, their work

was without incident, and the remnants of the raiding party spilled out onto the relative safety of their home base.

The Nort sisters wasted no time in dragging their dazed husband up the dunes and toward his tent; they were followed closely by Harald and the other Norts, leaving Alauren and Edlevin alone next to the sloshing waves. Both could do little but sit with wide eyes and slack jaws, shaking as the adrenaline finally bled from their veins. The air felt particularly frigid despite the warm sun and relatively still breeze, the cold adding to their quakes.

"What the *fuck*, Ed?" blurted the blacksmith, after some time.

Edlevin couldn't help but burst out in a dark laughter. "Well put. I don't know, Ally. I really, really don't."

Alauren shook her head. "Every time I feel like we're about to get answers, we just end up with more questions. They can't even tell me why they want me dead without giving the response in vague, meandering bullshittery." She punched the sand hard. "It's frustrating me to the point of insanity! I feel like I'm lost in a cavern."

"We all are, Ally," Edlevin replied, his shoulders sagging greatly. He was still hunched, and though the tightness in his back had let up, some pain clearly remained. "Seasons are changing, and the pillars of the old world are crumbling away in a frenzied tempest. More and more sense seems to be lost from our lives with every day." He sighed deeply. "Everyone has a point in life when things no longer make sense to them, when everything they thought was consistent and true disappears like the mirage that it is. For me, this is the second time." He shook his head. "Somehow, I feel more lost than ever, but at least I know what to do about it this time."

"The first time, you found Teth," Alauren replied quietly, looking out over the waves. "You found a world that made sense back home. Where will you find it now, when we're surrounded by madness?"

Edlevin chuckled lightly. "I didn't find it in Teth, Ally. It was always there, below my feet, in the here and now." He smiled warmly and placed a hand on the smith's shoulder. "I have kept up spirits, not because I am putting on a show or suppressing my sorrow, but because I cannot allow myself to linger on unsolvable problems. Painful as it may be to ignore them, some threads will only spool infinitely when pulled. We must simplify, take what we know, and focus on asking the right questions. Otherwise, you will join the madness around you." His eyes drooped to the sand, and he poked at it with a finger. "What I'm trying to say, Ally, is that instead of looking for a beacon of sanity in this vast dark of insanity, perhaps we should focus on finding our footing and taking comfort in what little light we actually possess. We have Nordiska, and we have enemies that, though mysterious, are bound to reveal more about themselves as time goes on. Just keep your wits and consider what you do know more than what you don't."

"I suppose," conceded the smith, biting her lip. "What about Xendra, though? We know her name, at least, and I think it's reasonable to assume she's not with them. She's probably our best chance."

"Possibly," Edlevin replied. "She seems agreeable enough, saving our lives and all. However, I am curious about the word Koro used: Eldari."

"You've heard it before?" Alauren asked.

"Only in some old manuscripts," answered the old soldier. "Even then, they simply referenced the name without further explanation or context."

"Old manuscripts?" queried the smith. "How old?"

"A few centuries, at least, but probably much more," Edlevin explained. "Fangirmish texts, mostly, speaking on the topic of the rise of their empire. I don't have any answers beyond that. Regardless, their leader seemed to recognize her instantly, and that's enough for me to be curious."

Alauren nodded and sighed. "Hopefully Xendra sees it pertinent to find us, provided she made it out alive."

"Hopefully," Edlevin concurred. He struggled to his feet with an agonized groan. "Now, come on. We had better check on Ronnok and take stock of our situation."

Alauren nodded, following the old soldier over the dunes, beyond the fields and into the makeshift Nort village, from the border of which the infirmary tent was only a short distance.

Valin sat on a barrel outside of the ruby red canvas and burst into a wide grin at the sight of his friends. He hopped down and bounded over with a spring in his step.

"They wouldn't speak t' me!" bellowed the Dwarf. "I kept askin' where ye were, but they were too focused on the big man t' see me. I feared the worst!"

Edlevin chuckled. "Not to worry. Ally and I have a shared habit of slipping away before the worst comes to pass. Ronnok, on the other hand…" He peered past Valin, into the tent, where the Chieftain lay still upon a cot, barely visible through an opening in the tent flap.

"Ah, yeah," Valin sighed. "He took a beatin', that's fer sure. The ladies gave him some sort o' herb mixture and he's out cold now."

"As long as he's alive," Edlevin said, a clear relief settling over him.

"Oh, he's alive, and I'm sure he'll be just as pissed when he wakes up as he was when he passed out," Valin huffed. "He was already demandin' t' go back out and find 'em that did this."

Edlevin nodded, biting his lip. "I hope his recovery is swift. We have much to discuss."

"Then discuss it with me," Eira stated, emerging from the tent. "While my husband is infirm, I speak for Nordiska."

"Few better, in my mind," Edlevin replied with a smile. "Our presence here is known, now. We should get the fleet moving and retreat to better positioning."

"We remain here," Eira replied calmly.

Edlevin cocked his head. "They will come for us, these men. They want Alauren."

"We know," Eira enlightened with some visible irritation. "We have not wasted our time in this place, Karlmaðr. This island has only three points of landing, two of them only small enough for a few craft. The third, our own landing zone, is hazardous and naturally fortified."

Alauren nodded exuberantly.

"Our best chance is here," Eira continued. "We will send the fleet away, unburdened and swift, and make our stand. All that we must do is spill enough blood to show that an assault against Norts is foolhardy. We have the advantage of a prepared position."

"We let them come to us and slam against our fortifications, yes," Edlevin mused with a scratch of his stubble. "I feel, though, that Niralan is about to be pulled into this conflict. You should move your fleet now, as they do not hesitate when there is an opportunity to be taken."

"I already have Thyra doing so," Eira assured. "Our ships are prepared to make sail as soon as our non-fighters and their escorts are massed."

"Very good!" Edlevin exclaimed. His tone was one of respect, as if he were advising a superior officer, and he was clearly tapping into the experiences of his past, something Alauren had rarely witnessed. "Make sure you leave a few openings in the defenses," he advised. "We'll want to funnel them in to kill zones."

"Your advice is valuable," Eira said with respectful appreciation, "but Northmen have been making war since before you awoke in this life. We are prepared."

Edlevin nodded respectfully. "Understood. Ally, best get to work on some weapons and armor."

"And a shield," added the smith. "I'm sick of getting punched in the face."

"Live and learn, eh?" Edlevin remarked with a snide smile.

"I suppose, Karlmaðr," Alauren replied. "Come on, I'll need your help prepping the forge."

"Sure," Edlevin agreed with a smile. "Valin, can you help the Norts with some runes? I'm willing to bet the beach defenses will be more reliable as stone than wood."

"On it!" the Dwarf yelped, bounding away towards the beach.

The two outsiders showed similar haste, hustling to the forge. As Eira had said, Norts buzzed to and fro with utmost urgency, each doing their part to blunt the severity of the coming violence. Even the children helped to carry wood and swords from place to place before heading to embark on their craft, out of harm's way.

"Word gets around quick," Alauren observed.

"It needs to, in a life like this," Edlevin nodded. "If only our people would answer a call to action in the same way."

"All we have is the person by our side," Alauren concurred. "At least the Norts understand that."

"Indeed. I admire their way of life, violent though it may be," mused the old soldier. "At least they can rely on each other fully and without question, through all of the blood and strife."

"I'm thankful we found them," Alauren said, arriving at her forge and ducking through the tent flap. "You were right. This place really can be-"

Her sentence came to a grinding halt. Sensing danger, Edlevin plowed through the forge's flap to find a figure dressed in black, bearing an unfurled hood around her neck while she enjoyed a drink from her seat on the surface of the workbench.

"Xendra," the old soldier muttered. "Or Eldari?"

Indeed, though she was now dressed in a double-breasted coat of wool and armored leather boots, it was the same woman from Alsara. She hesitated for a moment, looking over the two arrivals carefully.

"Xendra," the woman finally answered, her voice low and vibrating, a stark contrast to chipper Solvari they had met at Alsara weeks ago. Every part of her demeanor seemed to be darker, more gravely serious, and she held herself with an icy confidence in her sparsely displayed body language. "The Eldari are my people, my race."

"Eldari…" Alauren trailed off, looking to Edlevin, who was clearly sharing the same thought. "You look like me, in many ways. You said it yourself, back at Alsara."

"I do," Xendra confirmed.

"So, am I…?" Alauren posited, trailing off.

"No," Xendra stated. "You are not Eldari. Truth be told, girl, I don't know *what* you are. You don't look like any race I'm familiar with, and your song echoes through the world loud and unrestrained, instantly distinguishable from any other."

Alauren furrowed her brow in utter confusion. "My song?"

"You really don't know?" the Eldari asked incredulously.

Alauren shook her head in silence.

"I see," Xendra muttered. She picked up a half-finished chestplate from the table and turned it over a few times, running her fingers across the smooth metal as if she was searching for some unknown imperfection. "A song is what we call the innate potential in all living things, a fountain of power that ever bubbles up from within. From it, you have poured forth an enchantment along with your liquid metal, binding the magic within. Your creations are stronger for this feat, unlike any others upon this world."

"No, I'm pretty sure my crafts are so strong because I've been doing this for a couple dozen decades," Alauren said indignantly. "I've told you before that magic has nothing to do with it." Her gaze became stern and uncharacteristically angry. "I *do not* cheat."

"Think what you will," Xendra stated flatly, evidently having little desire to engage in a discussion on the matter. "But back at that creek, I witnessed your blade cut through the steel flesh of a pureblood, a feat of magic that none have seen before. My own eyes have proven the truth of my words, though I can hardly believe them."

Edlevin grumbled briefly before cutting in. "You mind telling us more than your people's name before we go into 'songs' and magic? How about telling us why you saved us, and what you are doing here?"

"Humans. Impatient, as always. As you wish, old soldier," Xendra acquiesced. "I am a last vestige of a time gone by, one of just a few who knew of a world before the young ones blanketed over the ruins of our ancient empires." She looked around the forge for a moment, searching for words. "My people were among the strongest of what we now call the old races, beings of life and innate power. I, for my part, am known as the last child of the Eldari."

Edlevin shook his head, unappreciative of the scant detail. "Which means?"

"Which means that I'm the only friendly being on these fucking islands who has any idea what is actually going on, so I'd appreciate if you listened rather than interjecting," Xendra quickly shot back, causing the human to cross his arms and scowl. She continued. "The Eldari, parents of all Elven species, used to rule the entire south of Odenseye. Before…" She trailed off for a moment. "Before the Thjodhild."

"Thjodhild…" Alauren repeated. "The men who attacked us?"

"Indeed," confirmed the Eldari. "The locals know them as the Augurs of Redja, but they are as much servants of the Arvynian god as Fangirmish Nobles are to their people."

"Who are they? What do they want with me?" the smith hastily questioned, eager for any kind of enlightenment.

Xendra motioned for the others to sit, which Alauren obeyed instantly. Edlevin, ever cautious, didn't twitch from his position at the door.

Xendra raised an amused eyebrow, but quickly moved on to the matter at hand. "As to your latter question, I have no idea. I'm sorry." The comment drew a frown from the smith as the Eldari continued. "I do have some answers, however. The Thjodhild, though ancient to you, are mere children to the elders of my race." She ground her teeth for a moment. "Once, the Eldari Hegemony ruled the south of a continent populated with mighty beings of everlasting life. We built a glorious empire in our own homelands and beyond, giving our culture and technology to the many closely related races that made up our home." Her mood suddenly grew darker. "A period of peace ensued when our work was done, and we lived in harmony with the other immortal ancients, until we began to consort with them, crossing our bloodlines." She met Edlevin's eyes. "What you call 'natural' death was the result, our offspring fading with time."

"Hold on for a moment," Edlevin rumbled, holding up a hand. "You're immortal? Really?"

Xendra nodded, as if the answer should have been nakedly obvious. "She is, too," she furthered, pointing to Alauren.

"What?" barked the blacksmith. "No, I'm not!"

"We'll talk about it in a few thousand years, provided we don't get killed," Xendra stated flatly, leaving no room for debate as she continued. "Though the Thjodhild are younger than us, we do not know of their origins, nor what lies beneath their cold plate. It was as if they had simply appeared from a fog, their atrocities foremost in their minds."

"Atrocities?" Edlevin questioned. "What happened? Did they make war?"

"Not just war," Xendra replied with a tremor in her voice. "They wilted crops. They leveled cities. They dried up rivers. They destroyed any trace of numerous races, from their lives to their art." She met Edlevin's eyes with an intense sorrow, the horrors of a hundred lifetimes bleeding from the depths. "Their crusade was genocide, and save for a few, it was successful. Hundreds of millions, as if they were never there at all. The Eldari Hegemony fell, and with it, my people."

"Why?" Alauren asked with shock, shaking her head. "What possible reason could they have to do that?"

Xendra shrugged heavily. "When dealing in atrocities, 'reason' is a malleable term. It can be shaped to fit any perverted vision or desire, until it eventually becomes insanity." She tapped the table lightly. "In the end, even insanity can seem quite reasonable to those who believe they have a greater purpose."

Alauren crossed her arms. "They obviously weren't completely successful, given that you're sitting here."

The comment drew a dark chuckle from Eldari. "As it turns out, genocide takes time. The old races, like the Eldari, were defeated during the tribulations, but the first generations of the young races, the earliest forms of human and Elven kin, our mixed-breed children, proved too numerous to be so easily wiped out, as they reproduced at a rate nearly triple that of any immortal." She smiled at amusement at the thought. "The Thjodhild, cornered and overrun by the young, fled this continent, knowing that they could not stand against a foe so countless and determined, even with the unwoundable purebloods that make up their leadership. The Eldari, for our part, retreated within the young ones' ranks, blending in well with the Alvari and Solvari, peoples who most closely share our genetics. We few cursed with survival made what lives we could in a new and unfamiliar world."

"Genetics?" Alauren repeated. "What does that mean?"

Xendra nodded. "Yes, I suppose you wouldn't know." She laced her fingers together. "Genetics are what makes one's hair brown, or their eyes green. They are what determines everything about us, even as we are still formed within the wombs of our mothers. The elves of the south are closely related to us, as our genetics created them, and so we found a haven among them, unseen and unheard, nomads cursed to wander, lest we be found."

"I get the feeling that the story doesn't end there," Edlevin observed. "They wouldn't just give up on your extermination, would they?"

"Indeed," confirmed the Eldari. "For a few centuries, we lived as normal: having children and families, trying to propagate our race beyond extinction under the cover of the scurrying young. We had hope, then, that the Eldari could persist." She ground her teeth for a moment and shook her head. "That is, until a violent wave of an unknown magic swept over Odenseye. Suddenly, any child born of the old races were boneless, dead or dying within the first moment of life. I was the last healthy Eldari who ever came into this world."

Alauren shook her head in disbelief. "I'm sorry."

"Don't be," Xendra quickly shot back. "My sorrow has long since been replaced by anger. That is why I saved you, and it is why I am coming to you with this information now. The Thjodhild stole my people's future, *my* future, and they must pay in blood for their crimes. Their endless lives must be cut short with brutal efficiency, lest they bring that fate to all other races upon this continent."

"Agreed," Eira thrummed, entering through the tent flap and taking up a position beside Edlevin. She stood tall and crossed her arms. "The Northmen will be happy to assist you in doing so, for blood must be repaid."

Xendra smiled. "You heard all of our conversation; I'm assuming?"

Eira nodded.

"Then you know that my anger burns as white-hot as yours," Xendra continued, standing. "They will come, for they already had begun planning an assault before you landed on the mainland. Would you allow a stranger like I to fight in your ranks?"

"We are strangers, but our enemy is a common one," Eira said with a nod. "We would be glad to have you beside us, as long as you do not mind our eyes ever being upon you."

Xendra smiled wickedly. "I do not, truly. The blood of the Thjodhild must paint the shores of Arvyn, of Odenseye, and of wherever else their feet may defile. I will report to the beaches and, as a gesture of good will, I will do whatever I can to strengthen the defenses there."

"Very well," Eira agreed. "A man named Harald is just outside. Do not leave his sight, and be clear about the goal of your tasks, down to the finest details. He will understand enough of the trade tongue to communicate."

Xendra nodded. "As you command."

She began to move out the tent's flap, but was cut off by Edlevin, who grabbed her by the shoulder with a coldly serious expression painting his face.

"What of Niralan?" asked the old soldier. "Why are they here?"

Xendra shrugged. "It matters little. Evil abided is evil itself. They have fallen in with the Thjodhild, and thus they will fall with them." Without another word, she hustled swiftly out of the tent.

"Do you trust her, Ed?" Alauren asked, once she was confident that the stranger was out of earshot.

"I don't know, Ally," Edlevin replied. "She saved us. That means something. But trust? Trust takes more."

Eira grunted in agreement. "She does not have to be trusted to kill our enemies. We must simply watch her closely."

The trio nodded briefly as each of them mulled over the situation.

Finally, Eira spoke.

"Our scouts report a fleet massing on the other side of the island, off the main city." She sighed deeply and shifted in place. "Our newest guest was correct. They are coming soon, within a week."

"Expect sooner rather than later, if Niralan has anything to say about it," Edlevin muttered. "Is Ronnok well enough to fight?"

"Ronnok is always well enough to fight," Eira quickly corrected, which drew a chuckle from the old soldier. "Fighting well, on the other hand? He will need some time."

"Will he be well by the time the Thjodhild get here?" Alauren asked.

"We hope so," Eira said with another sigh. "By the word of our scouts, the enemy fleet is still relatively unprepared by Nirali standards, and they have shown no immediate desire to attack. Every moment they delay will allow him to grow stronger. In the meantime, I need you and the Karlmaðr working to produce whatever our warriors need."

Edlevin nodded. "We'll do what we can."

"Oh!" Alauren yelped, opening a drawer on her workbench and rummaging through it roughly. She procured a small piece of parchment, rolled up and covered in wrinkles. "I almost forgot. I had an idea." She splayed out the paper on the table, looking it over carefully.

It was drawn by the shaky hand of a seasick blacksmith, having errant lines and hastily erased mistakes throughout. However, it still managed to show a device, seemingly little more than a wooden box with holes drilled into the side and sloppy text explaining the purpose of each part.

Eira's brow furrowed. "What is it?"

"A defensive weapon," Edlevin answered with a proud smirk, understanding the concept almost immediately. "I've seen something similar before."

"Are we sure that it will help?" Eira queried skeptically. "We can't waste a single moment."

"They won't take long to make, and they're reusable," assured the smith. "I won't make too many. Just enough to help stem the tide."

"Make them, then, and ready us for the storm," Eira said. With the words, she gave a nod and took her leave.

Alauren heated up the forge with urgency, using a small bellows to send the coals within surging into an intense glow. "Come on, Karlmaðr. Time to get your hands dirty."

PART FIVE:

THE OLD DARKNESS

CHAPTER THIRTY-ONE:

ANTICIPATION

35th OF THE MORN OF HARVEST
NORTHERN YEAR 715

The old soldier rustled around the bushes, placing the last of the intricate boxes in a hasty hiding place, buried in the sand at an angle, nestled within the thick grasses of the dunes. A cold wind, rolling from the east, pierced the exposed skin of his jittering hands while they armed the trap, pulling a tripwire taut across the trail behind him. The weather had turned sour in the days of preparation, the first full breaths of a cold winter, and the warmth of the sun was now wholly hidden by heavy grey clouds.

He cast his vision around, surveying the defenses one last time: pointed fences and pikes, turned to stone by the resident Dwarf, would force the imposing army into small kill zones. Runic traps laid hidden in the sand, a further courtesy of their stout companion (with some enhancement from their new Eldari ally). The Northmen had taken great care in making the approach on the main beach debilitating, digging out ruts and burying sticks to trip up the attackers. The landing would be difficult for the invaders, though not impossible, and the success or failure of their attack would, in the end, hinge on the mettle of those who stood to stop them.

Beyond the fortifications the ocean roiled, and upon its rough waves the Nirali fleet had massed in a blockade formation, something typical of their strategy. They were hidden behind a heavy fog now, cloaked in mist, yet they could be felt looming, like a bright-eyed predator skittering in the brush of a dark forest.

There was no fear within the soldier, but rather, a cold anticipation, an acceptance of what was to come. He had been here before, facing the end of all he knew, feeling as if he was truly in his twilight hours while the ocean gales stole away the warmth within him.

"You feel it too, Karlmaðr?" a voice said, subdued and gentle, as if the gusts themselves carried it along. "The wind cuts through, chilling to the bone. Your hands quake."

Edlevin turned and smirked. The Chieftain looked bruised and battered, having a deep purple mark across the right side of his face, yet a lopsided smile still poked through the damage, a reassuring sight in a time so unsettling.

"It's good to see you up and around, Chief," the old soldier said as warmly as he could in the frigid air. "I think you know well that my hands aren't shaking because of a little chill on the wind."

"We have something in common, then," Ronnok said, holding out his own quivering palms. "A side-effect of Nort life."

"Not just Nort life," Edlevin corrected quickly. "The empires, one and all, ensure that their young men feel our pain."

"A side effect of war, then," conceded the Chieftain.

Edlevin huffed a single breath of dark laughter, an action that carried more disgust than it did mirth. "Truth is, I don't know what to do without this feeling." He rubbed his hands together, begging them to calm. "It is such a horrible thing, isn't it? Knowing what is to come, knowing that we're facing a bloody struggle for our next breath. Yet, I feel comfortable, as if I'm sitting in front of a fire at home. These shakes and this anticipation make me feel like I have purpose again." He smiled and looked back to the dense fog over the ocean, reluctantly longing for what lurked beyond. "I feel alive."

"Karlmaðr," Ronnok rumbled, "I know you've wondered about Northmen life, how we live among such violence without complaint or resistance." His lopsided smile exploded into a thin grin. "You now understand."

"I understand, but I do not agree," Edlevin corrected with a carefully disarming smirk. "I much prefer to get drunk at an Inn and pass out on the ground somewhere, forgetting this need for purpose entirely. It gives me life, to be truthful, but a life I'd rather not have."

"Such conveniences are foreign when there is ever a knife at your back," Ronnok pointed out. "Even when the Nations came to the Norts to 'make peace', they were only interested in our ability to shed blood for them. If they are not killing us, they are using us. We cannot allow either to happen uncontested."

Edlevin nodded in agreement. "I suppose even my own life, containing those few years of joy and mirth, has been someone else's dream."

"Come now, Karlmaðr," chuckled the Chieftain. "Nobody dreams of being you."

"Har har, bastard," Edlevin huffed. "I don't know how your wives live with you."

"With many glares and frowns of embarrassment," Ronnok informed with a beaming smile. "Eira, usually."

"She is certainly an intense one," Edlevin thrummed. "She didn't miss a beat when taking over for you. No nonsense."

"She is a special person, like her sister," Ronnok said with a fond grin. "I've never told you of our lives before we led Nordiska, did I?"

Edlevin shook his head and gestured for the man to continue.

"They were the daughters of one of our greatest warriors, a man named Fiske," said the Chieftain. "He was by no means the strongest of us physically, but he had a mind that rivaled any Northman the world over. The man could look at a map and have a battle plan ready in mere minutes, a true genius of tactics. There was more to him, though; he was intelligent, kind, diplomatic, and one of the best mentors I could have ever wished for."

"I've known a few like that," Edlevin said with a firm nod. "They can be the difference between a narrow victory and a resounding defeat. They can save thousands of lives, with both their skill and their temperance."

"Easily," Ronnok concurred. "Were it not for him, we would have been wiped out by these… How did you say it?"

"Th-yo-d-hild," Edlevin replied phonetically, carefully remembering the pronunciation from a few hasty and abrupt conversations with Xendra.

"Right," Ronnok continued. "They attempted to attack our fleets first, to destroy our people's lifeline. Our embarked clanmates had no choice but to flee beyond the fjords of the north, leaving the rest of us to travel overland. Fiske organized brilliant rearguard action, creating pockets of resistance that took the attention of the enemy." He sighed deeply as a somber fog seemed to overtake him. "It was in one of these pockets that he fell, surrounded by blood spilled by his hands, in a battle that he had so adamantly refused to allow me to lead. We were able to find our way beyond the mountains, where we could await our fleet, because of Fiske."

"I'm sorry," Edlevin said. "He sounds like a great man."

"He was," Ronnok murmured. "He always looked out for his own, and he imparted onto his daughters as much knowledge as he could." He crossed his arms, shivering in the cold air. "It has served them, and me, well. Without their help, I might not be where I am today, leading my people. They've always been my guiding light, Eira for her fiery resolve and Thyra for her calm and reserved nature."

"I can see why you would entrust Thyra with the fleet, then," Edlevin said. "Calm and reserved is what they need. I just hope they managed to sail west unnoticed."

"They did," Ronnok confirmed confidently. "Else, why would the enemy be banging at our doorstep, rather than giving chase to our lifeline?"

"Good point," Edlevin said with a chortle. He mused silently to himself, grinding his teeth for a moment before speaking again. "You know, I had someone much like Fiske and Eira in my life, once. It seems an age ago now, but his words still cascade through my mind in times like these." His eyes fell to the sand as the memory rose; his voice was quiet and shaky, as if the words echoed off the walls of a deep well within his mind. *Do not despair at odds stacked against you. Simply focus and see it through. Their ego makes mistakes inevitable, while our desperation makes them impossible.*"

"Wise counsel," Ronnok rumbled with a nod. "Surely it came from a great man."

Edlevin smiled at the memory before letting it sink back into the depths of his thoughts. "Greater than any I've ever known."

The Chieftain and the soldier stood in silence for a while, listening to white capped waves as they crashed against the tidal pools with thundering booms. Seagulls swept over the beach, occasionally landing and grabbing a small crab or invertebrate before lifting off once more. All the while, the enemy mustered beyond the walls of fog, readying for blood.

"Come, Karlmaðr," Ronnok said, breaking the silence. "We must finish our preparations at the camp."

Edlevin nodded in agreement and, with one last look beyond the hidden horizon, turned to follow.

Frolì was alive.

Ronnok and Edlevin stood with mouths agape at the young Northman warrior. His brown hair was matted and bloody, and his eyes were bloodshot, as if he hadn't slept in days. His armor was tattered or discarded entirely, and his weapons had been lost somewhere between this island and Arvyn proper. Along his chest ran a significant and still very recent scar, sickly looking but clean.

"Ronnok," he quavered. "Ronnok, ìda vikr?"

Ronnok said nothing, staring on with a cold and guarded gaze.

"Ronnok!?" Frolì warbled.

Ronnok again remained silent.

"Ronnok, I am Alive?" Frolì said, switching to the trade tongue, rolling with the accent of the Northmen. His cadence was odd, uneven, and unable to choose a tone of voice or proper inflection as his words stumbled from his mouth. "I Am here Again."

"So it would seem," growled the Chieftain. "How?"

"I Swam!" Frolì exclaimed. "From the mainland? It took Me many an Hour."

"Something isn't right," Edlevin muttered, stating Ronnok's thoughts aloud.

"Frolì, what happened?" Ronnok asked, careful to keep his voice low and subdued. "I heard you die. I heard your scream of pain be silenced."

"You heard, But you did not see, hmm?" Frolì trilled in an uneven harmony. "I am alive!"

"He couldn't have made it here alone," Edlevin growled, his voice becoming ever more strained.

Ronnok nodded a single time in agreement. "Frolì, did the Thjodhild send you? Are you one of them?"

The young Nort recoiled on wavering feet, like he had suddenly been pushed by an unseen force. His eyes blinked rapidly as he nearly lost his balance, yet he managed to remain upright. "Why Would you ask Such a thing?"

Ronnok's eyes narrowed, practically burrowing through the younger Nort's head. "Because Frolì did not speak the trade tongue."

"Uh... th... Th..." the young Nort stuttered. "They did not."

"Frolì!" Ronnok demanded. "Truth."

"No?" Frolì asked, pulling at his own hair as his apparent stress grew. "No, no!"

"What do they want?" Ronnok thundered grimly. "Speak!"

"No, no, NO?" Frolì screamed, again failing to find an appropriate tone of voice. He procured a small dagger from the remains of his clothing and charged forward.

Ronnok disarmed the man easily, punching the weapon out of his hand before shoving him down and catching the knife as it fell. As Frolì landed on his back, so too did the dagger land in his heart, driven by the merciless hand of the Chieftain. The young Nort's gaze became wild, his eyes darting around in a deep and primal fear before they faded away into nothing midst the gurgles and groans of death.

"Frolì was a good man," Ronnok said once the body was still, his words flat and emotionless. He rose from the ground with blood dripping from his fingers. "He would not have willingly betrayed us."

Edlevin shook his head, eyeing the corpse with disgust. "No, not willingly. The paranoia of the locals is beginning to make sense. We'll have to do something."

Ronnok procured a cloth from his belt and wiped his hands. "One problem at a time, Karlmaðr. We have a battle to fight."

"þerre kom!"

The shout rolled through the camp, echoing off the stoic trees that surrounded the blacksmith. She put the finishing touches on a steel helmet, a small and smooth object, little more than a dome-shaped bucket with a small slit for sight and well-secured padding on the interior, crafted from quilts and leather. The rest of her body was protected by a shabby chain mail tunic, which drooped over her legs like a gown.

"It'll have to do," Edlevin said, hefting his heavy Nort shield.

"Looks like we're about to have company."

Alauren nodded and swallowed hard. The helmet rattled in her hands, moved by tremors that permeated her entire body as she took a final look at her creation. Her mind had been busy with her craft; now, there was nothing but the impending bloodshed to occupy her thoughts. "Are you sure it can handle this?"

"We'll be alright, Ally," Edlevin eased. "I've seen many a battle far greater than this one pass unscathed." He smirked for a moment and tilted his head. "Mostly."

"I'll stay close to you, then," wavered the smith. She plunked the helmet onto her head and found it to be a snug, comfortable fit. After securing the chinstrap, she held her arms out wide and spoke. "How does it look?"

Edlevin's response was a quick and hard backhand slap across the faceplate.

"*Ow!*" Alauren yelped, her voice muffled under the metal as she recoiled. "The *fuck* was that, Karlmaðr?"

Edlevin couldn't help but let his smirk blossom into a full smile. "Looks don't matter. Sturdiness does. How do you feel?"

The blacksmith shook her head and regained her bearings. "Fine, actually. The helmet took a lot of the impact out."

"Well, we can at least call your weakness to backhand blows conquered," Edlevin said with a chuckle. "Come on, we've got a battle to fight."

Alauren followed closely as they left the forge behind. The Nort village was little more than a ghost town now, inhabited only by a few warriors as they rushed to their last-minute tasks. All around, the wind whipped under gray skies, whistling here and there through the trees.

"Karlmaðr!" Ronnok called from the other side of the camp. "With me!"

Edlevin nodded and picked up the pace, trudging along as fast as his armor (and the slight pain remaining in his back) would allow. Still, he crossed the camp in a mere minute, even if the finish line found him panting and sweaty.

The Nort Chieftain impatiently awaited the duo, dressed in an angled silvery chestplate and shining vambraces, each piece patterned with the cascading waves typical of crucible steel. Tiny, individually crafted scales covered every gap, allowing for a revolutionary flexibility in the joints. The metal itself was solid and strong enough to repulse any attempts to sunder it, all while being thin enough to allow whatever movement that a Nort fighting style could require. The scales were connected to carefully laid chain mail, drooping over the waist and adding a final layer of steel skin beneath an already impressive creation.

"This armor, it is nice," Ronnok rumbled with clear admiration, banging on the center angle of the chestplate. "Strong, but light and flexible. It will assist me in killing many men."

Alauren chuckled darkly. "Warms my heart, knowing that my creation is so appreciated."

"As long as it helps keep us all alive," Edlevin stated matter-of-factly, speaking with a tone of experienced authority. His eyes shifted singularly to Alauren. "No heroes today. Stick with your company. We don't win a battle through a single leader pouring down orders from on high, we do it through the instincts of those who fight." His face became a stern, stone visage. "Don't get separated, and don't be afraid to pull back to better ground. Even a retreat can become a victory, should you pick your timing well."

Ronnok stared intensely at the old soldier, narrowing his eyes as if a secret had been whispered quietly in his ear by the passing of the frigid wind that whipped his hair about. He squashed the expression quickly, however, and moved to the matter at hand. "Strength comes from the many. My people know this, and they will place their trust in you. Use your instincts, but keep your wits and stay with us."

"Aye," Alauren nodded. "Let's stop the thinking and get to the doing, shall we? I'm going mad."

"Welcome to warfare," Edlevin huffed. "It's all mad."

"Big man!" Valin yelled from a distance down the beach trail. His stocky legs carried him rather well, however, and it was but a moment before he was on his knees, gasping for breath in front of the group. "Ships... closin' in... need t' get ready," puffed the Dwarf.

Ronnok nodded. "To the front lines, to battle, and to the glory of combat. May the Great Father protect us, or bear us to the halls beyond life." With a last look at the diverse faces returning his cold stare, he led the way to the shore.

CHAPTER THIRTY-TWO:

BLOOD ON THE SAND

*Warfare is deception. Before entering combat, you
must sufficiently light the shadows around you,
lest your arrogance allow them to consume you.*

- Karsus of Niralan, quoted from the Nirali Field
Manual, section 1, p. 1.

The Nirali Colonel looked at a large invasion map, bathed in candlelight on the main cabin of Niralan's local flagship, the *Koral*. Clear skepticism oozed from his narrowed, green eyes, and he made little attempt to hide his unsurety towards what lay before him. The Thjodhild professed themselves to be masters of tactics, true champions of glorious warfare beyond any mortal imagination, gods among the smaller races of this continent.

Looking at the battle plans, the Colonel couldn't help but wonder if it was all bluster.

He was a young man of twenty-five; even with his relative inexperience, however, he could see flaw upon flaw, like a generalized battle plan had been formed, yet never modified to suit the situation. It was amateurish, for lack of a better word, reeking of nescience.

"Go over it one more time," the Nirali requested.

"It is simple, Colonel Raevin," Koro hissed. As usual, a heavy accretion of ice clung to his voice like the mast of a fishing vessel in the dead of winter. "Three beachheads, three landing parties." He used two fingers to point to two small beaches flanking the main landing. "The pincer closes on the center. This is the last time I will enlighten you."

Raevin glared at the Thjodhild, daring him to remove his helmet, to unmask himself and stand before the Nirali as a true leader. Though the silent demand went unmet, the Colonel knew that his gaze was mirrored, for he could feel a matching intensity returned, as if the walls were closing in while he locked in a battle of wills with the gargantuan being.

"This plan may work for someone like you," Raevin muttered, turning his eyes back to the map. "For the Nirali, this could go south quickly. What if our flanks are unable to push through? What if we get bogged down?"

"You will not," stated the Thjodhild. "We shall observe and command you personally."

"Nirali are commanded by Nirali," the Colonel snapped, narrowing his eyes even further. "So it always will be."

"No," Koro rumbled, his icy words slicing the air like a ballista bolt. "Your Marshal has given us authority, yes?"

"He did," Raevin replied.

"Obey him, then," the Thjodhild growled. "You know well the cost of disobedience."

Raevin ground his teeth in frustration, but saw no choice save for concession. "Very well. What of the Northmen's fleet?"

Koro's armor creaked slightly as he crossed his arms. "They have fled to the west. We will not pursue them."

Raevin sighed, seeing yet another hole in the plan. "If we don't land successfully-"

"You will," Koro ordered.

Raevin grimaced and cleared a few strands of dark black hair from his face, focusing in on the Thjodhild's helm once more. His sneer was met with a stare that looked stern, even from its hiding place under the helm of the knight. There would be no alterations in the plan.

"As you command," Raevin sighed. "As Karsus commands."

"Good," Koro said, striding to a door and ducking through, reluctantly followed by the Nirali.

The *Koral* was a Galleon, a massive vessel with a decorated history, held in somber renown by its countrymen for extensive service in eastern waters. The towering deck gave the occupants a superb view of the island now that the fog had cleared out, becoming little but a transparent mist. The beaches were calm and quiet, a stark contrast to the loud bangs and grinding of saws that had occupied hours past. Below, over the railing, dozens of smaller square shaped craft made ready for an assault.

"Our covenant is sealed this day, with blood and metal," Koro thundered. "Our glory is at hand."

"*Your* glory," the Colonel corrected. "It can't be ours if you won't tell me what we're doing all this for."

"I will not," Koro growled. "Trust in us, for we will deliver you to a world of perfection."

Raevin looked silently over the white capped waves. "As Karsus commands."

"Sir!" A small, spindly petty officer clacked his boots at attention behind them. "The landing craft are loaded and ready to deploy."

"Good," Raevin nodded. "One more step."

"Ready!" Koro called, towering high enough to peer over the landing craft's rectangular door.

Raevin steadied himself on the rough waters. The swords and shields of his comrades in arms clacked against their armor in the waves, breaking an otherwise silent approach. All around, he could see the breath of twenty-five soldiers aboard, misting in the cold air and mixing with the spray of the sea. Behind them, at the rear of the vessel, two Nirali turned a waterwheel as fast as they could, propelling the boat along at a respectable speed.

"COMPANY, READY!" Raevin shouted vigorously. A bit of sea spray hit his face, sending a shiver down his spine that proceeded through his trembling hands in a needly cascade. He donned his shining silver helmet and secured it snugly with a leather chin strap. "Shields up!"

The men obeyed in unison, forming a large shell with their round blockers, closing off the flanks in their formation. While Niralan had largely moved away from shields, the vulnerability of soldiers during marine landings still called for the tactics of old.

"Remember your training," the Colonel instructed with a thundering authority, taking his place at the center of his unit. "Move quickly and engage at close range. Two Nirali to a Nort. They are much larger, so DO NOT rely on strength against them! They are savages, so outsmart them! Stay together and watch out for one another."

The troops shouted an affirmative.

"Marksmen, stay near the ships and pick what targets you can," Raevin continued. "Make ready, for this is our finest hour!"

"Welcome to the Dawn, Nirali," Koro roared, his voice booming through the high walls of the craft as it impacted the shore. Without another word, he kicked down the flat, forward door, sending it dropping to the beach with a wet slap. A deep rumble followed as the Nirali hurried onto their chosen battlefield, thirsting for the blood of their enemies. Raevin felt the soft sand smush under his boots while the surf rolled onto his ankles, and a sharp breath echoed in his helm as some of the frigid water made its way onto his sock.

Glancing through a crack in the protective shield cover, the Colonel saw several stone battlements ahead, too tall to climb easily in armor. Lines of Northmen formed shield walls in the few gaps to be found among the fortifications, hunched and ready to do battle.

"FORWARD!" Raevin cried. "GET TO THE SHIELD WALL! BREAK IT!"

The soldiers obeyed, closing ranks and surging forward. They were careful to keep their shields together, warding off a hail of arrows that thundered upon them from somewhere behind the dunes.

The sand was rough and uneven, and many carefully placed obstacles caused the Nirali advance to be slowed, yet never stopped. The forward companies crept across the hazards carefully, kicking away stones and rocks alike to ease the path for their fellows, diligently ensuring a smooth path for reinforcements.

There was something else on the sand, Raevin noticed: a small scrawling of what looked to be a fire within a cloud, as if a child had doodled something in boredom. Before any thought towards the origin could cross his mind, the boot of the second soldier to his left came down hard on an identical symbol, well hidden among sticks and sea grass.

For a moment, the world of the Colonel was nothing but white, a blank abyss for as far as the eye could see. He suddenly found himself lying on his back, dazed and confused, while a harsh ringing overtook his ears, like his head was inside of a vibrating bell. For a moment, he could do little but squirm and try to regain control of his surroundings.

Gathering his wits, Raevin noticed that the man who had stepped on the symbol was screaming in pain; his leg was severed at the knee, ripped to literal ribbons, while fragments of his greaves and sabaton had been scattered around amidst the concussed company. For the moment, the Nirali's shield wall had a hole blown into its front-left flank.

Raevin's eyes went wide, and he threw himself to his knees. The sun, mostly obscured behind clouds, had disappeared fully, and a pronounced whistling sound erupted over the chaotic clashing of the battlefield. "UP!" the Colonel screamed hoarsely. "SHIELDS UP!"

Raevin dug hard into the sand and raised his blocker with all of his strength. He could do little but grit his teeth at the screams of the slower soldiers as the wall of projectiles came whistling to the ground, finding many a gap in the armor of the Children of Niras.

"Reform!" Raevin ordered without hesitation, rising fully to his feet. "On me! Form a mass and be ready for more arrows!"

The surviving Nirali, roused by the familiar voice of their officer, regained their wits and dutifully obeyed, with even the newly legless man doing his part until he was forced by the medical teams to return with them to the landing craft.

"Shell formation!" Raevin yelled after a few heavy breaths. The shields came together over his head once more. "We have to move! We pause, we die! Eyes on the sand!"

The soldiers grouped tightly and thundered forth while arrows went ricocheting from their strong blockers. Each picked their steps gingerly, avoiding infuriatingly frequent scrawlings and trip-ups. After a small while, though, the sand was clear, and the enemy lines were in reach.

"Full forward!" Raevin shouted, causing his comrades to shift into a sprint, loosening their formation in the process. A Northmen shield wall lay ahead, waiting patiently for the arrival of their foe, an expected tactic. The Colonel readied himself for the impact. "Hit them!"

The Nirali company slammed into the Nortish wall with thunderous force, sending a wave cascading backwards in the enemy lines and creating a salient that lasted for no more than half of a breath. Without need for order, the Nirali troops shifted to an arrow-shaped formation, heaving their weight instantly upon the momentary weakness while diligently protecting their flanks.

The enemy was firm at first, meaning to hold them in place with force alone, but the numerically superior Nirali company was able to pressure the shield wall enough to draw out an opening. It was little more than a finger-width gap, yet Raevin reacted instantly, perfectly sliding his blade through the opening, rewarded with the satisfying resistance of flesh as he struck true. A scream of pain was followed by a larger opening in the enemy formation.

"Dirlan two-one!" ordered the Colonel.

Within a breath, twelve Nirali troops formed a wedge at the opening, forcing themselves through with their shields and splitting the enemy down the middle, two soldiers to a Northman. The orderly defensive wall became a fracas of blood and metal as chaos erupted; the fight had become something more even and balanced. The Nirali cried out with vigor, for the first step had been taken.

Raevin, grinning widely, was quick to pick a target, a burly, tattooed Nort with a blonde beard, wielding a sword and shield. The Colonel drove the attack quickly, striking hard at the enemy's buckler in an attempt send the much stronger man reeling. Instead, the enemy dug his heels into the sand and weathered the onslaught, grunting as he held fast against the impacts. Suddenly, the Nort forced his shield forward, sending Raevin stumbling clumsily backwards, though he was able to maintain his footing.

Another Nirali soldier, finding his way out of the fray, attacked the Northman from behind. The savage was quick to wheel on the new target, but found himself too slow to avoid a nasty cut on his arm as he brought his sword up to bear defensively. With a grimace, he kicked the newly arrived Nirali in the chest, sending him flying backward.

Raevin regained his balance and brought his sword down hard in an arcing blow, only to find it impacting on the Northman's wooden shield, swung back into position with remarkable speed. The Colonel's momentum carried the strike off of the center buckler and down to the sand, and though he nearly followed, the Nirali once again managed to keep his stability. The Nort was quick to drive the attack, moving forward rapidly.

At the apex of his stumble, Raevin was able to spot an opening: a gap in the man's chest armor was exposed at the belly. Reacting with impressive speed, the Nirali fell to his knees, stabbed up, and plunged his blade deep into the enemy's torso.

The Northman wailed in agony, a thunderous sound that was accompanied by a flying torrent of spittle and blood. His sword desperately cleaved at the air where his enemy's head had been an instant before; his momentum carried him forward and caused him to spin to the left, allowing Raevin to neatly slide his blade out of flesh with hardly a grain of his own effort.

Though mere minutes had passed, corpses of Nort and Nirali alike littered the beach, piling further with every passing moment. A drizzle began to fall, coating the armor of the combatants in drops that shimmered in the dimmed light of the sun, and the sprinkling rain formed rivers that carried blood through the sand and to the sea. Meanwhile, the second wave of the Nirali landing teams drove hard toward the Nort lines as the tide turned crimson behind them.

Raevin could only look on in horror as they ran headlong into the sand scrawlings, losing legs and lives at an untenable pace. The attackers discovered more traps, spikes that flew up from holes in the sand to impale them vertically in the belly, costing them precious time and reinforcements as they deafly charged beyond the frantic warnings of the medics and sharpshooters.

Infuriatingly, Koro had chosen to occupy himself in a duel with a much smaller combatant, seemingly oblivious to the need to push through the defensive lines. The hooded figure moved like wind around the knight, failing to find an opening, yet wasting time, nonetheless. Despite the fight being akin to one between a bear and a single bee, the Thjodhild was completely distracted.

Raevin scowled, but quickly returned to his own role in the fight. He picked a new target from the fray; a human, by the looks of it, clad in rusty armor and flanked by a smaller figure wearing a shabby helmet. One Nirali had already engaged in combat with the man, but was taking multiple stab wounds from the shorter attacker while he helplessly blocked heavy blows that thundered in from the taller. Raevin steadied his helm and charged.

The Colonel pushed past his underling and forcibly locked the enemy human into combat; the action, as intended, allowed his comrade a reprieve and a chance to focus entirely on staving off the smaller opponent. Raevin rained three arcing blows upon the man, finding each deftly deflected by the human's shield before being returned and intercepted in kind. The smaller figure shifted its attention to the Colonel, allowing the other Nirali a chance to breathe while both foes focused their assault upon the fitter of the two attackers.

The armored human suddenly thrust his weight forward and ran full speed into the Colonel. Raevin raised his shield and halted the charge with a heavy growl, taking the opportunity to stab at the man's waist as the two blockers collided. The blade hit flesh, as evidenced by the human's grunt of pain, but it seemed to be little but a minor laceration, judging by the force with which the Nirali's sword was batted away.

The human, unexpectedly, broke off his assault and bashed the Colonel firmly with his shield. Though most of the blow was absorbed, the Nirali still stumbled back awkwardly, taking a small blow to the chin.

Raevin felt a sharp, sudden pain in his waist. Instinctively, he elbowed out towards the source of the injury and caught the smaller fighter in the helmet. They went tumbling backward with a yelp, but were on their feet again in an instant, looking for an opening to jab once more.

The two enemies chattered back and forth, though the words were lost to the Colonel in the mire of battle. Raevin charged towards the human again, but found the enemy's shield thrusting him back onto his heels without delay, like a town guard warning off a drunkard with a shove. The two defenders, noticing a third Nirali wave arriving, took the opportunity to retreat, carefully backing away from their quarry.

Raevin heaved with breath and stumbled backwards; a laceration on the right side of his ribcage seared and ached, while the strain of throwing his armor around so heavily had drained his lungs. A regroup would be necessary, clearly, as the situation around him seemed to be grinding to a bloody stalemate. His soldiers, though they had broken the lines, were outclassed and on disadvantageous terrain. They were winning, but at an unacceptable cost.

Raevin turned, meaning to rally nearby troops, only to find one of his comrades caught in the massive pincers of a billhook crab, waving the soldier effortlessly back and forth through the air near the lapping sea. The man stabbed in futility at the creature's protective carapace as his own armored shell crunched under the weight of the animal's claws.

"For *fucks* sake," Raevin grumbled. He sprinted back down the beach and struck out at a small groove where the animal's arm met its carapace, displaying careful precision. The injured Nirali and severed pincer fell to the sand, causing the monstrous crustacean to erupt in a shrieking squeal. It trampled across sand and soldier alike, tearing back to the water and the safety of the depths below. Behind, however, its brothers and sisters bogged down reinforcements, drawn in by the blood in the sea.

Raevin moved to pick up his comrade, who still squirmed in his sundered armor, but the futility of assistance was quickly recognized by the officer. The claw had crushed the man's torso like the shell of an insect, making ground meat of his intestines. The Nirali footman could only scream in agony, a haunting wail that managed to drown out even the thunderous din of the battle.

Raevin stabbed his sword down hard on the soldier's neck and attempted to deafen himself to the gurgle as the man found his rest. There was no greater honor than to die for one's country, after all, and no Nirali needed to suffer unimaginable pain before they could do so.

Raevin looked up and again took in the scene. All around, his countrymen had rallied without need for the call of an officer and, with the help of reinforcements that enjoyed paths clear of traps, they were pushing the Norts back.

Most of the savages had retreated up a narrow path on the dunes, behind where the Colonel's company pushed the gap, though a few Northmen remained to hold back the tide. Meanwhile, a small contingent of meticulously armored Norts had pushed forward and managed to stay on the beach, killing more Nirali by the minute; they could do little save hold their small, circular pocket, however, unable to disrupt the advance as they were swarmed by silvery armor.

"PUSH!" Raevin yelled, charging up the sands as fast as he could. "PUSH THE ATTACK!" Any soldiers who heard obeyed without hesitation, assaulting the lines with a zealous determination.

Koro, having broken free from the smaller opponent, stalked to the choke point and hefted a savage by the armor, like the colossal northerner was a small child being lifted by the shirt. The Thjodhild took pleasure in his kill, clearly, holding the Northman aloft for a few prolonged moments. He suddenly plunged his blade through the enemy's chest and ripped it upward, splitting the unfortunate Nort in two; the heavy viscera shocked even the hardened Colonel of the Nirali, and he couldn't help but marvel at the sheer strength on display.

"Go!" ordered the Thjodhild, waving the company onward. He kicked at a group of Norts attempting to reform their wall at the choke point, shattering several of their blockers and forcing the remaining defenders to fully retreat, scurrying up the dunes before the enemy could take them. "Go now!" Koro lifted a section of stone battlements and threw them aside, allowing room for a full Nirali company to group up and charge, with their Colonel front and center.

Their victory was close at hand. Getting off the beach would cost the most blood, Raevin knew, being cramped and unable to flank. Once they could fight in an area that wasn't so controlled, when they could duck in and out of battle through the brush of the forest, their small company tactics would bleed their enemy dry, pressing on too many weak points for the onslaught to be survived.

The Colonel's eyes went ablaze with a sanguine determination; he let out a bloodthirsty battle cry, echoed by the men surrounding him as they stampeded up and over the sandhills: "ONE MORE STEP!"

In one moment, he was filled with the spirit of battle, the glory of victory seeming to be just over the passing crest of the sandy dune. In the next, his foot caught something hidden in the grass, sending him tumbling face-first to the ground with a clanking *thud*.

A whistling sound had erupted around him, followed quickly by sharp screams of pain and clattering armor as his company similarly fell around him. Regaining his senses, the Colonel spit a lump of sand from his mouth and attempted to rise, but found his helm once again plowed into the dune by a lifeless suit of armor crumpling upon his back.

Raevin suddenly felt a jabbing pain in his side, just below the laceration he had received earlier in the battle. He had been struck, though he could hardly tell how many times as the pain surged down his spine and permeated over his body. Agony tore through the entirety of his physical form, and every nerve seared like it was being touched by glowing metal.

The Colonel frantically pawed at his torso and found the jagged shaft of a broken crossbow bolt lying just under his skin, near the bottom of his ribs. It had shattered inside of him, he surmised, and each splinter caused a stinging quake that ripped through his body. He could do little but lay on the ground with shock as the blood of a dozen Nirali pooled around him, covering his shining silver armor with a sickly, sticky crimson.

The Colonel struggled to his knees, heaving the dead man off of his back. With quaking hands, he unfastened his chinstrap and removed his helmet in an effort to better catch his wind, dropping the helm absently into the pool of blood that lay before him. With all his effort, he raised his head to gaze upon the carnage, finding sweat-drenched hair hanging over his face as he desperately wheezed for air.

An entire company of his comrades had fallen in a fraction of a second, killed in action, each riddled with short crossbow bolts. The angle of fire was impossibly low, perfectly aimed at the gaps in Nirali armor, as if the Northmen knew every detail of their plate design. The sounds of the battle were little more than a muffle now, like a woolen hood had been pulled over his head and tied in place. Norts rushed by him, paying the dying Nirali little mind while they countercharged with their own bloodlust.

Koro. If they were to have victory, the mighty Thjodhild commander's assistance was needed. Raevin turned his head, hoping to see the giant of a man disrupting the Northmen assault.

The Thjodhild, already one foot onto a landing craft, met Raevin's gaze with a nod. He pushed the small skiff beyond the waves, turned it, and hopped inside, making for the security of the Nirali fleet.

Raevin, surrounded by the corpses of his friends and compatriots, looked to the gray sky before falling heavily into the sand as darkness swallowed him.

"What did I tell you about the helmet?" Edlevin exclaimed. "It works!"

"So I'm finding out," concurred the blacksmith, steadying the metal dome on her head. She regrouped with her old friend, backing slowly away from the distracted Nirali soldier while taking stock of their situation. She felt cold drops of rain land upon the back of her neck, finding their way through the solitary gap in her mail tunic. The world wanted to draw inward, to become cloudy and muffled in the midst of the carnage as it had at Alsara, but she willed herself to maintain control. "Is it time?" she asked, grimacing as a billhook crab tore an enemy soldier's armor asunder near the ocean waves.

"Getting there," Edlevin answered between heavy breaths. "They'll regroup. Center their troops in the chaos. We'll be splintered, which is what they want."

Alauren nodded. "Small groups can be managed, even if they're Norts."

"Exactly ri-"

The old soldier's words turned into a dull groan as an arrow tore through his hip. He dropped like a rock and hit the sand with a *thud*.

"FUCK," he screamed sharply, gesturing heavily towards his right side. "I'm hit!"

The smith was on him in an instant, lifting him from the blood-stained sands. "Use your good leg!" she howled. "Before another one finds us! Come on!"

Suppressing his pain for now, Edlevin hobbled beyond the last Northmen defenses and off the beach, practically carried by his old friend as they stumbled in the shifting sands. Once the hills and deadly traps hidden within were behind, they made haste to the second Nort defensive line, standing ready in the forest a short distance from the dunes.

"Hold on, hold on," panted the old soldier, breaking from Alauren's grasp and seating himself on a stump just behind the lines. "I need to breathe. Too much..." He coughed hoarsely from deep within his chest, like he was enduring a heavy bout of disease. "Too much exercise. Lungs are on fire."

Alauren waved at a few Norts, requesting a bandage, before similarly taking a moment to catch her breath. "Shit, that *was* too much. You need to lose some weight."

"Definitely losing some water weight right about now," Edlevin grumbled, palming his injury to find a pool of blood forming within. "This one is bad."

"It'll be fine," Alauren assured shakily, though she grew visibly worried. "We'll patch it up. You'll be fine."

Edlevin attempted to chuckle, but winced as the act sent a jolt of pain through his hip. "I've heard that one before." He swallowed hard. "Said it a few times, too. Only sometimes a lie." He shifted for a moment, pulling a small and smooth metal spike from his leg with an involuntary jolt. "Crossbow bolt, in one piece, thankfully," growled the old soldier. "Fucking Nirali, wanting me to bleed out. A clean hit, though, so not as bad as it could be."

"Got it!" a familiar voice yelped in the distance. "One fried Karlmaðr comin' up!"

"Oh *shit*," Edlevin gasped as his eyes ignited in genuine fear. "Oh, n-"

Valin already had the blade red-hot and ready, and his stout legs made impressively short work of the distance. He wasted no time, plunging the blade hard against Edlevin's wound.

Alauren grabbed her old friend, expecting him to squirm, but he simply ripped a loose leather strap from his armor and bit down hard, moving only in involuntary quakes.

"Done, other side," Valin instructed.

Edlevin rolled and allowed the Dwarf to cauterize the exit wound, maintaining a stoic face in front of eyes that screamed in fathomless agony. With both wounds sealed, he slumped back in his seat. "Water."

"On it," Valin chirped. "Lass, stay with him."

Alauren nodded an affirmative at the bounding Dwarf before turning her attention back to Edlevin's agonized tremors. "That was a bad wound, Ed," she quaked, unsurety flooding her voice. "I don't think cauterization is enough."

Edlevin shifted and looked to the point of impact. "It's just below the right pelvic wing, well above the femoral artery. Through the front and partially through the back." He slumped down once more. "It's alright. Must have slipped in a gap in the leg armor. Clean through, no major sources of bleeding…" He nodded several times in quick succession, his face pale and sweat-drenched. "It's alright. Good shot, though."

"Once Valin gets you some water, we'll get you back to camp and-"

Edlevin cut off the smith's words with a huff. "No. I'm needed." He tried to stand, but a clear, painful convulsion set him back upon the stump.

"No, you're really not," Alauren scolded, nodding to Valin as the

Dwarf arrived. "Drink."

Edlevin did as commanded, emptying the large wooden cup in seconds while sending a quarter of the liquid dribbling from off of his stubble. "I'm fine. I'm going," he persisted gruffly, still catching his breath.

"Look at you!" Alauren growled, slapping the man's shoulder plate. "You can barely stand, you're drenched in sweat and blood, and you can't even catch your breath!"

"I'm just fat, is all," assured the old soldier, rising to his feet successfully this time. "I'm good. Let's get back out there."

"The lass is right!" Valin said with a matching gruffness. "Yer an old man normally, already at a disadvantage. Now, yer an injured old man."

"I'm going," Edlevin thundered, stepping forward with a heavy limp, favoring his left side. "This 'old man' has endured far worse than a crossbow bolt from some damn Nirali fuckwit! They'll need us out there!"

Not a moment after the old soldier's words erupted from his lips, a detached Nirali head rolled towards him and rested at his side. He peered at the viscera with raised eyebrows before wheeling on the first of the dunes beyond the treeline. Ronnok stood tall and proud, drenched in blood of red and grey. Warriors flanked him, some wounded, others *very* much alive.

"I appreciate the sentiment, Karlmaðr," boomed the Chieftain, peering through the old human with burning eyes that had been fully refreshed in the feral fires of combat. He stepped carefully down the weed-covered hills of sand. "We held."

CHAPTER THIRTY-THREE:

TRUTH

"I don't... What?" Edlevin stammered. "There should be a second landing. Three attacks consisting of three waves each, as it always is with Nirali."

"Only one," Ronnok stated with grim confidence. "Their fleet has fled, seeking the safety of their fortress."

"It's Niralan!" Edlevin countered. "There's always a second wave."

"Not this time," the Chieftain replied with a thin smile. "A messenger from Nordiska found us shortly after the Nirali ran. Thyra, wisely, had gone northwest around the island, waiting for an opening. When their ships left port, she drew near to the capital, feinting a counter landing. The Eastmen scurried back to their hole, horrified that it had been threatened."

"Something is wrong," the old soldier warbled worriedly. "Very wrong. Niralan isn't this reactionary. It's never this easy!"

"Easy? You act as if our victory is without price," Ronnok growled, his demeanor quickly shifting from the glory of victory to severe offense. "You act as if we lost nothing."

Edlevin's gaze fell to the ground in a rare moment of embarrassment, lost for words.

"They wanted to disembark and hit us with a pincer movement, to defeat our shield walls by going behind," Ronnok explained. "The Northern flank, seventy-five warriors, were nearly wiped out. Five remain. Harald lost his son."

Edlevin nodded solemnly. "Yet, they held."

"They held," Ronnok repeated sternly. "Remember the name Bjorn when you speak of ease, for he had none before his journey to the halls of the Great Father."

"Fair enough, I will," the old soldier conceded in a soft murmur. "Still, we should be prepared. Niralan-"

"Is clearly not in charge here," Eira growled.

Ronnok nodded. "These tactics... Did they seem Nirali to you?"

Edlevin thought for a moment and shook his head. "No, not at all. They could have blockaded us with just a few ships, or chased down the fleet."

"Instead," the Chieftain said, continuing with the thought, "they launched a suicidal attack on a fortified position before leaving in a rush."

Edlevin ground his teeth and nodded in agreement, having no further argument.

Ronnok proceeded to direct his troops towards their duties behind the lines, though he stayed to watch over the front while others headed back to camp for medical care. Eira moved to tend to the more severely wounded (and her own superficial lacerations), her face as wild and grim as her husband's, even in the midst of such peaceful duties. The Nort warriors on the second line trudged forward to keep watch over the beach, looking to their fellows as they passed.

Gazes shifted from here to there as each Northman made eye contact with the others, exchanging intense glances. They would give a short nod and (occasionally) a mumbled word or two in their own language before moving on to the next fighter in line to repeat the action. Many looked to Alauren, expecting a similar reaction, yet she could only return a quick, confused, but well-meaning acknowledgement.

As the bulk of the warriors mingled back to camp, receiving specific orders from their Chieftain, Alauren got up the nerve to speak. "What just happened?"

"What?" Edlevin grunted.

"The sudden silence," explained the blacksmith. "The looks I got, as if they wanted to comfort me, yet no words came. I can read faces well enough, but that was lost in translation."

"Same here," Valin added. "I've seen a lot in me days, but nothin' like that."

Edlevin sighed and looked at Ronnok, who raised an eyebrow and stayed silent; the old soldier mulled the thought over for another moment before speaking, careful to choose the right words. "Just something you develop over time, I guess," he answered softly. "Empathy, I suppose, but mixed with an understanding you only get from experience."

"A silent, shared burden," Ronnok agreed. "Familiar to us.

Krimsgándr is our word for it."

Edlevin nodded. "I heard once that it loosely translated to 'Old Sorrow' in the trade tongue." He looked down at the blood on his tremoring hands. "A fitting name for such a feeling."

"One we can wait to discuss in further detail," rumbled the Chieftain. "We have work to do."

"Right," Edlevin concurred, letting the sorrow drain from his face (though the involuntary winces of pain remained). "They'll come again, sooner or later. I'm sure of it."

Ronnok cocked an eyebrow. "Why?"

Edlevin's brow furrowed. "What do you mean?"

"Why are you sure?" the Chieftain clarified in a harsh deadpan.

Edlevin looked confusedly, nervously, at the cadre of waiting glances. "I know Niralan," he grumbled, shifting uncomfortably. "I waded in rivers of blood that they created, bearing witness to the cold genius that lies in their slaughter. I don't want to talk about it."

"You must," Ronnok pushed. "Any detail can help us; any small crumb of knowledge can save a life. Have I done right by you, Karlmaðr?"

Edlevin sighed and pinched his brow in frustration. "Yes, above and beyond right." He bit his tongue for a moment before turning his gaze back to the stares, who eagerly awaited explanation. "Marakerlan," struggled the old soldier, as if the word itself was a bitter venom that took a mighty effort to expel from his mouth.

Ronnok and Valin's gaze grew cold, though the reason for such expressions was lost on the smith. "Educate me, Ed?" she asked.

"A walled city, on the border between Elysia and Niralan," the old soldier elaborated absently, his gaze peering beyond the smith while his voice turned low and subdued. "It was a warzone, constantly under siege. Thousands of civilians locked inside, rarely able to safely leave." His brow furrowed in a mix of anger and disgust. "Too valuable as hostages. I saw things there that I will never forget, cruelty beyond the imagination of most mortal minds on this continent."

"You never told me this," Alauren said softly.

Edlevin nodded. "I was trying to drink that pain away, to forget it. One of many things." He winced and gripped his wound. "Speaking of?"

"Right!" Ronnok bellowed, lumbering forward. "Back to camp

with you!"

"No, that's quite alright," the soldier chittered frantically, "I don't nee-"

His words became wails as Ronnok slung him across his shoulder, toting the old human down the path with speed.

"Shiiiii*iiiiit*!" Edlevin groaned, carefully crumpling down on a small cot in the medical tent. He had traded his armor for bandages, which had been wrapped tightly around his waist. "I'm *definitely* getting too old for this."

Alauren, taking a seat on a stool next to him, cocked an eyebrow. "He finally admits it."

Edlevin chuckled. "I admit nothing. It was an... intrusive thought."

"Sure," Alauren chortled. "You're in better shape than him, in any case." She pointed to an adjacent bed, where another human had been placed.

A severely wounded Nirali laid under a woolen blanket, lost in a fitful slumber. He looked stable, temporarily, but the paleness of his skin and the tremors that rocked his body showed clearly that he was teetering on the edge. Sweat rolled off of his forehead and moistened his sheets, and he could do little but shiver, as if he was left outside on a frigid winter night.

"He had better hope he goes in his sleep, first," Edlevin muttered. "It would be a shame to endure such pain just to be at the mercy of the Northmen."

"He needs to live," Alauren quickly snapped, surprising her old friend. "I need to talk to him."

"Oh?" Edlevin asked. "What questions would you ask such a person?"

"I..." the blacksmith began. "I don't know." She looked to her old friend, her gaze turning to steel. "What I do know is that I'm done running around like a scared little girl. I want to know what the fuck is going on here, why all of this is happening. If he has any answers at all, I need them, and so I need him alive."

"You and me both," affirmed the old soldier. "I can't say if you'd get much from this one, though." He pointed to the Nirali's bloody belongings, piled in the corner. "He's a Colonel."

"You can tell that from his armor?" Alauren asked.

"The large, thick threads attached to the shoulder plate, actually," Edlevin explained. "You see how each is colored silver, and how there are multiple of them entwined with each other?"

Alauren nodded.

"Silver means a commissioned officer, though one that has not risen to central command, which oversees armies," Edlevin continued. "Four threads twisted means four ranks up the command line. Colonel."

Alauren crossed her arms. "He's an officer, though. He has to know something."

Edlevin shrugged. "With Niralan, it really depends. Some Colonels run entire cities, answering to Generals, while some only command forward military units. We'll just have to ask him if he wakes up."

"If the Norts don't kill him, that is" Alauren pointed out.

"That was more of a jest than anything else," the old soldier explained with an amused chortle. "Ronnok is a practical man, and practicality says that this Nirali can be worth something. Provided he pulls through, we'll get our chance with him."

"Good to hear," Alauren said, standing. "In the meantime, I need to get started on armor and weapon repairs. Will you be alright?"

"Quite," Edlevin replied with a smile. "Go on."

With a nod, the smith took her leave.

Edlevin laid back and let his gaze fall upon the Nirali soldier. He was a young man, still walking the paths to true maturity. His once-handsome face was scarred by a single, flat laceration under his right eye, matched, the old soldier supposed, by a considerable number of wounds on his torso. Many splinters had been pulled from the man's muscular waist and shoulder in the preceding hours, each requiring its own careful incision to minimize the loss of his blood.

Edlevin shook his head in sorrow. The war had clearly been costly; while Niralan prided itself on allowing anyone to prove themselves, he had never seen someone so young trusted with so much. In his experience, even the lowest of Nirali officers had thirty winters to their name. They were adults, forged in the fires of war, trusted due to their experience and wisdom. He remembered their faces, still images that had been burned into his mind, each as ready to die as the last.

This one, though, was too fresh a face to be comparable to any that the old soldier had seen fall in years long past. Niralan loved their propaganda, telling the young that they should forfeit everything for nothing save their name engraved on a cold stone memorial. War was nothing but a waste, a quagmire of horror that had taken a lifetime of struggle to escape, and the reminder of the continuing cycle of violence plummeted Edlevin's heart deep into his chest.

He sunk his head, losing the strength to look on to the young man's suffering. It was too close to him, too painful, reviving memories that he had deceived himself into believing were dead.

He sat in silence for a while, stewing in his dark thoughts as his wounds racked pain through his hips. They would cascade outward, seemingly touching every bone and organ along the way, as if thousands of jagged splinters were slowly burrowing through his soft flesh. He gritted his teeth and pushed through, as he had done so many times before, taking as much strength as he could from the pain.

It could have been minutes or hours, as the agony bled each moment together into one, but the old soldier eventually heard two sets of footsteps walking in unison. They were heavy and purposeful, both Norts, yet they entered the tent as soft as the wind, careful and respectful of those who rested within. Ronnok led the way, followed closely by Harald; the latter Northman looked ragged and sullen, his heavy eyes pressing down upon any who gazed into them, clearly crushed by the loss of his son. Both took seats, side-by-side, between Edlevin and the foot of the Nirali's bed.

Ronnok said nothing for a while, choosing instead to watch the rise and fall of the young human's chest intently. After a few minutes, he stood and delicately unraveled the man's outer bandages before replacing them with strips of fresh cloth. Using a towel at the side of the bed, he then wiped the sweat from the suffering young Nirali's forehead with a gentle hand. Once the task was done, the Chieftain looked to Edlevin, nodded, and quietly took his seat once more.

The old soldier waited for a few minutes before speaking, unwilling to interrupt whatever was happening until he was sure it wouldn't be a major disruption. "Waiting to interrogate him, are you?" he ventured quietly.

Ronnok nodded. "We need him to survive. We have determined that he is valuable."

"Oh?" Edlevin asked, eager to push for whatever information he could get. "How so?"

"Our new friend is proving to be useful," the Chieftain explained. "Xendra managed to slip out on one of our skiffs after the Nirali fled. They landed at a forward base on the southeast coast of the island, to reorganize before returning to port." He smirked. "There, she stalked the shadows, overhearing that the Nirali force left one of their best commanders behind. A Colonel named Raevin, and a prominent figure on these islands."

"Raevin," Edlevin echoed. "At least I can greet him properly when he wakes up."

"*If* he wakes up," Harald growled.

Edlevin nodded. "I can let you know if he stirs."

Ronnok sighed deeply, chewing at the inside of his lip. "We'll see, Karlmaðr, but we have other business here. Raevin is not the only one we must interrogate this day."

Edlevin cocked his head. "Me?"

"You know too much," the Chieftain confirmed in a flat, serious deadpan. "Niralan's tactics, their culture, their people. You have known all of them naturally, hardly having to search your memories for this information."

"Know your enemy," the old soldier quickly shot back. "In Fangirm, we-"

"Stop lying to me, Edlevin!" Ronnok growled coldly, his patience fully lost for the old human's deflections. "Harald lost his only child today. Many others lost far more." He leaned forward in his seat intensely, bearing a menacing glare. "We've fought everyone, Fangirm included. Since when are Fangirmish men black of hair and tall of stature? When did they begin the tradition of ending their names with -vin?" He sat up straight as a board and locked eyes with the soldier. "Since when do Fangirmen wear rusted Nirali armor from an old war and preach the Eastern ways of small-company tactics? You *will* respect Harald and his loss with the truth, or you will be set afloat in open ocean, as we found you."

Edlevin's head sank. The Chieftain was sharp and inquisitive, noticing every detail, and expecting the truth to stay hidden was, in the end, nothing more than immaculate self-deception. "Fair enough," said the old soldier, his cadence still and calm. He met Ronnok's eyes and let the sorrow held within them display in full for the first time in decades. There were no tears, nor a quaking of the voice, only the frigid gaze of a broken man. With great effort, he spoke.

"In another life, I was known as General Edlevin, Chief of the Nirali military, friend and confidant to Karsus of Marakerlan."

Both Norts recoiled in shock. Ronnok's gaze became stern, locking in on the old soldier's averted eyes. "I knew you were Nirali, but a *General*, Karlmaðr?" he growled loudly. "A leader?"

"A lifetime ago," Edlevin murmured, quick to assuage any fears. "I believed and trusted in Karsus wholeheartedly, as well as his vision of a north free of the wars of the past. In reward for that belief and trust, I received only blood, suffering, and nightmares that haunt my every moment." He looked up to meet the Chieftain's glare, while tears finally turned the tide of battle against his willpower. His voice quaked and wavered, as fractured as his soul. "I was promised peace, in life or in death, and I received neither. I walked away." He grit his teeth to fight off the tears and poked heavily at his quilt to accentuate his words. "That is *not* who I am anymore."

"Karlmaðr," stated the Chieftain, softer this time, noticeably relaxing his tensed muscles. "We do not care about where you came from. Many of us bear scars of mistakes long past, too." He glanced at Harald, who nodded in agreement. "We do not, however, let those memories make us lie to those we are closest to. You should have told me this."

Edlevin nodded, a shallow motion. "I know. I just… I didn't want to risk Ally being burdened with those parts of my past. The things I've done…" He trailed off, not wanting to let the thought linger. "She sees me as an honorable old soldier, someone she can trust and love as a father. She uses my strength to support her own, and I give it willingly. If she knew that well was tainted… I don't know how she would react."

"And when she finds out you've been lying to her?" Ronnok asked.

Edlevin shook his head, blinking slowly. "I don't know."

"We are embroiled in something bigger than ourselves," the Chieftain pointed out. "Niralan is here. She will find out, Karlmaðr. Best that you ensure she finds out on your terms."

Edlevin nodded silently, though he kept his head hung in shame.

Ronnok breathed in deeply, pausing for just a moment. "Karlmaðr, I have another question: could your knowledge of the enemy have prevented the devastating losses we endured today?"

"No," Edlevin stated with clear surety. "I know their general battle plans, but so do you. The detailed troop movements were known to me twenty years ago, but we lost that war. Nirali weren't in command here, in any case, making my experience irrelevant." He looked to Harald, meeting the Northman's eyes. "Sir, Bjorn died fighting some of the finest soldiers in the world. He stood tall before a worthy enemy, and he has my respect."

Harald let a smirk of amusement cross his sullen face. "Sounds like a letter you Nirali would write to a grieving mother, or a widowed spouse."

"Yeah," murmured the old soldier. "It does."

CHAPTER THIRTY-FOUR:

PLANS IN MOTION

36th OF THE MORN OF HARVEST
NORTHERN YEAR 715

The blacksmith remembered her most difficult workload well, as it was in the aftermath of a powerful winter storm that had severely damaged many of Teth's fishing boats. For two weeks, she worked nonstop from dawn until dusk, filling her molds as fast as she could melt the metal, stopping only when the loss of the sun's light shrouded her work in too much shadow to properly address the finer issues.

Fitting, she thought, that her current, more difficult burden was the result of an entirely different kind of storm.

It seemed that every time she popped a dent or buffed a scratch, another piece of damaged armor would roll into her forge, needing, as the Norts would mumble, 'a good patch, not fancy'. Still, even the smallest of cracks took time to seal correctly, and even a small individual workload was overwhelming in numbers so great.

At least it keeps me busy, she thought. *No time to dwell.*

Indeed, when she wasn't working on something, Alauren was back to mulling the avalanche of information that had been dumped upon her in the span of a few measly days. The Thjodhild looked like they could crush mountains, yet their sole focus seemed to be on her. She was such a small, insignificant part of the world, yet they pursued her like their own lives depended on it.

Why?

"Dark thoughts lead to dark songs," a voice said, breaking through Alauren's insular ruminations.

"Xen," Alauren greeted, keeping her goggled eyes on a spout of molten iron that was being tipped from her crucible. "It's good to see you again. Eira told me you've been spying on the enemy."

Xendra grunted an affirmative. "Here and there, joined by a number of Nordiskans, but I needed a break. Northmen can be rather

loud, and the enemy only interests me in regard to how I can kill them."
She smirked and leaned against the tent's entrance. "You, on the other
hand, are quite the conundrum, and good company on top of it."

Alauren was focused intently on her task, but was able to speak.
"Always have been, on both counts."

"So, help me to find a solution," Xendra requested. "Humor me?"

Alauren nodded, finished her pour, and removed her protective
eyewear, letting the metal cool within the molds.

"Where are you from?" Xendra posited. "The north?"

"A place called Teth'Nerhol, on the coast of Se'Vikoral," the
smith said amidst a sorrowful shrug. "It's gone now. Before that, not
much detailed memory remains, so I've always thought of Teth as my
home."

"A human village, being in Se'Vikoral," Xendra said with a nod.
"Surely the people there thought you curious?"

Alauren nodded. "At the beginning, yes. The first things I
remember are people looking to me with suspicion, but that died over
time, especially as I apprenticed under the local smith, a gruff man by
the name of Fredi. Twenty years later and I was a perfectly normal
fixture." She snickered reservedly. "I was like the docks: always there,
always busy."

"You can't remember anything from before then?" the Eldari
pushed.

"No," the smith said with a shake of her head. "The first
Marchioness I knew, Sorun, said I was abandoned by transients when
I looked to be about ten. After a while, I figured that if I was cast away,
my past didn't matter. I was left behind, so I'd leave them behind, too."

Xendra nodded again. "I can relate, sometimes."

Alauren cocked an eyebrow. "Oh?"

"The Eldari are… practical," Xendra explained, a clear frustration
seeping into her voice. "Stubborn, and often uncaring. It isn't hard to
feel left behind. Our sole focus is on continuing our race, to seeing
another sunrise." She sighed, looked to the floor, and blinked a few
times. "I warned them of the Thjodhild presence here three years ago.
They scoffed, calling me a fool to think that the old, proud enemy
would stay in a backwater like this. Now we are left to fight alone, as
my people claimed that their resources are too limited to assist with
such a preposterous idea."

"How many others are there, anyway?" Alauren asked. "If they are immortal, as you say, there are surely still a good number of you."

"Immortal only in the sense that our bodies do not crumble before us," the Eldari clarified, looking back up to the smith. "We can still be killed. The Thjodhild have hunted us since the final days of our empire, taking more from our remaining thousands every passing morn, always stalking in the shadows for their chance." She grimaced and tightened her arms around her chest. "For the first time in millennia, the Thjodhild have shown themselves in great numbers. For the first time in millennia, we have a chance to strike them, yet the Eldari refuse to come out of hiding to do so. We are alone."

"We seem to do alright," Alauren pointed out. She snatched a rod and poked at a cooling arrowhead of steel, encased within the mold, testing its solidification. "At least, so far."

Xendra nodded. "We'll see if that continues. The Northmen mean to take the islands."

Alauren snapped up in surprise. "To… attack?"

"It is a good decision," Xendra said calmly. "The Thjodhild are using this place as a sanctuary, working their machinations too close to Odenseye's shores. This cannot stand."

"It's that important?" asked the blacksmith. "We could lose all of Nordiska."

Xendra shook her head, her face growing dark and cold. "You do not know them, young one," she rumbled, her voice akin to a rake being dragged over loose gravel. "They have killed untold myriads, numbers which were snatched from the jaws of death to be used against the remainder." Her eyes fell to the ground once more. "My father told me stories of holding city gates against a torrent of the dead. Waves upon waves of men, women and children, forced back to life to fight against their own." She paused, gathering herself, and looked back up. "We knew the Thjodhild would show themselves again, some day. Their crusade is beginning once more, and Arvyn is their first beachhead."

"Hold on, *the dead?*" Alauren yelped after snapping from a momentary state of absolute confusion. "Bullshit."

Xendra couldn't help but chuckle at the bluntness of the reply. "It is the truth," she asserted. "As much as I wish that it would not be so. It took the Thjodhild mere centuries of existence to pass us by in the scientific arts. They modified themselves, first, carving their bones and muscles into an unnatural image of perfection. They then modified their very blood, increasing their physical abilities and endurance." She shook her head and grimaced in a clear disgust. "They grew bored of that, after a while, and turned their talents to experiments on the other races as they captured and murdered us. Somewhere along the way, they discovered how to awake a being from death." She tossed a thought. "Perhaps that is why they crusade, because they believe that mastery over death begets mastery over life."

"Then what the *fuck* do they want with me?" snapped the blacksmith. "Why am I such a threat?"

"For that, I have no answers, Alauren," the Eldari replied. "You are something unknown. Perhaps that is enough for them to pay special attention. Your song is strong, and they have likely heard it." She shrugged heavily. "In this matter, your guess is as good as mine."

"My *song*," the smith repeated, letting the word hang for a moment. "You've said that before. I still have no idea what you mean."

Xendra took a moment, mulling over a thought in her head. "This is not a concept I can explain with ease, but I will try. Think of a pond on a summer's eve, bathed in the waning hours of the sun," she illustrated, looking to the canopy of the tent as she summoned the image in her mind. "The sounds grow louder and louder as the sky grows darker, each some creature or another calling to the fading light."

"We're the creatures?" Alauren asked.

Xendra smirked. "No, we're more like a drop of water in the pond, bound to the other drips around us. The pond, as a whole, senses everything that happens near its banks. Even the smallest of insects can cause a ripple; it may be tiny, inconceivably so, yet it is still felt by every drop of water within the pool." She paused for a moment, clearly taking great care to choose her words correctly. "We are rarely affected directly by the beat of the wing and the heart, but their vibrations are eventually passed on to us through the pond - the world that we inhabit. These disturbances are what most young races refer to as magic, needing only to be harnessed." She paused to swallow and take a breath. "Our song is defined by how we use those waves when they find us, which is, of course, up to the individual." She chortled, noticing the smith's increasingly absent glare of confusion.

"In short, power is drawn from the energy these ripples carry with them, and we can use that power in any way we choose. Using them to create a just, equitable world of acceptance constitutes a beautiful melody of a song, while using them for your own power and ego in a rejection of nature is a cacophony of madness."

"Where does the magic come from, then?" Alauren asked, content with the shorter explanation. "What is beating its wings or singing into the night?"

"You might as well ask me why the stars exist, or why a second passes on any given day," the Eldari replied. "Millennia of life have brought us no closer to that answer. We only know that the vibrations in the water find us, and that they can be harnessed." She sighed and shook her head in a barely visible disbelief. "This is why you are so interesting, Alauren; you seem to be closer than any other to whatever beats its wings, closer to the source, its power running through you before the ripples have a chance to diminish even slightly in the vast waters of the pond."

Alauren bit her lip, thinking. The deeper talk of magic and ripples were lost on her, and so she focused on creating a foundation for understanding. "Why call it a song, then?" she asked. "It doesn't sound very song-like, if we're not the singing creatures."

"It is a reference to harmony, in my people's traditions," Xendra explained. "We are taught to find a way to work within the bounds of the waves, harnessing what the world gives us, rather than trying to force it to serve us. The Paragons of my people, heroes of old, stood as examples of calm acceptance, dutifully working to better their changing empire, while the dark ones, known as Adwen, resisted the passing of seasons at every step and reaped a suffering song from it. They found only fear and isolation as they rejected the ripples that passed them by, and they became fountains of sorrow in the realm of magic, with even the physical world leaving them behind eventually."

"Hence the comments about dark thoughts," Alauren said. "You believe I'm resistant to the world that lies before me."

"In some ways," Xendra replied. "We are not fully in control of our own path. If you made your own destiny, would you not be with your people, back in your home of Teth?"

The smith nodded.

"Harmony, at its core, is an acceptance or a rejection of our helpless existence," Xendra continued. "We must find peace within the world, no matter what it chooses to give us." She attempted to smile warmly, but found it colder than intended. "This is another reason why you are a mystery to me. Despite knowing nothing of your own song, and despite your desire for the lost life you once knew, you display a temperance indicative of my own people, a strangely hypnotic harmony that can only come from inner peace."

Alauren paused for a moment, mulling the words, but shook her head after a few moments. "Bullshit," she stated firmly. "I know you don't know much about me, so I'll fill you in; I'm about the farthest from 'peace' you can get. I'm not part of some quaint pond in a forest, I'm part of a fucking hurricane!" Her words grew ever louder, ever more frustrated, with a twinge of fear within. "Every day is a frustrating nightmare, and my only desire is to go home! I sound more like some of your dark ones."

"In some ways," Xendra replied calmly, taking the words in stride. "Over time, though, the Adwen became another being entirely. They would give up everything and everyone to get one more day in a world that had long since died, or even one that had never existed anywhere outside of their own minds, rejecting reality for their own comfort." She tapped the workbench lightly. "During my lifetime, the Thjodhild have been the face of the Adwen. Are you like them?"

Alauren's head snapped up, clear fury seeping from her wild eyes. "Why would you even ask me something like that? They killed my only family, save Edlevin."

Xendra displayed a thin smile. "You share their pained, suffering song, holding on to a dead life. However, you also share our harmony, a true longing to let go of what once was and accept what is here now. In terms of desires, you are both at peace and at war at the same time, fighting successfully to move on, yet unable to budge your grip on the past. This something that my people would view as impossible."

"What does that mean?" Alauren growled with a quivering, confused voice, running her hands through her hair. "What does any of this mean?"

"It means you are holding on to questions that can never be answered; a search for a reasoning that is, practically speaking, irrelevant," Xendra elaborated, putting on her best soothing voice, but finding it hardly less low and grinding. "The question of why the

Thjodhild perpetrate atrocities is unimportant, as is whatever they, or I, see in you. The only thing that truly matters is the fact that the Thjodhild commit those heinous crimes, and that they must pay for them. The only path forward is one where you focus, harness the ripples, and use them to bring about justice to those who have spread their song of agony upon this world." She took a deep breath. "Try not to be overwhelmed by what I'm telling you, Alauren, and stay focused on the current moment. Focus on your own struggle and the just fight that is before us. Little else matters right now."

"Knowing the Thjodhild's reasoning can help us fight them, though," countered the smith. "It can show us weak points."

"Yes, if you operate under the assumption that there is value to be found within those reasons," Xendra retorted. "By what little we know of the Thjodhild, they are nothing more than the demented rantings of the insane, worthless and nonsensical. They make you feel…" She trailed off, grinding her teeth in deep thought. "Lost, I suppose, and afraid, unable to understand the world around you for what it is." She shook her head. "Your song, strangely, imparts these same feelings onto me, mixing in with a comforting warmth in your harmony. You are nothing that you should be."

"And what should I be?" Alauren snapped.

"One of us," said the Eldari, tapping her chest, "or one of them," she finished, pointing towards the peak of the big island. "You are neither Paragon nor Adwen. You are simply a stray drop of rain landing in the pond, lost to the vast world you have entered." She tapped her fingers against her leg, choosing her words carefully. "I do not know what you are. I know you hoped I had answers for you, but I cannot tell you who you need to be."

Alauren's head sunk, and she bit her lip in a barely hidden frustration.

"Just focus on seeing tomorrow and moving forward," Xendra reassured. "Your song is yours to craft. Do this wisely, accepting your life for what it is, and you'll be a paragon of your own making." She sighed and shrugged. "I'm sorry I can't impart these ideas upon you with more clarity. Our song and the emotions that define it are complex things, understood only by our own individual study of the concepts. It will be a long while before my words on your song, and thus, who you are, will begin to make sense. For now, smith, just focus on getting the job done."

Alauren nodded acceptingly. "Like Edlevin says, just put one foot in front of the other."

Xendra smiled warmly. "He carries a wisdom with him, one that would take my people centuries to gain. He is your Paragon, until you can become your own."

Alauren chuckled lightly. "Don't tell him that. He'd never shut up about it."

"I wouldn't think of subjecting you to such a thing," the Eldari said amidst a chortle. "Besides, I have scouting to do." She took a few steps back and smiled warmly once again. "Remember, the Thjodhild will pay. That is all that matters. Find your peace in their death, as I have."

Alauren nodded and stared forward for a moment. "Before you go," she said, "I've been wondering something. Back on the big island, you managed to totally disable the knights. Can you do that again?"

Xendra huffed a small, derisive laugh and shook her head. "We could only wish it that easy." She procured a small, cracked piece of two-pronged metal from her pocket. "The senses of the Thjodhild are greatly increased. Sight, smell…" She smirked wickedly. "Hearing. However, this gives them a notable weakness, as sounds at certain pitches can send them tumbling in agony." She laid the metal object down on the smith's workbench. "This is made of a rare metal called Orokite, fragile and difficult to mold. When it is struck, it will vibrate at the necessary pitch to harm a Thjodhild, maintained for a small period before cracking." She gnawed at her lips and shook her head. "If the Eldari were not so stubborn, we would have more. Unfortunately, my words have gone unheeded by my people."

"Figures," grunted the blacksmith. "It always has to be the hard way, doesn't it?"

Xendra chuckled. "Indeed." She moved toward the doorway. "One foot in front of the other, like the old man says. Let's get this done."

"Yeah," Alauren murmured, returning to her work. "Be safe, Xen."

The Eldari hesitated for a moment, turning back around reluctantly, as if the motion took the full force of her will. "Smith, there is something else. Something you must accept."

Alauren cocked an eyebrow. "What?"

"Whether you want to believe it or not, your blade is special, and no other weapon within Nordiska can do what it can," Xendra said. "When the time comes, I believe that only the wielder of that sword will be able to bring our most dangerous foe down." She smirked once more. "If that happens to be you, tear that bastard asunder, and make him feel the fear that he has set upon all of us."

The Eldari stalked out before any response could come, heading back towards the beach while the blacksmith was left within her own thoughts.

Pain was the world, and the world had no mercy.

Lightning shot through his spine, his nerves, every fiber of muscle in his body. His bones would alternate between feeling like icicles inside of him, crisping his flesh solid, before transitioning to scorching swords fresh from a forge, melting his innards back to liquid. Even the cold touch of water on his lips sent his teeth buzzing in agony, like a thousand knives had been driven into the nerves beneath.

Whether it was days or weeks mattered little, for all that he knew was the next moment. Still, he seemed to gain more awareness of his surroundings as time passed on. A figure watched over him, though he could hardly tell if it was Human, Nort, or something else entirely.

Stay with me, it would say, through a thick, muffling fog. *You are still needed, son of Niras.*

A calm passed over him, causing the voice to grow more frantic, begging him to remain even as he was tempted into the arms of this new feeling. It was a euphoric sensation, yet it felt wrong, as if it was a carefully crafted deception. After a time, he freed himself from the warm, enticing embrace, finding his way back to cold and ceaseless agony.

He shot up suddenly, a motion that brought the pain back in full force. He could do little but slump back and groan gutturally, enduring the searing nightmare of existence. Slowly, the world began to grow more defined and less confusing, the fog melting away from his hearing and his vision. He could tell which way was up, and after a moment, he managed to find his steadiness in his bed, brushing a few sweat-drenched hairs from his face.

"You're awake," the voice murmured. "I'm here to help you, Raevin."

The Colonel turned his head, finally able to glimpse another wounded man on the bed across from him. "Who...?" he questioned weakly.

"Edlevin," the figure introduced. "Charmed."

Raevin forced himself to sit up, fighting against the screaming will of every muscle in his body to remain still. "My soldiers?"

"Dead," stated the older man.

The Nirali fell back into his bed with a grimace. "All of them?"

"All of them," Edlevin confirmed coldly. "They fought to the last."

"They did their duty," Raevin said, looking to the tent's canopy as he tried to push away an entirely new pain. "They served well."

"I disagree," Edlevin quickly retorted.

Raevin fumed, even in his wounded state. "They died for Niralan, cur. They died for their country."

Edlevin shook his head and scowled. "They died because the Thjodhild wanted to test our mettle, to see how much resistance we could put up." Every word was carried within a snarl of hatred, memory tormenting him as he leaned forward in his cot. "Why was there no second assault? It is protocol."

Raevin shook his head and closed his eyes. "What do you know of Niralan, old man?"

"Quite a bit, actually," Edlevin informed with an eager smile. "I know that our nation was founded by Niras, the greatest of our people. I know that we came from beyond the shores of Odenseye in times long past. I know that the Memorial Wall of Farakan had exactly eighty-thousand, five hundred and twelve names on it just before the end of the last war." His gaze became dark, and his eyes nearly disappeared under the shadows of his brow as his voice became a thrumming, low growl. "I know that the Nirali Academy told you that I died at Marakerlan."

Raevin blinked slowly, trying to process the thought. "We do not abandon our nation. You cannot be him. You cannot be Nirali. Lies."

"I am, though only by my heritage," Edlevin replied, his voice returning to a stoic calm. "The life you lead gave me misery and death in return for my blood and tears. I left it behind, as I left Karsus behind. My home was no more, and so I moved on to a new life."

"Traitor," Raevin growled weakly. "Your duty is to your nation."

"My duty is to whatever I choose," the old soldier calmly rebutted. "Right now, that duty is to protect the people I hold dear." He sat back in his cot. "This is something you could help with."

Raevin scoffed weakly. "By betraying my people, I assume?"

"By betraying the Thjodhild," Edlevin spoke, slowly and clearly.

Raevin's head snapped up again. "What do you know of them?"

"Just that they've been trying to kill someone important to me," the old soldier explained. "They sent you against our fortifications to test us, to see if they could break through our lines with their current forces." He smirked. "The answer was a clear 'no'. Tell me, what reasoning did they deceive you with?"

"They said that destroying the Northmen was an integral part of the war," Raevin replied, heaving his weight to a full sitting position despite the visible difficulty of the task. "They told us that Niralan's fate depended on it. One less variable could win us the war. That makes sense to me."

Edlevin laughed boisterously. "They're after a spindly little Elven blacksmith, you idiot. One woman."

Raevin looked down, furrowing his sweat-beaded brow. "No. That's a lie."

The old soldier ground his teeth for a moment. "I wish it was. I fought them, back in my little slice of paradise, you know. They slaughtered everyone, and they have since made it *very* clear that my friend was their objective." He met the young Nirali's eyes. "You should have seen it, Raevin. Everyone huddled into our Marchioness' longhouse. Marks from their fingernails, scratching at the walls, trying to escape. Viscous fluid dripping from their mouths."

Raevin's eyes went wide, an expression duly quashed with a trained military efficiency. Still, it was enough for Edlevin to understand.

"You've seen them do it, haven't you?" the old soldier whispered. "It has happened here."

"They were organizing rebellion," Raevin mumbled, barely audible. "Our eyes found them. They left us no choice."

"Your eyes?" Edlevin asked.

"Wisps," Raevin said. "They found a way to use them. Clairvoyance, they called it." He put a hand on his forehead. "We had no choice but to give those people over, for they were traitors and insurgents."

"Maybe," Edlevin stated coldly. "Now, though, your ability to choose has returned. I think we both know that the Thjodhild care nothing for any of us."

Raevin nodded, keeping his head down.

"We're going to kill them," assured the old soldier. "All of them. We can free these islands and save these people from that fate. Help us."

"I... I can't," the Colonel stammered, looking up. "Karsus himself gave us orders to follow what the Thjodhild say, to the letter."

"Karsus is a brilliant man," Edlevin said, the tone of his voice as chill as a polar wind. "He is also the man who sent all of my friends to their violent ends, cursing me with a life of remembering each and every one of their dying screams, every day." He leaned forward and practically snarled at the younger Nirali. "He just did the same thing to you. Perhaps you should consider that Karsus isn't infallible in his decision making."

"What would you have me do, anyway?" Raevin whimpered, clutching his side in pain. "What could be done against their might, if even I could bring myself to do such a thing?"

"That depends on how high you rank," Edlevin said. "You and I know a Colonel can serve in many capacities."

"I'm the second in command of the islands, though I am the highest-ranking military official," Raevin answered. "The Thjodhild run everything, regardless."

"You can help, then," said the old soldier, standing. "You were betrayed, Raevin. Your men are dead. We are all you have left. Help us."

Raevin looked down, pondering over every word. The choice was one between an immovable object and an unstoppable force, his orders or his morality, his people or a command from on high. A lump formed in his throat, and he managed to speak.

"No."

Edlevin sighed and glanced to the floor. "More of your soldiers will die as we storm their keep. We can prevent that."

"It is their duty!" Raevin snarled, hurting his ribs in the action. "Their only duty!"

"Do not speak to me of duty when you ignore Karsus' first command!" Edlevin spat coldly. "Do tell, Colonel, what is it?"

"Wh… What?" the young Nirali stammered.

"What is Karsus' first command?" The old soldier repeated loudly.

Raevin looked at the canopy of the tent and sighed deeply, giving in. "Preserve the people."

Edlevin nodded quietly. He took a seat in a wooden chair closer to the Colonel, breathing deeply and recentering. "We have a guest at this camp, you know. She is Elf-like, though she is hardly an Elf."

Raevin closed his eyes again. "What of it?"

"Let's just say she has more experience with the Thjodhild than anyone else," the old soldier murmured. "Do you know what became of the corpses of your forces?"

Raevin looked up with a cold glare, staring intensely, practically ready to strangle the older Nirali if the wrong words escaped his mouth.

"We burned them," Edlevin stated flatly. "She ordered us to, without delay. She was afraid they would be used."

Raevin's head sunk again, his entire body shrinking in shame.

"Ah," Edlevin grunted darkly, with more than a little surprise. "You've already seen them do it, haven't you? Use the dead for their own purposes."

"No," Raevin said amidst a ragged breath. "Not dead. They were forced back, their mind snatched from darkness to inhabit a body that could no longer hold them." His weary eyes met those of the older human. "Those people were there, Edlevin, aware of all that they were doing, with no power to disobey the commands they were given. I watched a mother disembowel her own daughter, an accused rebel, in the town square." His head sunk heavily into his hands. "The tears and horror in her eyes were at odds with the plunging of her blade as it ripped her child asunder." He grimaced in disgust at the memory, and his words were unable to escape his mouth without a clear revulsion enveloping them. "She was *there*."

"Put an end to it, then!" Edlevin pleaded. "Unlike her, you can disobey. You can do the right thing for your people. They destroyed everything which I loved, everything that was good and right in my world. You think that they will spare Niralan the same fate?"

"They will not," a voice answered from the tent flap.

"Xendra," Edlevin greeted warmly. "Meet Raevin, Colonel of Niralan."

The Eldari hurried to the Colonel's side, where she knelt next to his bed and took his hands into hers. A warmth entered the Nirali, a feeling of healing as the pain was suppressed and his weakness shored up. It was as if a mere touch imparted to him an entire week's worth of mending.

"I am Eldari," Xendra said softly. "An old race of unending life, should we be able to safeguard it. I know of these knights, and their goals."

Raevin met her eyes. "The Thjodhild spoke of you. They were concerned at your presence."

Xendra smiled. "As they should be, for my existence proves their failure. They tried to wipe us out, Raevin. In many ways, they succeeded." She let go of his hands and sat back. "There are mere hundreds of us left, scattered and hiding among the young races. The Thjodhild wish us dead, along with any who do not share their blood. This is their mission: purity and an ideal world at the cost of every other life on this continent."

"Genocide?" Raevin asked in disbelief.

"Indeed," confirmed the Eldari. "A world of their own making, pure and free of what they deem to be imperfection."

Raevin shook head in disbelief. "Why would Karsus…?"

Before an answer could come, Ronnok barreled through the tent flap with a worried look etched onto his face. "The Dwarf is gone!"

CHAPTER THIRTY-FIVE:

COMPLICATIONS

"What do you mean, he's gone?" Alauren asked incredulously, her query returned with two blank stares. She tossed her hammer down and removed her goggles. For a moment, the crackling coal inside the furnace was the only sound breaking a still silence.

"He disappeared," Ronnok finally grumbled with a shrug. "Into thin air."

"Drell," Edlevin growled. "We were so caught up in whatever is happening here that we failed to account for him as a factor."

"Where did they go?" asked the smith. "Did he say anything before it happened?"

"He was drinking, with the weapon across his lap," replied the Chieftain. "The only message I received was the look of shock in the small one's eyes before he vanished."

"Great," Alauren sighed, rubbing her temple. "The last thing we needed was more trouble."

"Why? Why now?" mused the old soldier. "The timing is odd."

"Maybe Drell got frightened by the last battle and wanted to get away," the blacksmith proposed. "He probably doesn't want to end up in the hands of the Thjodhild."

Edlevin waved his hand in dismissal. "Why risk it, then? Why not just leave before the battle even starts?"

"It could have taken some consideration," Alauren quickly replied. "He thinks we can win against an assault and stays. But a siege of our own? He might not be so sure."

"Men like Drell are the type to plan five steps ahead, to leave well before they are in danger," Edlevin retorted. "I, for one, have read the written histories. Have you?"

"Yes, Edlevin," Alauren said sarcastically. "Because we absolutely had a well-stocked library in Teth."

"They had one on Alsara!" Edlevin exclaimed. "I may have borrowed a book before we left. Did you?"

"Too busy doing actual work, Karlmaðr," grumbled the smith. "I barely had time to look around. Besides, the last thing I want to do on a boat is look down at a text."

"That's what hammocks are for!" the old soldier bellowed. "Keep you stable, even on the rough, open seas."

"It was him," Ronnok said absently, wholly oblivious to the argument. He beckoned to a passing Nort woman. "Grìda, lìda leggjå Raevin ur Xen."

Edlevin and Alauren cocked their heads in unison.

"Elaborate?" requested the soldier.

"For a time, we walked free of the Thjodhild's pursuit," Ronnok explained. "After crossing the Tail," he said, referring to the mountains near Teth, "they began to fortify, to set up large camps. They let us go."

"They knew you would sail beyond the horizon, as Norts have always done in times of crisis," Edlevin concurred with a nod. "You'd be out of Niralan's way. I assume that changed?"

"It did," the Chieftain replied. "Over the last morn, the black-sailed ships of the Thjodhild have been seen by our scouts, shadowing our every move. We have kept this information close, for we did not wish to alert any who may have been treacherous towards us."

"Were they the ones who attacked us?" Alauren asked.

"No," Ronnok stated confidently. "These were larger vessels, galleons and heavy frigates who were last seen in the fjords of the north, attacking my people. They could not have kept pace with our swifter fleet, given their distance." He sighed and ran a hand through his hair. "Yet, reports from scouts always told us the same thing: since the events at Teth, our path was being perfectly followed, even though the pursuers were days behind us. I suspected you, Karlmaðr."

Edlevin nodded. "I understand."

Alauren shook her head and furrowed her brow in confusion. "I don't. Why would you suspect him?"

The Chieftain shot a glare at the old soldier, carrying with it the weight and pressure of a towering mountain. His opal eyes burned, and little more was needed for the human to understand the demand that was being made.

"Ally, I..." Edlevin began, before abruptly halting. "I haven't been completely honest with you when it comes to my past."

"Okay?" Alauren droned confusedly. "So, be honest now."

"Ally…" the old soldier struggled, averting his gaze and letting it fall to the ground. "I served Karsus, a time ago, as his Chief General. I am Nirali." He swallowed hard and shook his head. "Think of a battle from the last war between the Nirali and the Elysians, and it will be more than likely that I was behind that bloodshed. I'm sorry I didn't tell you sooner."

"Really?" huffed the smith amidst a cocked head and a single raised eyebrow. "That makes a lot of sense, actually."

Edlevin looked up and met her eyes sheepishly. "You don't seem as upset as I thought you might be."

Alauren chuckled. "It's odd, to be honest, knowing you came from the east. It also doesn't change anything."

"Ally, the things I've done-"

"You've always had demons, Ed," Alauren interjected with a warm smile. "I'm sure you used to be a violent, aggressive asshole like the rest of them, but I know you." She poked him playfully on the chest. "The *real* you." She tossed a thought about in her head, maintaining her grin. "Don't think you have to hide anything from me, Karlmaðr. Whatever you were then, you are a good man today. That's all that matters to me. Nirali, Fangirmish… does it really matter?"

Edlevin dropped his head and smiled, struggling to hold a whirlwind of emotions at bay. The blacksmith approached him with a chuckle and embraced him heavily, matched in kind. After a moment, she spoke.

"You've earned my trust and love a thousand times over, Ed," Alauren murmured. "Never doubt that."

Edlevin drew away and gathered himself. "Thanks, Ally. You have no idea what that means to me." He swallowed heavily and pulled himself back to the man of strength that was well known to his comrades. "I'll fill you in on the finer details later. Ronnok, you mentioned us being followed?"

The Chieftain nodded, content to watch until now. "We deduced that someone had to be reporting our position to the pursuers. We eliminated your betrayal as a possibility after you saved my daughter, Karlmaðr. Same with the Dwarf." He smirked at Alauren. "Her, I've always trusted. Too nervous to be malicious."

Edlevin nodded in agreement. "I assume you also made sure nobody betrayed Nordiska from within?"

Ronnok nodded. "Even Northmen can make fine spies when the time requires. We were uncompromised."

"Are we sure they didn't just follow tales of our passage?" queried the blacksmith. "The fleet wasn't exactly small."

Ronnok chuckled heartily. "Our city on the sea pales in comparison to the size of the Borean Ocean around us, smith. Despite this, they followed our journey exactly, observing the aftermath of our carnage, even when it meant turning to the wind and losing time."

Edlevin nodded and rubbed the stubble on his chin. "Our path was seemingly random, sailing north and south with the wind, even after the spur-of-the-moment decision to come to Arvyn."

"Oh, shit," Alauren gasped, slapping her forehead. "That decision came from Drell."

"It did," Ronnok stated. "The Eldari says the Thjodhild are tied into a world beyond ours. They can see and hear things in a way none of us can."

"Indeed," Raevin groaned, limping partially under Xendra's strength to meet the trio. He was wearing a black Alsaran tunic and pants now, secured by a leather belt; whether it was his health or his fresh garments, the smith could not tell, but he appeared to be much healthier than he was just a day ago. The Eldari sat him down on a wood stump nearby, where he hunched over. "Well, one did, anyway, a female they only referred to as the Dreamer. My soldiers often had to look over her as she fell into a deep meditation, and, when she returned, she would have knowledge of plots and thoughts across the entire island. Sometimes beyond." He looked up. "They knew exactly where you were. They knew you were coming."

Alauren rubbed her temple. "You don't think Valin was a part of this, do you? Did the Thjodhild ever mention a Dwarf?"

"They hardly mentioned anything to me, or any other human," grumbled the Colonel. "They told us where to be and when, and we followed their orders without question."

"They are not the only ones to hear whispers," Xendra said, a noticeable intensity about her voice. "For a time, I have sensed a beacon of power here, something unknowable. To put it into physical terms, I cannot look at it, for the light it gives off would blind me." She breathed in deeply, vainly trying to hide the extent that the new information had unnerved her. "This Dreamer is an elder of her race, known to me, and her song reaches out to touch a great many beings on Arvyn. If this is truly her, we have found our primary target. I need to get close and see what I can find out."

"Take Harald," Ronnok ordered.

"I would ask to do this alone," Xendra countered coldly. "I know that you have little reason to trust me beyond my assistance in our battle with the Nirali. However, I will need to move quickly and get uncomfortably close to our enemy in order to determine what this beacon is doing, and what can be done about her. Tagalongs will only hamper me."

Ronnok considered the words for a moment, looking deeply into the Eldari's eyes. "I am unsure. You have fought with us, yes, but how do I know that you did not do so just to gain our trust?"

The Eldari smirked and shrugged. "You don't. Sometimes you just have to trust." Her eyes narrowed, and a potent fury poured from her eyes. "I want the Thjodhild dead, Northman. Every single one of them. Look into my eyes and tell me that I'm lying."

Ronnok obliged, meeting the intensity of the Eldari's fury with a face of graven calm. "Your hatred burns bright and clear," he said after a prolonged moment. "Very well. Go, and good luck to you."

Xendra nodded and sprinted off towards the shore without delay.

"We now have an urgency that we could not account for," Ronnok said after a small while. "We must assume the enemy knows of our plans to counterattack. We need to strike as soon as possible."

"That could be foolhardy," Edlevin rapidly replied. "If they know we're coming, they can better fortify and prepare for a siege, as we did."

"Do you suggest we run, Karlmaðr?" asked the Chieftain.

"Not run, exactly. If we sail south-"

"They'll follow us," Alauren interjected. "As long as I'm with you, they'll keep carving a path of destruction to get to me."

"This is true, Karlmaðr," Ronnok concurred. "They also have the Dwarf, most likely. Would you leave him behind?"

Edlevin sighed deeply. "No. Yet, we cannot attack them head on when they know our plans, especially in our current state."

"We don't have to," Alauren pointed out, rubbing her chin. "They want me. They can come out and get me."

"Ally, no," Edlevin replied dismissively, like a parent scolding a child. "We're not using you as bait."

"They're going to chase us down anyway, Karlmaðr," the smith quickly riposted, a growing fire in her eyes. "I'm sick of running and hiding. You saw yourself how much they want me dead, how much their vision becomes tunneled when I'm near."

"The girl is right," Raevin said. "They are strong minded, but singly minded. They focus on their main goal, but often fail to see what lurks in their peripheral vision."

"A bold plan," Ronnok said proudly, with an admiring smile toward the fiery blacksmith. "A strategy fitting of my people."

"Get me back into the city," Raevin said in a calm growl. "I have made my decision; Arvyn must be protected. These islands, and their people, will be under the control of Niralan, not the Thjodhild. I will ensure that their defeat is final, and that Karsus' foremost commands are kept." He ground his teeth for a moment. "The people will be preserved."

"The Thjodhild would probably be wary of you, having spent so much time with us," Edlevin observed with clear skepticism. "They're just as likely to lock you up as they are to return you to your commission."

"I'm a gesture of goodwill," Raevin proffered, splaying his arms out as much as his aches would allow him to. "A sign that you want to bargain. If they can get the girl without fighting Northmen, they will attempt to do so. I am sure of it."

"Alauren," the smith corrected. "My name is Alauren."

Raevin nodded between heavy breaths. "My apologies, Alauren. I am Raevin, Colonel of the Nirali Expeditionary Force and Military Magistrate of the Arvyn Archipelago. A pleasure."

"I'll save the pleasure for when we kill these bastards," snapped the blacksmith. "And afterwards, you're going to tell me everything you know about them."

Raevin chuckled. "Your fire outshines even some Nirali. I'll tell you everything if we win."

"When we win," Alauren corrected, drawing confident smiles all around.

"Raevin, come with me," Ronnok ordered. "We'll formulate a plan." He gestured towards the smith and the soldier. "You two, keep your heads down until we're ready to go."

"Ronnok, I should be present," Edlevin protested.

"You should be resting and healing," growled the Chieftain. "You have Thjodhild to kill."

The crisp sting in the air intensified as the evening wore on, and the rays of the sun were rapidly disappearing behind the open horizon to the east with a final crimson blaze. These were, without a doubt, among the final breaths of the autumn, and the bite of winter was truly beginning to sink its teeth into the wind. A mere two days had passed since the disappearance of the resident Dwarf, and every second since had been filled with frantic preparations for what was hoped to be a mortal blow to the heart of their foe. There were few words spoken around the camp save for Ronnok's barking of orders; now, an eerie calm hung over the heads of the soldier and the smith as they lay in quiet contemplation.

They'd move first thing in the morning, following Raevin to Anduras, the capital. The bulk of the Nort fleet, still at sea, would stand ready, but would wait for an opportunity rather than engaging directly. The Norts would have a man inside. They'd flush the Thjodhild out and finish them. Their plan was desperate but solid; or, at least, they assured themselves of such.

Alauren looked at her hands, unsurely shaking about in the forge's dim glow. Whether it was the cold or nerves, she could not tell, as both felt as one in a body that was chilled to the bone.

"It's not the cold," Edlevin informed, seemingly reading her mind. He was bundled up in a small bedroll, enjoying the warmth of the smoldering furnace. "Mine are shaking, too."

"So, it's nerves, then," Alauren said, sinking back her own warm roll.

"It's not nerves, either, really," Edlevin quickly corrected. "It's…" He trailed off, struggling for words. "It's experience. The memories of what you've already seen seeping a dread of the future into your bones."

Alauren nodded. "That makes sense. I felt like I had seen the worst of it, Ed, back at Teth." She ground her teeth for a moment. "That changed when I killed a man, and it changed again when I saw a man be crushed like a beetle by a crab. We're apparently dealing with the dead now, and it seems like everyone save for the Norts wants me in the ground. What will I see tomorrow?"

"An end to the living nightmare we've been forced to carry out," the old soldier answered with confidence. "Valin, hopefully, as well. We'll be fine."

Alauren went silent for a moment, before taking a sharp breath and speaking. "I want to show you something, Karlmaðr." She grabbed a woolen blanket, covering a pile of metal under her workbench, and pulled it off. Underneath, there lay a full set of armor, sized carefully for the smith's lithe form. It was clearly based off Edlevin's Nirali uniform, ridged and smooth, but the design had been fused with the plate she had made for the Norts, with the overlapping scales fastened to a leather garment rather than chain mail.

"That's Ghaldeval armor," Edlevin gasped, noting the telltale bronze coloration. "It's been years since I've seen that."

"It's an alloy, actually," corrected the blacksmith, a strong pride in her voice. "The Ghaldeval gives it flexibility while maintaining strength. It is bonded with steel, making it hard to crack." She smiled. "I was going to have Valin forge a rune on it, to make it Nasgadh, but I guess I waited too long."

"It'll do," Edlevin said. "He'll give you a rune when we find him and end this."

"Yeah," Alauren muttered. "I hope we do. There's a lot on the line."

"Which is why we'll win," Edlevin said, a smirk creeping onto his face. "I've been in this situation before, staring down odds that aren't exactly in my favor. You hold on tight, you focus, and you get the job done."

"You make it sound so easy," Alauren said softly. "Not all of us are the mighty General Edlevin of Niralan."

"Edlevin of Teth, thank you very much," retorted the old soldier. "And Niralan hardly made me mighty."

"What was it like, anyway?" Alauren asked, striking a curious but careful tone. "Growing up there, fighting there? It must have been a nightmare."

Edlevin smiled warmly, surprising his old friend. "It was, on some days. Others, we were helping an infirm farmer haul his crops or assisting an old woman who couldn't fetch water on her own. Niralan is a violent, cold, and calculating nation when it comes to war and politics, but they are undyingly loyal to one another. Nobody goes sick without help; nobody goes hungry or without a place to sleep, even if that shelter is only a barn and the food only bread. My people are hardy, resilient and determined." He sighed deeply, and the smile bled from his face. "Put to work on something worthwhile, they could build a society unlike any other. It's unfortunate that their leaders would rather see the sons of Niras rot in the ground."

"Their leaders," Alauren murmured. "Like Karsus?"

The soldier stared blankly at the roof, and no answer came.

The smith cocked an eyebrow. "Ed?"

"Especially Karsus," Edlevin grumbled after a moment. "He has cost my people more blood than Elysia ever could."

"You hate him," Alauren observed calmly. "It's in your voice, a strained growl. I've not heard it before."

The old soldier nodded solemnly. "Before our first war with Elysia, I had thirty comrades in arms that I fought and bled with, side by side." He blinked slowly, fighting against a clear torrent of sorrow. "One remains, to the best of my knowledge. We were brothers all, forged in battle, as we believed all Nirali should be. Now we are shattered, with the two of us left to carry the splinters of the dead." He chewed at the inside of his lower lip intensely, holding back a typhoon of rage. "Karsus, and no others, ordered it so."

"Who is the other survivor?" Alauren asked. "Would I know of them?"

"No," Edlevin grumbled in reply. His eyes batted back and forth around the canopy of the smithy, as if they were trying to swat the memory away. "He was just another officer, like me, serving without a mind for glory. He became a shell of what he was, casting himself firmly behind Karsus' delusions despite the nightmares that were imparted upon us. For his sake, I hope he's passed on."

"Let me know a name, at least," the smith requested carefully. "Who was he?"

"Morvin," Edlevin rumbled after a moment of consideration. "My Lieutenant General, and one of my best friends. Lost to delusions,

Ally, like the rest."

"What was Karsus' delusion, then?" asked the blacksmith. "What does he want?"

"Peace, or so he would say," replied the soldier. "Niralan is a nation with many wounds, brought about by our struggles to survive in the north. For centuries, our enemies have been foremost in our minds. Elysia, Fangirm…" He chuckled lightly, darkly, at the thought. "If we could have slowed down enough to allow ourselves to heal, maybe we would have realized that the only thing making those nations enemies to Niralan was Niralan itself. Our old wounds drove us, no matter what 'greater good' Karsus claimed to represent. War can never lead to peace, just as hatred can never lead to love. Do not trust anyone who says otherwise."

"What of Raevin?" Alauren posited. "Can he be trusted?"

"I hope so, Ally," Edlevin sighed. "His choice is between his orders and his countrymen, a predicament that breaks his understanding of the world. He's seen what the Thjodhild have done, and he knows that it's us or them. Still, he has his orders, as all Nirali do."

"You think that would really make him betray us?" Alauren asked incredulously. "What good are orders if they let people like the Thjodhild run amok? Why would you follow them?"

Edlevin smiled. "That's much like the question I asked myself after Marakerlan, decades ago. It's the reason I'm here now." He shifted in his bedroll. "Raevin seems like a decent man, in a unique Nirali way. He'll do what's best for his people." He sighed deeply, as if he had suddenly been forced to accept a painful truth. "For *my* people."

"I hope you're right, Karlmaðr," Alauren said through a yawn.

"Yeah," replied the old soldier. "So do I."

CHAPTER THIRTY-SIX:

STRENGTH

The deep night grows on, yet I cannot yield to
sleep, lest rest be fitful.

- From the journal of an unknown Nirali soldier
during the Fifth Siege of Marakerlan, c. 643.

38th OF THE MORN OF HARVEST
NORTHERN YEAR 715

Arvynian had never been this silent. The familiar clucking of chickens
and the turning of wheels were not present, nor did the din of haggling
and conversation dominate the air upon the uneven dirt roads of the
community. Each farmhouse of the agricultural commune, one-floor
log huts lining either side of the wide main road, were sealed up tight
with wooden planks, leaving the bustling breadbasket of the islands
utterly still.

Everyone had been hastily pulled back, Raevin supposed,
readying for a siege that seemed all but certain.

The Nirali heaved each foot forward by sheer force of will alone.
He ached in the marrow of his bones and the depths of his heart,
increasingly unsure of whether his actions were right. The intensity
of the pain from the growing conflict within him easily overtook the
discomfort from the myriad of new bruises he had endured to properly
craft his story.

He was a token of peace, a tangible example that even the feverish
need for brutality among the Northmen was secondary to their
continued existence. The Thjodhild, though mighty, preferred to
intimidate their opponents into submission; failing that, of course,
they would rather fight with the blood of others. They could be
reasoned with, in any case.

He had hoped to find a horse or a mule, anything to take the weight off his burning legs. However, comfort was irrelevant, in the end, as was the Nirali way. Riding, walking, or crawling, his objective would be completed, in peace or in agony.

Anduras was a few miles more, a shimmering gem of black walls and white towers beyond the Örmur river and the vast, open prairie through which its waters snaked. The city itself sprawled high behind the defenses as it ascended the base of Redja's Mountain, where pockets of multi-story buildings were little more than blurry boxes from this distance.

The Colonel continued for a time, finding nothing and no one to ease his suffering. Only the cold whistling of the wind between the farmhouses called out to him and broke the eerie silence. The Thjodhild were playing it safe, saving their manpower. The Norts worried them.

Good, thought the Nirali. *They'll need me.*

"Oi!" a voice yelled out, a gargling warble of a sound. "Who goes there?"

"Tarvin?" Raevin called, recognizing one of his foremost scouts.

The soldier rounded a corner from behind an old, dilapidated farmhouse. He was a large, strong man, one of the few runners who could carry a suit of plate armor and move quickly on foot at the same time. Even now, on guard duty, he wore a concealing helm and standard Nirali mail.

"Is it you, Colonel." Tarvin droned, the inflection in his voice wavering between a question and a statement. "Koro would b-b-b-" he sputtered, struggling. "…be glad to Know that you survived?"

"Tarvin?" Raevin asked again, his eyes narrowing while his voice boomed across the commune, bearing the aura of respect that all Nirali officers carried with them. "Are you alright?"

"i am well, Sir!" Tarvin uttered, his voice again swapping inflections with every word. The first was worried, the second was surprised, and the third and fourth were distraught. "You should Go see the Thjodhild."

Raevin felt his spine go cold as a dark realization broke through the walls of denial in his mind. He stumbled backwards lightly, visibly unsettled. "Tarvin, remove your helm."

"I Would prefer Not to, sir." Tarvin demurred.

"Not a choice, Sergeant," Raevin barked. "Do it."

Tarvin hesitated for a moment, lightly quaking under his armor, yet he managed to obey the command of his superior. His arms shook with tremors all the way, like he was physically fighting against the dictations of something deep within to resist the clear and direct order. He held his helm to the side and looked up, smiling unnaturally.

His eyes were tortured, bloodshot and yellow. His skin, once a calm tan, was now pale white, as if the very warmth of his body had been scattered to the wind like the ashes of a bonfire. His hair, flowing and black, was now tangled and matted with blood. Seargent Tarvin was a man of strength, resolve and intellect, well-spoken and confident, one of the best soldiers an officer could ask for.

This was hardly a man at all, but a ghost inhabiting a corpse.

"Tarvin," Raevin muttered. "What did they do to you?"

"I died!" Tarvin rejoiced. "The thjodhild Gave me a second Chance. Another chance to serve!"

Raevin shook his head heavily, feeling a righteous fury brewing within his chest. "No. You did your duty."

"And now I Can do it Again." Tarvin propounded, struggling with every word. "My horse is behind The house. Take it To Anduras. I must Stay and greet Any visitors!"

"You do that, Tarvin," Raevin nodded, eager to go before the disgust could fully manifest on his face. "Kill anyone you see."

"aye?" Was the man's unsure answer.

Raevin left the dead man behind as quickly as he could, desperate to bury the righteous fury that whipped out of control within his rapidly darkening heart. A good man, a skilled man, turned into *that*, denied his rest. Any trepidation about the Colonel's coming actions left him in a moment, and his purpose became abundantly clear.

The rest, as it was called in the traditions of Niralan, was meant to be a reward, a peace in the knowledge that your loyalty was strong and your will unbroken. Despite a life of war and strife, every Child of Niras who served their duty could find solace in the encroaching darkness of the end, a calm quiet in the abyss. Desecrating such a thing, a sacred hope for all Nirali, was something unforgivable, and Raevin would see to it that the blood of the Augurs would paint the city in recompence for such a heinous crime.

Raevin pushed the furious thoughts away, mounting Tarvin's horse and kicking it hard. It sprinted out of Arvynian with speed;

though the repeated movement of its gallop sent a pronounced pain through the Colonel's torso, he kept his focus on the road and forcibly pushed the discomfort away. The terrain was relatively easy, and it wasn't long before the Nirali was at the doorstep of Anduras, peering at its closed gates furiously.

"Who goes there?" a voice cried out from one of the towers.

"Raevin," replied the Colonel. "Let me in."

There was silence for a few moments, but the wooden doors eventually swung open with a loud creak. Raevin dashed through the open portcullis, crossing into the city proper. The cobblestone streets were sparse, surprisingly, having little of the hustle and bustle that the he was accustomed to. Only soldiers stood in their places on the roads, and all parted before their Magistrate with a dutiful salute.

Raevin's ride came to an end at the base of Redja's Mountain, atop a small foothill, where the keep of Anduras overlooked the city. Rooftops of multiple colors cascaded down the slope behind him as he dismounted, and he plowed through the heavy, engraved doors of the grand building with a unique Nirali fury.

The inside was cavernous; multiple circular stories rose up and overlooked a vast foyer at their center, while a grand rotunda lay, in turn, above them. A few Nirali leaned on the railings on the floors above, talking, but most found silence as their commanding officer returned from what they had assumed was a sure death. Koro stood at the center of the room, in the mouth of an intricate dragon mosaic set within the marble floor.

"Koro!" Raevin growled. "I lived."

Koro was still, unmoving, intently staring at a cloth map in his hands. "Yes," hissed the Thjodhild. "We were told."

Raevin nodded. "The Dwarf did so, I assume?"

"His weapon," Koro corrected. "It speaks." He finally moved his helmeted head, cocking it towards the Colonel. "Why are you alive?"

"I'm a gesture of good faith," Raevin explained. "The Northmen want to negotiate. They want to get away without any more trouble."

"They can do so," Koro said dismissively. There was a seeping calm in his voice, as if the thought of a siege bothered him no more than an incoming attack by a chipmunk. "Our interest is not with them."

"They know," Raevin said. "They'll send out the girl, and you send out the Dwarf. An exchange at the city gates, after which they shall sail beyond the horizon."

"They lie," Koro growled. "They will want a fight, given how easily they killed your soldiers."

Raevin felt a rage growing inside him, but was quick to quash the fury before it could become a problem. "They are a practical people," he uttered calmly. "My continued existence proves that. They want to leave Odenseye behind. They'll send a small force by mid-day to make the exchange."

Koro stood silent for a moment, unmoving. "Tell me, what did you find at Arvynian, Colonel?"

"Nothing," replied the Nirali. "Nothing but silence."

Koro returned his gaze to the map. "Let them come."

Raevin's eyes narrowed. "What did you do, Koro?"

"They will be broken," the Thjodhild replied. "Their spirits will be dead, prepared for us. We shall finish this, once and for all."

Raevin's chest heaved, the containment of his anger becoming increasingly difficult. "Yeah, it's about time you stepped up and did it yourself."

Koro showed no reaction, simply folding the map in silence as the comment passed over him. "Come, Nirali," he rumbled. "You must see this." He moved toward a door near the rear of the foyer, next to a marble pillar.

Raevin obeyed, following the Thjodhild down a slippery, dank flight of circular stairs. They passed many doors on their way, but their destination proved to be at the bottom, where the stairwell terminated in a dark, damp room of stone, lit only by a single flickering sconce. Valin hung in shackles on the far side of the wall, his diminutive stature preventing his feet from touching the floor. His scythe was propped beside him, projecting an image of light that showed an old and clearly enraged human, like a ghost hovering in the air.

"Koro!" the projection snarled. "Release me!"

"This is Varsa Drell," Koro introduced coldly. "An old ally."

"We had a deal!" the sorcerer shrieked. "I brought you the girl. Unlock this weapon and give me a body, as you promised!"

"The Dreamer promised you such," Koro rumbled. "She is misguided. I will give you no such gift."

"What?" Drell growled incredulously; his voice was slathered in genuine surprise, raspy and light. "Koro, I saved your people! I destroyed my body to facilitate this crusade! Where is the Dreamer? Let me speak with her!"

"Yer a special type o' moron," Valin groaned weakly. "He's not gonna give ye shit, Drell. Yer as dead as I am, ye daft arse o' a wizard."

Drell's glance hopped between Valin and the Thjodhild. "Koro-"

Koro silenced the sorcerer with a wave, sending the projection tumbling back into the scythe. "These two will die after the Dreamer is woken."

"Why wait?" Raevin said, cocking an eyebrow. "Mercy is unlike you."

"We must always keep our assets close, child, until we find our destiny," Koro thundered, wheeling around. He pounded on the stone wall, sending an echo cascading up the stairs. Two Thjodhild knights appeared within seconds. "Keep them here," their commander ordered. "All three of them."

"What?" Raevin hissed. "Koro, I am the Military Magistrate! I am a part of this fight!"

"You should be dead, and thus I cannot trust you at your word," Koro snapped in reply. "You will assume command in time. Patience, child." The Thjodhild commander thumped up the stairs before any retort could be given, leaving the Nirali Colonel helpless.

"Ed, this is unnerving," Alauren said, clearly disturbed by the silent farms. Her armor and shield jangled in the still air and echoed off the vacant plains, joining in with the cacophonic clanking of the rest of the party as they moved ever forward. She could take a small comfort in their numbers, at least, as nearly one hundred Norts marched behind them, Ronnok, Eira, Arvid and Harald foremost among them. "It's like everyone just got up and left."

"They did, likely," Edlevin confirmed with a nod. "They took the animals and retreated to the city. They're preparing for a siege."

"Indeed," Ronnok concurred. "We have them worried."

"I don't know, Edlevin," Alauren said shakily, peering at the farmhouses. "You see the windows? Boarded up and sealed. There was real work put into locking this place down." She looked over the empty streets, feeling her heart becoming bound in frost. "This looks…"

The blacksmith trailed off, finding herself standing in a different time, a different place, beholding a familiar memory as if she stood physically within a time gone by. Teth suddenly bled in and surrounded her, its buildings burned and its square empty while the cold wind cut through her flesh as it whistled by. Her breath was short, shallow, coming and going with every rapid thump of her quivering heart. She blinked, an action which seemed to last an eternity; the knights of the Thjodhild appeared as her eyelids rose, waiting for her to come to them, to find the grim work of their hand, and to find her soul shaken by those macabre deeds. In the recollection, she found a striking similarity to her present, a realization that sent a chill through her spine: this emptiness had been seen before. She gritted her teeth and looked down for a moment, forcibly ripping herself from the echo of the past.

"They likely had soldiers come out during the last few nights and prepare the town," the old soldier said, his voice bleeding back in; it seemed that hardly a second had passed while the smith was lost in her own mind, her momentary drift unnoticed by her companions. "They are a smart enemy."

"Which means they are a dangerous one," Ronnok thrummed. "One we should not underestimate. Be on guard, until we find our prey."

It wouldn't matter, for they were found first.

"halt!?" A voice called, stepping out into the street, dressed in full plate. "You Are not welcome. you must leave." His voice was shaky and unsure behind his concealing helm.

"We are here to make an exchange," Ronnok replied. "The girl for the Dwarf. Let us through."

"That is not Possible?" the man demanded. "leave the girl and Go or die."

Edlevin cocked an eyebrow from beneath his helm. "Are you alright, son?"

"it Is not Your concern," the man trilled. "very Well. You have made your choice!"

He drew his weapon, which prompted the Norts to do the same. "You've lost your mind, Nirali," Ronnok snarled.

The man only huffed. There was a still silence for a moment, but the peace was not to last.

"Edlevin, do you hear that?" Alauren muttered. There was shuffling coming from inside the houses, growing in volume.

"I do," the old soldier rumbled with a growing urgency, the shuffling turning to quickly to violent banging as he spoke. "Fall in, now!" he screamed. The Norts obeyed instantly, forming a shield wall on either side of the ranks. The order was given in the nick of time, for the farmhouse doors flung open just as the last of the blockers came together.

Men and women, civilians, poured out of the houses, each with bloodshot eyes and pale skin. They were hardly armored and armed only with the sharp objects from their homes, yet they charged with a righteous fury, showing only cold determination in their actions despite a clear terror in their eyes.

"Fall in!" Ronnok ordered. "Close the wall! Tighter!"

The seasoned Nort warriors obeyed with haste, collapsing into the smallest circular formation they could muster.

"Edlevin, what-" Alauren began, finding herself near the center of the formation.

"Not now!" the old soldier scolded. "Focus!"

The blacksmith nodded and swallowed hard as the first wave struck the wall in front of her. She chose to keep low, in a half crouch, watching for any potential breaches rather than engaging directly. Edlevin, meanwhile, shoved his sword through a gap, eliciting a bloodcurdling scream from an older woman, who reeled back with tears in her eyes.

Peeking through the gaps, Alauren caught glimpses of humans with matted hair slamming against the wall, shortly before screeches of terror and pain would crack the air as the combatants fell to cleave and stab alike.

"Brìga!" Harald yelled from the back. "Breach!"

"ARVID!" Ronnok screamed. "Lì!"

The large Nort obeyed, letting his clanmates collapse to plug the hole that was left in the formation before running off to assist.

Alauren could do little but wait behind the wall of warriors, her breath uneven and ragged, though she was able to maintain some semblance of calm. She stood ready to act, if needed, but she could hardly reach past the Norts before her prospective target had already slammed and died against the seemingly impenetrable shields. It was to her surprise, then, that a small child of eleven or twelve years found his way under the wall, scrambling on his hands and knees amidst the bloody chaos, unnoticed in the violent fracas around him. "Are you alright?" said the smith, approaching slowly and cautiously in a careful shuffle.

The child looked curiously to the woman with a half-open mouth and bloodshot eyes. His brow furrowed and his head tilted, as if he couldn't make sense of what she had said, like a puppy attempting to interpret an unknown command. Abruptly, the curiosity was overtaken by a grimace of terrified confusion that took Alauren aback, even in the midst of a battle. Fear, often, is something clearly visible and easily recognizable to those who were experienced in its grasp, and the boy proved to be no exception for the smith.

"Hey," Alauren said with a soothing, calm tone, shuffling closer. "I can help-"

The child launched himself like a ballista, plowing the top of his head into the blacksmith's chestplate. Alauren, mid-step and off balance, couldn't help but fall onto her back with a yelp.

The boy procured a blade from his tunic, a small kitchen knife, and stabbed down hard on Alauren's chest. Her armor deflected the blow easily and sent it careening towards her left shoulder, where the tip found a narrow gap between the scales and plunged in. After a moment, the smith's mind broke free of the shock and confusion, only to be met with a sharp, stinging pain that radiated from the wound as the point of the weapon broke through the leather and punctured her skin. The child pressed ever harder and waggled the blade around, rending and lacerating the little flesh that it could touch.

Alauren punched the boy hard in the face, knocking loose a few of his teeth, but the heavy blow seemed to bother him no more than the bite of a mosquito. He pressed the knife down harder, trying vainly to force it through the gap.

Abruptly, the child was pulled from her and launched beyond the shield wall, tumbling through the air like a ragdoll.

"Get up, girl!" Eira screamed, hauling the blacksmith to her feet. "Get up and fight!"

Alauren grit through the lingering pain and got her bearings. All around, the Nort defensive wall had collapsed under the sheer pressure of the assault. Corpses, dozens upon dozens, lay piled around unevenly, enclosing the Northmen in a ring of gore. It was as if the entire town had been rallied to a mass suicide, for they seemed to care little for their own lives as they dove into combat with lumbering gaits and crazed attacks.

Alauren acted swiftly, picking a target that had breached the lines. The man, along with several others, was focused on a single Nort warrior who had lost grip of her sword; she bashed them away repeatedly with her shield, struggling to cover all of her angles, hoping for the eventual assistance of one of her clanmates.

The smith closed the distance quickly, unnoticed, and plunged her blade hard through the man's back, into his heart. He retched moistly before expiring, and he slid neatly from the sword as he slumped and fell forward.

Another Arvynian moved in, stabbing down with a shortsword. The blacksmith reacted quickly, raising her blade vertically and using her bracer to deflect the incoming attack to the right. A breath after the enemy's blade went tumbling, she brought her sword back down and slashed left, delivering a clean slice across the man's neck. He fell with a yelp and a spray of blood, and was still after a few moments of writhing.

The Nort woman gave the smith a curt nod of thanks as she finished off her own prey, the last of the group, with a cleave to the skull.

Alauren, taking the chance to grab a few hasty breaths, surveyed the scene. The bodies piled all around, mostly human, with Norts numbering in the dozens succumbing to the unyielding assault; the crazed innocents swarmed and crawled over the much larger warriors, quite like ants dragging their prey to the ground, each Northmen life they were able to extinguish requiring the sacrifice of a multitude. The Arvynians, despite the growing numbers of their losses, were still pouring from the houses, seemingly endless hordes of wailing farmers and merchants erupting from the doors.

"Edlevin!" cried the blacksmith, trying to find her friend in the confusion. Her eyes rested upon him after a moment, locked in combat with the armored Nirali who had spoken to them.

"Look at you!" the old soldier shrieked, deflecting a stab from the man with his shield. He was enraged in a way that the blacksmith had never seen before; his posture was hunched and aggressive, and there was little left of the typical calm with which he carried himself. "Mindless! Enthralled! Robbed of your rest!" He took advantage of an opening, punching the enemy hard in the helmet.

Alauren's view was suddenly blocked by Ronnok and Eira collapsing into a back-to-back formation. "Girl!" screamed the Chieftain. "Kill!"

Alauren nodded, picking another target, a young woman wielding a maul. The smith approached the enemy directly, meaning to use the foe's slow, untrained movements to her advantage.

The woman swung the axe clumsily to her right, a high blow which Alauren easily and deftly dodged under, feeling a rush of air as the weapon's edge sailed over her head. The smith, after a single, patient breath, sliced out and to her left, a strike that slashed the stumbling woman's belly, spilling her guts. Alauren stepped forward calmly and arced her blade upwards, continuing her motion.

The Arvynian woman's scream of pain was quickly and mercifully ended by a backwards, over the shoulder stab to the chest, puncturing her heart. The blacksmith let the enemy slide off of her blade, trying and failing to avoid being disturbed by the soft vibrations in the hilt as the edge dragged against flesh and bone.

Alauren, taking a few ragged, adrenaline-filled breaths, heard a noise behind her, a scuffling of feet, and wheeled to find another figure looking to face her.

It was the child once more, standing ready to engage, blood dribbling from his mouth and dripping off of his chin.

Alauren squared herself to the enemy, shaking her head. "Don't. I can help you."

The child's remaining teeth began to chatter wildly, but he gave no other answer.

The smith's shoulders sagged. She held herself low, readying to defend against the much shorter target. She silently pleaded with it to back off, to run, to do anything other than try to assault her.

The gaze that was returned to the woman was as helpless as it was fearful. The boy's eyes would strain to one side, then another, like he was futilely commanding his body to disengage and flee. His physical form, though, seemed as if it served the will of another, a sick puppeteer who would allow no such retreat.

The boy leapt up, snarling even as his eyes pleaded for mercy. There was none to be found, for Alauren's shield bashed him to the ground with little restraint.

The child struggled to rise, but little more hesitation could be found within the smith. Drowned entirely by instinct and adrenaline, accompanied by the cold realization of necessity, she did what this war demanded of her.

Alauren dropped onto one knee and stabbed down hard with closed, quivering eyes, grinding her teeth at a sickly feeling that seemed to emanate from her blade as it struck true. The boy retched and choked, but was mercifully silenced under the skillful placement of the sword's tip after a few protracted seconds.

The smith stood shakily, not daring to look at the ground. Instead, she surveyed her surroundings with heavy breaths and wild eyes, trying to keep her focus elsewhere while she slid her sword out of her deceased target.

She was greeted with the dying din of battle, the hundreds that once inhabited Arvynian finally being fully extinguished under the skilled blades of the Norts. Bodies lay strewn about, some still desperately gasping for life, while others faded into the dark with frantic screams of terror. Wails of agony joined in as the world became less blurry, forming a vile orchestra of suffering that fluttered across the open plains of the commune and beyond.

The cacophonic melody was forever gravened in the minds of those who had borne witness, and though the fight had been one of a mere few minutes, it was the bloodiest that many of the combatants had ever seen, something far beyond war, far beyond even what the darkest of nightmares could conjure. Alauren pushed the distress away, for a single thought began to dominate her mind.

Edlevin.

Finding the human proved to be simple, as his enraged voice carried easily over the suffering din of the battlefield. He screamed hoarsely at the armored Nirali he had been dueling; the enemy was now pinned under his leg, and Edlevin had managed to rip the man's helmet from his head. Heavy punches were repeatedly delivered by the old soldier, barbaric bludgeons that had little, if any, restraint behind them.

"WHY?" Edlevin thundered, knocking one of the man's teeth loose with a heavy strike to the lower jaw. He suddenly ripped his own helm from his head to reveal a maddened, enraged glare below his sweat-drenched forehead. "Why the *FUCK* would you let them do this?"

"Karlmaðr," Alauren said, approaching cautiously.

The words went unheard as Edlevin shook the man roughly, gripping him by the shoulders with intensely tunneled vision. Spittle flew from the mouth of the old soldier, sticking upon his stubble as he screamed in the face of the other Nirali. "They took everything from you! Your duty! Your honor!" He struck the man once again, cracking his nose in more than one place. "Your peace!"

"P... P... Please..." the man blubbered desperately.

"Edlevin!" Alauren snapped.

The only response was another merciless fist to the Nirali soldier's face.

"Hey!" yelped the smith, physically moving between her friend and the conquered enemy. "Enough! It's over!"

"No!" Edlevin growled, wheeling and shoving her away violently as he rocketed to his feet. "It is not!"

Alauren barely kept her footing, wide-eyed with shock as she stumbled heavily backwards. She locked eyes with her old friend, yet saw someone unfamiliar looking back, a stranger whose maddened glare tore through her like a volley of arrows. This man was shattered, angry, inconsolable, a revenant of pain inhabiting a sunken shell, with no effort to hide the agony that ripped through his veins. He was hunched, snarling, heaving with ragged, bestial breath, existing as something that barely seemed human in the moment.

"We have but one thing to look forward to after all the strife of life, blacksmith, our peace in death, in our rest!" snarled the old soldier. He spread his arms wide. "Look around you. These people, *innocent people*, have had that stolen from them!" His voice became low and grinding, breaking more than once as he ranted, and several heavy points of his finger were delivered towards the mortally wounded man on the ground in order to accentuate the coming words.

"The Nirali, like him, abided this atrocity!"

"There was…" the Nirali soldier said, still prone and clutching his belly tightly. "…silence. Peace. Now, I can't Go!" Tears ran down his cheeks, falling lightly into the dust of the road. "they told me I could Serve again. I could return to peace when I died again." He removed his hand from his gut, revealing a nasty stab wound which bled uncontrollably. "No? I can't go Yet! I have work to Be done. There is A duty. It Must be done… i…?"

His voice trailed off and his eyes went empty; he succumbed to the dark with a final, rattling breath, the fear never leaving his face.

Edlevin's gaze softened as he watched the man fade away. He knelt beside his fallen foe and removed a shim of metal from the inside of the armor. Without a word, he placed it into his side pack and stood.

"Edlevin," Alauren quaked, both in body and voice. "Who was that?"

Edlevin pointed to the dead Nirali questioningly, regaining his calm with great (and visible) difficulty.

"No, not him," Alauren replied shakily. "Whoever made that momentary appearance in your body."

Edlevin's eyes shifted their gaze beyond the horizon, staring into nothing, his face pale and expressionless. "It was me, Ally," he said amidst the deepest of sighs. "It was just the man Niralan made me, instead of the one I want to be. I'm sorry."

"Ed?" Alauren murmured, her voice still quivering heavily. "Are you alright?"

Edlevin sighed deeply, still looking far beyond his old friend. "No, Ally, I'm not. Are you?"

Alauren flinched as the pangs of pain from her wound surfaced above the rapidly draining adrenaline. "A shallow stab to the shoulder. I'll be fine." She looked over the carnage, wincing at the piles of death that engulfed her. "Physically, anyway. What the *fuck,* Edlevin?"

The old soldier looked down at his shaking hands. "Ally, I'm…" He trailed off. "I'm done."

"What?" Alauren asked, shaking her head. "What do you mean?"

"I can't do this anymore," Edlevin muttered. He collapsed to a sitting position and curled into a ball, gripping his legs as best he could in his armor. His eyes were sunken into the depths of despair, heavy, staring absently into nothing at all. "I've seen enough. I'm done."

Alauren said nothing. She knelt next to her old friend and hugged him closely. The tears poured forth as freshly branded memories sizzled in their minds, though their sobs could barely be heard above the unending screaming of the blood-soaked battlefield. Exhaustion overtook them; their hearts and bodies quivered while their lungs were robbed of air, and they felt as if their muscles could turn to liquid within them at any moment. Grief dominated them, grinding their stoic souls to a cloud of dust that seemed to blow away with the wind.

Alauren, after some time, took a deep breath, steadying herself as she caught her breath. With great effort, she spoke. "What are you done with, Ed? Me? The Norts? Valin?"

"The enduring nightmare of my life," Edlevin grumbled, staring blankly beyond the horizon. "Sorrow upon sorrow and pain upon pain. It needs to end. I want peace. I want to rest."

"Me, too," murmured the smith. "But Ed, you've spent the better part of a morn telling me that I have something to fight for, a will to live that I just had to dig out of the mud, another home to be found."

"I was wrong," the old soldier stated flatly. "Just like always…"

"Bullshit!" Alauren chirped, doing her best to regain her strength. "Look around you. The Thjodhild need to pay for this with every drop of their repulsive blood." Her voice went dark as something deep within her heart cast long shadows over her words. "This is going to end with their heads on pikes, Ed."

Edlevin huffed a pained laugh and shook his head. "Lost to a fantasy of violence, just like I was. It will lead you right to where I am, eventually. It is inevitable."

"Fantasy?" Alauren replied incredulously. "Ed, this violence is *very* real, whether we want it to be or not. Are we to simply lay down and die?"

"Easier that way," the old soldier grunted gruffly.

"Hardly," scoffed the smith. "Xen talked about the Thjodhild using the dead, and I think we just witnessed indisputable proof." She sighed deeply and fought off a sudden bout of nausea, running a gauntleted hand through her hair as she held back the bile in her stomach. "Edlevin, they made me kill a child."

The old soldier's blank gaze turned quickly to the smith. "You…

You what?"

"A boy. Human. He's the one that stabbed me." She looked at her old friend with steely, unfeeling eyes. "They used him as a weapon of war, Ed. They have to die. All of them."

"Ally, I…" Edlevin trailed off, meeting his old friend's hollow stare. He could find no more words, and instead hugged the woman tightly as more tears flooded forth. They sat for a while, sobbing, clutching each other tightly in an ocean of the dead.

"Karlmaðr," Alauren said after a while. "You've been my strength for so long, but you need to find that same strength for yourself, now. There is a will within you to continue. Find it."

Edlevin's gaze fell to the ground. "I'm not sure I can, Ally." He shook his head, closing his eyes. "I'm so tired."

Alauren nodded. "I've seen thousands of sunrises, more than my memory can possibly hold. But, for the first time, I feel my age. I understand."

The old soldier shook his head. "Not quite. Imagine how that age and that weight feels when you've seen so many fewer sunrises. Nearly all those dawns were filled to the brim with terror and death. I'm beginning to think that my greatest mistake, for all of my years, was thinking it could be escaped."

"It can't be," the blacksmith agreed softly. "The world is changing around us, Edlevin. The greatest empire in the north has fallen. The dead walk, desecrating themselves without even knowing it. It seems that even the air has taken a sour taste as of late, as if the winds themselves are growing deadly."

Edlevin nodded silently.

"Life will be difficult for us," Alauren continued. "I understand that. I accept it. Odenseye is moving beyond what we were. We have a choice, now, to change ourselves with it or to be left alone and scared in a world we cannot recognize, dead or enslaved within death. For all our desires of peace, the moment calls for justice."

"The girl is right, Karlmaðr," Ronnok rumbled, approaching with weary eyes. "We did not take you in simply because you needed a home. You showed us kindness where fear was warranted. You behaved with practicality in a world where such a trait is increasingly absent." He sighed, wiping blood from his hands with a cloth. "You are who you need to be. This is valuable."

"We need you to fight," Alauren said. "Find strength in the people around you. You've always told me that."

Edlevin nodded once more.

"Valin needs us. The Norts need us. Your people need us," the smith continued. "You can't say no to that any more than I can. You are needed."

Edlevin sat for a while, staring beyond the horizon, but eventually rose with a sigh. "You're right, of course," he relented. "I can't let these people be condemned to something worse than death. Evil abided is evil itself, as we've recently heard."

"Good to hear it, old man," Alauren thrummed, similarly rising to her feet. "Keep the nightmares behind and persevere."

Edlevin nodded. "One more step."

"Karlmaðr," Ronnok said, coldly suppressing his disgust at the gore surrounding him as he waded through. "I need you now. Come." He walked to the entrance of a farmhouse, whose door had been splintered off its hinges and scattered around the threshold.

After a moment, Edlevin hurried to the entrance, finding a single, black-robed man sitting in the middle of a dirt floor, facing away. On a table nearby, a dead woman with a knife jutting from her chest lay prone, her eyes only partially bloodshot.

The old soldier circled the mysterious figure, inspecting him closely. His hands, contorted into stiff claws, twitched uncontrollably, as if each thin, bony finger was coursing with pain. He wore a concealing black hood, under which a wide mouth breathed in and out erratically, sending a fog billowing forth with every exhale. He smelled strongly of mildew, though the source of the odor was nowhere to be found.

"Who is he?" Edlevin asked.

"We do not know," Ronnok replied. "He will not respond to us, and even Arvid cannot remove him from his place. It's as if he's attached to the ground itself." He sighed and shrugged. "He wants to speak to the 'Savage Nirali'. His words."

Edlevin nodded, circled a few more times, and knelt. The man's square jaw was painted purple, and a beard grew in small patches here and there, unkempt and encrusted with blood.

"Who are you?" asked the old soldier "Thjodhild?"

"No," the man replied curtly. His voice was reserved, quiet, yet the acidic bite within seemed to melt the armor from Edlevin's body.

"Nirali, then?" the soldier questioned.

"Once, yet no longer," the man growled, rolling back his hood. His eyes were a deep purple, remarkably milky and speckled by shining pins of white, looking akin to the clusters of stars that smudged the night sky. "They made me more."

Edlevin betrayed no emotion, delivering his words calmly in a flat deadpan. "So then, what are you?"

"A servant of a pure world," the man replied. "An Anointed. The Thjodhild showed me visions of the coming paradise, a place free of any but those undying. We would not fight wars against Elysia, or anyone else, and our people would prosper under the rightful rule of the Old Lords. There will be a cleansing, of course, but a glorious world will be borne upon it, the bodies of the unworthy fertilizing the fields of the future."

"And you believed them?" Edlevin asked incredulously. "Why?"

"We are weak," the man answered with a venomous chortle. "We die, all on our own, as our frail forms crumble in the tumultuous weather of existence. The Thjodhild, however, have lived for eons. They are greater than any mortal alive, true gods of another age. Who else but gods could make the dead walk, and extend that precious power to the undeserving young?"

Edlevin shook his head in disbelief. "You desecrated these people so those bastards could commit genocide? I can't imagine even Karsus, for all his flaws, would allow that."

"This is the truth," the man replied calmly, words which visibly surprised the old soldier. "Karsus is but a servant, a tool for a greater purpose, like me. He will bend to the will of the gods, whether he deems it fit to or not."

Edlevin smirked. "I see. He doesn't know the extent of all this, does he?"

The man returned the smirk in kind. "No. When the time comes, all of us will help to transcend the world to its natural, beautiful existence." He splayed out his arms, gesturing wildly, like a devout Priest delivering a bombastic sermon. "The Thjodhild, glorious gods, have granted the power of resurrection, the power that brought these people to be loyal servants, to any who would submit to the Dreamer's will. Through that power we will see the vision of our masters to a successful conclusion. Through us, the Dreamer guides the action of those risen by our hand, ever toward a world of life."

Edlevin cackled madly. "Life? You call this life?" He pointed to the woman on the table. "It's nothing more than servitude, rewarded with torment. You've condemned them."

The man laughed loudly, a cold, raspy sound. "You act as if it is forced. I call them back from the void, and they choose whether to answer." He tilted his head toward the woman. "She refused."

"And the rest of them?" questioned the old soldier. "Did they understand what you were asking of them? Did they understand the price? Did they even know they were dead?"

The man grunted lightly. "Does it matter? We dangled life in front of them, and these wretched children snatched it like the ravenous, wild dogs they are." He grinned wickedly. "We of the young races value life, even our temporary jest of an existence, above all. Our masters see beyond that, and that is why they will inherit the new world. That is why each of the risen who lay outside deserved to di-"

His words were interrupted by a spray of blood, black and runny, accompanied by a gurgle as his head separated from his shoulders. Edlevin recoiled from the mist for a moment but snapped his eyes back forward quickly.

"Enjoy your new world, you piece of shit," Alauren growled, her armor freshly painted with viscera. She kicked the man's decapitated head across the room like a ball and roughly shoved his body prone with her foot. "We need to move as soon as we can."

"Our losses have been heavy," Ronnok stated, leaning on the doorframe, content to watch until now. "Only a few dead, but many injured. To fight humans, we could risk taking seventy men. For Thjodhild..." He trailed off. "We only have about thirty fit to fight."

Edlevin shook his head and rose to his feet. "I don't know if that's enough. How did we not see this coming?" He rumbled an indistinct growl, visibly frustrated with himself. "Why didn't Xendra warn us, for that matter?"

"We have not heard from her since last she departed," the Chieftain replied. "Given what we've seen, we must assume she is dead, captured, or treacherous." He shook his head, similarly irritated with himself. "The Thjodhild surprised us. We assumed that even they had limits to their depravity. We should not have done so."

"Their secrecy and the element of surprise has been their advantage," Alauren pointed out. "They're in the light now. We can't waste this opportunity. We need to get them outside of the walls." She took a deep breath and chewed her lower lip, holding back an ocean of rage that surged from the deepest abyss within. "They have to die, and they have to die today."

Ronnok nodded in full agreement. "There will be no better opportunity for blood repaid. We are with you."

CHAPTER THIRTY-SEVEN:

FALL

*"I alone can fix it" is the final
cry of the confident fool.*

– Nirali proverb

The air was crisp and clear as the small cadre of Northmen approached the city gates, though there was an ever-hanging twinge of burnt flesh carried along with the wind. The carved black walls of Anduras rose far above the trees that flanked them, and the white towers of stone rose, in turn, far above them. The city was quiet, oddly so, with nary a sound escaping from beyond the great gates that towered above. Even the birds seemed afraid to announce their presence for fear of the coming bloodshed.

"Have they seen us?" Alauren asked.

"They have," Ronnok replied. "The smoke plumes from the pyres at Arvynian will be seen across the island. They know we survived."

"Still, either voices or arrows should be coming from those towers," the smith pointed out. "What are they doing?"

"Calculating," Edlevin rumbled from under his helm. "They know they're safe. They want us to make the first move. We'll need to get creative."

"Fine," Alauren grunted. She stepped forward, careful not to stray too far from the protection of the Norts. Even as her determination moved her along, her heart fluttered with adrenaline and anxiety, and each step blended together into a single, focused moment in time. "Thjodhild!" blared the smith, her voice echoing in the eerie silence. "You've been after me for too long, sending others to do your bidding. We've killed them all." She spread her arms wide. "Now I'm at your doorstep. As we speak, we burn all that you left behind in your commune. What food you have is all you will get for the duration of our siege."

Only the whistling of the wind replied. The blacksmith took a breath, letting the acrid odor in the air fuel her anger.

"We are battered and bloodied, horrified by what we have seen and done," she continued. "The Eldari told us what you want, to purify the world. Our goals are similar. If you hide, if you allow my existence, I will spend every moment of my life annihilating your very bloodlines. The grey mucous that flows through you will run as rivers to the oceans, and your people will join all those you slaughtered in the dark abyss." She cackled madly. "Your fate awaits. Come out and be cut down like the weeds you are." After a wicked smile, held for a few moments, she wheeled back around and returned to the lines.

"Rousing," Edlevin praised with a chuckle and a smirk.

"I just went with insane bravado," Alauren replied. "I think I did pretty well."

"We'll see," said the old soldier. "Just be alert."

For a while, silence was the sole answer, broken only by the whipping of the wind and the occasional shuffle atop the walls. A voice would echo from the towers now and again, speaking softly before cackling with subdued laughter.

"ïptyr!" Eira yelled suddenly. "Behind!"

Alauren wheeled, finding a line of heavily armored Thjodhild fading in as if they had materialized from thin air, with a few knights thundering to fill a gap that had been intentionally left in the road, big enough for the invading band to march through. They closed ranks around the Northmen war party quickly, forming a half-circle that terminated at the city's walls. Each enemy held towering, rectangular shields, shimmering a rustic gold color in the sun.

"Edlevin?" Alauren muttered with unease. "Were they there the whole time?"

"Probably," Edlevin stated flatly. "We've made one mistake too many, I think."

"It's as bad as it looks?" asked the blacksmith.

"Yeah, Ally," the old soldier said through a debilitating quiver in his voice. His breath was heavy and ragged, and his eyes, barely visible through the slats of his helm, were glossed over, lost in memory. "It is."

"Brave," a voice thundered from atop the city gate. "I almost admire it."

Alauren recognized it instantly as Koro, igniting her heart with fury. Hatred was a new feeling to her, carried into her mind on the wings of anguish, yet she felt no resistance to the dark thoughts that the sound of the knight conjured. His death was a necessity, a just punishment, and it would come.

"However, the long epoch of the night has ended," continued the Thjodhild. "Dawn brightens, and our march can begin in full! The end of our exodus has come!"

On cue, the shield-bearing knights planted their blockers, forming a concave wall. Slowly and steadily, step by step, they pushed forward, perfectly synchronized in their movements.

Koro leaped from the one of the towers, landing behind his troops with a thunderous impact that sent vibrations through the ground and dust fluttering into the air.

"Rìg Vall!" Ronnok cried. "Fall in!"

The Norts reacted instantly, creating a small bulge against the main gate with their shields. Edlevin and Alauren were pushed to the back by the larger Northmen, having only just enough room to stand.

Surprisingly, the Thjodhild stopped. They held their ground, keeping their own wall seamless as the air fell still, leaving a hanging silence for a few elongated moments.

"Your tactics are admirable, effective," Koro yelled from behind the enemy shield wall. "We have learned from you, and your ways of war shall help deliver us upon the golden roads of paradise."

"Are you sure those roads are golden?" Alauren taunted, spitting her words with a caustic bite. "Or is it the sun's reflection from the armored corpses that litter the ground?"

Koro did not respond. Instead, he barked a single order to the gathered knights. "Forward!"

Alauren, finally, found a better view through a small gap near the front of the Nort wall. The enemy shields had begun to move forward again, inch by inch, step by step. The knights kept each towering blocker together firmly, gapless, their discipline immaculate and well-refined. When the contracting wall would grow too small to accommodate every soldier, one Thjodhild would silently slip out while his comrades closed to cover the gap in an instant.

"Edlevin?" Alauren huffed. "What are they doing?"

The old soldier's breath was heavy, ragged, and his head was practically sunken into his shoulders. His single word was delivered with a cold, matter-of-fact surety, disturbing and unsettling.

"Winning."

With the word, the Thjodhild wall finally impacted upon the Northmen. Contrary to what was expected, the hit was soft, barely making a ripple in the solid Nort formation. Alauren readied, waiting for the telltale sounds of bloodshed to start trickling through as combat erupted.

Such sounds never came. The eerie silence of the battlefield was filled only with the clanking of armor.

"Push!" Koro commanded.

The Thjodhild obeyed, pressing against the seemingly immovable Northmen wall with the full brunt of their might. The Norts in the front, Arvid and Ronnok among them, grunted in equal parts strain and pain, overpowered in strength by the colossal knights that faced them. The feet of the Northmen slid back in the dirt, as the ground below proved quite unable to hold in place the iron wills that battled above.

There was a loud *crack* on the right flank as a Nort warrior's shield splintered to pieces under the sustained pressure. Before any of his clanmates could act, the Thjodhild wall opened and the Northman was pulled through the gap like a child being towed by his mother, his scream of surprise silenced soon after.

Eira plugged the hole as soon as she snapped to her senses, pressing hard against the unyielding shields that towered above.

"Edlevin?" Alauren yelped desperately. The free space had begun to close, pressing her tightly against the wood and metal of the door, her position at the rear of the formation becoming tight and claustrophobic.

"Just push, Ally!" screamed the old soldier. "Help them!"

Try as she might, Alauren could not find a way to support the warriors around her. The collapsing wall took away any room to maneuver, and more space seemed to be lost by the breath. Another Nort's shield gave way to the pressure; he fell behind the enemy wall, causing the Nort lines to shrink and force the smith even further against the door.

"Edlevin!" she shrieked as panic overtook her. "Edlevin, help!"

No answer came. Another Nort was pulled out and the pressure increased, again and again.

"I... I can't..." Alauren sputtered. "I can't breathe! Edlevin!"

The light seemed to grow dimmer with every word, blocked out by the towering Norts around her as well as a growing, heavy darkness in her eyes.

The Nirali Colonel could do little in the dim light of the dungeon save frantically searching his thoughts for a solution, for some way to recover from his miscalculation. The Thjodhild guards, pressed against the far wall near the stairs, stood perfectly still, like great statues of bronze, presumably watching his every move. Their chests didn't heave with breath, nor did their muscles twitch with fatigue. They were always watchful, always ready to move at the slightest provocation.

A mistake had been made. His presence hadn't allowed a deception at all, it simply made the Thjodhild more vigilant, more suspicious, as he had been warned. Without him, the Norts were as good as dead, and the sinking feeling plunging ever downward in his gut was a firm reminder of how little he truly knew of his enemy.

"Dwarf," Raevin whispered, pushing the dread away and kneeling next to the dangling Priest. "I've heard you can move yourself from one place to another with a thought. I need that now."

"Not me…" Valin groaned, nodding weakly towards the scythe. "Him, and he can't."

"No talking," growled one of the knights.

"Not with them here," the Dwarf finished.

Raevin winced. "Yeah. Figures." He sighed and bit into his lower lip, keeping his mind focused on his duty rather than the uncomfortable details of what it likely entailed. "I'll take care of it."

"Nirali!" the knight snapped angrily. "No. Talking."

"I'm going get you out of here, Dwarf," Raevin said aloud. "As soon as these idiots get themselves killed by the Northmen."

The knight moved forward and roughly grabbed the Nirali by the shoulder, meaning to tow him backwards.

Raevin, with a smirk at the Dwarf, wheeled wildly. He procured a small dagger, serrated and straight, from the inside of his belt. He plunged the razor's edge into a gap in the Thjodhild's neck armor without hesitation, pressing it as far into flesh as it would go.

The knight stood in silence for a moment, letting his putrid gray blood pour from the fresh wound to slather Raevin's hand. Unfazed by the pain, he ripped the human to the side, throwing him at the wall with force.

The Nirali, though, held firm to the ridged leather handle of the blade; as he was tossed, so too did his dagger move, rending the Thjodhild's neck with its serration. A single blink later, Raevin hit the wall with force, impacting shoulder-first just beside the Dwarf.

Crack!

Bolts of pain shot through the Colonel's chest, waves of agony that made it feel as if his body had split in half. His head, thankfully, had been spared by the cushioning of the stout Priest's belly, though the impact ripped the air from the lungs of both prisoners. Raevin maintained consciousness, rolled himself over and surveyed his handiwork, struggling for every wheezing breath all the while.

The injured Thjodhild clutched his neck wound, feebly trying to stop the river of gray blood that escaped down a drain in the middle of the floor. He was crumpling into a stiff heap, wriggling in panic and terror as he gurgled profoundly.

The first knight's companion shook his head and chuckled. "Pathetic. Bested by a Nirali." He thundered to Raevin, picked him up, and launched him into the wall near the stairs.

Pop-crack!

The Colonel impacted leg-first, taking the brunt of the pressure on his left calf. Like a fresh birch branch, it splintered and shattered into multiple pieces without snapping completely; the damage spread out to foot and hip, tearing through the lower left of his body with an easily audible crunch.

Raevin shrieked in agony as he hit the ground. There was little time for anything further, for the knight grabbed him by the neck and held him well above the damp stones of the floor, upon which the wounded Thjodhild finally expired.

"You are strong willed and cunning," the armored titan complimented with a thrumming chuckle. "But you still break easily." His grip tightened, cutting off Raevin's breathing and causing his head to turn a pronounced indigo color. He brought the Nirali's face close to his helm, nearly touching the metal slats of the faceplate. "You spilled blood more valuable than your entire race." His grasp tightened further, threatening to crush the Colonel's windpipe like the exoskeleton of an insect. "I like how you die. Slow and panicked. Just like all your-"

A jet of grey blood scattered across Raevin's face. A blade had been driven up and through the guard's torso, the tip visibly jutting from the front of his neck, where it was wiggled and twisted violently. The knight gasped, the air knocked out of him, and he rapidly went limp. The strangling grip released, causing the Colonel to fall heavily to the floor.

"*Fuck*!" Raevin wailed. Though he was able to land on his one good shoulder, the vibrations of the impact made certain that his spiking agony was only slightly lessened.

"That was foolishly brave, Nirali," a voice said.

"Xendra?" the Colonel asked through heavily gritted teeth, attempting to ignore as much as the pain as was possible, his mind focused on his purpose. "I thought you'd be with the Norts."

"I went where I would be most effective," the Eldari replied, ripping her blade mercilessly from the limp body of the Thjodhild as it fell to the floor. "Making sure you kept your end of the bargain."

"In progress," Raevin muttered, hobbling onto his good leg. A burning sensation akin to molten metal seared his veins, seeming to spill onto exposed nerves with every one of his quaking movements. Each step was pure agony, but one more was taken, ever toward the Priest, ever toward the doing of his duty. "Dwarf," said the Colonel, "we need to go to the front gates. I need to retake my command."

"Drell can do it," Valin mumbled weakly. "You have t' take me weapon."

"Usually, I would advise against that," rumbled the Eldari. "Magical weapons are not to be trifled with, especially one with a living soul within. Now, though, you need to go help the girl. Koro must die."

Raevin hesitated. "What about you?"

"I'm going to be killing every fucking Thjodhild I can find," Xendra growled venomously. "You're in no shape to do so, and we need some chaos behind the lines since things have gone south."

Raevin eyed the scythe warily and sighed.

"It's Drell's choice who he burns, usually," Valin assured, his voice ever weaker, fading under the continued pain of his wounds. "He's pissed as can be, but not at ye. Take it."

Raevin's hand was hurtling towards the weapon before the Dwarf's sentence was finished. A radiating warmth ran up his hand as it gripped the ivory handle, and he could hear a faint voice whispering lightly, unintelligibly, into his ear. There was no burning, though, just a tingling that ran down his spine like charging cavalry.

"Dwarf is, this-?" the Colonel began, only to be interrupted by a flash of light. He abruptly found himself just inside the gates of Anduras, where the cacophony of a bloody struggle echoed through the air. "-normal?" the Nirali finished after a confused blink. He tossed the scythe down with an incredulous nod of thanks.

"Colonel?" a voice yelled from atop the doors, recognizable as a Major named Fara. "Is that you?"

"It is!" Raevin bellowed, wincing at the effort to project his voice. "Code: Dirlan one-seven-eight, eight-eight-one, four-four-three. This command is now mine alone."

The Major replied instantly. "Good to have you back, sir. Orders?"

"What's going on outside the gate?" Raevin asked. "Doesn't sound like a battle."

"Thjodhild are crushing them to jelly against the door!" Fara yelled boisterously. "I've never seen anything like it!"

"Open the gates!" the Colonel thundered urgently. "Now!"

"Sir, we can't," Fara replied tepidly. "The Thjodhild ordered us to keep them shut."

"Did I mumble?" Raevin countered in a harsh deadpan. "Who do you serve, Son of Niras?"

No response came, save for the rumble of the gates as they opened toward the stoic officer of the Nirali.

The darkness gave way to light, and the smith could breathe once more. The world was a blur for a moment; her vision twinkled like the night sky in front of cascading colors, yet she willed herself to rouse.

The Norts' shield wall had collapsed backwards, and the Thjodhild, in turn, had tumbled forward in surprise. The blacksmith had lost her own shield somewhere along the way, finding the bonds that held it to her arm severed cleanly.

Ronnok and Eira, ever ready, were already at work spilling blood during the confusion. Ronnok's axe cleaved one Thjodhild at the neck, decapitating him. The Chieftain punched the now-detached helm, sending it flying towards another enemy. Eira, moving like lightning, plunged her blade deep into a gap in the knight's belly armor as his arms rose instinctively to bat the helmet away. The Norts, though bearing the full brunt of bloodlust, made sure to carefully retreat further into the city as they fought, putting distance between themselves and the chaos.

Alauren was suddenly aware of shouting, two distinct voices, both strained and dire. The first was Koro, booming in the enclosed portcullis. "Regroup! On me!"

The second, far hoarser and more desperate, was Edlevin. "For *fuck's* sake, Ally!" shrieked the old soldier. "RUN!"

The smith's senses finally returned. She blinked the rest of the fog away, finding herself lying prone on her back.

A shadow loomed over her suddenly, a towering Thjodhild knight who had burst through the remaining Nort defenders, singly focused on his helpless prey. He raised his sword high and brought it down in an arc, leaving the blacksmith naught but a single breath before it cleaved her skull. She raised her wrist instinctively to block the blow, closing her eyes and gritting her teeth.

Clunk-Crack!

The sound echoed throughout the portcullis and into the streets. The Thjodhild's blade was deflected away, clanging as it was intercepted with a mere arm's length to spare before it struck true.

Harald, wounded badly in the chest, ditched his now-dented axe and snatched the Thjodhild's sword by the crossguard, ripping it away while plunging a dagger into the knight's shoulder. The Northman growled primally as the weapon was driven deeply into flesh, savoring the blood that spilled forth. He was shouldered away roughly, and, with a wink to the smith, he prepared to meet the Great Father.

The Thjodhild, leaking gray ichor and blinded by rage, changed his focus entirely to the faltering Nort. Harald delivered a few more clean blows, but his battle was a losing one as his breath faded more and more, taking punches and lacerations as the knight inflicted as much pain as possible upon the one who had dared spill his blood.

Alauren rose to her feet without further hesitation and sprinted down the cobblestone street, scrambling away from the violence with heaving breaths and wide eyes.

Ronnok, Eira, Arvid and Edlevin alone had made it to safety, a devastating blow to their already weakened force. Koro, meanwhile, rallied, missing no more than a handful of his knights. They closed ranks and set up a wedge formation in the safety of the portcullis, readying to move once again, seeking strength in numbers.

"What happened, Raevin?" Edlevin growled furiously. "You were supposed to hinder them, not us!"

The Colonel ignored the words entirely. "Nirali!" he thundered. "Drop the gates!"

His troops obeyed instantly, plunging the heavy iron doors down with a thundering boom, enclosing the Thjodhild within a makeshift prison.

Koro simply shook his helm, seeming no more concerned with the situation than a drunk who had just spilled a splash of ale onto a dirt floor. "The pup finally shows his teeth," he hissed with a potent annoyance. "My doubts were correct."

"Raevin?" Edlevin tremored unsurely. "What are you doing?"

"Something local," Raevin replied flatly. "Something out of protocol." He cupped his uninjured hand to his mouth and barked an order. "SAP, NOW! LIGHT 'EM UP!"

A number of loud bangs rang out, the sounds of axes impacting wood, to be swiftly followed by a viscous black liquid pouring like loose molasses through a few trapdoors in the roof of the portcullis. It covered the Thjodhild from head to toe, drenching them in inky ichor.

"What is this?" Koro snapped, inspecting the substance as it dripped over his arms.

A small leaf on the wind served as the sole answer, dropped from above by an unseen Nirali. It glowed brightly with an ember, while flames licked from every side, consuming it slowly. With a single touch of the fire upon the sable fluid, the midday shadows of the portcullis became a sun.

The Thjodhild fell into a mass of writhing agony. Their screams echoed off the walls of the mass crematorium, filling the air with an otherworldly howl that carried through the streets with haunting reverberations, making it seem as if the city itself was wailing in pain. Most of the ragtag group of allies could only look to the brutality with wide eyes and gaping jaws, beholding the awe-inspiring end of their mighty enemies. Alauren, however, focused intently on a single silhouette inside the inferno.

Koro still stood. Even as the flaming shadowbeech sap ran over him, even as his armor beaded into liquid, he towered like a golem of southern legend, his shoulders squared and his posture perfect. His eyes, fixating on Raevin with a pulsating fury, gleamed an intense emerald as his helm began to sag and droop,.

"Nirali," the Thjodhild growled. "You have betrayed your oath."

"No more talking," Raevin replied calmly. "Burn."

Koro simply stood silent, letting the crackle of his fellows' burning flesh fill the air while the last of their screams died to nothing. After a moment, he spoke. "I do not share the blood of the rank and file, cur. I am pure. Flame nor blade can bring me grievous harm." He picked up the iron portcullis, lifting it as if it were made of paper, and ducked underneath.

He removed his melted, sagging helmet, revealing a grim, pale-white face with a squared jaw and high cheekbones, from which the hairs of a beard were still glowing as they burned to the roots. His features were perfect, artificially so, looking as if he was sculpted from marble by a master Alvari craftsman. His armor ran in beads down his body, badly malformed, while the sap licked over his unharmed skin with small flames. His irises glowed an ever brighter green color, two burning dots whose intensity only seemed to strengthen within the lasting inferno.

"Come on, then!" Edlevin screamed, bringing his blade to bear. "Prove it!"

Koro stalked calmly to the man and towered over him. "Try."

Edlevin complied, bringing his sword down hard with a swipe across Koro's chest.

It was *supposed* to be a swipe, at least. The old soldier's sword stopped dead, held easily in Koro's bare hand as the last piece of his gauntlet sagged and melted from his flesh. A small cut erupted on the knight's palm, barely noticeable, yet a small amount of gray blood trickled from the hairline wound and boiled in the running flames. He hardly seemed to notice; his eyes stared blankly, emotionlessly, towards the small human, shining an intense green glow onto the old Nirali's face.

"Did you not listen, child?" Koro hissed. "Your weapon is powerful, I admit, yet not enough." He suddenly kicked Edlevin hard in the right side of the hip, sending him flying into a market stall with a scream.

The three remaining Norts reacted before the old man touched the ground. Arvid grabbed Koro's arms, ignoring the searing pain of the burning sap as he pushed forward with all of his might. The Thjodhild accepted the challenge, keeping his full attention on the massive Northman.

Ronnok and Eira, meanwhile, tried to find openings with their respective weapons. They struck at the legs, the arms, the chest, anywhere they could fit their blades between the melting fragments of armor. It was fruitless, as their edges simply blunted against the enemy's adamant skin.

Koro smiled and brought his forehead down upon Arvid with unnatural speed, sending a brutal, moist clunking sound cascading through the street. The colossal Nort was knocked out cold, going limp and tumbling forwards as his momentum carried him.

Taking advantage, Koro grabbed the Northman by the shoulders and spun, lifting him into the air as if he were a wooden doll. Arvid's legs caught Eira in the head, knocking her to the ground and eliciting a scream from her husband.

Having the Nort Chieftain's location revealed, Koro released Arvid with force, sending him spiraling into his clanmate. Both tumbled heavily through a bush, where they could do little but groan, each of them half-conscious. The field was now empty, save for Raevin and Alauren.

The Colonel stood tall despite his injuries, his eyes betraying no fear as he stared at the knight with a visible, palpable hatred.

"All you had to do was sit and wait, Nirali," Koro hissed with wide, unsettlingly blank eyes. Soft, orange fire still licked from his back, fueled by the liquid beads of metal and sap on his flawless skin, making him appear as if a mythic demon of flame had stepped out from the storybooks. "You only had to follow your orders. You and your people would have been brought to glory."

"We would have been killed," Raevin countered in a harsh growl. "You cannot hide that fact any longer. Your 'glory' is damnation."

Koro smiled. "For you, child, death is a gift." He tightened his fist and, in a blink, sprinted to Raevin, throwing the blow hard.

The Nirali, even in his injured state, reacted instantly, ducking to his right. While he saved himself a killing head blow, the strike impacted his injured shoulder and sent him tumbling to the ground, where he writhed helplessly in pain, his arm hanging twisted and useless by his side.

Alauren instantly flicked her sword up and stabbed out towards Koro, catching only air as the Thjodhild desperately avoided the blow with a backwards lunge. Using his longer reach, he snagged the blacksmith by the arm and tossed her towards the portcullis.

She landed with a heavy *smack*, stealing the air from her lungs and knocking her helm roughly from her head. She could do little but cough and sputter with her face against the cold stones of the road; while her armor had saved her from the worst of the damage, the smith could only heave as she attempted to lift its weight with unfilled lungs and shocked muscles. She could feel Koro closing in on her as she struggled, each step from the monstrous knight sending thunderous vibrations through the ground.

Use me! a voice screamed in the head of the blacksmith. *You must!*

Alauren blinked, trying to focus. She gripped her sword tightly, relieved to find it still in her hand.

You know who I am, the voice continued. *Help me kill that bastard.*

Koro was upon the woman with the final word, kicking downward toward her head with a crushing force. Alauren's arm shot out, following the direction of the voice, and found the warm handle of Valin's scythe.

In a single moment, the smith's senses were returned to her, like a bucket of icy ocean water had been dumped onto her head after a day of drinking. Drell, appearing as little more than a transparent shadow in the center of her vision, smiled wickedly and cackled.

Koro's foot thundered into the ground, sending chips of rock scattering all around as the forceful blow carved a crater into the road.

A squelching sound tore through the air, moist and grotesque, followed by a lingering silence.

The Thjodhild's leg, resting firmly on nothing but dirt, was leaking grey liquid around a single, small blade, which quickly retracted back through the rear of his calf. Koro wheeled, confused, but found nothing save for a second blow that tore through his waist, again from behind. He swatted in the direction of the pain, feeling a whoosh of air as the strike missed by a hair. For his effort, he was rewarded with a stab in his uninjured leg.

"No blade can harm you, huh?" Alauren thundered madly, wielding Valin's scythe in her left hand and the sword in her right. She stood tall and firm, ready to dodge even the slightest of attacks. "You are one *damn* good bullshitter."

Koro dropped to his knees momentarily, gritting his teeth in agony. His body heaved with breaths, growing ever more ragged as he forced himself back to his feet, carried along on a torrent of rage. Pain was unfamiliar to him, clearly, a sensation that had faded from his memory. He wheeled on the smith, shooting her a glare that was meant to be fiery and enraged as his hatred burned bright and true under the assault of agony.

Instead, it only betrayed the truth.

"Fear," Alauren snapped, her words slathered with derision. "I can hurt you. That's why you want me dead." She shook her head and uttered the darkest of chuckles. "All of this has been because you're afraid of me."

"You would wish it so simple," Koro replied calmly. "It is not."

"Koro," snarled the blacksmith, bearing a thin smirk. "Death seems pretty simple to me."

The Thjodhild ran forward in lieu of further conversation, forcing his legs to carry him despite the significant damage to his tendons. Alauren steadied, controlling her nerves and waiting for a chance. As Koro took his last step to close the distance, she raised her sword at his chest.

The knight stopped with a skid and lost his footing. He lunged to his left, punching out towards the woman while desperately attempting to avoid her blade.

Alauren dodged to her left and sprung into an arcing blow, using her momentum to carry the blade up and forward, an attack that managed to catch only a glancing slice on Koro's passing fist.

The smith vanished and appeared again a blink later, just under Koro's other arm. She maintained the upward momentum of her sword, sending the blade sailing through his flesh like a hot knife through wax, separating the appendage at the elbow.

Koro landed and clutched at his wound, the stump bubbling forth grotesque blood like a mountain spring, spilling putrid gray ichor onto the streets. Undeterred, he rose, turned, and charged once more.

Alauren vanished again before reappearing a few steps forward from her original location, getting much closer to the Thjodhild than he had anticipated. As he turned to try and dodge, she delivered a heavy, deep slice across his gut, which sent him tumbling to the ground with a gurgling groan of agony.

Alauren's eyes blazed like twin suns as the knight gasped in shock, sprawling out on his belly before her and attempting to rise despite the efforts of his entrails to escape through the grievous wound on his belly.

A moment passed, and then another. The blacksmith felt like she could do little but watch, giving herself over to a passenger that had, until now, been content to lurk in the shadows, feeding from her misery and growing mighty. She tossed the scythe down and moved forward, feeling a numb calm as her movements carried her mind along with them. An inferno of fury guided her hand towards justice, towards the fitting punishment for the crimes of this vile madman.

She flipped her sword in her hands, holding it with an underhanded grip, and stabbed down hard, eliciting a squelch of gray liquid and a piercing wail from the once-powerful knight. The sound brought her comfort, a peace that felt, put simply, right, as if the sheer brutality of her action affirmed her very existence, giving her an indisputable purpose with which to carry forward. She twisted the blade to and fro, cutting through Koro's spine, eager for a few more moments of her enemy's suffering, savoring it like a mouthful of sweet mead. His screams were akin to music, flowing and beautiful, healing in their shrill melody.

An ardent darkness flickered in the heart of the smith; while it lasted only for a moment before it vanished into nothing, she knew instinctively that it would someday return.

"Ally!" Edlevin's astonished voice broke her trance, snapping her from her bloodlust.

Alauren removed her sword, stepped back, and nodded. "Karlmaðr."

"You..." the old soldier's face was covered in various shades of disbelief as he limped forward. "How?"

"I'm a good blacksmith," Alauren chortled, holding up her viscera-smeared sword and shooting it a floppy, goofy point.

Koro wailed. "I can't... I can't feel my legs!"

"Your spine is severed," Raevin growled weakly, amidst an intense pain that caused his eyelids to flutter uncontrollably. He could barely walk, hefting all of his weight upon his single functional leg, and his arms seemed to work only with great distress. Beyond all explanation, though, he had managed to stand, hobbling on the final solid part of his body. "The mighty Koro of the Thjodhild, leveled to the ground by someone a third of your size. Fascinating."

"Not so fascinating when you've known her a while," Ronnok groaned, rising from a now-ruined garden. He was dazed, but alive. Eira, tending to a still unconscious Arvid next to him, nodded silently in agreement.

"Are you alright, Karlmaðr?" Alauren asked with heavy breaths. She felt increasingly weak and shaky, but she stood tall, nonetheless, fighting off the effects of the waning adrenaline as it bled from her veins.

"Banged up, Ally, but I'll be okay," Edlevin replied. "We need to get him bound."

Raevin nodded and made a twirling motion in the air with his hand (an effort which he paid for in pain), in response to which Nirali troops on the wall dutifully rushed off to grab restraints suitable to hold their newfound prisoner.

"Amazing," Xendra said, striding down the street in clear and unrestrained disbelief. "You just made history. Simply amazing, girl."

"Valin?" Alauren asked, ignoring the praise entirely. "His scythe was here. Is he alive?"

"He'll be fine," the Eldari replied. "A family near the keep agreed to care for him temporarily. He is hardy."

"Yeah," Alauren nodded, kicking a moaning Koro in the ribs with a visibly malicious intent. "We all are."

"We should..." Raevin said, faltering. His consciousness, strained far beyond the human breaking point, finally gave way as the adrenaline bled fully from his veins. He crumpled forward and was caught by the arms of the smith before he could topple over.

"Xen, come," Alauren beckoned. "Help me get him inside."

CHAPTER THIRTY-EIGHT:

RECOVERY

39th OF THE MORN OF HARVEST
NORTHERN YEAR 715

The fog of sleep was blinked away by the blacksmith, who stirred in her chair and let go of the merciful darkness as it dissipated like mist under the early morning sun. The light beamed through soft white curtains that seemed to extend its reach, leaving hardly a shadow to be found in the traditional Arvynian two-story home. It was a modest structure near to the gatehouse, hurriedly quartered and converted into a makeshift hospital for the local Military Magistrate. The smell of the Thjodhild's burned flesh still colored the air outside, thick and bitter, wafting like smoke from a hearth as it seeped in through every crack on the wooden windowsill.

They couldn't move the Nirali any further than this place without risking additional harm. Raevin's wounds were grievous; his left shoulder was smashed to bits, while the leg on the same side was cracked and splintered. His knee was dislocated and had pushed partially through the skin, causing profuse bleeding that, thankfully, seemed to have let up during the night. Only his right leg was somewhat intact, with little but a few bruises upon the skin. For the moment, he laid relatively still in his bed, enjoying a few moments of minimal pain before he would once again, inevitably, fall into tremors.

How did he even give orders during the battle? Alauren thought, watching the sweat on the man's forehead glisten in the light. *How did he even stand?*

She chuckled to herself and shook her head. Her mind hadn't been awake for more than a minute, yet it was already filling with questions, racing from thought to thought in an unrelenting determination to find answers.

She could do naught but yield to them. Edlevin, temporarily bound to a wheelchair, had left with Ronnok to prepare their defense strategy in case a counterattack came, while Valin was recovering closer to the keep. All her normal distractions were far from her reach, leaving only a void behind.

She had chosen this path willingly. Enduring the memories that flashed through her mind with every conscious moment was a gritty war of attrition, yet there was a value to be found in these experiences. The atrocities that had been thrust upon her were still freshly branded into her mind, the very flesh of her brain still crackling under the blistering heat of the iron. She let them sizzle and sear, for within were lessons that she would not allow herself to forget.

They had been lured into a trap by the Thjodhild, outsmarted and outmuscled. They had made mistake after mistake, driven to each folly by desperation and a misguided, righteous fury. Were it not for Raevin, Drell, and Xen, she knew, they would have ended as nothing more than a smear on the main gates.

We thought we knew them, the blacksmith mused to herself. *The abominable knights would come out like the boorish fools they are, and we'd slaughter them on open ground!* She grimaced, grinding her teeth. *Idiots, all of us. Never again.*

Raevin shifted, tensing his left side as a new wave of pain soared through his nerves. Even if he survived, it was clear that he had already lost his ability to walk comfortably. He would be lucky to be able to raise his arms over his head, and wielding a sword was surely out of the question. He would be crippled.

'He should be dead,' Edlevin's voice echoed through the dark room, dredged up from the last evening in the memory of the smith. 'He would want to be dead.'

Good, Alauren thought, feeling a brief surge of anger soar through her chest. Raevin was a bringer of unthinkable horrors, a man who stood by while innocent civilians were made into helpless shells of fear. He was, to her reckoning, a monster in a man's body, regardless of his assistance in the final moments of this fight. *He deserves to be broken before he dies.*

Broken or not, he would provide answers, everything he had gathered about the Thjodhild. As enraging as it was, he was valuable. Alauren needed to know the enemy as she knew herself, down to the finest details, and there were few with more knowledge to give than this cretin.

Where do they come from? What do they truly want? The questions raced through her head like charging mustangs across the fields of Se'Vikoral. *How can they be shaken, as we were?*

The door creaked, startling the woman out of her ruminations. Seeing that it was Thyra, she settled back into the cushy leather chair and nodded a greeting. The Nort took a seat on the bed, next to Raevin's left leg.

"He survived the night," Thyra said softly, a subdued admiration carrying in her voice. "I thought he looked dire, even before I was told what happened. I am glad nobody else had to die this morn."

"I am, too, as he is needed," Alauren murmured amidst a sigh. "Truthfully, I don't know how any of us survived. We walked directly into a trap."

Thyra nodded and dabbed the Nirali's forehead with a moistened cloth, procured from a small basin next to the headboard. "I am grateful that my place was among my fleet, away from such a battlefield. I am as strong a warrior as the next, but my blood does not boil like theirs." She smirked at the weary blacksmith. "Like yours, I hear."

"I guess my blood did boil, huh?" Alauren mused. "When I plunged my blade into Koro's spine, I felt something I had never experienced before. A calm, or a peace." She shook her head, clearing a tangled mess of hair from her eyes. "I'm not really sure how to word it."

"Kìr," Thyra said with a soft smile. "The rush of victory, of blood repaid. You avenged your people." She wrung the cloth over the basin, letting the drops splatter lightly into the water. "Many of mine, too."

The smith's soul was heavy, able to take only a precious few more stresses upon it. Still, the question would eat away at her mind far more than the answer ever could. "How many of your people fell?"

"The official count is one hundred and eighty-one, across all battles," Thyra replied with a solemn ice about her voice, letting sorrow overtake her for a moment. "Many died of their wounds at Arvynian. It is a paltry number for Niralan or Elysia. It is a devastating one for us."

"I'm sorry," mumbled the blacksmith. "I'm sorry that it had to come to this. I've caused your people so much pain."

Thyra shook her head quickly and heavily, fully refuting the thought. "No, quite the opposite. What do you know of the Nort afterlife?"

"Just what I was told," Alauren replied. "They go to drink with the Great Father."

"Our lives travel beyond the world of flesh and blood, to drink and celebrate, but also to train and ready for a time when we are needed to march forth from the halls to save the living world," Thyra explained. "They await another purpose, a duty that is robbed of them should the Thjodhild steal them away."

"Ronnok told you everything, then?" Alauren asked, letting the lingering weariness pour into her eyes.

Thyra nodded. "As he always does."

"When Raevin first awoke, Ed said he had indicated that the people the Thjodhild raised from death were still there, within the body," Alauren recalled, shaking her head. "I wasn't sure what he meant, initially. I understand now. I hesitate to call these creatures dead; the mind that is trapped within is unmistakably lucid."

"This is why we are grateful to you," Thyra thrummed, dabbing the Colonel's forehead once more. "Your determination kept you alive, and your blade brought their leader low. His punishment was made possible because of you, avenging the loss of our fallen and our stolen."

"He will be followed by the rest of their forces, hopefully," Alauren rumbled with a dark chuckle. "The glory is not mine, though. Your people bled and died for this victory, and they should have songs sung about them for the rest of time. The Norts, for their deeds, deserve the whole north more than any empire."

"We don't want it," Thyra rebutted with a warm smile. "We only want to continue on to a better life, a life back in our homes. This cannot happen without the destruction of the Thjodhild, and so we will aid you in any way you need."

The smith shifted uncomfortably, trying in vain to hold in a deep sigh.

"You have something to say," observed the Nort. "Let it be said."

"Yeah, alright," Alauren murmured. "I want my path to be of my own charting, is all. I have a feeling I'll have to fight to keep control. Even you, with no offense meant, see my prominence in these events as a way to get back to your homeland." She glanced at the floor and shook her head lightly. "I do not want to be held to promises I can't keep."

"Do not make them, then," Thyra soothed, wiping Raevin's forehead with a freshly dampened cloth. "It is in the nature of nations and tribes alike to look after their own, to see the best future for a new generation. Yes, we see a way home in you, but we will do so by following the choices you make, not by making them for you. Your heart is a stormy sea, but it is good and just, as well. You will be well guided in even the darkest of times."

"I know," Alauren replied softly. "My focus, though, is on protecting what I have, not retaking what was lost. I have a home and a family again, something to drive that next step forward. I won't lose it."

"Fair enough," Thyra replied with a reassuring nod. "I cannot ask for any more than that."

The two sat in silence for a moment, broken only by the ragged breaths of the Nirali.

"They will execute Koro today," Thyra stated, after a while.

Alauren's face turned from solemn memory to absolute shock. "He survived?"

"He is unlike anything we've ever seen," Thyra confirmed with a slightly furrowed brow. "His wounds covered themselves over and his blood replenished, all in a matter of hours. He even regained feeling in his legs." She gritted her teeth and looked at the floor. "You need to speak to him before he dies."

"I know," Alauren replied, rising. "Where is he?"

"The grand foyer of the keep," Thyra said. "I will watch over the Nirali. Follow Redja Street all the way."

The heavy, iron-banded doors of the keep flew open with ease, parting before the storming blacksmith as if they were little more than single planks of wood. Her fury carried her steps and her strength, propelling her eagerly towards the last hours of the Thjodhild's life.

Koro hung several armlengths off the ground in the center of the room, bound with thick anchor chains which wrapped around the grooved marble pillars supporting the keep's structure and its grand rotunda above. He still wore armor, though it was not by the good graces of the Northmen; much of the metal had melted into his pale skin, fragments permanently trapped beneath his rapidly healing flesh. Edlevin sat next to the Thjodhild in his wooden wheelchair, while Ronnok paced back and forth in thought.

Koro's glowing emerald irises focused immediately upon the new arrival. "You."

"Indeed," Alauren growled sternly.

"He's been a right bastard all night," Edlevin spat, spinning his chair around. "Constant threats and cryptic nonsense. He's miserable!"

"I'm going to kill him," Ronnok deadpanned. "Such a mood is expected."

"It makes little difference," Koro said, his eyes unblinking and his gaze unwavering. "Your impurity will rot this world from the inside. We will win."

"Impurity..." Alauren mused, approaching the massive man. "Koro, you say that as if your actions aren't an impurity of their own. The things you've done-"

"Are in service to a better world," Koro snapped. He gestured towards the soldier and the Chieftain with his head. "Their bodies fall and rot." He stared into the smith with starry eyes and an expression that she could have sworn was wonder. "Ours do not. Ours is a world of *only* life."

"What do I have to do with this?" Alauren asked, largely ignoring the rantings of the deranged zealot. He needed to be steered toward more useful topics. "You came after me with great caution, driven by either fear or respect. Both, perhaps."

"You can kill us," Koro replied absently. "Your blade is powerful."

Alauren shook her head with a knowing smile. "One person doesn't cause this much mass hysteria because she makes a half decent sword. What am I to you?"

"An aberration," spat the Thjodhild. "A mistake. Our greatest shame, and an impurity to be cleansed. She must be woken by your death."

Alauren crossed her arms and huffed in annoyance. "Are you capable of having a point, or do you speak entirely in dogmatic bullshit?"

Koro simply stared at the woman and furrowed his brow.

Alauren paced slowly around the Thjodhild, observing every statue-like feature that peeked out from beneath the fused armor. His skin was pristine, seemingly undamaged by the melted slag, and there was hardly a mark wherever his new flesh met with the malformed metal armor. "Who is she?" asked the smith, returning to her place in front of the prisoner.

"What?" Koro rumbled.

"You keep talking about someone who needs to wake," Alauren's said coldly. "Who, and what does that mean?"

Koro averted his eyes and looked to the floor. "I will humor you no further."

Alauren drew her sword and walked around the fallen knight, letting the edge slide dangerously near to the Thjodhild's bare belly. Save for his severed arm and melted armor, his blade wounds appeared as if they were never there at all, with only the lightest scars appearing on his pale skin. Koro recoiled from the cold steel of the blade, breathing in sharply.

"How many more are there for me to kill, Koro?" growled the smith. "How many more until I can count you extinct?"

Koro breathed heavily, raggedly, offering no answers.

Alauren turned the blade and ran it lightly along the knight's belly. Another wound opened where the other had been mere hours earlier (though more superficial this time), leaking gray blood across the ornate mural of the floor, running into the mouth of the mosaic dragon. The knight grunted, but said nothing.

"You will die today, abomination," Alauren stated, turning the blade to run down the side of Koro's leg. "Will it be painful or swift?"

Koro suddenly shook his head, keeping his eyes ever downward. "It matters little, for the end is the same."

Alauren, holding her blade midway through a brush down the Thjodhild's right leg, snapped the edge of the weapon inward, severing the limb with a single slice.

"Well?" the smith snarled as the Thjodhild's leg slapped against the floor, followed swiftly by dribbling grey fluid. "Does it matter?"

Koro grunted and strained against the pain, again refusing to alleviate his suffering.

The splattering sound of the Thjodhild's blood hitting the mosaic echoed throughout the room, bouncing from the walls and the dome far above, a vile waterfall of putrid slime. Alauren readied her blade next to his remaining leg. "Well?"

"No, it does not," Koro heaved. "I have no more words."

"You do not, maybe," Ronnok replied, breaking his meditative silence. "Yet, we have found another."

Koro's eyes went wide with a wild wrath. Their soft glow turned to a burning emerald light, as if a discolored bonfire had been lit inside them. "Do not harm her, you *feckless* crow!" spat the knight, leaning forward as best he could in the bindings. "She represents the experiences of a million of your meager lifetimes, a bastion of wisdom in an ignorant world."

"Sounds like we hit a nerve," Alauren said, bearing an evil smile. "I suppose a chat wouldn't hurt."

Ronnok nodded and beckoned the woman into a stairwell at the corner of the room, lying next to the anchoring base of one of the grooved pillars. The smith ran her hands across the white marble as she passed, savoring every small crack and bump that was sensed beneath the light touch of her fingers. Emotions whipped within; fear and trauma, sorrow and hatred, all boiling over as if there was a furnace burning white-hot below. Her fingers lifted from the rough surface, and she pushed the fury away.

After descending a few stories, Ronnok guided her through a small, green door and into a room that was dim and heavy with incense. Opulent silk curtains of many colors hung from the walls, drooping to carpets that were expertly woven from a material wholly foreign to the smith; it was soft and malleable, like sand under her boots, but it seemed to be a solid object rather than many individual grains. She moved forward curiously, while Ronnok waited quietly near the door.

Xen stood vigilant watch over a golden-skinned female figure kneeling on a small red pillow in the rear middle of the room, her eyes closed. The woman was quite tall, meeting Alauren's lower chest even while sitting, and her brilliant hair flowed like molten gold onto dark robes which were decorated with tassels and studded gems of a dozen colors. She was quite beautiful at a glance, yet she looked as manufactured and unnatural under close examination as Koro did, like her features were purposefully molded around her natural skull, ridged and thorough in their design.

The Eldari nodded in greeting. "Meet the Dreamer. A Thjodhild scryer of sorts, older than most of her kind, one of a council of nine."

"You," said the Thjodhild. Her voice was calm and mellow, drifting like a soft wind. Her eyes opened, revealing deep, black voids accented with bright specks of light and a dull, milky glow that seemed to shift like a tempestuous storm cloud behind the tiny stars. Her gaze was locked onto the smith's face before her eyelids ever rose, as if she could see through them. "At last."

Alauren approached cautiously. "You sound like you've been waiting for me."

"I was," the Dreamer replied. "I knew I would have you."

"You do not have me," Alauren rebuffed. "Nor will you ever. In fact, it looks like I have you."

The Dreamer chuckled. "You act as if this was an unexpected outcome, rather than one of only two futures. I dreamed of your arrival, girl, hundreds of morns ago, knowing that you would either be cleansed or prove the superiority of the Thjodhild. The others did not wish to believe, but..." She smiled widely, looking on in amazement. "There can be no doubt now. It is proven."

Alauren scoffed heavily. "We just beat you. We're going to kill Koro. Your 'superiority' is a joke."

"Even through your victory, you solidify our place in this world," the Dreamer replied brightly, her tone one of wonder and respect. "You aren't a blight to be cleansed, like my less gifted brothers and sisters had so pessimistically assumed, but a gift. I was right!"

"Just like Koro," Alauren growled. "You speak in abstract monologues and provide no answers."

"Koro could not provide answers because he will not accept the truth," said the Thjodhild woman. "He is a soldier, but much like the others of our military leadership, he is blinded by his own dogma, seeing salvation only in your death. I, on the other hand..." She trailed off with an infuriating chuckle, the sound carrying off the walls and vibrating through the blacksmith's skull as if a hummingbird were trapped inside. "I see you as so much more. Koro wished to 'wake' me from my idea that you are who I thought you to be, to get me to see the light of his own arrogant 'Dawn', yet I could see the truth. You have seen through this onslaught with an unbroken body and spirit. I was right."

Alauren moved in, close enough that she could feel the sickly cold of the woman's breath. "I know you carry knowledge. I can feel it, like the sun burning in front of me." She gazed deep into the Thjodhild's eyes, her own wide and bloodshot as they bled fury. "Answer me, then: what am I to the Thjodhild?"

The Dreamer returned the question with a thin smile and an amused glance toward Xendra. Relenting, she shifted her attention back to the smith, nodded deeply, and spoke. "The creed of the Thjodhild is purity at all costs, standing in opposition to the ways of the Eldari, who cursed this world with rot and decay through so-called 'natural' death. We bred only within our own race, preserving immortality, as was our duty. For this reason, we are superior." She chuckled again, heavier this time, a deep and rumbling sound that vibrated through the blacksmith's chest. "Yet, who cares less for duty than mere adolescents, caught up in their own hearts?"

Xendra recoiled visibly. "What are you saying, wretch?"

"This woman, this simple smith, is a child of shared bloodlines, Eldari," the Dreamer replied with a beaming grin. "She was born of a Thjodhild mother and an Eldari father."

Xendra's wide-eyed stare darted between the two women. There was a clear disgust in her face, impossible to hide, even if she wished to do so. She found no words, and could muster only a cold stare that settled in on the blacksmith.

Alauren simply shrugged, sharing little of Xendra's shock. "Why does that matter?"

"We assumed you to be young. Long-lived, yet young all the same," the Dreamer thrummed, grinning in entertainment at the unsettled Eldari. "Now, here you are, immortal and perfect beyond our imaginations. You have bested a pure blooded Thjodhild in direct combat, the only time in history that this has occurred." She shook her head in amazement. "You are purity, a glimpse of the world we seek, proof that our natural power and our gift of life expands even to our mongrel offspring. You are superior, even to us. You are my dream, child, foremost among those who will inherit this world, an example of perfection for all living things to behold."

"Fuck your dream!" Alauren spat hatefully, allowing every bit of pent-up rage to color her words. "You killed my friends, everyone I ever cared about. That's not a dream, it's a nightmare."

The Dreamer chuckled again. "We didn't kill your pitiful little village, girl, else they would be under my thrall, risen for a glorious purpose." Her mouth hung agape for a moment, sending cold breath hurtling towards the infuriated blacksmith. "It is foolish, though, to think we are the only ones who stalk the darkness of the cold forests. Even the Thjodhild find themselves in service to others, from time to time." The milky abyss of her eyes swam about, the bright pins within moving as if they were being tossed about by a tumultuous current. "Even the darkest creatures of this world require sustenance, do they not?"

"Who?" Alauren demanded, grabbing the woman tightly by the robes. "Answer me!"

"Patience, child," the Dreamer grumbled, roughly pushing the smaller woman away. "She has seen you. She knows you. You will have your answers, but they will not come from me. Through pain or death, whatever you may threaten me with, you will hear no more."

Alauren drew her sword and leveled it with the Dreamer's neck. "I can kill you," she snarled, feeling the heat of her wrath burning wild and unbridled in her chest. "I would love to, actually. Give me a name."

The Dreamer shook her head slowly, ploddingly, as if she were goading the woman on. "It is not my place, for she is greater than even I."

Alauren's knuckles went white as they squeezed the hilt of her sword ever harder, her chest heaving with ragged breath. Her pupils dilated, bloodshot streaks reaching forth from the edges of her eyes as rage tore through her mind and heart.

"Smith!" Xendra barked with a grave gravity in her voice. "She is useful. We need her alive!"

"*You* need her alive," Alauren corrected. "I need to send them a message."

"No," eased the Eldari, reaching out and gently pushing Alauren's blade away from the Thjodhild's neck. "She can be used as a bargaining chip, or an informant, despite the danger she carries with her. Smith, I believe that she may be the only one who can facilitate the raising of the dead, not to mention the ancient knowledge that she carries with her. Her people value her beyond their own lives, beyond the world its-"

Alauren, needing to hear no more, snapped her blade forward in a one-handed arc, removing the Dreamer's head with a single flick of the wrist. The Thjodhild slumped backwards into death while the heat left Alauren's chest, sated and replaced by a soothing calm. A heavy wail, sorrowful yet thunderous, carried through the keep, drawn out of the Thjodhild knight chained above.

Xendra recoiled in shock as grey blood splattered across her face. "Dammit, girl!" she screamed, a potent rage and unease infecting her voice. "Do you know what you just did? They will hear the silencing of her song! They will know that the wisdom she carried in her dreams is lost forever to the void." She wiped the gray viscera from her eyes. "You just declared war!"

Alauren scoffed incredulously and wiped her blade on the hanging silks. "That happened when they killed my town, and when they tried to kill me. I simply hit them back for the first time." She slid her weapon back into its scabbard. "I am willing to take no further risks with these monsters, nor am I willing to allow any more of their subterfuge by keeping them among us. We will no longer fight on their terms."

"You always fight on their terms," Xendra retorted. "Millennia of a losing war has proven that as fact."

"How many of this kind did you kill in that time?" Alauren snapped, gesturing to the headless corpse. "Beings so important that the others would give their life to protect them?"

Xendra sighed and brushed her hair back in defeat. "None."

"Indeed," Alauren continued, ignoring another howling wail from Koro. "Their world just changed, as mine did at Teth. The sorrow and despair simmered within me and tunneled my vision, causing me to err."

"The same happened to the Norts," Ronnok added, content to watch silently until now. "Our losses enraged us, and our thinking became unclear."

"The same thing happened to you, Xen, supporting our foolhardy attack because of old anger," Alauren pointed out. "Our victory here was miraculous, and such a stroke of good fortune won't happen again. The Thjodhild will need to be dealt with, and our only hope is to shake the foundations beneath their feet, as they have done to us." She glared toward the corpse. "They need to be as lost as we are."

Xendra bit her lip, thinking, and nodded. "I see your point, misguided as I believe it to be. I suppose there is no argument now, as our road has been irreversibly chosen."

"Yes," Alauren muttered, shooting a final, hateful glance to the motionless corpse on the floor. "It has."

CHAPTER THIRTY-NINE:

JUSTICE

The smith opened her eyes as a heavy cloud of incense washed over her, filling her senses with a potent, pleasant fragrance. Still in the silk-draped room (minus a corpse), she sat opposite Xen on a red pillow, cross-legged. For a time, both women were lost in their own heads; the Dreamer's words had struck the Eldari deeply, and she had requested time to study the blacksmith's song, while Alauren simply tried to relax and enjoy the quiet. For the first time in weeks, her mind was able to rest, sated by blood and justice. Still, there was a final, nagging annoyance at the back of her mind, one last job that remained undone.

"I have to go," Alauren said, snapping Xendra from her meditation.

"He is about to die," the Eldari observed calmly. "You wish to be present."

"I *need* to be present," Alauren corrected. "The Dreamer's death was one of necessity. This one is close to me."

"Go, then," Xendra said. "The calm you feel is temporary. Enjoy it."

Alauren nodded at the woman and quietly paced out of the room. After ascending the stairs and crossing the (now empty) foyer, she found herself on streets that were bustling with the relieved faces of hundreds of locals, each carefully enjoying their newfound freedom now that their oppressors had fallen. Following the crowds, she hustled her way to the central square, where Koro was chained upon some gallows in the center, moored on the trunks of twin oak trees. Behind him, the rope typically used to hang criminals now held two large billhooks, which dangled in the wind.

A crowd had gathered, fascinated by the unmasking of their tormentor, gawking in awe at the fused metal upon (and under) his flesh. Nirali, Nort, and the Arvynian Islanders mingled together, sharing stories of their journeys as they waited for the sun to rise to midday. Curiosity and justice had united them for the moment, eager to see their nightmares put to rest.

Alauren, spotting Edlevin's wheelchair (and a boisterously laughing Valin) at the side of the gallows, pushed her way through the gathered masses and found a small wooden seat next to the old soldier, reserved for her with a small placard that was simply labeled "blacksmith".

"Ally!" Edlevin barked. "I hope Xendra didn't interrogate you too much."

"Not at all, actually," the smith replied with a shrug. "She's a strange one." She leaned forward and raised an eyebrow at Valin. "Still alive, I see."

"For the moment, anyway," the Dwarf grumbled with a hearty chuckle. "Damned wrists will ache fer weeks, though." Indeed, both were wrapped under heavy bandages, while his arms were marked up and down with pronounced bruises. He glared at his scythe, safely recovered for him, and rolled his eyes. "Oh, yeah, sure, I'm so happy yer no worse fer wear, ye wooly wank."

"In any case, I'm glad you're still with us," Alauren chuckled, taking her seat. "Drell, of course, is excluded from that statement."

"Hah!" Valin chirped. "As he should be. Damned idiot almost got us all killed."

Alauren shook her head. "He was only one drop in an ocean of mistakes." She sighed deeply and rested her chin on her fist. "Ed, as a military commander, tell me: how foolish were we?"

"We won," stated the old soldier. "Sometimes, that's all that matters. Mistakes are mistakes, and as long as we live to see the next dawn, we can learn from them." He chortled heartily. "Still, we couldn't have made it easier for them, I think."

"I guess yer right, lass," Valin relented. "Still, we'll have t' discuss what t' do with the bastard. He betrayed us all. Our own mistake or no, he did what he did." He shifted in his seat. "It's as much me own fault as it is his, honestly. I shoulda caught him talkin' t' the big arses."

"Don't blame yourself," Alauren quickly soothed. "You couldn't be expected to control a being like him. In fact, the least he could do is apologize."

Valin's attention was drawn away. He focused on the scythe intently, while his brow furrowed deeply.

"Valin?" the smith inquired. "What's wrong?"

"He showed me somethin'," Valin said in a half-absent drone. He moved to hand the weapon to Alauren. "He wants t' show you. Says it's yer apology."

"Ally, you should probably be careful," Edlevin cautioned. "He might try to kill you again."

"He's had another chance already," Alauren quickly dismissed. "He didn't take it."

Valin, with little more hesitation, offered the white handle of the ancient weapon. The smith accepted it carefully, feeling the soft glow of warmth as her palm contacted the surface. The world melted around her, and she found herself on a white plain opposite a silhouette she immediately recognized as Drell.

"Your trust is appreciated," said the sorcerer. He waved his hands, summoning dripping colors to fill in the blank canvas of his vacant reality. After a moment, the two were standing on a mountain pass in a horrible storm; rain and sleet were frozen in time over a treacherous, jagged trail which snaked downwards into a bank of fog. Above, the road terminated at a peak that was cracked in two, as if an unfathomably large giant had cleaved the mighty stones with a maul.

"I don't remember how long ago this was," Drell mused. "Four thousand years? Six? Twelve? Time is different here, dragging on and on. I suppose it doesn't matter."

The sorcerer waved his hands again, causing two figures to appear in the violent winds of the storm. The first was wearing robes that made him recognizable as Drell, though his physical form was far younger than the one kept in the scythe. He was joined by another being, a tall man that would have looked like a Nort, were it not for his Elf-like features and golden skin.

"Who is-" Alauren began.

"Thjodhild," answered the sorcerer. "From a time before they reached their self-crafted 'perfection'. Joined, of course, by a shade of the man I once was."

Alauren studied the Thjodhild carefully. A soft, long face was complemented by waving brown hair and further accented by bright green eyes. His features looked much more natural, still jagged, but not carved, and his irises didn't glow like Koro's had. Other parts of the man, though, were blurry, such as an insignia on his chest, and the armor beneath.

"Drell, what is the mark he wears?" Alauren asked. "Why can't I make it out?"

"This is a memory, smith," Drell replied. "Imperfect and winnowed by time. This one's name is Einar, and I remember little but his face." He waved away the thought. "No more questions, please. Simply watch."

Alauren nodded and turned her attention to the whisper of the past as the world around them snapped into motion.

"We had no problem killing the rest!" Einar thundered, his voice easily overtaking the roaring storm around them. "It's the damned young. Your people breed too quickly for a race so inferior!"

"Inferior?" the shade of Drell scoffed. "Even you can't use the magic I've learned, Einar. Magic, may I remind you, that is about save your people from the very young you curse."

"You are talented, I admit, and you have our thanks," Einar relented. "Whether a hundred years or ten thousand, our new world will await. I will see you there, Varsa."

Drell's shade nodded. "In good time."

Hundreds more Thjodhild bled into the vision, stretching down the rain-slicked trail. Drell's shade planted his weapon in the ground, thundering the rocks around it as he started to chant in an unknown tongue.

A point of light began to emerge from the air, four-pronged like the bright northern stars, appearing as if it was drawn out by the sorcerer's indecipherable words. It grew in intensity, larger and larger, until it collapsed into a single, almost imperceptible, pin of darkness. The pin, in turn, began to grow into something Alauren could only comprehend as a black void, expanding until it was just larger than a Thjodhild's size.

One by one, the hooded members of the old race stepped hesitantly through, each venture into the mysterious abyss causing Drell's shade to age, older and older, until his once-young face became marred with wrinkles and scars, looking more like the specter that now inhabited the scythe.

Einar, the final entrant to the portal, stopped for a moment. He patted the sorcerer on the shoulder and smiled. "We'll find you, my friend. You have my word."

With the passing of the final Thjodhild into the unknown, Drell's body turned to ash and blew away in the wind, leaving only the scythe behind. It tumbled roughly to the ground, sizzling the rain and melting the rock beneath, plunging ever down into the depths of the mountain. The portal collapsed upon itself with a thundering roar that echoed across the vast, obscured lands beyond the storm.

In a blink, the vision turned white again.

"I serve them no longer," Drell declared hatefully. "Their people exist because of me, and they spat in my face."

"Why?" Alauren asked, her voice bearing a pronounced incredulity. "Why would you save them?"

Drell sighed and shrugged lightly. "A consistent, solitary world can be alluring, young one, for someone who has known only exile, as I did." He crossed his arms and looked down in sorrow. "Their dream was a world where everyone is as perfect as the last, where even death itself could fade away into the sands of time. Tell me, if you could end the changing of the seasons, knowing only plentiful summer, would you not?"

Alauren shook her head. "Summer is nothing without the spring rains, just as the fertile ground of spring cannot be without the melting of the winter snows. Anything else, Drell, is a world that can never exist. Time cannot be halted, no matter how intensely we demand it so."

"I suppose," the sorcerer replied with another deep sigh. "Go, now. You have a ceremony to attend."

"Wait!" yelped the smith. "One more question."

Drell, though surprised, nodded.

"Back at Teth…" Alauren began. "You could have helped them. Instead, you killed one of them. Why?"

Drell thought for a moment before speaking. "While they shared the same goals, in the end, Koro and the Dreamer held wildly different ideas when it came to you." He ruminated for another few breaths, searching his memory for details. "Koro's only desire was your death, while the Dreamer wished to pursue dominance through you, thinking you to be purer that even she, some sort of god figure." He chuckled darkly. "Koro thought her deluded and felt the need to 'wake' her, for he believed the bloodline of his people to be the purest; having command over their knights, he had the advantage of manpower.

Lacking forces of her own to pursue you, the Dreamer came to me with a deal: a successful transfer of my soul into an immortal body in exchange for getting you close." He interlaced his hands behind his back. "They had been silent toward me for millennia before that offer came. For me, smith, every one of my actions were desperation, a last throe to escape this maddening void of a prison."

"Why not just teleport me, then?" Alauren questioned. "I held your scythe."

Drell nodded. "Greed, plain and simple. In that, I saw an opportunity to bypass the Dreamer, instead of taking you to her. Your body can clearly, unquestionably, survive the transfer of my soul without need for her influence, much to my own surprise at the time. You are a powerful vessel, Alauren of Teth."

The blacksmith stepped back carefully, suspiciously, unwilling to take any risks when it came to the sorcerer.

"Worry not, for I can no longer find a desire within me to return to the world of life," Drell murmured. His demeanor became noticeably more somber with the words. "Go, now, please; leave me to my confinement and enjoy this day."

Alauren awoke back to the physical world to be greeted with a worried gaze from her old friend. "Ally, are you alright?"

"I'm fine, Ed," the smith replied, handing the scythe back to Valin. "Just fine."

Her words were bookended by the ringing of the town bell as it echoed through the streets, loud enough to rattle the glass and frames of any windows nearby. Mid-day had come, and with it arrived the thunder of the Nort Chieftain's voice.

"Ikrìt Va!" Ronnok boomed, emerging from behind the gallows in a painstakingly sewn, snow-white garment of fur. It draped over his head and torso, forming a fine hooded coat from under which a red-painted face peeked out. In his hands laid an ivory blade, carved into the visage of a wolf and a serpent, each locked in combat with the other, twisting in a beautiful dance up the weapon until their mouths poured forth a sharp tip of silvery steel.

Ronnok was flanked by a few Norts that Alauren hadn't met, three older women and an equal number of older men, each wearing white furs and face paint that matched their Chieftain.

"Shamans," Edlevin commented, noticing Alauren's curiosity.

"Envoys to the gods. I'm glad we finally have enough of a break to see true Northmen culture."

Ronnok and the Shamans, midst the heavy pounding of a few table-sized drums, climbed the gallows and took their places behind the bound Thjodhild prisoner. The older Norts began to chant in unison, repeating a Nortish phrase in careful rhythm, fast and steady, with the drum.

Ekka fol hata

Fjor un Flìv

Ekka dol Mata

Iss thjal Kur

"A treatise to the gods, a request for their attention," Edlevin whispered. "I don't know what it means beyond that, but I've always had an appreciation for this ritual."

For Alauren, the words felt alive, as if they crawled through her mind in an intent search for something unknown. There was a power in them, a tingle that ran up her spine, yet one that relaxed her and made her feel at ease.

"You feel it too, Ally?" Edlevin asked, drawing out a nod from his friend. "It feels like I can finally rest. Like there's nothing more to do."

Abruptly, the drums stopped and Ronnok spoke, choosing to use the trade tongue.

"Koro lies before you, a false Augur of Redja and commander to the Thjodhild," thundered the Chieftain. "Who among us was not victim to his violence, his depravity?"

The crowd, no matter their backgrounds, grumbled as one.

"He stole lives. He stole peace. He stole everything we hold dear," Ronnok continued. "Today, we steal that which he holds close. Today, Koro of the Thjodhild dies. Today, Arvyn sees an eagle of blood."

"Do what you will," Koro murmured. He looked noticeably sunken; his defiance had evaporated and his body slumped dejectedly in the binding chains. "Tomorrow is another day."

Ignoring the sulking of the Thjodhild, Ronnok turned, pointed to

Alauren, and beckoned her onstage.

Though surprised, the smith felt no hesitation, rising and climbing the soft wood of the gallows in seconds.

"Your blade, please," Ronnok muttered. "For the initial cuts."

Alauren nodded, drew her sword, and handed it to the Chieftain.

The Northman smiled wickedly, gripping the hilt with one hand while pawing at the Thjodhild's bare back with the other. Finding a flat spot near the right shoulder, he plunged the blade into flesh. It cut deep and easy; gray blood ran from around its shining edges, beading over the melted fragments of the knight's armor like wax running down a metal candlestick.

No scream came from Koro, as one would expect. There was only a destitute whimpering, accompanied by involuntary twitches of pain as the metal edge dug into his back.

Ronnok, proceeding without delay, dragged the blade in an oval-shaped slice, amazed at how flesh, armor and bone were dissected with only a gritting resistance, as if they were wet sand beneath a mighty Nort axe. He formed a neat and careful hole, an arm's length vertically on the Thjodhild's back, and discarded the scrap of ribcage that once occupied the space under the shoulder.

Repeating the process on the other side, the Nort Chieftain found his handiwork quite suitable, and so he returned the sword to its rightful owner. Behind him, one of the Nort shamans procured a bowl of vile black liquid, crusted over in salt, which Ronnok turned and plunged his arms into, elbow deep.

Ronnok ripped his hands from the fluid without delay and immersed them into the Thjodhild's chest cavity through the left cut on the back. This time, Koro wailed in pain and seized up, straight as a mast, unable to ignore the mordant burning of the substance as it brushed against his exposed nerves. His voice carried across the silent crowd, echoing like the shriek of a banshee, otherworldly and unnaturally high.

The Chieftain, undeterred, fished around inside with a distinct squelching sound, audible even above the wild wails of the prisoner. Finding a grip on something, Ronnok slowly shuffled backwards, keeping his arms straight while pulling a heaving pink mass carefully from the wound.

The organ, which Alauren sickly recognized as a lung, was

enormous, slathered in gray blood and pulsating vessels, many times the size of even the largest domestic animals. It inflated in ragged, uneven breaths, growing to be the size of a Nort torso before retreating again into a fold of quivering flesh.

Ronnok held up a hand, beckoning a shaman, who duly fetched one of the dangling fishhooks and placed it within his ruler's hand. The Chieftain delicately pierced the lung, ensuring that the hook wouldn't rip through, before signaling another shaman to hoist the organ aloft, lifting it above Koro's sunken head.

Ronnok expertly repeated the same steps on the other lung, being rough when he could and careful when needed. He was, Alauren observed, careful to avoid pushing the Thjodhild into unconsciousness, keeping Koro awake and alert through slow and deliberate injuries, rather than quick and traumatic ones.

Ronnok hung the second lung from its hook and signaled for it to be hoisted, completing the gruesome visage of vengeance. The shamans, led by the drums, began repeating their chant again, more intensely this time, dancing in circles behind the tortured prisoner.

Koro's lungs heaved with ragged and increasingly gurgling breaths. The radiant sun of midday shone through the flesh of the softly quivering organ, exposing a multitude of shadowy veins and vessels that cascaded across the surface as rivers do continents.

Alauren, mouth agape, walked forward, encouraged by a nod and a lopsided smile from the Chieftain. She stood front and center before Koro, the arbiter of her pain, the hand who had delivered her into a nightmarish world of suffering and death. The gurgling and heaving as he struggled for life was refreshing, a pure and calming picture of justice, and she hoped that her old friends from Teth were fortunate enough to look on from beyond and find a more tranquil rest.

The smith found that the ritual did, indeed, form an eagle; the wings were raised high, just preparing to take flight while the body heaved below. In the most gruesome and grisly of ways, it was something of beauty, a punishment uniquely fitting for this vermin's crimes. Alauren leaned in, feeling a surge in her spine as the chanting of the shamans reverberated through her mind. She was at peace, utterly calm, feeling nothing but relief as she whispered into the fallen knight's ear.

"As it ends for the Dreamer, so it ends for you. The rest will follow."

Koro heaved with gurgling breath. "You are…" Sputters of grey blood erupted from his mouth along with the words. "…the Dream." His consciousness gave way, and his eyes became heavy.

Alauren punched the knight in the mouth with all of her might, knocking loose several teeth. Without another word, she returned to her seat and flopped down.

"Quite the view," Edlevin said with a chortle.

"It was better up there, believe me," replied the blacksmith. "He deserves every bit, and more."

Edlevin chuckled darkly. "As long as he dies, Ally. I'll sleep easier when we no longer have his shadow looming over us."

"In good time, Karlmaðr," Alauren assured. "For now, let the bastard suffer."

The next few hours were ones of careful celebration, with the common people taking the previously unthinkable opportunity to see an unmasked Augur up close. They gazed on in a disturbed fascination as he heaved and groaned in agony, while the tireless chanting of the shamans behind him seemed to preserve the last thread of life that remained within.

Alauren, who quickly lost interest in the viscera, chose instead to watch the gathered masses carefully, noticing the fear and sorrow that darkened their eyes being slowly muscled out by a newfound hope and determination. For now, they were not strangers of different races, seeing little common ground between them, but friends and allies joined behind a common condemnation. The smith, for the first time since Teth, felt her heart swell with genuine confidence.

"We made so many mistakes, Ally," Edlevin said, drawing his old friend from her thoughts. "Looking at these people, I'd make them all again. We did far more than just kill a few Thjodhild, I think."

Alauren nodded and allowed herself a thin smile. "We've gained many an ally. We've earned trust."

After a while, Alauren opted to once again approach the Thjodhild, just as the chanting of the Nort shamans dwindled to nothing. His breath became ever shorter, shallower, and the last forces of life inside his body were clearly beginning to fade.

The blacksmith sat cross legged in front of him, close enough to allow herself to feel the sickly cold and smell the molten nickel of his breath. She closed her eyes, taking comfort in the decreasing length of each of the fallen knight's inhales, until the respiration halted and the wings of the eagle finally became still. The nightmare, for now, was over, and the wheel of justice had completed its first grinding revolution.

Alauren opened her eyes and stood, taking one last look at the corpse while a final, peaceful calm overtook her thoughts. Thunder rumbled in the sky above, somewhere quite distant, yet it seemed to evaporate the last of her rage and carry it off to the horizon. She returned to Edlevin and Valin, flopping heavily onto her chair. "It's over," groaned the smith.

"Yeah," Edlevin nodded with a warm smile. "It is."

Ronnok, removing his furs and cleaning his hands a final time, beckoned an older woman, bearing a bowl of gray blood, and joined the trio of outsiders. He was followed closely by Eira and Thyra, having completed the last of their duties around the creaking gallows.

"This is Brida," the Chieftain said. "She, and she alone, can make others one of Nordiska."

Alauren chuckled and smiled warmly. "About time, big man."

Ronnok returned the laugh, which was in turn echoed by Eira and Thyra, and nodded. "Long past, in my mind."

Brida, an older woman of wrinkled, dark skin, approached Alauren, dipping her finger in Koro's blood. The Shaman brushed a few strands of hair from the smith's face and used the greasy fluid to draw a waving line on her forehead, like a snake. "Mät uv ŏrekker," said the Nort, speaking her native tongue.

"The Mark of the World Serpents," Ronnok translated. "For your blood bears the strength of dragons."

Brida moved to Edlevin and drew a hulking, four-legged figure on his forehead. "Mät uv Bjǫrn."

"The Mark of the Bear," Ronnok said. "For your body and spirit are unbreakable."

The shaman moved to Valin and drew what looked like a small cup on his large, bulging forehead. "Mät uv..." She hesitated, suppressing a smile. "...uv Aleinn."

Ronnok and his wives chuckled in unison. "The Mark of Ale, for you bring us joy in dark times."

"Seems fittin' t' me!" bellowed the Dwarf.

Ronnok nodded in full agreement. "You bear your marks now, each showing the strength you add to Nordiska. You are to be outsiders and outcasts no longer, but brothers and sisters to the Northmen. You are of Nordiska, now and forever. You are our family."

Alauren sprung up and hugged Ronnok tightly. "Thank you," she said softly, fighting back a torrent of tears. "For everything."

CHAPTER FORTY:

ACCEPTANCE

42nd OF THE MORN OF HARVEST
NORTHERN YEAR 715

The docks of Anduras were normally a place which flowed with the hustle and bustle of hundreds of workers and fishermen. Now, though, it had grown quiet in the dying light of the day, falling into a peaceful serenity. The only sounds were the lapping waves and the cackling squawks of seagulls, who regularly dove into the frigid water in search of a meal.

Most locals, the smith assumed, were still celebrating newfound freedom, or had made themselves busy by picking up the pieces of their home now that the looming shadow over their lives had been removed. There was, for the first time since Teth, true quiet, and even the Nort fleet peacefully bobbed here and there with an atypical stillness, holding just outside the boundaries of the city's wide bay. Beyond the furled sails, a brilliant sunset dominated the eastern horizon of the Borean Ocean.

Alauren, seated upon the left side of a long, level fishing pier at the north end of the port, eyed the water warily, hanging her bare feet just above the sloshing waves. After some hesitation, she plunged them in, forcing herself to keep them submerged, despite her body's clear and forceful command to the contrary. The frigid shock dulled after a moment, regardless, leaving a numb tingling in its place.

"Ally!" Edlevin called, rolling himself across the dock on his chair. "Little chilly for a dip, isn't it?"

"To sane people, yes," Alauren chortled, swishing her feet around in the glacially cold water. "Besides, I thought your chair couldn't get out here. Figured I'd make you work for it if you wanted to see me."

Edlevin chuckled. "Well, it wasn't an easy sale, but that Arvid fellow was willing to give me a ride down here. Hefted my whole chair up on his shoulder, me included."

"Sounds about right," Alauren said flatly. "How is Arvid, anyway?"

"Oh, he'll be fine," Edlevin replied with a dismissive wave. "A mild head wound, burned hands, and some damaged pride. I feel the latter would keep him down more than either of the former." The old soldier rose from his chair with a groan and hobbled his way to the end of dock. He sat, careful to keep his feet out of the icy water.

"Beautiful, isn't it?" Alauren murmured, pointing towards the masts and riggings of the Nort fleet. They were perfectly silhouetted against a falling sun of orange and pink, like a masterwork dreamed up by a great Elysian artisan, missing only the strokes of a brush. "I've never seen anything like it."

Edlevin removed his shoes, speaking only after they had been carefully plunked far back from the edge of the pier. "Enjoy it, because you'll never see anything like it again, believe me." He sighed deeply, smiling at a resurfaced memory. "Such experiences are more than just what our eyes behold, in the end."

Alauren nodded quietly. "Try putting your feet in, Karlmaðr."

Edlevin, initially hesitant, chose to oblige, sinking his toes slowly into the lapping, dark waters. "Shit, Ally!" yelped the old soldier, tearing his flesh from the waves and lifting his feet well clear of the surface. "That could wake a stonebound Dwarf!"

The smith smiled and looked down, seeing that her own feet had grown pale and white in the cold. "It's refreshing," she said softly. "It reminds me I'm still alive. That all of this is still real." She sighed deeply and shook her head. "No matter how much I wish it was a dream."

"That would be convenient, wouldn't it?" Edlevin mused, finally bearing the cold and slipping his toes into the water once more. "To wake up, have a drink and make some nails for the boats, all while I chatter about this or that." He shook his head, letting his shoulders sink. "Honestly, Ally, what I felt at Arvynian, that crushing dread and sorrow, wasn't new to me, it was simply the strongest wave I've endured. In the end, I'll curse every sunrise that doesn't bring the old peace of Teth with it."

"Valin. Ronnok. Eira. Thyra. Solveig. Alvilda," Alauren stated flatly. "Arvid. Xendra. Harald. Bjorn."

Edlevin raised an eyebrow and cocked his head, equally curious and confused.

"Ed, I've been telling myself for weeks that I'd trade everything for another day in Teth, another day with my friends and family," the smith continued, keeping her gaze on her feet and the swishing black depths below. "I realize now that doing so would require sacrificing all those names, all those faces. They'd be dead without us. Shit, some ended up dead *with* us."

Edlevin nodded silently.

"It has been the hardest battle I've faced, that realization, but I now understand that going back to those days in Teth would require more than I'm willing to give," Alauren continued. She looked up and met Edlevin's eyes with a gaze of calm anguish. "We would have to trade all that we have now for what is, in reality, only memory." She ground her teeth for a moment, thinking deeply. "Edlevin, the Thjodhild made that choice."

"And look where it got them," concurred the old soldier, nodding quietly with the words. "Look at the cost."

"I won't fall into the same trap," murmured the blacksmith, swishing about in the water once more. "My world died, as did yours. For Valin and Ronnok, their worlds died long ago. We are not unique in our suffering."

"We are only the latest to experience it," Edlevin finished.

"Exactly," Alauren affirmed. "None who have lived our lives can avoid that sorrow; we can only carry it to greater deeds. We can't bring Martin or Sortul back, but they will still drive us. They will remind us of what can be lost if we don't take that next step. If we don't keep moving forward..." She trailed off, a slight darkness weighing upon her eyes.

"What, Ally?" Edlevin asked. "What do you know?"

The smith shook her head and grimaced in frustration. "Not much, other than the name Einar and the fact that there are more of them out there, more Thjodhild, somewhere. Drell helped them to escape Odenseye." She dropped her head into her hands and rubbed her eyes. "They never seem to end, do they? The mysteries and the questions. One after another."

The old soldier huffed a laugh. "No, they do not. The key is realizing that you don't need answers to find peace. Remember that."

"Yeah, Karlmaðr," Alauren murmured softly. "I will."

Edlevin put an arm around his old friend and hugged her tightly. "In the end, the world that we loved has turned to dust. There's nothing we can do but get out the brooms and help make way for the new." He smiled warmly. "One more step."

The two old friends clutched each other tightly as the dying light of the sun vanished fully behind the waves, carrying with it the last vestiges of the past.

EPILOGUE:

SPECTRE OF THE PAST

Western Elysia

2nd OF THE MORN OF BARE TREES
NORTHERN YEAR 715

Morvin's heavy boots clunked upon the creaking wood of a rickety bridge, upon which hairline fractures erupted under the weight of his armor. A stream bubbled below, flooded from the last rains of autumn as the waters surged south, towards the ocean. Many soldiers hardly cared; they eagerly waded through the muddy current with no trouble before emerging on the other side, thinking such an action to be harmless. Morvin, though, knew well enough to keep his feet dry.

His soldiers were used to fighting in Elysia, a temperate and navigable theatre of war. Se'Vikoral, the last collection of kingdoms in Odenseye, would be different, less organized and more savage. Ahead of them the great shadowbeech forest known as Mayahina waited with an open, hungering maw; in the Lunari language it was known as the 'Forest of the Blind Moon', and its shadowy lands stood as one of the few sanctuaries in the world left for the elusive Elves of the dark.

The jungle-like forest was hot and wet, even in winter; its piercing shadows and merciless environment had stopped many an Elysian campaign in its tracks over the long centuries. Even the simplest fungus on a man's foot could put them out for days in such a place or, worse yet, get them killed. The ease in logistics that horses brought would be nullified in the barely navigable rainforest; even now, many days before they would enter the darkness, the Nirali high command weaned their soldiers off such a convenience. The sons and daughters of Niras would learn hard lessons in the coming days, and Morvin would be happy to let the wisdom of experience take its full effect upon his armies. Those that were cunning and aware would survive.

The bridge led to a dirt road, beyond which a small farmhouse lay nestled in the woods. Shadowbeech trees were sprinkled around, but they had not yet become the dominant feature of the landscape. Niralan's armies were, for now, still in the safety of the new Elysian Province, not yet beyond their newly established boundaries. There were still hearths here, peaceful havens like this remote home, but they would not last as the westward march of the Nirali continued forth.

Morvin plowed through the rickety wooden door of the farmhouse, wildly flinging it open before emerging into the musty interior of the home. A table was in the center of a single, perfectly square room, lit dimly by a large ceiling sconce. A map was splayed out, being looked at by two Nirali, a man and a woman.

"I thought you might have ended up dead," the man growled. His booming voice nearly shook the walls, the standard volume of his words ever seeming to be triple that of his fellow Nirali. He was tall, head and shoulders over Morvin, having to hunch awkwardly under the low farmhouse roof. A scowl was ever-present above a black braided beard which still held brown streaks of dried blood within.

"It's good to see you, too, General Tarkus," Morvin rumbled with annoyance. He nodded to the woman, whose short, black hair trickled over a face pocked with scars, each a history of the last throes of those who had stood before her, and each adding to the crushing force of her gaze. "General Silena."

The woman nodded silently, offering no further pleasantries. Instead, she pointed to the map, which showed the large wall of forest that separated them from victory. "We need to push through, and fast," she stated, her raspy voice matching the intensity of her much larger comrade with ease, though the sheer volume of the words was noticeably lower. "The Se'Vikoran leaders cannot be allowed to reach the castle of Gaillard'Gor and fortify."

Morvin shook his head, mildly puzzled. "What of the Thjodhild? Have they not established themselves in Se'Vikoral yet?"

The other two generals looked to each other, trading worried glances.

Tarkus was the first to speak. "You haven't heard?"

Morvin shook his head and furrowed his brow.

"Makes sense. Just heard a few minutes ago, myself," Tarkus continued. "They got spooked, or something else got their attention. We only know that they disappeared into the night, without a word."

"Karsus was right, again," Silena confirmed with a shallow nod. "He was wise to keep them at arm's length, to distrust them."

"...*Fuck*!" Morvin thundered, slamming the table with a gauntleted fist that sent a crack soaring through the old wood. "For the first time in decades, I wish he wasn't. Our timetable was just moved forward by weeks. We must move soon."

"Agreed. We can't afford any more delays," Tarkus prodded, smirking. "No more Vulmoors."

"Blunt your edge, General," Morvin snapped sternly. "Vulmoor was handled, and I'm in no mood for lip from a subordinate."

Tarkus half-bowed respectfully. "My apologies, sir. Just heard you got bogged down, is all."

"I tried to solve things with words instead of bloodshed for once in my life, Tarkus," grumbled the General. "It could have gone better."

"It is behind us now," Silena interrupted, hiding a clear annoyance in the typically flat, unwavering cadence of her voice. "We must focus on the future. If they reach that castle, it will cost us entire regiments to take it."

"We will drive them out," Morvin stated with confidence. "Gaillard'Gor was an Elysian design, which the great library of the Capital held many secrets to. The traps and fortifications are known to us. Mayahina, in any case, comes first, and we must maintain our focus on the nearest obstacle."

"As you command, sir," Silena conceded. "There is one other matter you must be made aware of. We have a visitor."

Morvin crossed his arms. "Who?"

Tarkus and Silena again traded unsure glances.

"It is in the woodshed outside," Tarkus rumbled unsurely. "It's probably best you see for yourself, sir."

Morvin nodded and spun, walking out the main door. He directed Skarde, just arriving with the Elysian recruits, to set up camp on the edge of the farm, before moving on to find a small structure standing within a clump of bushes next to a wagon.

The woodshed door was partially open, and so the Nirali General stepped through without hesitation. The building, little more than a dirt floor and wooden walls, held a corpse, which hung upside-down from the dark rafters above. It was a Lunari, male, bound by the feet, having each major artery slit carefully. His blood ran down and off his shaved head, collecting into a large trough below him.

A woman knelt to the left of the threshold, dressed in flowing robes that reached easily to the floor. She held a dripping knife, which she carefully used to make another, deeper incision on the Lunari's wrist, seemingly unaware of her visitor.

The patterning of her clothing was perfect, having no extra fabric, wrinkles, or popped stitches, as if each strand of woven thread was carefully chosen and sized for her specific form. Several green silk sashes accented the heavy, black material of her robes, twisting like vines around her lithe form before meeting at the center of the chest, where a large amulet of the sun glowed a bright emerald from its jeweled center.

The woman noticed Morvin's presence, stood, and turned; the movement flowed as if her feet were not touching the ground, like she was hoisted aloft by the wind. Her face was obscured by a mask made from a vaguely human-looking skull, its hollow eyes each containing soft flames that flickered like the fire of a wax candle. Both of the gentle flares matched the color of her amulet perfectly, and their glimmer in the metal ridges of the jewelry sent pins of light skittering across the shed.

"Morvin," the woman trilled happily, as if the General was a long-lost friend come for a reunion. The flames in her eyes lit up and dimmed with the coming and going of the words, glowing brighter as her enunciation reached its peak. Despite the lightness of the sound itself, her voice crawled through the General's head like a migraine, lingering and unsettling. "I've heard so much about you."

"Who are you?" Morvin demanded with crossed arms, having no time for pleasantries.

"A wanderer, once with the Thjodhild, and now with you," the woman answered. "You may call me Jor."

Morvin narrowed his eyes. "Niralan does not accept wanderers, especially those of the damned Thjodhild."

Jor chuckled, her subdued voice seeming to distort the air around her with vibrations. "Yes, I've heard you've had some problems with them. I know them. They are..." She paused to make a fresh gash on the dead Elf's femoral artery, slowly and with precision. "Single minded. Unchanging. Not like you."

"Where did they go?" Morvin demanded. "Why did they renege on their word?"

"Fear," Jor stated, chuckling again. "Primal and unfamiliar to them. If they return, it will be with a feverish bloodlust and a hatred toward any not their own. Assume your pact to be broken."

"And you?" asked the General. "Why did you not go with them? Do you mean to fight with us?"

"No," Jor replied calmly. She slipped the dagger back into her robes, evidently happy with the level of mutilation on the Lunari corpse. "Only to observe and teach, taking my payment as I see fit."

"Payment," Morvin echoed. "Elaborate."

"No," Jor growled. "You do not command me as one of your mere infantry soldiers. Karsus himself has so decreed."

"Is that right?" Morvin scoffed. "I'll make sure to get his official word on-"

His sentence was interrupted by a rap at the door.

"A message for you, sir," Skarde said, poking his head through the threshold and wholly ignoring whatever business was playing out in front of him, for he knew it was none of his. "Direct from Marshal Karsus, delivered minutes ago."

Morvin took the letter and waved his Lieutenant away. The message was sealed with a purple wax, stamped with a dual visage of Niralan and the new Elysian territory, a color and mark reserved for the highest levels of the new northern government. The General broke the wax and read the letter, his eyebrows raising more with every word.

"Well?" Jor asked. "Does Karsus command it so?"

Morvin, though his face showed nothing but a perplexed bewilderment, nodded. "Yes, Jor, he does." He beckoned. "Come. We have much to discuss."